A Pattern of Swallows

Russ Hawton

Copyright © 2022 Russ Hawton

All rights reserved.

Russ Hawton has asserted his right under the Copyright, Designs and Patents Act 1988 to be identified as the author of this book.

This is a work of fiction. Names, characters, business, events and incidents are the products of the author's imagination. Any resemblance to actual persons, living or dead, or actual events is purely coincidental.

No part of this publication may be reproduced, distributed, or transmitted in any form or by any means, without the prior written permission of the author, except in the case of brief quotations embodied in critical reviews and certain other non-commercial uses permitted by copyright law. For permission requests, contact the author.

ISBN: 9798367581140

'Cover illustration includes a detail from 'Pendennis Castle - Falmouth in the Distance' by John Callow (1822-1878

Chapter 1

It had snowed again during the night. She remembered the sticky, white flakes clinging briefly to the casement window. Now as the sky lightened imperceptibly the snow turned to rain which she could hear falling persistently into the grey white slush of the yard. The window was slightly ajar, just the way Samuel preferred it, even in winter.

She had lain awake for much of the night, her eyes half-closed or staring vaguely through one half of her small, mullioned window. Her cap had rubbed off as usual and, with her long, greying hair, lay on the pillow behind her. She had had a dream, or a recollection perhaps. She could not be sure. All her dreams now and all her memories were of a kind, of the family, the family she had once so loved and nurtured. In her dream she had been sitting upright in a large canopy bed, this bed she supposed, for surely it could have been no other. Samuel had come in, large and unkempt and smiling, as he always was.

'So now, Mary has come back! She is risen. I tell you, she is risen!'

She had been puzzled, but then something had prompted her to look down to the tiny baby she held in her arms. Mary. Yes, it was surely Mary. And though she was tired and still in pain from the birth, she knew it was true, and her heart lifted. And Samuel was there sitting beside her, buckled and belted and ready for work. And it was daybreak then too and perhaps too, it had been raining persistently into the snow.

She lay perfectly still listening to the rain, smiling a little to herself at the memory, until she heard Janella's bedroom door creaking open on the other side of the stairs. Even alone and unobserved and cosy in her feather bed, she began at once to feel uncomfortable. 'It is only Janella,' she told herself. But

Janella no longer offered friendship, was not even deferential as once she had been, and Alice constantly wondered why. Without turning from the window, she reached behind her for the warmth and solace of Samuel's hand, knowing in her heart of hearts it was not to be found. Instead she closed her eyes, pursed her lips and pretended to fall asleep. But she could still hear Janella, herself half asleep as she stumbled down the last stairs and into the kitchen. First she would light the fire. Then Arthur would come and they would eat and gossip and warm themselves.

But soon Janella would bring her bread and hot milk so, after an interval, she began to rouse herself again in preparation, straightened both their pillows, sat upright as she had in her dream, as if in so doing she might somehow recapture it. But as she waited patiently for Janella, it was not one dream but all her dreams that came back to her at once. Dreams and memories, for so long indistinguishable, vague, no longer vivid as once they had been. And always Mary, not her image just the consciousness of her presence. Mary as a child. Mary as a young woman.

Another creak on the stair, and then a cursory knock. Janella came in and placed the wooden tray beside her on the bed. Neither spoke. 'Once we had been friends,' she reflected bitterly. 'Now we hardly speak.' Modestly she adjusted her tray, looked up surreptitiously, hoping Janella might catch her expression of gratitude. Failing to catch her eye, Alice concluded Janella was sick. She did not look at all well, still ruddy complexioned but heavy-lidded now in the mornings. She had lost weight, looked more than her thirty years or so.

'Janella', she said, but only in her mind, so Janella did not turn at the door to face her, dutiful, expressionless. 'Mary was my third child and my fourth.' The thought came suddenly and without bidding, a belated explanation of her dream. And although it was Mary that preoccupied her, she made an effort to recall the others. 'First,' fastidiously she prodded the covers as she placed them correctly in the order of their birth. 'John, then Robert, then Mary...' She paused in her recollection, 'and then Francis.'

The bread was not of the quality to which she had once been used and the milk she sipped from her pewter jug was barely warm. Before the fighting, she reasoned to herself, Mary had loved her, but then Mary had married and gone away. Samuel had explained everything to her, but she had not properly understood. She finished what remained of the milk, disregarding the bread with a slight toss of the head and a rueful glance to the other side of the bed. 'I am not hungry,' she said aloud, 'but I drank the milk.'

The rain was noisy, intrusive, splattering in the yard. The day was breaking but the clouds still hung low and heavy over Venterdon. She heard Arthur go out to the barn, boots squelching in the mud. Why then had Mary never come back?

***

At the Rectory, by Clymestone church and little more than a hundred yards from where Alice lay, the Reverend Richard Clarke had risen even earlier than usual. There had been a knock at the door, an urgent knock from a nervous and sympathetic neighbour. The news imparted that General Fairfax, at the head of a substantial body of troops, had been seen approaching the environs of Lanson, had come as no great surprise. Ever since the defeat at Naseby in June, he had been half expecting it. And then after the carnage of Bristol and more recently the Torrington debacle, he had become convinced the people would soon submit. Cornwall would submit. Those who had left their farms to fight for the King and had been fortunate enough to survive, had long since returned for one harvest or another. The fight had gone out of them.

The maid being slow to rise, he had dressed and briefly breakfasted. He was not a man given to hesitation, nor to excessive formality. His duty now was to warn all those in the Parish most likely to be threatened by the new order. There would be a new order. Of that he had no doubt. There would be arrests, sequestrations. As for his own position, well that was not something he would easily relinquish.

He regarded himself critically in the mirror above the heavy oak sideboard, adjusted the lace ruff at his throat and then, with a certain inevitability, picked up his two silver-backed hairbrushes. It had become a kind of ritual, this lengthy, vigorous brushing of his thick mane of white hair. A vanity, he would have acknowledged that, but also over time it had become a necessity. It helped him prepare for the day, bolstered him in his self-belief. This day would be no more challenging than many others. He would come through. Had he not always come through? Had he not falsely taken the Protestation Oath before Justice Gewen in Lanson? Had he not witnessed the taking of that same Oath by every man in Clymestone, even encouraging those who had hesitated? Had he not sworn, the words swirled about his mind in spiteful repetition, 'to defend ...the true Reformed Protestant religion against all popery'? He paused to examine his own increasingly severe features, staring back at him in the mirror. How was it then, that before the triumph of Lostwithiel, he had been so rudely threatened with ejection from his living, for being 'scandalous in his life' and 'ill-affected' to Parliament? His life had admitted no scandal and if he had been 'ill-affected' to the rebellion, how was that to be discovered? No art, short of Confession, had yet been devised, he grimaced to himself in the mirror, to reveal the nature of a man's true Faith. 'And only God,' He spoke aloud to his reflection, 'is my Confessor.'

It was after all fortunate, fortunate for all the Parish that he had had the determination to remain. Fortunate also, if truth were told, that he had loyal friends on the County Committee. But he would not concern himself with all of this! He discarded the hairbrushes with impatience. He was well able to look after his own affairs, Fairfax or no Fairfax. That Puritan cleric skulking in Burraton would enter this Rectory over his dead body! But there were others, especially those who shared the Faith less able than himself. They would need him now more than ever.

One of them in particular came to his mind with mounting concern, Mary Hawking. Her husband had fought bravely for the King at Bristol and had undoubtedly been killed. At least that was what was generally believed. But Mary was stubborn and had refused to accept her loss. In despair, she had turned to him for succour and in his desire to comfort her he had lost all caution and revealed to her his own secret Catholic conviction.

They had celebrated Mass together in her cottage by the river. He had heard her Confession, at the same time urging her to secrecy. But Mary, he soon found, was not inclined to subterfuge. It was not in her nature. If arrested, she would openly espouse her Faith. He would be implicated.

Sitting just inside the great studded door to the Rectory, pulling on his boots, he became increasingly mindful of the danger posed, not only to Mary but to himself. He must think clearly. He could not go to her now. Besides, she would not listen. She would not understand that the County was about to be turned upside down one final time and that, at the merest hint of her Faith, the Puritans would sequestrate her husband's substantial property along the Tamar and throw her out. Mary's lonely life by the river, hopelessly, obstinately awaiting her husband's return was already, in the febrile imagination of the times, arousing suspicion. To continue to draw attention to herself now would be to court certain arrest in Lanson.

His most prudent course, perhaps his only course, would be to call on her mother, Alice Pellow. She had not been well since the death of Samuel but perhaps he could persuade her son, Francis, to look out for his sister. John, the carpenter and the eldest would not involve himself. Robert was not to be trusted. That only left Francis, damaged goods, but the only one Mary would be likely to listen to.

He closed the huge Rectory door behind him and fastened his cloak. The rain was only light. The lane circling Clymestone church was deserted. Snow still clung tenaciously to the churchyard wall and beneath the high hedgerows which marked the lane to Venterdon. The Reverend Clarke was supremely conscious of his own brisk and dapper figure as he hurried towards the Pellow farm. As to his precise course of action, there was no doubt in his mind.

***

Janella was not busy. The fire had been lit and there were spare logs to hand. Alice had her bread and milk and Arthur had been dispatched after what Janella liked to call his 'usual attempt at lechery', to get the sheep in or put them out or whatever he was going to do. Now she was dipping rushes in the bowl of tallow beside her on the kitchen table. It was work she found relaxing, but it would no more take away the aching cold and dull hunger than a rush light on the wall. She was sitting in unladylike fashion astride the kitchen bench to be as close as possible to both her bowl of tallow and the limited warmth of the newly lit fire. Someone was in the yard, an early beggar perhaps. Janella continued with her dipping.

'Mistress Pellow! Are you there? Mistress Pellow!'

Janella, only mildly surprised, recognised the rather high-pitched yet oddly masculine voice of the Reverend Clarke. She rose unhurriedly, straightened her cap and adopted, without difficulty, her usual air of composure.

'Good morning, Reverend. You are early for a day such as this!'

The Reverend entered without closing the door behind him or, to Janella's infinite annoyance, troubling to scrape his boots, and made purposefully for the fire.

'Janella, is your mistress about? I would speak with her.'

The Reverend tended towards peremptoriness. That at least no longer offended her. He took off his cloak and laid it unceremoniously on the table, turned his back to the fire and stamped his feet. She could not for the life of her understand why the Reverend Clarke never, even in the middle of winter, wore a hat of any kind.

'Mrs Pellow keeps to her bed, Reverend.'

'Janella, you must understand,' His voice had already slowed and softened, lost its customary briskness. It was a trick he had frequently used to great effect from the pulpit, 'Mrs Pellow is melancholic. It is more than a year since Samuel...Her humour is unfortunate in a widow.'

He turned, crouching a little to warm his hands, and became abrupt again, 'Tell your mistress the Rector has come with news of soldiers in Lanson. Perhaps that will rouse her.' And then as Janella moved to the stairs, 'If she will not come, bring Francis.'

Alice was on the side of her bed. Janella saw she had used the pot and decided to leave it until after the Reverend had gone.

'The Reverend Clarke is here. He wants you to come down. He says there are soldiers in Lanson.'

With surprising agility Alice swung up her feet and manoeuvred herself back to the oak board of her large canopy bed. Through her window she had watched the Reverend carefully picking his way across the yard, but now found it simpler to feign surprise.

'Oh, but I'm not well Janella. You had better wake Francis.'

Janella, it seemed to Alice, had briefly regarded her with contempt before closing the door behind her. She wondered if Francis would choose to emerge from his attic at such an early hour. But that was no longer her business. Her youngest son was no longer her business. Francis was, had always been, a disappointment. Samuel's favourite perhaps, but not hers. When Francis had chosen not to fight, Samuel had begun to understand. 'Dissolute,' Samuel had said. 'My son is dissolute.' She had not understood exactly, but had an idea what Samuel meant. The Reverend Clarke would no doubt leave, but in that she was not altogether pleased. She had an idea at the back of her mind, that the Rector was a friend, a friend of Samuel's

Janella ascended to the attic and banged on Francis's door. As she expected, there was no response. He was probably asleep. Seeing the necessity, she knocked and entered. Against expectation, Francis was already dressed and at his desk, quill in hand, a blanket round his shoulders. Only writing when he should be out with Arthur in the fields, thought Janella, but kept her counsel.

'The Reverend is downstairs. Soldiers in Lanson, he says.' Francis mumbled that he would come down. Soldiers, Janella thought, Soldiers is all he thinks about.

***

The Rector was sitting close to the fire in Samuel's chair. Francis was momentarily taken aback. It was his father's chair. It was sacrosanct. But the Rector seemed unconcerned, uncharacteristically at ease. 'Francis.' The Rector looked up from the fire, flushed cheeks and immaculate silver hair, a welcoming smile. 'I understand your mother is indisposed. But no matter. In truth, it is you I came to see.'

Feeling slightly dishevelled in the face of Clarke's consummate neatness, and consequently at a disadvantage, Francis sat down awkwardly in his mother's chair.

'General Fairfax will shortly be in Lanson. I believe there are no forces sufficient to obstruct him. Hopton and the rest will capitulate. The Puritans will control the whole of Cornwall before the spring is out.' The Reverend paused for effect, seeming to take pleasure in the relation of news which otherwise must have caused him acute concern.

'The end of the war. It will be a blessing,' Francis replied. taking advantage of the pause.

'A blessing for some. For others a torment! Those who do not bend to the Puritan yoke will be hung or, at the very least, incarcerated. The Duchy itself will be dismantled!'

'It does not concern me.'

'Does not concern you!' The Reverend almost rose from his seat. 'Did you not fight for the King? Are you not your father's son?'

Francis did not respond and the Rector took cognisance of the fact that he was not in the pulpit and had strayed somewhat from the purpose of his visit. He became aware that Janella had placed two jugs of ale within reach of them both on the kitchen table. He collected himself, leaned back comfortably in Samuel's chair, the better to contemplate the nervous but implacable demeanour of Francis Pellow. He waited for Janella to go about her business and then began again, leaning forward and lowering his voice.

'Your sister Mary is thought to be a papist. She does not obscure the fact. What is more, she is the widow of, some would say, a famous Royalist officer, perhaps even a papist himself. She lives in ostentatious isolation, the sole inhabitant of her husband's substantial property. She has no servants and eschews all personal intercourse.'

There was a pause. The Reverend could perceive his words were beginning to have the intended effect. 'Do you believe, Francis, that our new Puritan masters will entirely ignore such a woman? I tell you they will sequestrate her land, arrest her and if nothing else have her for a witch!'

Francis had stood and begun to walk about the kitchen. He picked up the jug of ale. 'What would you have me do?'

'Francis, you are kin. Forgive me, but your brothers will not take a risk. Your mother is bedridden and George Hawking is dead. You are all she has. You grew up together, did you not? Would it not be better for Mary if she came here to live, if she relinquished her property before it is taken from her, and above everything else,' The Reverend Clarke lowered his voice still further, 'if she denies all sympathy with the Catholic Faith? You appreciate she is only one of many in this Parish I must seek to protect. I believe she will listen to you, her brother, more than to me who am merely her vicar.'

Without waiting for a reply, the Reverend rose, took a swig of ale and readied himself to leave. Francis had nothing more to say and only stood discomfited while Janella showed their visitor out. Once they had all encouraged her. George, an experienced soldier was sure to come home. But it was more than two years now, nearly three since Bristol had fallen. So many had come back, but George had not been among them. He had been presumed dead by everyone, except Mary. She was like her mother, Francis thought. Neither of them understood. In a war people died. He knew that well enough, had witnessed it at first hand. Like everyone else, except for Clarke it seemed, he had long since lost patience with Mary. Did Clarke really care for his sister more than he himself? Was Clarke really busying himself about the Parish, warning all and sundry of the Puritan menace, or was he rather more concerned in some way about protecting himself? Was he not some curmudgeonly old man obstinately usurping the rights of James Marten, now languishing in Burraton? Did General Fairfax not have better things to do than prosecute his sister for popery? But Mary... it was true, was needlessly drawing attention to herself. Francis mounted the narrow stairway to his bare attic room. It was too cold to sit, painfully recapitulating his own bitter account of the Lostwithiel campaign. He resolved once again that, when the ink dried in the well, he would commit it all to the flame. But the Rector's words would not go away. 'If nothing else, they will have her for a witch!'

In the chamber below, Alice, unconsidered by her son, was standing motionless at her window, watching as the Reverend Clarke picked his way through the mud to the lane. While Janella, equally unconsidered, ascended slowly to Alice's chamber to remove the pot from beneath the bed.

Chapter 2

The Puritan cleric regarded so contemptuously by the Reverend Clarke as 'skulking in Burraton' was in fact Minister James Marten who had formally been granted the living at Clymestone more than a year previously, Clarke having been found scandalous in his habits and 'ill-affected' to the Parliament, as indeed he was. But Clarke had obstinately refused to quit the Rectory and had continued, outrageously, to collect the tithes and benefit from the glebe. Cunning, stubborn, yet popular with his congregation, the incumbent priest had proved quite impossible to remove and as a result Marten had been forced to purchase a property in Burraton and content himself with what he was wont to describe as 'the pains of the cure.'

Marten, in contrast to Clarke, was not at all ill-affected to the Parliament and indeed had preached with some success in Puritan London. In the capital, his sermons had been published, distributed and enthusiastically acclaimed. He was already a man of substance. But when the unexpected offer of a comfortable living at Clymestone had been made he had, surprisingly perhaps, welcomed it as 'manna from Heaven'. He was not, after all, an ambitious man, had never coveted worldly success. The tensions, the distractions, the sectarianism rife in the capital had begun to sap his energy and strength.

The stewardship of a Parish such as Clymestone had seemed ideal. Had it not ever been his wish to spread the word of God to those who needed it most, to those at the furthest reaches of this restless, unhappy Kingdom?

But he had reckoned without Clarke, nor had he expected to encounter in this western Parish so rich a vein of, what seemed to him, mindless Royalism. And naively perhaps, Marten had underestimated the apparently indestructible power and influence of the Duchy, wherein much of the Parish lay.

Nevertheless, he had decided to sit it out. He was not a poor man and he would not be defeated by Clarke's intransigence. In due course, his appeal to the House of Lords would be successful. Peace would come. Clarke would be ejected. He, together with his wife and children (whom he had temporarily abandoned in London), would at last enter the Rectory, not in a spirit of triumph but rather, he told himself, in one of sober anticipation, of being at last able to fulfil his promised, his sacred duty to God.

Minister Marten was a patient, undemonstrative man, in many ways the antithesis of his somewhat mercurial rival. He was serious, restrained and genuinely thoughtful, a man altogether without spontaneity, lacking also it might be said as a result, the experience of natural friendship. To compensate perhaps, he would even in his isolation, read aloud from the Holy Bible and pray for peace.

It would be an exaggeration though to say he suffered 'the pains of the cure.' Sadly, Minister Marten's spasmodic attempts at bringing the word of God to his rustic neighbours in Burraton had done nothing but arouse suspicion, or in some cases outright rejection. The Parish had not yet come to understand that Richard Clarke, not he, was the real imposter.

Despite his forbearance, for many months and through a long, cold winter, Marten had at times been close to despair. Only his Faith, together with the messages of encouragement which occasionally reached him from his wife in London, had sustained him in his determination.

Only one regular visitor came to his new home in Burraton, a woman who at once both flattered and disturbed him, the pious, yet to his mind all too feminine, Christina Pellow.

Marten Looked up from his well-thumbed Book of Common Prayer, guiltily conscious of its recent replacement by Parliament with the new Directory of Public Worship. He had, in a spirit of forgiveness natural to him, been attempting to reconcile the one with the other. As was his custom, he had seated himself with a view of the lane and observed Christina Pellow's coming with a mixture of confusion and anticipation.

She had brought from her own kitchen and quite unnecessarily a basket containing fruit and bacon, a combination determined as much by the contents of her larder as by an uncertain interpretation of religious observance. Did the Minister recognise Lent?

'Minister,' she blurted as soon as Marten opened the door, 'General Fairfax is in Lanson.'

***

It had been a full nineteen months since that other great Parliamentarian invasion of Cornwall. There had been no time then for the people of Clymestone to mull over the news, no time for visiting, no time to discuss the implications. It had caught them entirely unawares.

But everyone in Clymestone remembered that day, the 26th July 1644, when a huge Parliamentarian army of 10,000 men had crossed the Tamar at Horsebridge and then marched through the village, past Almshouses on their way to Linkinhorne and Bodmin. Some had watched from behind the hedgerows, a few had fought briefly alongside Greville's tiny detachment of horse, which had been so easily swept aside.

Most had stayed at home or simply come in from the fields to pray.

But on this day in late February, another harsh winter to run its course, the bridge remains silent, untrodden, almost abandoned. Only the river moves, full and unperturbed, beneath the seven grey, granite arches, following its inevitable course to the sea.

But since the rain has now ceased, a little further downstream and on the Cornish bank, a single diminutive figure might just be discerned, close to some trees which at this spot overhang the swollen stream. It is the figure of a young woman, distinguished by a dark blue shawl, white linen scarf and a light-coloured petticoat. If you were close enough you would notice her clothes are dry in spite of the rain and as there is no proper dwelling nearby you might conclude she has been sheltering in the ruin a little way across the meadow and used more commonly now for sheep or pigs. The woman is making her way beside the stream to the area of scrub where the lane from Lidwell approaches the bridge. Now she seeks out the higher land, a kind of narrow pathway close to the stream, hitching up her skirts, stepping with caution around the treacherous roots and pools of icy water.

At the bridge she pauses and then begins to walk across. Halfway she pauses again, as if afraid to continue. On the Devon side to her right the steep, bare, wooded hillside rises up from the river, she knows to follow its meander without interruption, to Morwellham and beyond. To her left, the lane skews away past the 'Packhorse Inn, once a nunnery and even now bleak and silent in the late afternoon.

The woman assures herself that the lane is empty and, as is her habit, turns to look north, up the narrowing stream.

After a while, the small patch of blue sky over her head contracts and disappears, darkening the river and sending a shudder through her bones. A few drops of rain. The woman pulls the blue shawl tight around her and begins to wend her way homeward.

Mary Hawking is a familiar figure by the bridge. The farmers, packmen and occasional carriers who come by Hampt and Tutwell all know who she is and why she still comes every day, rain or shine, to the river. 'This is the way,' her husband has told her in the agony of parting, 'This is the way I will come.' And so, obstinately, Mary waits for him. That Captain George Hawking fought valiantly at Stratton, Lansdown and finally Bristol is not in doubt. But that was a long time ago and George has not yet returned.

Storm clouds are moving in from the west. She takes one more glance down the lane past the inn, and then turns once more towards Hampt where she lives alone.

Much of the land hereabouts is still in her husband's name, but the small, whitewashed cottage is old and winter stained. The thatch, where it is not white with snow is green and sodden. She has removed here from the farmhouse, only to be closer to the bridge and the river.

The fire burns despondently in the grate. She takes off her scarf and thick, blue shawl and hangs them together on the door. Her hair is light brown and falls in delicate ringlets the full length of her back. The outer one of her petticoats which is damp is removed and draped over the back of a chair. Automatically, she stokes the fire, puts on an extra log and then, ignoring both her chairs, sits herself comfortably on the rush matting by the hearth, to tend the incipient flame. In the gathering gloom her face, caught in the wavering glow of the fire, is small, pale and like her mother's, entirely unfathomable. But you can see, she is more resolved than Alice, the eyes are darker and still might blaze with unpredictable fervour.

When the fire has taken hold, she lights a taper and, shielding the flame, rises and steps towards the door to her chamber. This, her only other room is sparsely, yet incongruously, furnished. On the far wall a small bed with a straw mattress, feather pillows and expensive looking covers. Above the bed, a rough piece of sacking which hangs crookedly at the window. The room is extremely cramped, but behind the door to her right and set against the wall is a small table, carefully draped with a folded rectangle of pure, white linen. At each end are silver candlesticks and between them an elaborate, silver crucifix.

She lights the candles, closes the door and, crossing herself, kneels before the gleaming crucifix. Mary prays silently, first as she has been taught for the soul of her father, Samuel. And then for George and his imminent homecoming. She does not pray for the remainder of her family who have abandoned her. Rather she prays, of her own volition, for one with whom she feels a bond, a shared loyalty to the true Catholic Faith, a shared loyalty perhaps to an absent husband. She prays too for her namesake, Queen Henrietta Maria.

Her prayers are not long and do not vary from day to day. But like the occasional visits of the Reverend Clarke, they give her strength and hope. Perhaps soon she will again make her confession, receive the sacraments. The Reverend Clarke's words sound gravely to her ear:

'The body of Christ.'...'Amen.'

'The blood of Christ.'...'Amen.'

A sudden flurry of hail against the window disturbs her reverie. Again she crosses herself and with a renewed spirit of determination returns to her place by the fire. The long night has hardly begun, and there will be many more, but she will not weaken in her resolve.

***

Mary Hawking was not at all aware nor would she have cared that earlier on the same day General Thomas Fairfax, at the head of a large Parliamentarian army, had crossed the Tamar at Stratton and ascended the hill to Lanson, only eight miles away. As expected, there had been only brief skirmishing in the steep, narrow streets. A handful of Royalist militia were killed but many more taken prisoner, an indication if any were needed of the overwhelming efficiency of Cromwell's New Model Army. The following day, employing the same tactic as at Dartmouth in January, Fairfax would free all his prisoners with a shilling each and a free pass home.

In Lanson, the town's leaders, including MP, JP and powerful Cornish Committee member, Thomas Gewen, did not hesitate to welcome the General. Nor were peasants from the outlying villages, perceiving no doubt where their best interests lay, slow to bring in much needed provisions for the army. As The Reverend Clarke had accurately foreseen, there was little stomach left for the fight in Cornwall and a new order was irrevocably taking shape.

Nevertheless, Fairfax was cautious. To ensure the strength of his position, 'Black Tom' who now appeared less darkly threatening than he had on the other side of the Tamar, despatched an emissary to Plymouth to arrange for treaty with the local gentry. The emissary, army chaplain Hugh Peters, a veteran of Lostwithiel and said by some to be coarse and 'without taste and refinement,' was however known to Fairfax as a persuasive cleric and, more to the point, a Cornishman.

Fairfax clearly knew what he was about. There was no possibility whatsoever of this Roundhead army being trapped, like its predecessor, and mercilessly cut down in the heart of Cornwall.

Chapter 3

When they had at last brought his father home, carried him through the door and upstairs to his bed, Francis, overcome with shame, had been unable to confront him. In any event, Alice had taken control, asking only for Janella. It was naturally supposed Samuel had been wounded at the bridge. Others, mostly of Grenville's troop, had already been brought to the churchyard to await burial. But the nature of Samuel's wound was unclear.

The following day the Reverend Clarke had arrived and later a physician from Lanson, but apparently to no avail. Francis had continued to hide away in the attic. It was only with the news of the King's army now in hot pursuit of the Parliamentarians that he had perceived, in the midst of his shame, an opportunity for absolution.

In the night he had picked up his father's sword, discarded in the buttery, sneaked out to the stable, taken one of the packhorses and headed for Lanson. At length he had been directed to Trecarrel where the whole of the King's army lay encamped about the manor. His loyalty was not questioned and so he had been steered towards a ragbag of Cornish volunteers grouped in a nearby copse. At dawn he had even caught sight of the diminutive figure of the King, emerging from the tiny chapel close to the manor.

But that had been only the beginning. For three frustrating weeks the two armies had manoeuvred for position. It had taken until the end of August before Essex's army had become fatally surrounded. They had attacked in heavy rain and Francis, albeit briefly, had experienced the satisfaction of revenge. But it was short-lived and not so sweet, and absolution was nowhere to be found. Instead, what followed had appalled him beyond measure and, no matter what, the scars refused to heal.

Francis bowed his head once more to the words he had just written:

'...in their defeat, they were allowed to march away but as they passed they were much abused and reviled by the people. They were spat on by the women. They took away their cloaks and hats and many struggled to walk, barefoot and half-naked in the rain. Our officers tried to prevent this cruel humiliation, but it was of no use. And their hangers-on, their women, fared even worse..'

His throat tightened. The words seemed inadequate. He was ready to tear them up. But then he became aware of Janella's step on his narrow creaking staircase. She paused at the door to catch her breath. 'Master Francis,' Her breath was not yet recovered, 'you must help Arthur get the fodder from the loft.' He could not bring himself to reply, absorbed as he was. She waited a little, then opened the door. These days, Janella would not be ignored.

'There is not much hay left but it must be taken out to the sheep, what remain of them. You may not have noticed, but there has been more snow in the night.'

He considered how to respond, but did not look up. He had intended, he had positively resolved, after much thought during the night, that he had a responsibility to his sister. He could not ignore the Reverend Clarke's warning. But then he had set all that aside and started writing again preferring, he knew, to dwell on the past rather than deal with the present. Well, he supposed the farm must not fail. The sheep must not be allowed to die. And Janella would not be ignored.

'Janella, I apologise. I understand about the fodder. I will come down and later go to Mary.'

'I'm glad you're listening more than usual, Master Francis,' Janella retorted, and then out of sheer malice, or so it seemed, 'The Reverend says she's a witch.'

He stood up in a paroxysm of rage, unexpected even to himself. His chair fell back. His pen and papers scattered. He took Janella by the arm, spun her round and screamed in her face.

'Mary is not a witch!' His lips were trembling. He could hardly enunciate the words. 'The Reverend Clarke said, 'they will have her for a witch.' He does not believe her to be a witch! He does not believe in witches! He is an educated man! He was warning me. The war is lost. Do you not comprehend, Janella? Everything is lost!'

He picked up the chair, ignoring his papers, and sat down heavily. More quietly he added, 'You should not have been listening.'

Their eyes met fleetingly. Janella had been determined to go, but somehow his explosion of passion had recalled to them both a time before the war, a time of harmless flirtation which had come to nothing. How different they had become. Janella softened visibly, in spite of herself.

'What are you writing?'

'You remember father coming home?' His voice was breaking with emotion. 'And then I went for a soldier?'

'There was a great victory.'

'Yes, but it wasn't really a victory, Janella. It was like a hell on earth. That is what I am writing about.'

'Why write about it? Better forget.'

'I can't forget, Janella. I don't believe in fighting any more, not for anything...I can't forget.'

He picked up his papers, conscious of drawing too much attention to himself. He understood how it must appear to Janella, who could not read a word, let alone write.

'We have both suffered,' he said. 'But you are the real hero. I ran away. I was a coward. You stayed here. I know what you did.'

He looked down at his papers without noticing them. Janella stood motionless, close enough to touch, close enough to read his words however inadequate, had she been able. In the muffled stillness they could hear the snow as it fell slowly past the attic window. Janella, as she had been well used, held back her tears.

'I will help Arthur with the fodder,' he whispered. 'Then I will see if Mary will not come home.'

They descended the winding stairway together. At the landing they could hear Alice mumbling in her room. Unprompted, Janella went in to her.

'Janella, I don't understand. The Reverend Clarke says there are soldiers at Horsebridge. You told me, there are soldiers at Horsebridge.' Alice was standing at her window, her hair loose, her hands wildly fluttering.

'No, there are soldiers in Lanson, not at Horsebridge. That was a long time ago.' To her surprise Janella found she had not lost all of her compassion.

'Then where is Samuel? Why has he not come back? Please Janella, why has he not come back?' Janella was at a loss but Alice had, as if not requiring an answer, already turned her attention back to the window.

'That is Francis. Where is Francis going?'

'To Mary.'

Somehow that seemed to satisfy her and, after adjusting the window a little, Alice returned to her bed and ostentatiously settled herself down, to sleep.

***

Arthur acknowledged his presence with characteristic incoherence and they began to bring the hay down from the loft. Half would be kept back for the white mare and the two scraggy oxen which had somehow survived the winter. The mare was harnessed and they walked slowly beside her along the slithery, rutted lane and between the white hedgerows. In the long field abutting the lane to Lidwell, they found their remaining twelve ewes, splattered and begrimed against the immaculate snow, but otherwise unharmed. The snow was very light now. After looking over the sheep, in a rare burst of surly optimism, Arthur expressed the view that the worst was over. If it wasn't, then there was a problem. The fodder was all but finished.

On the way back to the barn, Francis explained he would have to go and see if Mary was well.. Arthur grunted, as if he understood, as if he understood the problem of a wayward sister. Francis felt his temper rising again. Arthur seemed to understand that too and turned diplomatic.

'Take the mare,' he said. 'I 'ave no use for 'er now, not till the snow's gone.'

He watched Arthur shamble off to the kitchen for another breakfast and saddled the mare. He decided to follow the lane, through Lidwell to the bridge, and then make his way to Hampt. If Mary was not to be found at the Hawkings' farmhouse, he would ride down through the trees to the cottage where she was said to be living.

By the time he reached the river the snow had stopped and, improbably, a cold winter sun came splashing through the trees. He thought how he and Janella had, equally unexpectedly, come to some kind of truce. Perhaps he and Mary would also become reconciled. Though why they had grown so far apart, he could not properly explain. There was no sign of Mary at the bridge. He was further reassured and proceeded to Hampt, allowing the mare to pick her own way along the slippery lane.

George Hawking had inherited the farm at Hampt from his parents and it was here that George and Mary had spent the early weeks of their marriage. As it had turned out, the only weeks they had ever spent together. Now the farm seemed deserted. No sign of life. No footprints in the snow. No sound or trace of livestock. But as he entered the farmyard, a man in a green doublet, adjusting himself over his paunch as if he had just been roused, emerged from the front door of the farmhouse. Without prompting the mare halted, out of curiosity perhaps.

'I am looking for my sister, Mary Hawking.'

By way of reply, the man further straightened his breeches and pulled down his hat. 'She is at the cottage, sir.'

'And who are you?'

'I am John Wright, Mrs Hawking's servant, sir, 'trusted with the farm, sir, at the present time.'

'Are you resident in the house?'

Francis bristled but was not surprised. He rather expected Mary to have made some unusual arrangement. As the man did not immediately respond, he persisted; 'My sister does not live here?'

'She stays at the cottage, sir. I take 'er what she needs.' And then recognising a difficulty. 'This very day, sir, I take 'er what she needs, a flitch or two, bread, milk, whatever she might need for 'er fire. Every week, sir, I take 'er what she needs.'

To Francis, the man appeared unpleasantly servile and hence unreliable, so belatedly he became the protective brother. He picked up the reins.

'Then I expect to see you before the day is out at my sister's cottage, with everything she needs!'

He did not wait to observe the man's response, but set off at once down the track and through the trees to the very edge of the woods, to within sight of the greyish, white meadowland bordering the river. The cottage looked desolate, as he peered through the bare branches of oak and ash. There was no smoke from the chimney. He tethered the mare and, with a growing sense of foreboding, approached the cottage door. It was unlocked.

Inside it was colder and dark. There was an empty chair facing him and another turned to the fire, but the fire was dead. He could see the top of Mary's blue shawl protruding like a cowl above the back of the chair. In one movement, he hardly had to take a step the room being so small, he snatched the piece of rough material away from the window. The white light reflected from the snow streamed into the room as he came to face her. She was hunched and pale and for a moment he believed she was dead. But she was breathing lightly. He fell to his knees and took her hands, like ice to the touch, in both of his.

'Mary!' Her eyes remained closed, maliciously he thought, and immediately repented. 'Mary,' he repeated more softly. And this time her eyes opened slowly, reluctantly, and she took away her hands.

'Francis. What is it? What do you want? Her voice was clear, genuinely curious, unheard for so long.

'It is freezing,' he said impatiently. 'I believed you were dead. You have no fire.'

He looked round the bare room, the rough, whitewashed walls, a single shelf by the window with some pots and plates. Apart from the chairs there was no other furniture, save an old forlorn-looking oven in a corner by the fireplace. No spare logs on the hearth.

'Why are you here?' he stammered. 'There is nothing here. You have nothing! How do you live?'

She saw she would have to reply in one way or another, or he would continue to badger her, and she was tired. 'There's no Walt and Digory now. I pay John Wright to bring me food from the farm, and logs when I need them. Last night they ran out. It's been cold,' she added unnecessarily.

'I met him at the farm. He is clearly not doing the work for which he is paid.' Why did he sound so pompous? 'I told him to bring what you need, now.' Then realising that was hardly enough, that in truth he had not told Wright to come immediately, that moments before he had believed his sister frozen to death. 'We must get some warmth, or you will freeze. Have you an axe?'

She seemed profoundly unconcerned, not in the least grateful, had not thought to stir from her chair.

'Perhaps. There is a lean-to at the back.'

He went out, found the axe and cut some wood from some broken saplings, blown over in the winter. When he returned she brought out a flagon of ale from behind the oven. He sat on the rush mat close to the grate, as she had the night before, and managed to stir the embers into life. They watched in silence until the flame took. As she leaned toward the fire, he saw the flush had returned to her cheeks.

'They say you are a witch.' Mary did not react in any discernible way. 'You have made a Covenant with the Devil. When you walk alone by the river, you are communing with the Devil. You pray constantly for his army of Demons to cross the bridge and infect the Parish.'

This time she caught his eye and gave a cynical, close-lipped smile. She knew when he was embroidering.

'I know it is superstition, but they have hung witches in Lanson. Have you not heard of the witches' tower? She stared into the flames. 'If you continue this way, you risk arrest. To answer your question, that is why I am here.'

After a while she spoke. 'There must be something else. I have been waiting a long time for George. I am not yet taken for a witch.'

'General Fairfax is in Lanson,' he replied somewhat portentously. But she only raised her eyebrows and put her head to one side in mock amazement, as he remembered she had been used as a child. It was obvious the news had not yet reached her. How could it have done? John Wright's was probably the only voice she had heard in months. And the name of Fairfax clearly meant nothing at all to her.

'Fairfax is Parliament's General. It is expected the whole County will soon fall to the Roundheads. In a matter of weeks the war will be over, the fighting, thank God, will be over.'

Mary was not slow to take in the implications. Isolation had not at all impaired her intellect. She seemed immediately buoyed up and, even before she spoke, he saw the reason. 'Then all the soldiers will be coming home. You see, I am not such a fool for waiting, for not giving up! George I am certain is a prisoner. I have always known it! Prisoners will be exchanged.'

He was about to say that Fairfax had already released many prisoners in Lanson, but changed his mind. George would not have been in Lanson anyway. George was dead.

'Mary that may be, but listen to me!' She looked him in the eyes and tried to concentrate. 'Everything is about to change. Unusual behaviour, forgive me Mary, unusual behaviour like yours will be noticed. People will ask questions. Rumours, however false, will be taken account of. There will be a new Puritan order. The Reverend Clarke..' She seemed to take a new interest at the mention of the Reverend. 'The Reverend Clarke is concerned for your safety. There will be arrests. Land belonging to

Royalists will be confiscated. George was, is.,' He corrected himself quickly, 'a well-known, well-respected officer in the King's army! And though you no longer tend it, Mary, your land is rich and valuable. Do you understand? They will…'

He had become increasingly excited, as Mary had become increasingly troubled and confused. Her normally passive features had become tensed in a frown. She looked away from him towards the cottage door, as if seeking some means of escape.

'What would you have me do?'

It was the same question he had put to the Reverend Clarke and he gave her the same answer. 'Come back to Venterdon, before it is too late. Give up your land before it is taken from you. Do not wait by the river. When your husband returns, if you are not at the farm, will he not come at once to Venterdon? Where else would he look for you?'

She replied more quickly than he had expected. 'I will consider what you have said.'

There was a loud knock at the door. John Wright. He had brought milk, cheese, butter, ale, bacon and pickled beetroot. In the bags on the packhorse were dry logs, some of which they brought in to the hearth. What remained John and Francis took out to the back where he had found the axe. As Wright was about to leave, Francis took hold of his arm.

'John, I thank you. Please make sure my sister has what she needs. If you do, I will not forget. You knew my father, I think.' John Wright assented. 'You may trust me as you trusted him.' It was not the first time he had made use of Samuel's good name. And then as an afterthought. 'My sister has heard news her husband is kept a prisoner. That is why she waits...you understand?'

Wright nodded and touched his cap, but Francis was unimpressed by the man's obsequiousness, a man, he was convinced, not at all to be trusted. When Wright had gone, he re-entered the cottage. She handed him some of the bread and cheese and continued sorting out the food and drink along her shelf and on the oven top.

'You will think about it?' He should not be impatient. She had not rejected his proposal.

'Yes.'

He prepared himself to leave .The light was already failing. He would come again. They were parting on amicable enough terms, Perhaps she would do as he, or to be more accurate the Reverend Clarke, had advised. Then he remembered.

'The Reverend Clarke said there was talk, that you were turned papist.'

Again, as he had come to expect, she did not reply at once. It occurred to him she was debating with herself how to respond.

'Well, are you a papist? You do not attend church.' He felt her steady gaze. She would say just what she wanted to say, and no more. She made him sense his own inadequacy. He tried again. 'When the Puritans come they will root out Catholics. Was George a Catholic too?' She appeared to consider carefully.

'George was not a Catholic when he left. Now, I don't know.'

'Mary, I don't care about your Faith.' He raised his voice in frustration. 'But if you are a papist you had better conceal it. That man Wright is not to be trusted. If the Reverend Clarke thinks you are a Catholic, then perhaps others do. You do not understand the danger you are in!'

'You have already cast me out, you and our mother, you have cast me out.' Her voice was hard, contemptuous, controlled.

He was shocked. They had said nothing at all of their mother. Why had they said nothing of their own mother, who was sick, bedridden?

'She does not understand what has happened,' he muttered shamefacedly. 'She does not remember what happened. I think she is losing her mind......I cannot bear it any more. I think she needs you back. I think one day soon........She never leaves her bed now.'

He felt the tears coming to his eyes, grasped briefly his sister's hands. 'I'll come back,' he said and rushed out into the gathering dusk.

*

It was still light across the meadow. What remained of the snow had begun to freeze and crackle underfoot. The white mare stood patiently among the trees. He mounted, and not wishing to encounter John Wright again, set off down the gentle slope to the river.

When he reached the stables at Venterdon, Arthur was nowhere to be seen and the house was in darkness. Perhaps his mother was watching at the window. He could not tell. Where was Janella? Perhaps already gone to her chamber. There was some stew in the pot, which invariably hung over a dying fire, of a winter evening. He took some into a bowl and found some fresh bread. He was hungry, aching from the ride, glad to have found Mary well but uncomfortable in the knowledge of her likely Faith. She had avoided his question. How could she have become a papist? She spoke to no-one. Who could possibly have corrupted her? She clearly did not understand the danger she was in. Or perhaps the Reverend had been exaggerating. And why, out of all the people in his Parish, had Clarke been so concerned about Mary? Perhaps the Reverend Clarke was, in some obscure way, more concerned about his own future. Perhaps now, James Marten would finally have Clarke removed from the Rectory. It was strange they had not even spoken of their mother until the end. John and Robert, that was understandable. The questions came haphazardly. He was too tired now to think. His cot beckoned.

At Alice's door, he stopped to listen. If he went in she would feign sleep or ask where Samuel was. He could not bear that. He glanced across to Janella's door. She would welcome him into her bed. No more could he bear that, not now.

Instead, he mounted his cold, creaking stairway to the attic. His room looked different, the bed neatly made, the floor swept. His quill was returned to the well and his papers were meticulously stacked, waiting.

Chapter 4

As February turned to March, the merest whiff of optimism spread hesitantly along the valley, from Lanson to the Lynher. For several days the rain came in only the mildest of showers, soon blowing away to the east. And here and there a patch of blue dared to show itself behind grey, scudding clouds.

On the farms there was a predictable flurry of activity, a renewed sense of purpose. There were fields to be ploughed, hedges to be coppiced, fences to be repaired and a host of other tasks accumulated over the winter months and though, as everyone knew, the snows might yet return, the worst, as Arthur had surmised, was surely over.

In Lanson, Fairfax did not have to wait long to hear from his emissary, Hugh Peters. The Eastern Gentry would not after all rouse the peasantry as they had once rashly claimed they might. And so on March 1st, the General was able to advance from Lanson, safe in the knowledge that the New Model Army would not be trapped in Cornwall like its predecessor, and destroyed. As for the local gentry, they were summarily instructed to surrender to Fairfax in Bodmin where the remnants of Lord Hopton's Royalist army had already slipped away in the night, retreating in some disorder as far as Truro.

The following day, as Fairfax was duly being welcomed into Bodmin, the Prince of Wales who had been lying low at Pendennis Castle, was finally persuaded to sail from Land's End to Scilly and eventual exile. During a momentous few days, virtually the whole of Cornwall had fallen into Fairfax's hands. The Civil War in the South West was now set to reach its inevitable conclusion.

At the Pellow farm in Venterdon, even Alice seemed affected by this slight though distinctly palpable mood of optimism, this sense of the past being another place. When Janella brought her milk and bread or stew at dinner, more often than not she would find Alice sitting by the window, curiously peering out as if the world had completely changed, not just that the rain had stopped. Janella would pick up the shawl which had slipped from Alice's thin shoulders and though invariably few words passed between them, at least the silence was no longer strained.

Janella thought, 'Her memory is coming back very slowly. She has an idea now what happened to Samuel.'

Francis spent long hours in the fields with Arthur and sometimes a labourer from the village to help with the ploughing and the sowing of the oats which had been delayed by the weather. He had stopped writing, partly from sheer exhaustion or perhaps it had at long last served its purpose. Occasionally in the evening, he would summon the courage to enter Alice's room and in the few words they exchanged, he became aware, like Janella, of the change in his mother's demeanour.

'I think she remembers, Janella said. 'She's trying to put it all together.'

He nodded. 'Perhaps if Mary came home...Perhaps that would help.' And in expressing that thought reminded himself of his promise to return soon to Hampt.

But Mary of course, was otherwise preoccupied, still waiting for George whom she now expected daily. George had not been released yet, had not been one of those released in Lanson by General Fairfax. She had learned of that from John Wright, a less sensitive soul than Francis. Well he would come soon.. More prisoners would be freed and would return as the fighting came to an end.

Mary had briefly considered moving back to the farmhouse, now occupied during the day by John Wright and his wife. She had even contemplated returning to Venterdon, as Francis, or rather the Reverend Clarke, had advised. She smiled to herself at her brother's naivety. Well, nobody would ever know. So, the Reverend Clarke was a papist. The Queen was a papist. And even the King. It was not a sin to remain true to the old ways.

So Mary made no decision but stubbornly resumed her lonely walks along the river, and in the evening knelt at her makeshift altar and murmured the same prayers for the soul of her father and the return of her husband.

*

The glimmer of hope that had lightened the valley had not however spread as far as Burraton and Whiteford in the far west of this sprawling Parish. Christina Pellow had returned dejected from her meeting with James Marten. Unexpectedly, the Minister had not been at all roused by the news of Fairfax's arrival in Lanson. In all truth she had found him not a little tiresome. Power, he had explained dully, sometimes has only the appearance of changing hands. Beneath the surface, the same figures pull the same strings. How had the Reverend Clarke illegally maintained his position at the Rectory, except by some influence of the County Committee? And how would he most likely continue to do so?

'My appeal to the House of Lords is unlikely to be successful, ' the Minister had lamented. And then gone on to explain why.

Marten had been altogether unbearably long-winded, Christina supposed because no-one else would listen to him. At one point, the Minister's pessimism had been so overwhelming that she had been afraid of his giving up and returning to London, and then where else would she possibly find spiritual sustenance in such a God-forsaken place?

She had stayed at Burraton much longer than intended, constantly reassuring the Minister of his rightful place at the Rectory and of the new order which would soon prevail to his advantage. And then hurrying along the darkening lane to Whiteford, the crunch of freezing snow beneath her feet, Christina had thought how strange it was that she should provide consolation to the Minister and not the other way around. After all, though Robert had no intimation of it, was it not she who was most desperately in need of spiritual comfort? The Minister must not continue to disappoint her, or she was truly lost.

After that, as the weather improved, Christina had wisely stayed away from Burraton. At first she had turned to her Bible, but for the first time in her life it would not comfort her, any more than the Minister. To Christina, it was as if the very Word of God had failed to offer solace, the words of the Gospel that had hitherto coloured her whole life. Robert would not understand that. Nobody in this backwater of a place even had the capacity to understand, only Minister Marten. And yet he himself seemed only drowned in a sea of troubles, troubles of his own making.

For days on end, Christina kept to herself. Thomas was consigned to the perpetual care of Liddy, his one-time wet nurse and now servant to all their needs. Robert, seeing but not understanding, went out at dawn with his dogs. And at night she turned away from her husband, and tried to sleep.

When once he returned from hunting, in his buff coat and floppy hat, to triumphantly lay a great brown hare on the parlour table, Christina could only burst into tears and flee to her chamber. It was not the hare, Christina screamed to her inner self, but Robert's simple enjoyment of the pleasures of life, his disregard for all the rest, that stubborn inability to understand his own depravity. Christina had always known about depravity, not least her own. She had grown up with the knowledge that to be saved a person must believe the Gospel and repent. She had never questioned this. Her first husband, a Minister of profound conviction, with whom she had prayed solemnly until the very end, had taught her this above all. Frequently, she recalled his words, as she did now, lying alone in her bed.

'None of our capacities can lift us from this abyss of our fallen state, only an act of free Grace from God.'

Robert did not follow her immediately to their chamber. Christina, though often self-absorbed, did not usually weep. When she did, in his presence, it left him taken aback and confused. He knew there to be a gulf of understanding which he could not fathom. Now he could only lower his large frame, much like that of Samuel, his father, to sit by the fire and take off his boots. The dead animal of which, only moments before he had been so proud, stared back at him vacantly.

'One for the pot,' he said to Liddy curtly when she came in from the brew-house with six year old Thomas. And then seeing his son's small, worried-looking face, at once relented. 'Liddy will show you how to skin him, Thomas. And next time, if mother allows it, you shall come with me and catch another.'

Thomas brightened and Liddy diplomatically picked up the hare by his hind legs and motioned for him to join her in the kitchen. Robert stayed by the fire, warming himself, plucking up courage. Christina was normally so self-controlled, severe even, everywhere save in their chamber. That made it all the more shocking when she lost her temper or wept.

The country life he knew did not suit her, but he could never leave Clymestone. That would be unbearable. And no matter how much Christina urged him, he had no desire for position, no wish to make his way in the world. Her first husband, the Minister, had been an older man, serious, admired. Christina had been at the heart of his congregation in Lanson. It was understandable if sometimes she should think of her previous life and regret its passing. Her husband, the Minister, would not have been so pleased to spring a hare and set the hounds on him. And then bring him home, over his shoulder. The contrast for Christina must sometimes be all too apparent.

But then, Robert reflected, there were compensations for both of them.

Christina, in her anguish, had thrown herself on the bed, then kneeling unsteadily had pulled the curtains around her, shut everything out. She had tried to think clearly but sleep had quickly overtaken her. When she opened her eyes, Robert was standing over her. It was the drawing back of the curtain that had caused her to wake. He had taken off his coat and jerkin and now stood beside the bed in shirt and breeches, his gaze roaming from her wide, brown eyes along the full length of her tightly secured but unmistakably supple body. His face, she saw, bore a mixed expression of lust and contrition.

'This is what it always comes to,' she thought. 'It is Robert's solution.

But at the same time she felt her breathing quicken, her lips part and her body arch spontaneously towards him. Now he was clumsily undoing the bow to her cap which he pulled off and threw to the floor, revealing her short, pale hair. He removed the kerchief from her throat. His hand was on her breast.

'Thomas,' she murmured, suddenly afraid of discovery.

'...is with Liddy,' came the gruff reply. He was unbuttoning her bodice, 'skinning the hare in the yard.'

Afterwards, fully sated, they lay together quietly, though Christina clung to him in a kind of desperation of which Robert, true to his nature, was perfectly unaware.

'You stay away from Burraton now,' he said lightly, as if to provoke her.

'Perhaps I will go back.'

'Why do you go to him?' Robert persisted. 'Does he remind you of your husband?'

'You know I hate this ungodly place!' She pulled away from him, her former mood returning with a vengeance. 'Your Rector is an imposter!' Her voice had become harsh, gutteral, in its anger. 'He does not even preach the Word of God!'

He was further taken aback. He had never understood how such things could so overwhelm her. Christina had started to rise from the bed, in a kind of fury. But he pulled her back.

'Christina, I do not understand you. Do we not love one another? Do we not obey the will of God? What has that to do with these men of the Church? Why, for Heaven's sake, do you say this place is ungodly?'

Recognising his distress, she allowed his embrace but would not return it.

'Can this be God's will?' Her voice had shrunk to a whisper. 'I love you Robert, but you are not righteous. You do not seek salvation, and so it will not be given.'

His mind plunged uncertainly into a distant past to grasp a long lost memory that had once given him pause for thought, and which Christina's words had somehow revived.

'He who desires to be righteous, is righteous. He that would repent, doth repent.'

At least he had aroused her curiosity. 'Why do you say that, Robert? Is it written in the Scripture? Is that the Word of God?'

Robert could not say but he was able to repeat the words and it seemed to calm her and bring them closer together. Somehow they had reached a point from which there was no going back. For a time, they were able to talk to one another spontaneously and without fear. Robert admitted his lack of religious conviction. He could see no difference between the Reverend Clarke and Minister Marten. He was a God-fearing man but had no sense of shame and had no doubt that salvation would be theirs, according to God's will.

Robert had no reason to dissemble and Christina could only listen to her husband with trembling affection. But she was not convinced. God knew she had been got with child out of wedlock. What had she done to expiate her sin? What had either of them ever done to merit God's Grace. And how would God take into account this, their life in Clymestone? The world was changing quickly. Everything they knew would soon be swept aside in the wake of Fairfax's armies. Did God intend them to stay in Clymestone for ever? Must they not rather, in compliance with His Will, commit themselves to this new order? Or else it and God would surely pass them by.

They fell silent. They could hear Liddy's voice in the yard. He rose from the bed and hitched up his breeches. Standing at the window, he could see Liddy and Thomas by the brew-house door.

'I have always lived here in Clymestone, and my family for generations. You cannot ask me to go to Lanson.'

'It would not be the end of the world.' Her voice wavered half way between derision and frustration. 'At all events, you take no real account of your family. You never see them, not even at church.......which they do not attend.'

'My mother is ill,' he said hesitantly, still looking into the yard.

'She has lost her mind, and that is why you never see her,' Christina retorted, re-buttoning herself. 'Francis is a no-account,' she continued in a matter of fact way, 'and Mary tramps the riverbank in search of her dead husband! Your family is nothing to you.' She let her head fall back on the pillow, sneering almost.

'You forget my brother, John.'

'...who is in Callington.'

'Perhaps I should become a carpenter and set up shop in Callington. Is that what you want?'

'I admire your brother. He has made his own way.'

Robert came back to the bed but refrained from discussing his elder brother further. It was true. John had married, left the Parish and made his own way. He had not concerned himself with the rights and wrongs of the war, but rather sought to profit from it.

The armies that had passed through Callington, unused to the rough Cornish roads, had needed to repair their broken wagons. The bereaved had unexpectedly found themselves in need of a coffin. And John Pellow had always been happy to oblige. His workshop had expanded; he had taken on labourers in search of work, of any means to support themselves. Now he had opened stables. Was this what Christina wanted of him? Surely not. John Pellow was the kind of man who attended church simply because it was required. A purposeful man, but without conviction. His God was Mammon.

'I will consider what you have said. I will mend my ways. You are right. When my father died the family fell apart. Perhaps we need not stay.'

Robert thought perhaps that half promise would suffice as, by way of emphasis, he took her into his arms once more. But Christina had other ideas.

'It is Lent.' she said, struggling to free herself. 'It is a time of abstention. I must take care not to submit to you,'

***

Liddy had taken Thomas through to the kitchen where she had paused to pick up a sharp knife and some string, and then through the brew-house to the yard. At the side of the well, she had laid the hare down and quickly cut off his feet. There was a nail, set at head height close to the brew-house door, to which

Liddy expertly attached the hare's right hind leg. The hare dangled with his long, brown back towards them, long ears flopping just above the cobbles.

'Your pa's caught a good'n 'ere,' Liddy remarked, taking the knife from her apron. 'e's a real March 'are. March is the time for 'ares, see.'

Thomas listened carefully, all the time intent on what Liddy would do next. His father would ask.

'We 'ave to take 'is jacket off first,' said Liddy, reaching up to his hind leg and cutting into the skin.

And before Thomas knew it, Liddy was peeling the skin back down the leg and then the other leg and in one swift movement the white scut was removed and discarded.

'That's what the dogs see when they're after 'im, 'is white tail bobbin' up an' down. 'e's fast min', an 'are is faster'n any ol' rabbit.'

Thomas tried not to flinch as Liddy turned the body of the hare this way and that, alternately cutting the sinews and pulling the fur, to reveal the dark flesh beneath. When Liddy came to the head she did not, as Thomas feared, chop it and send it rolling round the yard, but instead cut skilfully around and down the front legs so that what Liddy called the jacket came of neatly in one piece.

' 'ow about that then, Master Thomas? Liddy said, proudly holding the hare up by the shoulders for him to see, the skin and the head slumped without the body.

Thomas wanted to run, but stood rooted to the spot, wide-eyed and gaping. In her satisfaction at a job well done, Liddy did not seem to notice.

'Now we've got somethin' we can eat,' she said, leaving the skin at the well with the feet, and turning to the wall. 'But we got to get 'is guts out first.'

Thomas could only watch in horror as Liddy cut open the animal, allowing the entrails to spill down the wall. Reaching inside, she pulled out first the liver and after that the heart.

'That's 'is 'eart, see, Thomas. 'e's got a big'n too. That's what makes 'im run fast, see.'

But now for the first time, Liddy saw the horror in the little boy's face, pale and draining of blood, like the hare, and understood how brutal it must seem to one so young and to one so cosseted. His father, Liddy thought, should not have told me to do this.

'We'll leave 'im now,' she said quietly, 'for the blood to drain,' and took a cloth from her apron to wipe her bloodied hands.

Later, warmed and in the kitchen with Liddy, Thomas had become quite reconciled to the fate of the hare.

'When are we going to eat him, Liddy?'

'Well,' Liddy considered, sucking her teeth, 'I've a min' to roast them loins and put the rest in a stew for later.'

Thomas's curiosity was unappeased. Doubtless, his father would want to know all about the hare.

'Why do hares come out in March, Liddy?'

Liddy knew that in March the hares sought each other out in order to copulate, but considered that an unsuitable explanation.

'Mad as a March 'are, they say. That's because they do their fightin' in March, see. 'a'n't you never seen two March 'ares standin' up to one another, an fightin'?'

'I only ever saw one hare,' Thomas replied, ruing his lack of experience, 'and he's hanging up in the yard, where we left him.'

'Well,' said Liddy, encouraging, 'that's why we catch 'em in March. They got it comin' to 'em, see....so we catch 'em to stop 'em fightin'.'

Liddy thought obscurely that this simple explanation might, in Thomas's eyes, somehow make allowance for her earlier brutality. At least Thomas saw no objection to the logic.

'And people stop fighting in March too,' said Thomas, knowledgeably. 'It is the will of God.'

Chapter 5

'George?'

It was barely more than a whisper and even as she spoke she knew she was mistaken. The man lying with his back to her on the dirt floor was not her husband. George's hair was darker, streaked here and there with grey. The brown leather jerkin, full breeches and stained yellow stockings might well have been those of a soldier in the service of the King, but it was not George.

Mary stood transfixed. The man seemed to be stirring. Realising her mistake, her hand slipped to the place in her petticoats where she kept the dagger, the dagger George had given her before he had left.

'These are dangerous times,' he had insisted. 'Do not hesitate to use it.'

She thought to flee, but something prevented her. Somehow, although it was not George, it had already become in her mind, a fateful encounter. A sudden shower, soaking her blue shawl and white cap, had brought her once more to seek shelter in the ruined cottage close to the river. During all the months of waiting, she had come to regard this place, this ruin, as her own personal refuge. Now its only dry corner was occupied by this intruder, this stranger who was not George.

Disappointment turned quickly to anger and frustration as, grasping tightly the dagger in her skirts, she waited for the man to wake, to give a proper account of himself. She stepped forward a little, the better to observe him. He was young, much younger than George. He lay huddled, facing the stone wall and clutching a kind of leather satchel, which served as his pillow. His hair was brown, curly, neatly cut. She watched him open his eyes, slowly as if from a very deep sleep, and at the same time, with a start, saw the brightly decorated hilt and thin blade of a rapier, lying in the dirt close to his right hand.

The soldier, for so she imagined him to be, made no further move, though she could tell he was awake. Unconsciously, she loosened her grip on the dagger. In all likelihood, he was a soldier in the King's armies and therefore, she reasoned falsely, would not threaten her. After some minutes, the man heaved a great sigh and hoisted himself to a sitting position, his back to the wall. Only then did he open his eyes fully and look up to her. To avoid the rain, splattering through what remained of the roof, she had moved more closely to him than she had intended.

So they regarded one another with curiosity. His eyes, which settled frankly on her own, were unusually blue, his small beard, it appeared to her, fastidiously trimmed. Though clearly exhausted, his face was pale and drawn, there was a calmness about him which led her to release the dagger silently into her skirts. When he spoke, it was with the accent and confidence of an educated man.

'You do not have to fear me,' he said softly. 'I will not harm you.'

'Who are you, sir?' It was unnecessarily brusque and brought the hint of a smile to his lips.

'I might ask the same of you,' he retorted, rising to her challenge. 'I had not expected to encounter an angel in a pigsty.'

'You blaspheme, sir!' She took a step back, into the rain.

'Forgive me.' His voice was again soft, beguiling. 'I meant no offence. As you may have concluded, I am nothing but a poor fugitive, though not I assure you, a fugitive from justice. That is what brings me here. I am hiding. As you can see,' he gestured towards his right thigh, 'I am a little discomfited.'

There was blood across the front of his breeches, some of it fresh, which she had not noticed. She was not shocked having seen wounded soldiers before, but she was confused. There had been no fighting. According to John Wright, Fairfax had already advanced peacefully from Lanson towards Bodmin. Yet this man appeared to have been wounded, and recently. From the way he spoke, he was a gentleman, an officer doubtless in the King's army.

The shower was blowing itself out across the river. She was certain he would not prevent her from leaving. And yet, at the back of her mind was the thought that this officer might just have news of her husband. Perhaps it was only this invisible thread that detained her.

'You must explain yourself, sir. Who are you? What has happened to bring you here? You must understand....' She was backing towards the opening in the wall, where once there had been a door. 'I risk my reputation...my life,' she added disingenuously.

The man observed her. She could not make out whether he was amused or saddened by her aggressive, if calculated display. He made no move towards her but rather seemed to be considering his position. What should he tell her?

'It is true,' he said at last, without emotion. 'You risk your life. The officers of the King's regiments hereabouts would have me shot. Thomas Fairfax, on the other hand, being a civilised man, would first have me arrested and then hanged. As you may imagine, I prefer to avoid them both equally. If you are found in my company, you will certainly be arrested yourself, one way or another.' He paused, perhaps to allow her to flee, but Mary simply waited for him to continue. 'I will explain.' He picked up the rapier, not to threaten her but rather, it seemed to her, to convince himself of the rightness of his cause. 'The King's regiments in these parts have seen fit to surrender to General Fairfax. I am,' he corrected himself, 'was an officer in Colonel Edgcumbe's Regiment of Foot which has for some time been engaged in the defence of the Tamar. 'I did not assent,' a slight tremor entered his voice, ' to this cowardly submission. I fled into Devon and received a musket ball..' He paused again to judge her reaction. 'My name, which I recommend you to forget, is Andrew Hampton.'

Hampton had spoken, for the most part clearly and concisely, perhaps underestimating Mary's capacity to assimilate. Mary for her part, had listened carefully and understood perfectly well.

As far as she could tell, Hampton's account of himself was plausible enough. But what should she do? Leave him to his own devices? Bring him food and water? It was not likely she would be caught. Help him on his way? Her eyes strayed to the wound in his thigh, now further staining his breeches.

'It is no more than a graze. The ball did not lodge..but we made a bargain.'

'A bargain?'

'You claim to be no angel. I accept I am merely landed in a Cornish pigsty. But who are you then? And what are you doing here?'

She hesitated. 'I am Mary Hawking. I am waiting for my husband. I came here to shelter from the rain.' The contrast between his explanation and hers almost caused her to smile, but not quite. And again it occurred to her there was something fateful in their meeting.

'Then if you are to meet with your husband Mary, you must leave now. I have told you of the danger. Go! I beg you not to betray me.'

He had struggled to his feet, pulling himself up against the wall, and was now peering intently through the hole which had once been a window, towards the river and the bridge. His face contorted with pain. Clearly he was quite incapable of taking flight or even of defending himself.

'Sit down!' she hissed. 'Nobody is coming! My husband...my husband will not come today...now. It is too late. I promise you. You need have no fear, sir.' She took his arm and helped him resume his former position against the wall. In the urgency of the moment, she had, unwittingly, taken control. 'You must stay here.' The man looked dubious. 'My husband fights for the King, sir. I will not betray you. When night falls, I will bring you food and water. I will clean your wound. You will be safe till then...'

Whether or not the man believed her, she could not tell. When she turned at the entrance his eyes had already closed. He was in her hands, like it or not. Quickly she made her way across the meadow towards the treeline, conscious she might already have been observed. The rain had cleared but the sky hung low and uniformly grey. Strangely she had not thought to continue her way to the bridge, as had been her unvarying habit, in expectation of her husband's coming.

At the cottage she found some bread and fruit and hastily wrapped them in a cloth and then took a jug and filled it with water. She stirred up the fire and added some logs, took off her shawl and cap and hung them close to the fire to dry. She thought perhaps she would pray, but her mind was too much in a whirl. Instead she went to her bedchamber, not to pray but to comb the damp straggles from her hair. She felt unkempt, unworthy even of the task she had set herself. She might have left the man to his own devices, but then she had been certain he would die. Perhaps he would die anyway. Perhaps, she thought with sudden horror, she should be tending him now, not wait till nightfall. Perhaps he was bleeding to death even now, as she sat on her bed, prettifying herself.

But no, she had made the right decision. The meadow by the river was a wide open space. If she were seen entering the ruin a second time, suspicion would be aroused.

With this held firmly in mind, she returned to her chair by the fire to wait for the night, still some hours away.

As the day wore to a close, Mary became convinced the man could not be left where he was, nor could she bring him food every day to the ruin, until his wound was healed. That way, sooner or later, she would be found out. She therefore resolved the man Hampton must be brought back here, to the cottage. She could, Mary persuaded herself, conceal him without difficulty. Her only visitors, John Wright and perhaps Francis, would not be a problem. The Reverend Clarke, for reasons best known to himself, had apparently set her aside.

At dusk she slipped out to the woods and found a suitable length of ash. Hampton would need to support himself as they crossed the meadow. And when the grey afternoon finally gave way to darkness, she stoked up the fire, put on her shawl and cap, gathered together the articles she had prepared and stole down through the trees to the meadow.

No moon or stars lit her way, but the path being so familiar, so well-trodden in her fruitless quest, Mary had no need of guidance. Only the wrapped food and stick in her left hand and in her right the jug, which she tried in vain to hold upright to stop the water slopping on her skirts, slowed her pace. When she came to the tiny, crumbling ruin with the gaping hole for an entrance, she paused and held her breath. Perhaps he had gone. Perhaps he was already dead.

But then from the doorway, she could just hear the sound of his regular breathing mingling with the familiar, dark rush of the river. As her eyes slowly grew used to the pale light reflected from the broken stone walls, his form appeared to her exactly as she had first encountered it. She said nothing but watched as he gradually became aware of her presence and hauled himself to a sitting position against the wall.

She offered him the bread and fruit and told him to drink from the jug as much as he needed. Then she explained, with the cloth and the remaining water, she would clean the wound. She allowed him to eat and drink without interruption. That he neither spoke nor smiled in acknowledgement unsettled her. She stood by the doorway, preferring the sound of the river to that of his eating and drinking. Already she resented him. She lingered a little, listening to the river. Perhaps she was making a mistake. When she returned to him, he had finished off the food and drunk most of the water.

'You are a brave woman, Mary,' he said. 'Does an angel carry a knife?'

She was at once flattered, startled and angry.

'The dagger in your skirts will suffice.' Still she did not comprehend. He smiled grimly. 'To slit open my breeches.'

He took the weapon from her, considered it critically as she imagined a soldier would, and then where the stain had dried and spread and dried again, with the point ripped open his breeches. Then with his two hands he pulled the tear wide to reveal the streak of torn flesh beneath. The wound was not large and the blood had dried and congealed. Kneeling at his side she dipped the cloth, squeezed out the excess water and began to wipe away the grit and dirt from where it had become embedded. Hampton observed her, silently. The wound appeared superficial. The musket ball had apparently caught him only a glancing blow.

'Shall I bandage it?'

By way of reply, Hampton raised his knee a little, the better to examine in the pale light, the dull, red smudge on his thigh.

'No, I think there is bruising. See.' he pointed to where the ball had penetrated the flesh most deeply. She peered closely into the wound and saw that the skin around it was darkening blue and grey. 'I must cut it out or it will rot,' he said bluntly. 'The dagger is no good.' He handed it back, almost dismissively. And she knew, though his life might depend on it, he would ask nothing more of her.

'Mr Hampton,' she began rather pompously, 'I have already considered your position and mine. If I leave you, you will die. If you come with me, I take a risk, but we might both be saved.' She paused for Hampton to protest but he refrained. 'I live alone. I have few visitors.......and......and I am not afraid of you.' Still Hampton said nothing. 'I have brought a stick.' She reached for it to show him, forcing him to raise his eyes to meet her own in the gloom.

'I do not believe in many things, Mary. But I do believe the light of God touches us all.'

Not reflecting on Hampton's words, she perceived them nevertheless to be his way of accepting her terms and so helped him to stand and handed him the stick. There was nothing more to be said, nothing more she could say, though her heart soared.

A handful of stars consented to light their way but the journey of no more than half a mile was tortuous enough, Hampton stumbling continually on the lumpy surface of the meadow and more than once slithering in agony to the cold, wet turf, only for Mary to help him to his feet. As the ground rose to the trees, though drier underfoot, it seemed impossible he would continue.

'This is my cottage, sir, through the trees,' she encouraged him. 'There is a warm fire.'

Strangely enough, it was exactly as she had imagined it, sitting in her chair by the hearth as the afternoon drew on. For Mary, it was a kind of triumph. So when the time came, it was almost with reluctance that she opened the cottage door and brought him to her chair by the fire. It was not George. She did not even bring George to mind. But in the act of placing Andrew Hampton in her own, comfortable, upholstered chair by the fire, her obsession at last began to dissipate.

'A knife,' he said, his breathing still fitful from the exertion, 'for meat or bread....Put it in the fire.'

To her consternation, he had manoeuvred himself to the rush matting on the floor. There was a desperate urgency about him now. He was tearing at his breeches, to reveal the whole of his thigh. She held the blade to the flame as he instructed, until he leant forward and took it from her. She looked away and after a moment fled to her chamber.

When much later, she summoned the courage to return, she found the knife bloodied on the floor and Hampton unconscious. She brought herself to examine the wound, where the flesh had been cut away, where the bruising had been cut away.

Hampton recovered consciousness to find his thigh had been cleaned and bandaged. There was a pillow beneath his head and a cover over his legs. He reached automatically for his rapier which still lay untouched by his side, the hilt and cup glistening in the firelight. His leather satchel hung at the door, casting small hesitant shadows in the first blush of morning.

***

Something momentous was happening. Alice had sensed its coming as she had the Spring, before its time was due, before the sap had risen to the leaf. Samuel, the real Samuel, whether in her dreams or in her memories, but returning nevertheless. Spring was only the harbinger of Summer and she had always connected Samuel with the Summer, and not just its warmth. Summer could be harsh too, she knew that. And she remembered perhaps, a sequence of events that only Janella would be able to confirm. Janella, Alice thought, knew everything. And she was kinder now. That, she reflected, had something to do with Francis.

'Janella.' she said lightly, plucking idly at her counterpane. 'I have been dreaming, or perhaps remembering, I am not sure which.' Janella said nothing. 'Janella,' Alice pursued tremulously, 'if I told you something would you........would you tell me the truth of it?' Janella nodded. 'And Janella, will you, though I am your mistress, call me Alice, as once you did?'

'I will call you Alice,' Janella replied, though it was not something she had ever done or thought to do.

Alice got up from her chair by the window and clambered into bed. 'You care for me more than I deserve,' she remarked, pulling the covers up to her shoulders. 'Sit by me please.'

Janella sat on the bed and Alice took hold of her hand. And then she began, quickly so she would not lose the memory, lose Samuel for ever.

'One or perhaps two years ago, perhaps more, there was a rumour that soldiers were coming. The Reverend Clarke came to warn us, there would be fighting at the bridge. We had to stay inside.' Janella brought her other hand to Alice's in acknowledgement of the truth of her words. 'The Reverend Clarke knew what was happening. I listened to them. The Queen was in Lanson, he said. They were coming to take her. He had to pray.' She was already becoming confused, losing her thread.

'Alice!' Janella interrupted. She had never addressed her mistress thus. 'You must not upset yourself. It is true what you say.........'

But Alice would not be deterred. 'Samuel became angry. I tell you. Do you not recall Janella, how his anger filled the room? He was so loud!' Alice visibly shrank into her pillow. 'John is a coward!' he said. 'Robert is hitched to a Puritan whore!' 'Francis is a debauched bastard!' I remember his words, Janella, Janella...'

Alice was breathing rapidly. Her eyes wept, the tears washing down her cheeks. She looked to the window, as if for some means of escape, but Janella grasped her meagre body tight to her bosom.

'I remember, Janella.' Alice would not be comforted, nor restrained. "They are all debauched!' He put on his sword. He would not be cowardly. I begged him. Do you not recall, Janella? He pushed me aside. 'Woman,' he said. And that..was the last I saw of him.'

'But he came back, Alice...'

'I waited. I waited. Francis came. I remember Francis came. I heard the soldiers, tramp tramp. From the bridge to Almshouses. Horses, the jingle of horses...Afterwards they brought them to the churchyard. Francis went to look. Nobody there. They buried the Puritans by the bridge.'

Janella wished it to be night time. But the day had hardly dawned. Arthur and Francis had breakfasted and were out on the farm. She would rather have dealt with her housework than this uncontrolled outpouring from her mistress. The day promised to be fine, fine as ever it was likely to be in March. She had bedding to wash. Though the sun was weak and unpredictable, the sheets might still dry on the hedgerows. But Alice was beginning to remember. She would have to see it through. Relive it all, once more.

'I waited all day for Samuel. He did not come back.' Alice seemed annoyed. 'He kept me waiting. 'Woman!' he called me. Francis went to look. There were forty or fifty dead, he said, brought up to the church.....Then they found him in a hedge!' Alice gave a snort. 'His legs were sticking out into the lane!'

Janella could tolerate it no longer. Gently she released herself and stood away from the bed. Alice seemed in a kind of daze. Janella no longer had the strength either to encourage her or to urge her to stop. Alice would not stop anyway, but her normally thin voice had deepened and reduced to little more than a croak.

'They brought him back. Yes, he came back Janella. You are right. It is all true! They brought him back and took him to his bed.' Janella saw that Alice was now coming to understand. His bed was her bed. Samuel had been brought to lie exactly where she herself now lay. 'He was not dead,' Alice looked to Janella for confirmation. 'But there was something wrong. I looked to see where he was wounded, but there was nothing. Only he would not speak to me. His face was twisted.' Alice twisted her face by way of illustration. 'He listened to me but would not answer.' Her face was bathed in tears and perspiration. Janella took off her clean apron, all she had to hand, to wipe away the tears. 'He would not answer me, Janella.'

She closed her eyes. Her dreams were no longer dreams, but memories. Janella, for her part, had never forgotten the events of that terrible day nor of the months that were to follow. Alice would speak to her again, she had no doubt. She would have to be prepared.

Chapter 6

When later that night, Mary had returned to Hampton lying unconscious in the flickering firelight, it was with a sense of profound horror at what she had done. The man sprawled before her dying fire in the dead of night, the colour drained entirely from his pale, twisted face, seemed far less prepossessing than the gentleman soldier she had discovered in the ruin.

Gingerly she had placed more logs on the fire, not wanting him to wake, but realising nevertheless that having come thus far she could hardly now retreat, throw him out and allow him to die, as he surely would, one way or another.

Kicking the bloodied knife aside, steeling herself, she had knelt once more to examine the wound in his thigh. It was larger, bloodier now, but the creeping darkness of the flesh had been ruthlessly cut away. Compassion had unexpectedly overcome revulsion. As before, she had cleaned it as well as she could and then had torn her white, linen scarf to make a bandage. Awkwardly, for she would hardly have removed his breeches, she had wound the scarf around his thigh and tied it tight. The blood had spread inexorably to the surface, but what more could she do?

Hampton was becoming restless, gabbling unintelligibly, his body drenched in perspiration, his head twisting this way and that on the rush matting. She had gone to her bed and taken one of her two feather pillows to place beneath his head. Above all he must not wake!

Throughout the remainder of the night she had lain awake, dreading the dawn when she would have to speak to him, when she would have to come to terms with what she done. Although she now had unlimited power over this man; she could have him arrested, let him be taken away, still she felt herself at a disadvantage, perhaps because he was a gentleman. Or perhaps it was his manner, which she could not grasp. He had not behaved, nor spoken in a superior fashion as gentlemen commonly did. Nor had he begged or threatened her, but instead had warned her of the risk she was taking. He had seemed to regard her openly, honestly, admiring her supposed bravery it was true, but not to cajole or flatter but simply as an expression of belief. She had been led to say, entirely without encouragement, 'I am not afraid of you.' she regretted that most of all. It made her feel weak, exposed.

But that man, the man she had so determinedly brought across the meadow, was surely not the same as the one she had just left unconscious, only a few yards from her bed. It was almost as if she had been dreaming. Perhaps she had. The first man had never existed.

As the day broke, cold and hesitant, reluctantly lightening her tiny chamber through the tattered, makeshift curtain, Mary found herself at last drifting into sleep. Only to be woken moments later by a sudden, indeterminate screech. She half rose, wide-eyed and in that instant remembered she was not alone. Without further thought, she pushed back the covers and reached for her clothes. The screeching had stopped. She dressed quickly, pulled a comb impatiently through her curls and failed to find her cap. But she was too tired to care and so, resolutely, went in to face him.

He was struggling to sit up. The noise which had woken her had been the scraping of her chair on the flags, as he had attempted to lean against it. She brought the chair up to him.

'Sit in the chair. I will help you.'

With difficulty she helped him to his feet and into the chair. She could see he needed to keep his leg straight but there was nothing except a large log by the grate which she manoeuvred into position so that he might rest his foot. Then she sat opposite him in the rickety spindle chair by the hearth. He was still recovering his breath. She had noticed before his tendency only to speak as he found it necessary. It irritated her now as it had then, in spite of his evident pain.

Perhaps she should take advantage of the circumstance and relieve her irritation at the same time. Perhaps she should interrogate him. What was he doing here? He had never properly explained himself. Why had he fled into Devon and promptly returned to Cornwall? It did not make sense. But she was too late.

'You do not look so kindly on me. Did you change your mind in the night?'

'No,' she replied unconvincingly and more aggressively than she had intended.

'You live modestly, frugally even for the wife of an officer,' he persisted. 'I have no wish to impose on such frugality. I have money.' He nodded towards the leather satchel, hanging at the door.

'I am not poor,' she interrupted.' I choose to live this way.' And then more softly, 'My husband is Captain George Hawking. He fought from the beginning with Sir Bevil. Perhaps you know of him?'

Hampton did not answer at once and seemed reluctant. 'George Hawking. I know the name. Where is he? When do you expect him? He may not take kindly...'

'I have not heard, since Bristol...' she stammered.

She wanted to weep, wanted him to see her tears but could not summon them. Then to avoid explanation, she determined rashly to assert herself, to show him she was not to be trifled with, and blurted out that it did not concern her how she was regarded by him or anyone else. In her anxiety for self-justification, and because Hampton drew no unnecessary attention to himself in spite of his wound, she seemed to have entirely forgotten the events of the previous day She would wait for her husband, she said, come what may, and he would return as he had promised.

Hampton, sometimes grimacing in pain, nevertheless listened carefully without comment or judgement. And slowly, as it became clear he would not ridicule her, she could not help but reveal to him the way of life she had chosen. She began to relax. There was a kind of safety in speaking to a stranger. It was like a confession, but whereas with the Reverend Clarke she had sobbed in desperation, with Andrew Hampton it was different.

Hampton did not instruct or counsel or judge, nor pretend to act as God's true representative in Clymestone. Hampton just listened and as a result slowly built up a picture of Mary's life: The farmhouse she and George Hawking had briefly shared and which a year previously she had abandoned, unable to bear alone its terrible familiarity; John Wright who supposedly brought her all the necessities of life, as she needed them ; her long walks by the river ; her solitariness and virtual estrangement from her family.

'Now I have told you everything!' She smiled as if a great burden had been lifted.

'Not everything, though you are wise to be cautious. Are you and your husband both of the old Faith?' She was taken aback, became flustered again. 'Your wedding ring,' he explained, also smiling, 'is on the finger of your right hand. I suppose it was your husband put it there?' She nodded, feigning unconcern. 'Mary.' He leaned forward and gave a sharp intake of breath as his foot toppled awkwardly from the log.

Promptly she set it right, feeling guilty as for the first time she registered his distress. She brought him some water and as an afterthought, some bread and cheese from the shelf on the wall. It was all she had left.

'Mary,' he continued after taking some of the cheese, 'you take too many risks, without knowing what you are at. It is already five years since all Catholic priests were banished. If they are found now they are summarily executed. You and your husband are at serious risk simply for your Faith, particularly now that Fairfax is in control. To make matters worse, you take into your house a soldier you know nothing of and who is sought by both opposing armies. What is more, 'He half turned towards her empty shelf, 'you do not even have food for yourself.'

He had indeed brought her to a strange pass. Instead of trembling with fear, as no doubt had been his intention, Mary had begun to laugh out loud for the first time in years, at the incongruity of it all. It was Hampton's turn to be taken aback. She seemed to be afflicted by a kind of delirium.

'Mary,' he said in a serious tone when she had settled herself. 'Who can you trust?'

'You,' she retorted tremulously, 'though I have no idea why, The Reverend Clarke and my brother Francis. That's all.'

'Does anyone else come here? John Wright, I suppose.'

'Yes, but my brother says he is not to be trusted. Nobody else comes. They believe I am mad.' She could not help but grin wildly, as if in confirmation of popular opinion. '...that I have made a Covenant with the Devil,' she added, recalling Francis's words.

Hampton had to force her to consider their situation seriously. He no longer thought of leaving, not that he was capable, sensing that Mary needed his protection every bit as much as he needed hers. Nobody, he insisted, must know he was there. She must not alter her habits. She must continue her walks by the river. John Wright must continue to bring her everything she needed every week. There could be no question of moving back to the farmhouse. That too would arouse suspicion. There remained the problem of food. She was already undernourished. Wright was clearly not caring for even her most basic needs. Now they needed enough food for two or they would both starve to death.

Eventually, it was Mary herself who came upon a solution. She would break into the farmhouse and take whatever she could find. She had allowed Wright to make use of her kitchen where she knew he breakfasted, sometimes together with his wife. Wright was after all running her farm, albeit indifferently. There was certain to be food in the kitchen, and in the larder, fruit, vegetables, pickles and herbs she herself had long since stored away. Surely it could not all have been consumed. It was Saturday. Tomorrow, during morning service, the farm was certain to be unoccupied. A vagrant, of which there were many, breaking into an isolated farmhouse, would barely be noticed.

Hampton did not like the risk but could think of no better solution.

'You must leave no trace,' he said, 'no trace of yourself, not a hair from your head.' And then as an afterthought. 'Honey, get me honey...for my leg. I am useless until it heals.'

That afternoon, she took her walk as usual to the river. It was damp and misty, though she hardly noticed. Nor, when she came to the bridge did she so much as glance up the lane towards the inn, shrouded as it was and barely discernible through the mist. Apparently, she no longer expected her husband to appear, as he had promised. Idly, she continued her way past the bridge towards Tutwell, with only the huge oaks, spaced regularly along the riverbank to guide her way. She was glad to be alone again. The proximity of Hampton had both disturbed and excited her. He had appeared from nowhere, sent by God or so it seemed, to draw her back into the real world which she had so resolutely rejected.

Or was his mission a more earthly one? Was he a secret messenger from her husband? he had seemed to know the name. With a start she found herself wishing that not to be the case. Something strange was happening to her. She felt as she had when George had abandoned her for the war, that her life had become dislocated again. On her return, she asked him outright.

'Do you know my husband?'

'I only remember the name,' he said. 'An officer I believe, not in my regiment.'

She was relieved, but could not help noticing how Hampton had altered his gaze. His normally frank expression had faltered. But Mary accepted his reply, perhaps because it was no more than she expected or even wanted. Besides, there was something else he had not told her.

'You have not told me truly. Why are you here? You fled into Devon and are now returned to Cornwall. The river is wide. You could hardly have mistaken your whereabouts.'

She was conscious of adopting his tone, his manner of speaking, aware of her growing confidence. This time though, Hampton did not hesitate, nor avoid her question in any way.

'Lord Hopton instructed my regiment to move to the west and regroup. Instead, as I have explained, the so-called Eastern Gentry have seen fit to capitulate. I have not. By now, Hopton will be in Bodmin. As soon as my leg is as willing as the rest of me, I intend to join him there.'

***

At Venterdon, Alice had given no further indication to Janella that her memory had returned. Yet she had seemed less desultory, more inclined to sit by her window than to lie in her bed. She spoke kindly to Janella, whose every care she seemed to value, rather than ignore as she had for so long. And she ate and drank greedily all that was offered. Janella made no attempt to persuade her, but knew before long Alice was bound to make the journey downstairs to the hearth, perhaps when it all came back to her. But when it did, would Alice have the strength to bear it?

'You should go in to her. Perhaps she will speak to you.'

Francis had struggled to wake. By the time he had clambered downstairs in the darkness, Arthur had already breakfasted and gone out to the barn. Janella handed him his morning pottage and resumed her work which was not onerous and allowed her to remain sitting and close to the fire. Francis looked askance.

'We have enough light now for all next winter.'

'She would like to see you. I am her only companion.'

'She threw us out, remember.'

'I remember well enough, sir.' Janella did not deign to raise her head from her bowl of tallow. 'I was at the heart of things, you might say. When you came back from Lostwithiel, it was all too late. Your father had deteriorated. He would admit no-one. None of you understood that.'

Francis had no wish for the conversation to continue and so finished his breakfast in silence, took up the bread and cheese which Janella had prepared for him and left without another word. Janella was right of course. He should stop avoiding his mother. Alice had suffered as they all had from the war. She had lost a husband, he a father. Janella said Alice was recovering her mind. Perhaps one day they would all be able to share their grief together. Perhaps one day all would be well again.

By late afternoon, the gauzy, clinging mist had turned to a thick, impenetrable fog such that in the fields they hardly knew their whereabouts. He and Arthur, sweaty and dishevelled from threshing the wheat, decided to call it a day.

In the kitchen, Janella was nowhere to be seen but there was a pot of stew over the fire. Janella he thought, pretended not to care for them but always did. He took a few spoonfuls of the stew and then went up to his mother's chamber. As usual, she was in her chair by the window. The shawl Janella had placed around her shoulders hung loosely, not quite discarded. He thought, with a shudder, how they might one day find her close to her window stubbornly ajar, frozen to death. He went to sit on the bed.

'Mother, you should come down to the fire. In the kitchen, it is warm...as always it used to be.'

At first she said nothing, but then turned to him. 'I will soon. I will speak with the Reverend Clarke the next time he comes. I was not well before.' Her voice was stronger, more determined than he had expected. He reached out tentatively to pull up her shawl.

'Janella says you are feeling better.'

'I will come down soon,' she said, looking out of the window into the fog. 'Soon.'

There was a long silence. He was at a loss and prepared to leave for his bed. And then she spoke again.

'I like to see you. Francis...and Mary. Where is Mary?'

'Mary will come and see you. I will ask her....' He paused, wondering whether to continue with his train of thought. 'She is well. She waits still for her husband. He has not yet returned.'

'John is in Callington, I know. And Robert. They have families. Samuel says they are cowards.'

This time, Francis could not bring himself to reply. He resented the vehemence in her voice, fearing again she was not altogether well.

'I will go now. The farm is busy. I...Janella...'

'Janella is my friend,' Alice interrupted harshly, turning her head to face him once more. 'Janella is my friend.'

***

Mary had woken to a deathly quiet. She thought the snow had returned, but pulling aside her makeshift curtain she saw nothing but a thick blanket of fog. It occurred to her at once there would be little need to wait for morning service to ensure Wright was away from the farm. While the fog remained, few would be astir, even to attend church. Nature it seemed, had joined in their conspiracy.

Hampton lay on the matting, apparently asleep. It was unnecessary to disturb him.

'I will go now,' she whispered softly, taking her shawl from its customary place at the door. 'No-one will be about. There is fog.'

Once outside she trod carefully, her feet barely visible on the sodden turf, but she was certain enough of her way. She had resolved to enter the house at the back by the buttery door, knowing the lock to be broken.

She climbed the slope without accident until at last her outstretched hands touched the familiar wall of the farmhouse. She followed the wall round to where the stone became more uneven, indicating the older part of the house which she had so much preferred over the newer, grander addition facing, too proudly for her liking, into the yard and within sight of the lane. She brushed past the familiar laurels which stood up boldly against the rear of the house, and knew then why she had had to leave, why she could not have borne this comfortable familiarity alone. As she had expected, Wright had not seen fit to repair the lock on the buttery door.

Inside, apart from the rats' droppings by the door, there was no sign of life, only that stale, dank odour which comes from long disuse. She could hardly complain. This house had neither master nor mistress now, each having deserted it separately and of their own free will.

She moved to the larder and in the dim morning light something brushed against her shoulder. She gave a shriek, which seemed to echo endlessly around her, and took a step backwards. It was nothing more than a rabbit, hung in the cold, clammy air by Wright or his wife, to improve the flavour. Why, she wondered confusedly, had she been happy to provide Wright with a better life than her own?

In the larder, she also found a number of woodpigeons recently killed and hung, and then cheese and fruit she remembered having preserved herself and, she had not forgotten, a large pot of honey. In the kitchen was a flitch of bacon and a loaf, untouched and still fresh from the day before.

She took off her shawl and spread it on the table and placed upon it all the food she could find, then pulled the four corners together and dragged it to the floor. Then back through the larder to the buttery. The door to the buttery was still open as she, imprudently, had left it. A little out of breath, she paused to listen. From this part of the house there was no sound, not even from the barn or the henhouse. She felt suddenly tempted to go up to her bedchamber, their bedchamber, she corrected herself. It might be for the last time.

Perhaps she was only now beginning to heed the warnings of the Reverend Clarke, Francis and now Andrew Hampton. Perhaps it was true. Perhaps they would take it all away. Perhaps George would never return. She slipped back through the kitchen and into the hallway. The familiar staircase, the chamber to the right at the top, overlooking the yard. Nothing had been touched. It was all there, just as it had always been, the canopy bed with its feather mattress, the oak chest by the window. She could take up residence again, now. There was nothing to stop her. She could wait for George here, in the comfort of her own chamber, mistress of Hampt!

A noise, boots trudging up the lane, then voices brought her quickly to her senses. It would be time for morning service. Some at least were undeterred by the fog. The Reverend Clarke would not fail to deliver comfort to his parishioners, as he always had done. He touched so many lives, she reflected, not just her own.

Her eyes fell on the oak chest, its dusty lid for so long unopened. She found George's clothes and her own laid out neatly together. As she bent down she caught a movement in the corner of her eye, as if from the far wall someone were watching her. The lid slammed shut and her heart missed a beat before she realised it was her own reflection, in the small, ebony framed mirror George had brought from the Low Countries, his deep, confident voice came back to her, 'but made in Venice.'

Recovering herself and now, without her shawl, beginning to sense the cold again, she took from the chest her bonnet and woollen cloak and hurriedly put them on. Then, at random, she took out more clothes for herself and Hampton.

Before leaving she caught sight of her reflection again and, unable to resist its lure, came close to examine herself. Her cloak and bonnet looked clean and expensive, as they were. But as for herself, the eyes which stared back at her were wide and startled, the face pale, unwashed and distraught, her hair twisted and bedraggled. Was this what she had come to? What would George think of her now? No wonder she was regarded as a witch. And yet Hampton seemed to admire her and Francis even, wanted her by his side at Venterdon. Mary could not make herself out.

As she dragged what were nothing more, after all, than her own possessions secretly down the hill to her cottage in the fog, Mary could not have known, any more than the rest of Clymestone, how events beyond their tiny world were taking shape.

It was then Sunday 9th March and Lord Hopton, whose army Andrew Hampton was so anxious to join, had already agreed to surrender to General Fairfax in order 'to procure,' Hopton wrote, 'the peace of the Kingdom and the sparing of Christian blood.' True most of Hopton's footsoldiers, somewhat in contradiction of their commander's fine words, were sent to Pendennis Castle together with considerable ammunition and supplies. But the surrender was real enough. Each trooper giving up horse and arms was to receive twenty shillings in return. Officers, yet further evidence of Fairfax's political skill, were duly allowed to retain an allowance of horses, arms and servants and could go overseas or compound for their estates.

By the time news had trickled through to Clymestone, the formal surrender had already taken place at Tresillian Bridge. On the same day, St Mawes Castle at Falmouth was also delivered up to Fairfax. And five days later, Sir John Arundell, Governor of Pendennis Castle, would equally be summoned to surrender. The reply from Arundell was immediate, unexpected and uncompromising:

'I resolve that I will bury myself before I deliver up this Castle to such as fight against His Majesty.'

And so the siege of Pendennis began, by land and by sea, the only part of Cornwall still remaining in Royalist hands.

Chapter 7

Throughout the night Alice had observed the fog, nudging and fumbling at her open window, slipping its invisible tendrils into her room, already damp with winter. She was unabashed, comforted rather that this great unfathomable blanket should so enfold them. How strange it was that even as this cloud had descended on the valley, the cloud so long obscuring her mind had lifted at last. Samuel would not have credited it. Yet now that fog of the mind had quite dispersed to reveal in minute detail the truth which lay beneath.

She could now recall with absolute clarity the cart standing in her yard, in the waning light, the back unlatched to expose its sole occupant, hunched awkwardly on the flimsy boards.

Samuel being a large man, his rescuers had struggled to bring him up the narrow stairs, depositing him like a sack of potatoes on the bed before hastily taking their leave. Francis had followed them up.

'Tomorrow Francis. For now let him rest. If I need you I will call.'

Her words were ghostly now, yet how self-possessed she must have seemed as she closed the door to their bedchamber, excluding Francis, not even thinking of Janella who waited below to see if she were needed. She supposed, thinking back, it was just that she had to be alone with him.

He seemed only half-conscious, his eyes were closed, his beard wet with mucus, the right side of his mouth oddly twisted down. Dragged from a hedgerow, to be transported up the dry, rutted lane in a dilapidated cart, it was only natural, she reasoned to herself, that his clothes should be torn and stained, his cheeks bloodied, his face twisted in pain. She took two pillows from her side of the bed and managed to push them beneath his head and shoulders, propping him up a little to make him, in her eyes, less like a corpse. Then she pulled off his boots, stockings and breeches and, so far as she dared, inspected him for injury. Finding nothing, she covered him hurriedly where he lay, persuading herself he was unharmed.

Standing by the bed, still breathless from her exertions, softly so as not to wake him, she called his name. But Samuel did not stir. It was at that moment, the moment of his not stirring, she became conscious of the world beyond their bedchamber. She could hear voices from the direction of the church, carried on the still, warm air. It was barely dark. The height of summer. She did not want to leave him, but she should at least bathe his face, which was scratched and bruised. So she opened the door and called for Janella.

'Janella, we must at least bathe his face.'

Afterwards, when Janella had gone, she had undressed to her shift and curled herself up on the mattress, close to Samuel. She remembered taking his hand beneath the covers and squeezing it tight as she had always done. But this time there was no response.

In the morning she woke early to the mixed blessing of another hot day, and to the unexpected stench of urine. She lay motionless, almost panic-stricken. But Samuel, she reminded herself, was alive. Whatever his injury she would have to face it and be thankful for God's mercy. The sheet, his underclothes, her shift were all damp with urine.

She rose and dressed quickly, not noticing until she reached the door, that Samuel was wide awake and alert to her every move. He was trying to speak but only managing a series of faint grunts, dismal attempts at words. Now, catching her eye, he was gesturing with his left hand and shaking his head. Tears flooding down her cheeks, in relief or despair or both, she took his hand in both of hers.

'Samuel! You will be well soon! Can you hear me? Do you understand?'

He was staring at her, wide-eyed, in a kind of intense desperation. Then, coming to himself, he nodded vigorously.

'Samuel, you have been hurt...in the fighting. But all is well. I will look after you, but not alone. I have not the strength. Janella...' Samuel shook his head, pleading. 'Then Francis...'

Samuel would not have Francis either, such was his humiliation. But Alice knew what she would have to do and would not brook opposition, even from her husband. On the landing she called for Janella, who had already risen to prepare breakfast for Francis and Arthur.

For Alice and Janella that first day was to pass in an unending maelstrom of tears, frustration and elation, all in equal measure. Slowly, by trial and error, they discovered what Samuel could and could not do. What had happened to him and why was pushed, of necessity, to the back of their minds. While Alice was still mistress in her own house, sometimes peremptorily issuing instructions to Janella, her maid, she had long since learned to value the younger woman's calm, almost stern practicality. Janella had always been loyal to a fault, possessed shrewdness beyond her years, and was unafraid to express an opinion.

First they had to change his clothes and bedding, discovering in the process and to Alice's delight that Samuel, with a little support, was able to stand. But Samuel's right arm, though apparently unscathed, refused to straighten and so remained crooked and useless at his side. The anger and humiliation on Samuel's frightened, twisted face, both Alice and Janella instinctively ignored, resulting as the day progressed in Samuel's reluctant acceptance of their constant invasion of his privacy.

It became apparent before long that while Samuel could stand to use the pot, he could give no reliable warning of the need. And so his bedshirt and sheet had to be changed again and again. Janella, anticipating what might lie ahead and with her mistress's permission, broke open the seat of one of the two bedroom chairs and made a sling of cloth in which the chamber pot could be suspended. It was an invention for which Alice was to be eternally grateful

Still, most frustrating of all, Samuel would not utter a single word, but could only nod or shake his head.

'Do you want to drink?'

'Do you want to sit?'
'Do you want to lie down?'
'Do you want to see..?

To the last of these, the answer was always a violent shake of the head. When John and Robert came together, naturally concerned for their father, Samuel waved them away with his left hand and with what seemed to them both, utter contempt. When Francis sidled in, while Janella on hands and knees was for the second time scrubbing the floorboards around the bed, Samuel spotted him at once and looked away in shame.

In the late afternoon, as long shadows spread across the yard Mary, still they supposed living in some style at her farm in Hampt, arrived on horseback. Alice went down to greet her, leaving Janella to feed her husband supper. Even with his left hand, they had discovered, Samuel could not safely direct the spoon to his mouth.

'Do you want to see Mary?' Alice had asked.

Samuel had hesitated, the pottage trickling down from the corner of his mouth and into his beard, then holding back his tears, had shaken his head decisively. Alice took her daughter into the kitchen and tried to explain, but Mary she could tell, did not understand or even sympathise with her mother's dilemma. George had already been missing a year. Was she not now allowed to speak with her own father? Mary, understandably, left in high dudgeon, making it clear she had no intention of returning.

By the time the Reverend Clarke arrived, darkness had fallen. Alice was lying exhausted on the bed next to her husband who was sleeping noisily. Francis had disappeared and Janella was midway between washing sheets and kneading the dough for the bread she would bake in the morning. The Reverend had spent the day visiting the wounded and making arrangements for the burial of the dead, but looked as calm and immaculate as any man could in the circumstances. Only his black, buckled boots, spotted with dirt from the innumerable yards and lanes he had trod since Essex's army had marched through the village, gave any hint of his commitment to the Parish .

Janella went to fetch Alice and was then instructed to remain with Samuel until the Reverend had gone. Seated comfortably in Samuel's chair by the fire, the Reverend Clarke listened patiently to Alice's detailed account.

'Samuel is apoplectic,' he concluded sagely. 'It comes with his fiery temper. He is not the first in the Parish.' But that sounded too dismissive and the Reverend, perceiving Alice's distress, quickly altered his tone. 'It is the war Alice. He might just as well have been struck down by a Roundhead. The result is the same...'

Alice wanted to ask if Samuel would die, but knew from experience of the Reverend's ways to hold her tongue.

'...Sometimes they recover,' the Reverend continued, leaning forward to take her hand, 'There is no knowing. You must pray Alice, pray for his recovery. And if he should die, pray then for his mortal soul.' The Reverend's mellifluous voice seemed to linger on these final words, bringing Alice to the point of absolute despair. It seemed to her, though she could hardly express it, that the Reverend took a certain relish in the power of his authority. 'But,' The Reverend sat up straight, released her hand and adopted a brighter tone, 'there is a physician in Lanson. I will ask him to come.'

So they waited and everything was very much as it had been on the first day, except that John and Robert and Mary did not return. It had rained all that summer but now, in the last days of July, the sun beat down remorselessly. Flies constantly buzzed and settled all around Samuel's bedchamber and however much Janella scrubbed the floor, the smell of urine would not go away Early on the last day of the month, Samuel began to fidget and point towards the door. After the usual period of mutual frustration, Alice finally understood.

'Do you want to see Francis?' Samuel nodded vigorously.

Janella was gossiping with Arthur. There was no sign of Francis, so Alice remounted the stairs and knocked on his door. If he was not awake, he should have been. Soon it would be harvest time. Even confined to his bed, Samuel would be thinking of that. She knocked again and then impatiently thrust open the door. Francis had gone.

They searched high and low. Janella discovered that Samuel's sword, discarded in the buttery, was also missing. And Arthur found one of their two packhorses had been taken in the night. Alice had no time for this, her heart too full of Samuel, but she had the presence of mind to explain to her husband that Francis had set out to join the King's army and avenge his father, a fact, though true, she could scarcely have believed.

It was Arthur who reacted most bitterly. The harvest would not come to much after such devastating summer rains, but he could hardly retrieve it alone. without the harvest, how were they to survive the winter? The farm would go under. Alice unhesitatingly handed over all of Samuel's savings without a murmur and told Arthur to employ whoever he needed. And then promptly turned her back on everything and everybody outside her husband's bedchamber.

Soon after, as the Reverend Clarke had promised, the physician from Lanson arrived, to concur with the Reverend's diagnosis of apoplexy. A mincing, apologetic yet somehow overbearing man of a distinctly puritanical demeanour, the physician insisted, on production of a neat set of lancets and and flint cups, that bloodletting was the only possible cure.

Alice could not bear it and fled downstairs, ordering Janella in peremptory fashion, to stay with Samuel so that he was not accidentally done to death by the unprepossessing physician.

On completion of his work, the surgeon explained mildly that he would, as a matter of course, need to return at regular intervals. But Samuel, much to the man's disappointment, made it abundantly clear by means of furious gestures that he would not countenance it. At least the physician did not ask for payment and that was something else, Alice reflected, they had the Reverend Clarke to thank for.

When he had gone Samuel, his left arm scarred and still bleeding, lay more helpless and dispirited than ever, the unmistakable smell of fresh blood mingling now with the reek of the pot.

In mid-September, all the talk of the village was of the King's triumph at Lostwithiel. The army of Lord Essex which had tramped so arrogantly through their Parish on the road to Linkinhorne was now all but destroyed. It was said that Essex himself had escaped on a fishing boat, coward that he was. The King's victorious army had passed out of Cornwall and, according to some, had been seen approaching Tavistock, only a few miles across the river. The Cornish volunteers meanwhile, including Francis, were gradually returning in equal though less celebrated triumph to their homes.

Francis did not say much on his return. He had joined the King's army at Trecarrel. He had been with them at Lostwithiel. The Parliamentarian army had been defeated and yes, Essex had escaped on a fishing boat, most likely to Plymouth. He seemed altered, more troubled even than when they had brought Samuel back from Horsebridge. Whatever impulse had driven him to fight had now gone right out of him.

'Francis is back,' said Alice to her husband. 'It is true he fought for the King.' She did not add, as she might have done, 'You should be proud' or 'It was a great victory.' But merely, 'Do you want to see him now?'

And Samuel shook his head sadly. Rather he would have had Francis visit him daily, keep him up to date with the farm, get him away from Alice and Janella and all their suffocating care. He would rather have had that than Francis leave him, and at harvest time too, merely to fight for the King.

Winter set in early. Alice would not leave her husband's side. Janella came when she was needed, to help move Samuel to or from his chair, or to change the bedding, or bring food, or to scrub the floor. And Alice, almost inevitably, began to take Janella for granted, forgetting that she herself had discarded all responsibility for the household. She forgot that Janella, apart from helping her with Samuel, was daily baking, curing, salting, brewing, milking, feeding, cleaning and looking after them all. Without Janella, none of them would have survived the winter. Francis merely skulked in the attic, causing Arthur to complain vociferously. What did he expect? Janella retorted. Should she slaughter a pig or muck out the barn, whenever she had a minute to spare? The truth was Arthur, like Janella, had nowhere else to go.

Christmas passed without notice except for a visit from the Reverend Clarke, but even for him Alice would not come down, nor admit him to Samuel's presence. Francis stayed in his room, leaving Janella to toast the Reverend with the ale she herself had brewed and which they all drank every day. Well, Janella had concluded philosophically, Cromwell had abolished Christmas anyway.

As the village dragged itself into spring, Samuel's condition began to worsen. He would sit on the side of the bed, the curtains having long since been stripped away, and allow Alice and Janella to change the sheets or take off his white linen shirt to wash that pale emaciated body which had once so towered over them. Samuel could no longer stand, nor could they move him to his chair and get him up again. From time to time he would, though conscious, begin to tremble and shake, his eyes staring wildly into space. And Alice would hold him desperately, talking, just talking until he came to himself. And then he would sleep and nothing would wake him. At night she would notice how his right arm and leg had become stiffer and more crooked, inadvertently pushing her to the side of the bed, his fingers stiff and increasingly curled so that she could no longer place her hand in his. And Alice wept.

Janella, ever practical, said there was a woman in Tutwell who understood these things. She would come and they would not have to pay. Alice agreed and the next day Arthur was sent to bring Mrs Bowhay to the farm. She was tiny, wizened and distinctly unwashed but had a kindly, beguiling air. Janella brought her to the fireside for something to eat and a jug of ale and explained to her how Samuel had been. Alice would still not leave her husband for a moment. Mrs Bowhay nodded and smiled and seemed to understand and, without difficulty, to accept Samuel's need for privacy. She only asked to witness once, perhaps from the landing, when the shaking started. Until then she was content to wait in the kitchen, warming herself and periodically accepting pottage or a drink from Janella. It was not until the evening that Samuel began to shake and Janella brought Mrs Bowhay to the landing, as agreed with Alice, and opened the door to Samuel's bedchamber. For a minute or two , Mrs Bowhay watched expressionless, and that was all she needed.

Downstairs, she brought out two jars from somewhere in her skirts, one containing crushed pink and white, sweetly scented petals, the other an equally crushed but dark and evil-smelling root. Samuel, Mrs Bowhay explained, was undoubtedly possessed by demons. Janella was to mix a little from each of the jars, pour on hot water and then allow the liquid to cool. Samuel was to imbibe this concoction daily and without fail. The potion, Mrs Bowhay stated categorically, if taken as instructed, would drive the demons away with immediate effect. It was otherwise known, she added mysteriously, but with a twinkle in her eye, as the 'King's cure-all'.

Alice was doubtful but since the physician had been rejected, what else were they to do? So Janella followed the woman's instructions and brought the foul mixture for Alice to administer.

Samuel grimaced, had more difficulty swallowing even than normal, but did as he was told. Later he would vomit repeatedly but Alice persisted and each day administered Mrs Bowhay's mixture, and each day Samuel vomited. But miraculously the trembling and shaking stopped and Samuel, when he was not vomiting, seemed much more himself. Samuel, Alice concluded, was no longer suffering as he had and for a time she believed he would recover entirely and be his old self again. But when Janella returned to Mrs Bowhay, it became clear the woman's skills had been exhausted. It was too late now, she said, to cure Samuel's apoplexy. Bloodletting was all she could recommend, but the old-fashioned way, with leeches, 'Put them on 'is arms an' neck,' she said, handing Janella another jar. 'P'r'aps they can do what no physician from Lanson can. The old ways are always the best.'

By this time Samuel was visibly fading and would have allowed whatever Alice and Janella chose to inflict. In their presence he had no more dignity to lose. They took off his shirt and Janella, unflinching, placed a dozen dark brown leeches along his forearms and neck. Alice turned away and sobbed and in the evening ordered Janella to take them away.

Alone again with Samuel, it seemed strange that for all her caring and perhaps because of it, they had drifted finally apart. Samuel knew and she knew it would soon all be over. Their eyes met in what seemed to her some final, dreadful, tearful embrace. And then Samuel turned away, apparently preoccupied, his left hand moving feverishly almost, across the counterpane.

'Do you want something?' she asked inanely.

Samuel nodded weakly, but with determination in his eyes. Eventually she understood. Samuel wanted to see the Reverend Clarke, urgently. It was June, almost Midsummer. At Naseby the New Model Army had already given notice of the inevitable outcome of the war. Samuel's decline had coincided fatefully with the rout of the King's armies. Janella found Arthur attempting, without much success, to teach Francis to shear a sheep.

'You must go to the Rectory,' she said, 'and fetch the Reverend. Your father....'

It took some time, Alice recalled, for the Reverend, who was forever attending to his parishioners, to be found. When he finally arrived, typically unflustered, he explained to Alice he would have to speak to Samuel alone. So Alice and Francis and Janella waited, hardly exchanging a word, for what seemed a very long time. When the Reverend finally descended, he took Alice to one side and in low, confidential tones assured her that Samuel had made his final wishes known. She did not understand. How had the Reverend been able to determine her husband's wishes, when Samuel could utter not a single word?

'Your husband is a fine man. He has made his wishes known,' the Reverend repeated. 'You have nothing to fear.'

Samuel knew he did not have long. When the Reverend Clarke had taken his leave, they almost expected him to have already expired. Janella tactfully busied herself, allowing Alice and her son to mount the stairs together, with some trepidation. But Samuel they found alive and well, almost cheerful. They kissed him solemnly in gratitude, and watched him promptly fall asleep. During the night, Alice listened for his breathing. It had lately become so shallow, barely audible, and sometimes would stop entirely and then start again.

Samuel was propped up now, almost to a sitting position, commandeering all the feather pillows in the house. Alice lay curled up flat on the mattress, turned away from him, straining to listen and watching the stars from her window.

The nights were short, the days long. Samuel took Mrs Bowhay's concoction, but little else. He was fading away.

'Samuel, I love you, 'Alice whispered during the night, but there was no response.

*

And then, Alice supposed, becoming aware that the fog had now replaced the stars, Samuel must have died. She remembered a coffin painted black on the kitchen table and tried to remember Samuel's face at the end, but it would not come to her. The Samuel with whom she had lived for thirty-five years would not come back to her. She supposed he now lay by the church in Clymestone, but had no recollection of his burial.

'Samuel,' she murmured privately to herself. 'It will not be long. I swear I will come to you.'

The fog remained, but she could tell the day had already begun. She listened now for Janella, for Arthur in the yard, Francis dragging himself down the stairs.

***

During the day the fog cleared. When Francis came in, exhausted from threshing the wheat, Janella was nowhere to be seen but Alice was sitting calmly by the fire.

'Mother!'

'There is stew in the pot,' Alice replied barely looking up, as if her presence in the kitchen was quite an everyday occurrence.

Francis slowly took off his boots and hung up his jerkin, thus containing his astonishment. Then he ladled out the stew and brought it to the table.

'I want to see Mary. It has been so long. She should come home,' It sounded very much like an instruction.

'I will..'

'And the Reverend Clarke. He does not visit now. Do you remember Francis? He said your father had made his wishes known. But what were your father's wishes? That was months ago.'

Francis was tired from the threshing and then elated to see his mother in her old place by the fire and then immediately subdued by the responsibility he felt towards Mary, and his mother. He knew nothing of wills or the lack of them. How could his father have made a will? And if he had, what would come to him or to his mother or to John, who was after all the eldest?

He took Alice back to her room, vowing to her and to himself to bring Mary home and to seek an explanation from the Reverend Clarke. Afterwards he lay awake in his attic bed staring emptily at the sloping ceiling, burdened by he knew not what.

Chapter 8

Christina was seething. Robert sat opposite her in the parlour, oblivious, wearing that sober, Sunday expression he was convinced she would appreciate but which, in reality, drove her to distraction. She could no longer bear to look at him and though it contradicted her own view of the Sabbath, suggested, with barely a hint of tension in her voice, that he should take Thomas out with the dogs. That would, she justified it to herself, release Liddy to make the dinner which otherwise would never be ready. Luke, Chapter 6, verses 26-28 would have to wait. Liddy could help Thomas with his Bible reading later.

Robert tried but failed not to look pleased. Christina, he reflected, would at least be spared the unmitigated delight of Thomas and Liddy, both now hunched uncomfortably over the kitchen table.

'Robert.' He turned at the door. Christina could always change her mind. 'The Minister did not attend service. Only sickness could have prevented him. If the rain clears, I may go to Burraton.'

Robert, leaving the door ajar, did not reply, simply calling for Thomas from the hall. Christina had paid no attention to Minister Marten for a while. He thought she had finally lost patience with the man. Well, something must have got into her, the Reverend Clarke's sermon perhaps.

When she heard they had gone, Christina rose at once to close the parlour door, the privacy thus afforded at least allowing her some measure of relief. Unthinking, she flung off her cap, to reveal her short, pale hair, flat and straggled, damp on her scalp. Like a panther in a cage, trapped and untamed, she paced the room. Liddy, unlike Robert always sensing her torment, would keep well away. She paused at the window. The rain still spat viciously against the panes. Perhaps she should not visit the Minister after all. She must not be over hasty. On the last occasion Minister Marten had offered no spiritual guidance whatsoever. All she remembered now was begging him, on her bended knees, not to leave Clymestone, reassuring him about his hopeless petition to the House of Lords and, on her way home, the crunch of freezing snow beneath her feet.

Yet she still regarded the Minister as an ally. It was only unfortunate she was not better appreciated. She began to pace the room again. This was all Clarke's doing. The morning service had been an outrage. The man was an imposter, had already been ejected, was doubtless a papist. Why then was she the only one, aside from the Minister, to care?

They had sat together in their usual pew, close to the pulpit. She recalled with a shudder Clarke's high-pitched yet clear and assertive voice, his sermon devoted to the Feast of the Annunciation. He had taken his text from St Luke, referring to the very same verses she had instructed Liddy and Thomas to read together, on their return. She was familiar enough with the Gospel, had required no reminder from the Reverend Clarke. The Annunciation, Lady Day, the 25th March, now fallen conveniently on the Sabbath. 'The day our Lord entered the world', Clarke had stated with easy conviction. 'Et homo factus est!' She recalled with distaste how his strident tones had reverberated eerily around the little church, a challenge to anyone who cared to deny them. And then, like some wilful magician, Clarke had asserted Lady Day to be the day God created the Earth, the day of the fall of Lucifer, the Crucifixion, the creation of Adam and Eve and God knows what else! The day above all, he had solemnly pronounced, when we must honour the Virgin Mary. What, Christina wondered, would Minister Marten have made of that?

The church as usual had been full, the congregation attentive, and yet from where she had been sitting the Reverend, such a short man, had been barely visible in the pulpit. She had glimpsed only his immaculate grey hair and occasionally, as he leaned forward to fix his gaze in every corner of the nave, his confident, slightly florid and, to her, pugnacious countenance. She had looked for doubt, at least for some indication of critical thought, in the features of those around her, but saw none. The Reverend had the whole community it seemed in the palm of his hand. In the face of such conviction, she had begun to doubt herself. She needed reassurance.

'And do not forget,' the Reverend's words intruded once more, unbidden. She stood stock still in the centre of her parlour, inwardly squirming, 'Lady Day is for sowing your barley, or you will have no beer!' The Reverend had paused, like any true performer supremely aware of the value of timing. 'The consequence, my friends, is not something I wish to dwell upon.' There had been a ripple of appreciation to which the Reverend had appeared not at all to object. 'And if you are lucky enough to have victuals on your table,' Clarke had persisted by way of conclusion, 'remember to set aside the last Wednesday of the month for fasting, by order of Oliver Cromwell!'

The painful recollection of this last remark positively set Christina's teeth on edge, such that she swore on the spot never again to attend Sunday service, until Clarke was well and truly ousted. But after a few moments had passed, she picked up her cap and began preparing for her visit to Minister Marten. It had occurred to her and with much satisfaction that whatever friends the Reverend Clarke boasted in so-called 'high places', he had now overstepped the mark. He had begun, in effect, to dig his own grave, unassisted. It would not, Christina reasoned, be inappropriate now to hasten his end.

*

From her privileged position, close to the pulpit, Christina had been unable to gauge accurately the congregation's reactions to the various parts of Clarke's outrageous sermon. Positioned elsewhere she might have been surprised, even puzzled, to observe her brother-in-law Francis, blatantly sitting together with the servant Janella, and as far away from the pulpit as possible. Janella it was true usually attended but Francis, like his papist sister Mary, not at all, a fact that had long scandalised her. And at the end of the service, departing by the central aisle, she had been conscious only of Thomas and Liddy, hand in hand in front of her. So full of contempt had she been for Clarke's superstitious nonsense and yet simultaneously aware of the need to control herself, she had shut out entirely the rest of her surroundings. The church might just as well have been empty. Though Janella had stood almost beside her in the crush at the porch, separated now from Francis who had lingered behind, Christina had failed to notice.

In fact, Francis had hardly risen from his pew, holding back awkwardly from the throng. Only as the church emptied did he step tentatively down the side aisle and in roundabout fashion cautiously approach the pulpit. He need not have been so circumspect. The small, whitewashed door towards which he had been edging his way opened as if on cue and the Reverend Clarke, accustomed to retreat to the vestry at the conclusion of every service, emerged unsurprised and smiling.

'Come in Francis. I see you have something on your mind.'

The vestry was tiny but, there being a high arched window to the outer wall, unexpectedly light and airy. Entirely in keeping with the character of its principal occupant, the room was scrupulously ordered and uncluttered. Fixed to the far wall was a folding table accompanied by three rickety chairs and to the left an ancient oak chest with three impressive-looking padlocks.

'For the registers,' the Reverend explained, observing the direction of his gaze. And then, without ceremony, he lifted off his neat white surplice and hung it carefully on a hook, clearly set aside for the purpose.

Close to and in such a confined space, the Rector looked older, his face more deeply lined, the pouches beneath his eyes darker, the skin more transparent. And yet in this, his own private domain, he was even more animated than usual, jocular almost and, to Francis at least, all the more intimidating. Without understanding why, he shrank within himself, scarcely able to explain the reason he had come. The Reverend, however, was in no doubt.

'Mary. You have come about your sister. I read it in your face! You have persuaded her to return to Venterdon, I trust. She will be safer with you. If she has papist tendencies, they will be less evident. You will be able to protect her. Bring her back to the world, accept, sadly, that her husband is no longer with us. No more maundering along the river, eh? Tell me, Francis, you have followed my advice?'

'I...Mary,' Francis stammered, the conversation not at all taking the course he had intended, 'I have been to see her. She is well, but I fear does not look to herself...but only waits for her husband still.' He hesitated. The Reverend had abruptly adopted a more serious expression. 'Our mother looks forward to Mary's return. It is that. That is the purpose...Our mother is happily much improved. She sits at the fireside and no longer keeps to her room.' The Reverend continued to listen patiently, blankly observing his petitioner. Then for no apparent reason rose from his chair and took a step towards the door. For the first time Francis noticed the ornate gold cross and delicate chain suspended over his cassock.

'I will come to Venterdon, Francis. But..you understand, I am sometimes hard-pressed. There are many in the Parish who seek relief, of one kind or another..'

Somehow, the Reverend Clarke had allowed the mask to slip and Francis became, all at once, aware of the older man's vulnerability, the cross deliberately hidden from the outside world, the increasingly rash remarks from the pulpit, the undue concern for Mary which he had wondered about before. Francis no longer felt intimidated, pursuing his mission with added confidence.

'My mother has asked me. She remembers now the friendship you showed to our father at the end of his life. You told her 'Samuel has made his wishes known...' Reverend, I must ask you, does my father have a will? What were his wishes?'

The Reverend resumed his seat at the table, appeared for a moment disoriented, not looking up, apparently avoiding the question. 'The will must be proved in the Bishop of Exeter's Court. You understand, with the war, there are delays. In due course, your mother will receive a sealed copy. She has no need for concern, Francis. Samuel, your father, was a good man...'

Francis got up to go. 'Wait. Listen.' Clarke sounded weary. The voice which had reverberated so confidently round his church had grown weak, as if it had used itself up with the effort of preaching. 'This is a dangerous time, more dangerous even than the war itself. There are many in this Parish...' Normally so fluent, he seemed to have lost his thread and became, to Francis, momentarily incoherent. 'Quia sunt in servicio domini Regis. They are already amongst us. You understand, Francis, they will take no more risks...'

Francis thanked the Reverend and took his leave, unconvinced at the reassurance and disturbed by the Rector's behaviour. The Reverend Clarke, once a figure to be relied on if not always admired, had inadvertently revealed to him the weakness and confusion which lay behind the public facade. It left Francis strangely unsettled.

***

Lady Day was marked by events even more stirring than the Reverend Clarke's controversial sermon in Clymestone. On that very day, Sunday 25th March, Thomas Fairfax and Oliver Cromwell led a triumphal procession through the streets of Plymouth in celebration not it must be said of the Feast of the Annunciation, but rather of the successes of war. Three hundred 'pieces of ordnance' were said to have been discharged as part of the ceremony. By the end of the day, Christina for her part, had determined upon a salvo of her own,

Her visit to Minister Marten had taken much the course she had anticipated. She had presented him with a bottle of some herbal mixture or other she had discovered in the larder, whereupon he had predictably sniffed and moaned his thanks. Then by way of recompense, she had insisted upon his judgement with regard to the significance of Lady Day. As expected, the Minister had firmly agreed that the Reverend Clarke had somewhat embroidered the Gospel. The precise dates on which Lucifer fell, on which Adam was created and suchlike had not yet been revealed to man, in spite of recent scientific advances. All that the Minister had been able to do was to refer her to the Scripture, while at the same time reminding her that, according to the Directory of Public Worship, Festival days were 'no longer to be continued.' The celebration of the Annunciation was nothing more nor less than a tradition and as such inherently suspect.

But Minister Marten had nevertheless been unable to resist the temptation of reading aloud to her the very same verses which the Reverend Clarke had drawn attention to earlier:

34. Then said Mary unto the angel, How shall this be, seeing I know not a man?

35. And the angel answered and said unto her, The Holy Ghost shall come upon thee, and the power of the Highest shall overshadow thee: therefore also that holy thing which shall be born of thee shall be called the Son of God.

'The man is an imposter!' Christina had not been concentrating, causing the Minister at first to misunderstand. 'The Reverend Clarke!' Christina had not been able to contain herself. 'He spouts superstition as if it were the word of God, and Minister, from your pulpit!'

Whereupon Minister Marten had counselled patience and wisdom, as he was bound to do.

'The ways of the Lord...'

But by then Christina had stopped listening, again. Nor did she, on this occasion, stay to absorb all of the Minister's woes. But something had been nagging her. On the doorstep, she remembered.

'Minister, it is said that he who desires to be righteous is righteous, and that he would repent doth repent. Is that true?'

'No, my child,' the Minister had replied, a little sniffily Christina thought. 'It is false reasoning for surely it cannot be said that if you would be happy, then you are happy, or if you would love thy neighbour, then you do so? Only an imposter would say that.' And having scored a point, the Minister smiled and closed the door.

Christina had set off rapidly down the lane, adjusting her bonnet as she went, determined not to look back to where the Minister would doubtless be watching from his customary place at the window. Nor did she look up to the thorny hedgerows, still bereft of green, which topped the ancient banks of the lane to

Burraton. The banks themselves, which so hemmed her in, were not yet dotted with the flowers of spring. Not that Christina would have noticed as she bowed her head against the drizzle.

How she hated the lanes! How they swallowed her up, however much she tried to disregard them. She thought of Marten and Clarke and Robert, one by one, impatient with each for their various inadequacies. And then, by way of contrast, she thought of those men who were in full possession of themselves, men who enhanced the world they lived in; General Fairfax, a brave and generous leader in time of strife, Thomas Gewen, her uncle, in peacetime perhaps the most powerful man in Cornwall, Her former husband, dedicated to the true faith. His words came back to her.

'Only an act of free Grace from God can lift us from the abyss.'

She dared to look up from the rutted lane. The banks on either side seemed to press in on her, the lane ahead narrowed to make her way all but impassable. And then another voice from further in the past.

'All the wisdom we possess...' She had stopped in her tracks, ignorant of the spitting rain, struggling to remember. 'All the wisdom we possess.....is the knowledge of God and of ourselves.'

Of ourselves. The knowledge of ourselves. There was a break in the clouds, and though the rain did not cease, spring sunshine slipped secretly into the lane, casting its subtle light along the hedgerows. Slowly the shadows of the banks parted and, in the warm sunlight, she saw the way ahead was clear.

For the remainder of the day, Christina maintained the severe demeanour they had come to expect of her on the Sabbath. Though beneath the surface she was burning with a new excitement. Soon after Liddy had taken Thomas to bed, Robert, increasingly morose since she had withdrawn her favours on the pretext of Lent, also retired. Christina, apparently absorbed in some mysterious calculation of her own, pointedly ignored his muttered, 'Good night.' She waited for half an hour, until the house was quiet, then crossed to what she had liked to call her 'escritoire', which had admittedly since her former husband's demise, seen little use. She selected a quill from one of its drawers, eventually found some ink and settled down to write.

Whiteford
25th March 1646
To Thomas Gewen MP of Bradridge

Dearest Uncle

Please forgive my recklessness at addressing to you this short note when matters of far greater import must ever be your concern. I write to you, both as a beloved uncle and as a leading member of our County Committee on whose shoulders so much will rest as Cornwall strives to throw off the heavy yoke of Royalist tyranny.

I write not without qualms and with all the humility appropriate to my sex, but feel bound nevertheless to inform you that our Rector, the Reverend Richard Clarke, has on this very day, a day of unprecedented celebration throughout the County, chosen from the pulpit to insult the military leadership of Parliament in the west. In the same shocking tirade, the Rector of this Parish advised his congregation, in contradiction to Acts of Parliament and to the Directory of Public Worship, to celebrate the so-called Feast of the Annunciation. The Reverend Clarke also claimed that this day was also that on which Lucifer fell, on which Adam was born and on which the Earth itself was created!

You will recall, dear uncle, that the Reverend Clarke is already seen as an imposter, having been ejected from his living many months ago. Minister Marten, his worthy successor, lives humbly and in some degree of poverty in the Parish to which he was appointed. The Reverend Clarke, as you will know, persists in refusing to leave the Rectory.

I know that the County Committee has the power to remove the Reverend Clarke on the grounds of his being ill-affected to Parliament. I therefore request as a simple parishioner, that you use your influence to bring this about. Minister Marten's application to the House of Lords has unfortunately been too long ignored.

As I am subject to some mild inconvenience at present, my husband, Robert Pellow is the willing bearer of this message. I hope and trust you will find the time to consider this petition and speak with my husband who will await and accept your advice on this as on all matters relating to the future of our Parish.

I remain
Your affectionate niece
Christina Pellow

By the time Christina had finished, the candle at her desk had almost sputtered out. She read the letter through. It was written in the clear, flowing hand she had once employed to such effect on behalf of her former husband. No part of it would be mistaken. She applied the seal, blew out the candle and prepared herself, with something akin to relish, for what was to come.

Robert lay abed, the curtains drawn around him, but she could tell he was not asleep.

'Robert, are you awake?' Robert indicated, with a degree of deliberate incoherence, that he was. 'Robert, I believe I have wronged you for too long.' She heard him turn over and imagined his eyes opening wide in expectation. 'Lent,' she said, undoing her bodice and letting it slip, without ceremony, to the floor. 'It is too much for you to bear.'

She stepped out of her petticoats, one by one, casting them aside until they lay in a heap on the carpet. When he pulled back the curtain, she was standing only in her shift. And before he could fling away the bedclothes, she had lifted that one remaining garment over her head and slid in beside him.

Christina was elated, ravenous, a revelation, a resurrection almost. By the middle of the night, the small hours of the morning, Robert had come to deem the privations of Lent entirely acceptable. Christina, fully sated and lying half alongside and half over him, whispered in that deep, velvety, caressing way he loved so much.

'Robert, I can do this again, if you wish. I ask just a small favour in return. Easter is almost upon us and my uncle will be as usual at Bradridge.' No response. 'And you know how that man Clarke upsets me. He is an imposter,' She could not suppress her contempt, 'and must be replaced.' Now she was conscious of the tension in her husband's body. But she dragged him back to her, pressing herself against him. 'You know, I do not give a fig for Marten. He is a no-account, but he and his kind are the future and we must be part of that. I want you to take a note to my uncle. I wrote it while you slept. I wrote that Clarke is an imposter and must go. My uncle is a powerful man.'

Robert was exhausted, could not fathom her, but as she roused him once more, assented.

'I will be yours,' Christina whispered, 'whenever you want.'

Chapter 9

Easter Saturday, Francis was saddling the white mare in the yard. Lambing, such as it was, had finished, Arthur, having borne the burden as usual. So by mutual consent rather than government edict, or even tradition, the work of the farm had ceased for the weekend. Francis could no longer procrastinate. The Reverend Clarke had once more filled him with foreboding. Mary was alone in her cottage and his mother sat by the fire in stony silence. He had reassured her repeatedly, Mary would come home soon. And as for the will, that had yet to be proved at the Bishop of Exeter's Court. Then it would be sealed and delivered to her. The Rector had promised.

'Francis!'

His mother, looking frail and paler even than usual in the brutal spring sunshine, had come into the yard in her shawl and slippers. She had not stepped outside for as long as he could remember. He took her back inside to the chair she had adopted now, that had once been Samuel's.

'Bring her back, Francis,' she pleaded. 'Her husband is long since dead. Does she not understand? This is her home now.'

The mare, carrying him sedately down the lane to the bridge, seemed to share his reluctance. He replayed endlessly the scene with his mother in the yard and then by the fireside, at the same time dreading the encounter with his sister. Whatever else, he was certain she would not easily be persuaded to come home, would remain as she had been for so long, stubbornly obsessed with her dead husband.

The mare picked her way cautiously down the last steep slope to the bridge. As the lane opened to the meadow, he heard, as if for the first time, invisible birds chattering in the hedgerows. He could not, in spite of himself, ignore the season. He looked across the river to the forest of oak and ash now coming into leaf and rising from the water's edge in anticipation of summer, and his spirits were lifted. Across the water meadow, south towards Hampt, there was no sign of his sister.

But for no particular reason, he rode briskly up onto the bridge. The river was full and flowing fast, down towards Morwellam, Calstock, Gunnislake and the sea. It was a thought which never failed to excite him. He pulled the mare round slowly and much against her wishes, his eyes set on the widening stream. It was only on looking up towards the lane, ready to retrace their steps, that he caught a glimpse of her.

A woman walking smartly along the path towards him, from the direction of Tutwell in the north. It was a woman, but not at all like Mary slouching in her drab shawl and grey skirts. On the contrary, she wore a smart, green cloak and matching bonnet and strode with a purposeful air, stooping now and then to pluck whatever flowers of early spring happened to lie in her path.

He could not help but watch her. As she approached, such was his concentration that he was able to catch the exact moment when she, in her turn, espied him dismounted now and observing her intently from the parapet. As he led the mare back over the bridge, the woman visibly slowed, almost stopped in her tracks and then apparently resigning herself to their encounter, continued towards him. She was not twenty yards from him when she stopped again and looked up boldly into his eyes.

'Mary!' He was dumbfounded. 'What has happened?'

She came to him where the bridge dipped into the meadow, smiling awkwardly. 'Francis, were you on your way to see me? I thought you would come back. Well, it is lucky you have found me. I was picking some flowers,' she continued unnecessarily. 'It is truly spring now. Don't you feel it? Her cheeks were flushed, her voice tremulous. 'How is mother? I have not yet decided. Tell her........tell her I will come soon........Are you well? Does Janella look after you?'

He waited until she had run out of things to say. It could not have been more apparent that she was concealing something.

'What has happened, Mary? You look so well. The last time I saw you, you were pale and starving. I thought you were freezing to death in that cottage of yours...

'It must be spring,' she interrupted, but saw at once that he would not be so easily persuaded. 'The house was broken into.'

'Your cottage? There is nothing to steal.'

'No, the farmhouse. I thought you would have heard. It did not surprise me. There are many without food, tramps, soldiers with nowhere to go. John Wright took me up. The larder and kitchen were plundered. You can hardly blame them. And,' Mary hastened to explain, 'our chamber was ransacked. I picked up some extra clothes while I was there, and some food...So you see, perhaps it was all a blessing in disguise.'

She had recommenced her walk along the path towards Hampt and he had followed meekly, though it was not the way he had intended. The mare might easily have stumbled on the lumpy surface of the meadow.

'Stop, Mary. Stop a moment. Our mother has begged me to bring you back. You are already halfway. She thinks of nothing else...except our father's will, though how he could ever have made one, I cannot imagine.'

They had come to an ancient oak close to the stream, its huge roots rising up in their path and on the other side, down almost to the water's edge.

'I remember this tree, she said, looking up. 'It was when John was apprenticed at Luckett. We were walking home. You and me and father. I think even then I was drawn to the river. Father lifted you up to that branch, the first one, and you stood up, proud as punch.'

He tethered the mare, not entirely sure where Mary, let alone himself, was headed. The sun was already high in the sky, its rays seeping through the nascent foliage and twisted branches of the great oak. Mary took off her green woollen cloak and bonnet and laid them on the turf. And then arranging her skirts with care, seated herself. Confident and coy, he thought unfairly, but at least prepared to parley.

He found a spot for himself between the roots at the foot of the tree. She wore a blue sleeveless bodice with no kerchief or scarf. Her hair, released from her bonnet, tumbled in wayward fashion about her shoulders. He could not help but admire her. If he had not known better, he would have said she had a fancy man. She would hardly be taken for a witch now. More likely she was breaking some new ordnance of Parliament, alone with a man in a meadow, and on Easter Saturday too.

'You need a woman,' she observed slyly, reading his thoughts.'

'And you look so different,' he defended himself. 'You look as if you have everything you need. Do you still wait for George? Or have you given up?'

He could see it unsettled her. She would not be able to admit, after three years, that George was not coming back. She had been trapped by her own obstinacy.

'George would prefer me like this, do you not agree Francis, if ever he should cross that bridge?'

Perceiving her dilemma, he relented. 'If you would come home with me, our mother would be equally happy to find,' He struggled for the words, 'that you look so well. Come with me now, and then whenever you wish, I will take you back to Hampt.'

Mary did not answer at once but when she did it was clear from her tone, she would not change her mind.

'I cannot come now. Take the flowers. Tell her I picked them for her. Tell her, when I am ready, I promise I will come.'

Francis unconsciously changed tack, following whatever thought came into his head. 'The Reverend Clarke is still obsessed with your safety. I can only think it is because you are a papist.' He shrugged his shoulders and adopted a supercilious air. 'Clarke knows it and wants to protect you.' She was arranging the flowers studiously beside her on the green cloak. 'And if you are a papist, how does that come about? I can only think it is George. You and George are both Catholics.' Mary had now turned her attention to the far riverbank, as if something especially interesting had caught her eye. 'You don't have to tell me, Mary. But I am your brother. Who else can you trust?'

There was a long pause. They could hear the rustle of the stream close by, nagging the bank.'

'Do you remember the Easter Saturday services before the war? The vigils?' Francis could not bring himself to reply. 'The candles to celebrate the Resurrection. The promise it brought of the life hereafter. There is no more of that now...'

'I don't believe you even think of George now,' he retorted. 'It's all a pretence.'

Her gaze remained fixed on the far riverbank. 'I sometimes think there is no difference between absence and death....Do you remember when John went to Luckett and then Callington? Well, after that, after a time, I never thought of him at all. And anyway we have hardly seen him have we, over the years?'

'We were children,' he frowned. 'And John is not dead...but George is. It is not the same. Is that what you think about Mary, alone in your cottage or walking along the river..? If I am in need of a woman,' He was breaking a twig into smaller and smaller pieces between his hands, 'then you are in need of company, company of any kind. You must not think…'

'John just took himself away,' Mary did not appear to be listening and was following her own train of thought. 'John always went his own way, always knew what he wanted. I think Robert was jealous. I can't remember John even raising his voice.'

'He never did. You're right. He always knew his own mind.' Francis had given up. She would not listen to him. But then immediately he became frustrated by his sister's wilful contrariness. 'Why are we sitting here?' he burst out. 'Come home, or go to your cottage!' He stood up, impatient, but Mary would not budge.

'Take the flowers,' she said softly. 'Put them in water or they will die.'

'Then I will leave you!' He untethered the mare. 'Since you wish us to part......but you cannot remain here, alone.'

'Wait!' She scrambled to her feet. 'It is true. You are my brother. I trust you. I am a papist...' She was close to tears, seeming even in her confession to doubt herself. 'George told me we must always confess our sins!' He held her close to him, conscious of her confusion. As they stood together, the words of the Reverend Clarke, the words she did not properly understand, rang in her ears, 'Dominus noster Jesus Christus te absolvat.......ego te absolvo a peccatis tuis in nomine Patris et Filii et Spiritus Sancti...'

She must have swooned and only gradually became aware that Francis too was speaking to her, holding her tight where she lay in his arms, whispering in her ear. Her spring flowers were scattered and broken all around her. And then her own voice came to her from afar, 'Forgive me Father, for I have sinned.' 'Come home now,' Francis whispered. 'Come home.'

The sun had slipped away somewhere. The mare had grown restive and wandered away, leaning her neck now and then to nuzzle fastidiously at an occasional shrub or clump of furze. After a while, Mary was able to take back possession of herself, releasing herself from his grasp.

'The Reverend Clarke used to come, to the farmhouse, before I moved at the start of the war. He brought me the sacraments. I confessed and he gave me absolution. He visits others.'

Francis held his breath. Mary did not appear to understand the enormity of what she had said. The Rector's anxiety for Mary, his strange behaviour in the vestry, was not then to be wondered at. If found out, a closet Catholic priest, he would certainly be hanged.

'I must go.' She was fixing her bonnet and motioning to him for her cloak. 'You need not accompany me, Francis. I am quite recovered,' Her ever-changing demeanour was astonishing to him. 'You too should pray, Francis. For the dead, for our father Samuel, and for the living, for the Queen. George taught me how to pray. And the Reverend taught me how to confess.'

They were about to part. The mare had ambled over to where they stood and was looking from one to the other in mystification.

'You have never had anything to confess,' he stammered.

'Perhaps you are right. You are always right Francis. You keep your feet on the ground now. But I think I always felt sinful, cast out. You will say I am foolish but I believe mother never really cared for me...Well, now you know it all. But next time, next time I will come home, when the war is over.'

'The war...' He did not bother to finish, to explain that the war was already over in Cornwall. She had stepped away from him and continued on her way across the meadow to Hampt. He could only watch her striding confidently away, pausing only to select her way across the knobbly field, and wonder what on earth was in her mind.

Returning to Venterdon the mare, aware of his consternation, became ruminative herself, picking thoughtfully at the hedgerows as they ascended the slope. Mary had taken him through a whole gamut of emotion in the short time he had been with her. From surprise and pleasure at her appearance through to confusion, frustration and ultimately shock at her casual revelation of the Rector's papistry, and then tenderness when she had inexplicably broken down

Her altered appearance and sudden changes of mood convinced him that she had still not been open with him, as she had claimed. He thought of how he had not recognised her from the bridge. Surely it was inconceivable that George had appeared after all this time. But he could think of no other explanation.

His mother would be waiting. He remembered almost the last words Mary had spoken, that she had always felt sinful, cast out. She had used the same expression before, 'cast out'. Was it true his mother had never cared for her? Janella would be waiting too. She would keep her thoughts to herself, but he knew Janella had no time for his sister who she regarded as self-indulgent. Janella had long ago concluded that Mary cared not a jot for her husband. And that, he thought confusedly, is what I too have just accused her of. His own words came back too him, 'I don't believe you think of George any more. It's all a pretence.'

*

She did not look back. He would be watching her still, as he had from the bridge. At first, she knew perfectly well, he may not even have recognised her. Coming back from Tutwell, as carefree as she could ever remember, Francis would hardly have taken her for a woman bereaved, or pining for a lost husband. Everything after that, at least everything she had said intentionally, had been to put him off the scent. She had stopped by the oak on impulse, to prevent Francis accompanying her all the way to Hampt.

Her mind was racing. But there was no cause for alarm. Deliberately, she slowed her pace, pretending to pick her way through the scrub, though by now she imagined Francis would have mounted the white mare and be slowly ascending the steep slope to Venterdon. After all, Francis had changed too, a picture of sobriety. Not at all as he had been before their father's death, before Lostwithiel. She was not the only one.

But Francis had not been convinced. In her effort to protect Andrew she had revealed truths she should better have kept to herself. She had hardly denied what Francis had called her 'pretence'. And she had gone further than she would ever have intended, admitting her papistry and that of George and the Reverend Clarke too. And somehow, confessing to Francis had brought back to her what she had thought to have discarded, and when she had least expected it. George's insistence on the need for prayer and Confession and the Reverend's words of absolution, once recalled had overwhelmed her. Well that was done with now.

She could see the grey smoke from the little cottage chimney, rising above the trees and almost invisible against the grey of the sky. Andrew would be waiting and it came to her, with a pang of guilt, that she should not have spoken in the way she had about absence and death, nor about the war not being over.

That had all come from Andrew. It seemed false now and a kind of betrayal.

He would be restless, walking round and round her tiny room, to exercise his leg, anxious to be gone. To Pendennis, he said, now that Hopton had surrendered, but for reasons she would never understand. When he had tried to explain, to describe to her the castle, its location, its construction, its absolute inviolability, she had known at once it was all a myth. 'They will have to surrender in the end.' He had shrugged and pursed his lips, as if to say that was neither here nor there, that he had no power over the truth or otherwise of her claim. 'It is something I have to do,' he had explained, as if that was enough. Why? Why? Why? He had no answer.

Andrew, she had soon learned, looked at things differently. he did not look back, as she had done for so long. Nor in a way did he look forward from one day to the next. When each day arrived, Andrew took it for what it was, no more no less. And so he had entered her world truly by accident or, she could not help wondering, was it fate rather than chance? 'When the cards are shuffled,' Andrew said, 'no man knows what the game will be.'

And from the beginning he had accepted her for who she was, never said she should do this or that, and had made no attempt to change her. That was what she loved most. She was an angel in a pigsty and proud of it. She smiled broadly as she approached the bare and stately trees surrounding her cottage. He was no papist. She would surely have recognised that, nor atheist as at first she had feared. 'The light of God is in everyone.' She remembered that too. Of course she loved him more than ever she had loved George, who seemed to her now so old and bigoted.

To her shame, she had even offered herself to him, but he had refused. It had stung her to the quick. She had accused him wildly of other women, of caring not a fig for her, though she had saved his life.

He had silenced her lightly, with patience and with poetry.

'For I had rather owner bee

Of thee one houre, than all else ever.'

But still he would not take her. One day soon he would leave. He would find a way to reach Pendennis and might never see her again, and so he would not take her. Stubbornly he continued to sleep on the mat by the fire, where she had first tended him. She still thought of him wounded and helpless, as he had been when she had first encountered him in the ruin. But now, after a month in her care he was, on the surface at least, much altered. The wound was almost healed. The beard she had once found so neat and trim, he had deliberately allowed to grow. The torn and soiled clothing had been exchanged for George's stockings, breeches and red doublet, a country gentleman's attire, which fortunately had fitted him well. And whenever, cautiously, he had strayed outside the cottage, perhaps to collect firewood, he had donned George's grey sleeveless jerkin which had once been so familiar to her. From her window, it might have been George himself.

Sometimes she wished she had not dragged so much of her previous life down the hill in the fog, the day she had invaded her own home. She knew he would be gone soon. He was adamant and not slow to remind her that her own life was at risk, every moment he remained. Perhaps, the thought gripped her with awful suddenness, he had already gone...

Chapter 10

At the South Gate Robert brought his horse to a halt and dismounted. The pikemen at either side studiously ignored him but a man, whom he took to be an officer, had emerged from the shadows beneath the arch. Though peasants, small traders, beggars and hangers-on of every kind came and went freely, a gentleman on horseback was a different matter.

The officer was a large, heavily-bearded man with a black, wide-brimmed hat set squarely and a rough leather jerkin, only partly obscuring the distinctive red coat of the New Model Army. He was completely unarmed but nevertheless wore an air of absolute authority.

'Name?'

'Robert Pellow. I'm...'

'What is your business here?'

'I bear a letter, for Thomas Gewen at Bradridge.'

The officer extended an open hand to receive the letter, without releasing him from a cold, appraising stare, the natural prerogative of those with absolute power. Robert was left in no doubt that this man might commit him to the deepest dungeon of the Castle prison and throw away the key, if he had a mind to.

He took out Christina's carefully sealed letter on the outside of which she had written in her practised, formal hand, 'For Thomas Gewen M.P.', and placed it in the officer's hand.

'My wife is Thomas Gewen's niece.'

'Name?' Being unused to interrogation, Robert was slow to respond. 'Name?' The officer was handing him back the letter, thankfully unopened.

'My wife,' he mumbled uncertainly, 'Christina, Christina Pellow.'

The man seemed satisfied or at least sufficiently appeased and reluctantly presented him with a small square of paper, which already bore his signature.

'Show this whenever you are stopped.'

That was all. He was free to continue. The officer had already returned to the shadows beneath the archway of the Gate. Not wishing to appear conspicuous, he did not remount but led his horse, with some trepidation, through the Gate and into the town. To his left the Castle, which he had once been used to ignore, now loomed threateningly over the town. Lanson itself was as busy as ever, the compact maze of streets and alleyways crammed with horses, wagons and travellers of all kinds, but it was more subdued as if the townsfolk had not yet decided, under this new regime, exactly what was to be tolerated.

There were knots of red-coated soldiers here and there, not at all boisterous as might be expected of an occupying army, but serious and vigilant. As he entered the square, the strong smell of new-baked bread emanating from a nearby bakery and somehow a welcome remnant of normality, briefly lifted his spirits. He paused, together with a group of fellow travellers, to watch a company drilling in the centre of the square, mesmerised for a while by the regular tramp of boots and simultaneous clatter of muskets drowning out the more familiar sounds of the town, the raised voices of traders selling their wares, the clip-clop of hooves and rattle of harness, the hammering of a shoemaker or blacksmith.

A quartet of young women giggling on a corner to attract attention, a pair of ragamuffins scampering down an alleyway struck him, amidst this sober, business-like atmosphere of the town, as a kind of profanity.

Unhurriedly, he led his horse away from the square, past the church of St Mary Magdalene and then, as the crowds began to thin, remounted. At the northern extremity of the town, he was stopped again as he had expected, but on presentation of his pass was allowed to proceed.

Once on the open road he felt nervously inside his jerkin for Christina's letter as if this, his only justification for riding to Boyton at all, might mysteriously have become lost or stolen in the bustle of the town. Reassured, and as the road straightened down the hill from Lanson, he encouraged his mount to a canter. It was late morning. The sun was struggling to cast its light from behind high streaming clouds.

Gewen's house at Bradridge in the parish of Boyton was less than six miles away. The sooner his mission was completed the better. Christina, he knew, had sealed the letter before he had even known of its existence. Yet he had not asked to read it. Christina was the politician and he would not have had the fluency to contradict her. If she had merely, as she claimed, written a ferocious criticism of the Reverend Clarke and of the Lady Day service which had so enraged her, then who was he to disagree? Clarke was certainly an imposter. There was no doubt about that, though he had to admit, a popular one.

A brief shadow of uncertainty crossed his brow. He reined in a little as the road began to twist and turn between high hedgerows. Popular or not, that was hardly his concern. 'I do not,' he told himself self-effacingly, 'pretend to be a religious man.' But he did hope that Christina had not referred in her letter to more personal matters. Before his leaving she had taken the trouble to remind him that the inheritance she had received from her late husband, the Minister, would not last for ever. For this reason if no other, he knew Christina would wish him to return with some kind of position or at least the assurance of one.

All too soon, the house at Bradridge came into view. He had visited once before when, in seeking Christina's hand, she had half-invited him, but he had no recollection of Gewen himself.

Gewen's manor was substantial, situated on a rise and with a fine view over the woods to the Tamar. The two storey building rose to the left and right of a walled forecourt entered via a modest, arched gateway. There was a number of musketeers lounging about the entrance, less disciplined apparently than those in Lanson. He dismounted and showed his pass, whereupon a stable boy was summoned to take his horse. In the court a soberly dressed man, with a long nose and heavy jaw and not without an air of importance, asked him his business. He took out Christina's letter which, after a moment's consideration, proved sufficient for him to be ushered into a small room, immediately to the right of the gateway.

The room, entirely panelled in oak and having only a single window set high in the wall, was unusually dark. There was a dark blue upholstered bench following its circumference and three soberly dressed men sitting as far apart from one another as possible. His presence went unacknowledged. The man who had taken his letter had disappeared through another door, presumably leading to Gewen's inner sanctum.

Half an hour later there was a stir of anticipation from his fellow petitioners when a squat, innocuous-looking man wearing a dark cloak and hat of indeterminate shape emerged from the sanctum and, without so much as a glance, passed between them and out into the court. The petitioners shared a sigh of mutual frustration and then, by degrees, returned to silent contemplation of whatever it was that had brought them there. A few moments later the man who had taken Christina's letter also emerged and beckoned him to enter. He had acquired an unexpected priority.

The room to which he was admitted was in complete contrast to the one he had left, it being large, light and airy, and benefiting from a row of arched, mullioned windows through which now streamed a confident afternoon sun. The oak panelling was relieved by a scattering of maps and portraits. In the corner facing him and close to the windows was a large table and behind it, now rising to greet him, was the very same squat, inconspicuous man whom he had taken for a secretary only moments before.

'Robert, come in. It is such a pleasure to meet you again.' The voice was unexpectedly deep for such a small man. The words, in contrast to their sentiment, spoken without emotion. 'You do not remember? Is it so long ago since I attended your wedding in Lanson?'

'Sir, it took me a moment, I confess,' he stammered. 'It is some eight years.'

Gewen bade him sit, enquired after Christina's health, his journey and so on, the natural concerns of a well-loved relative, and then Gewen came to the letter which lay on the table in front of him.

'You must thank my niece. This letter is most useful. It will no doubt help us to discredit the Reverend Clarke and so hasten his ejection. The Rector has been flouting the wishes of the Committee and, by implication, Parliament itself, for far too long. Of course, he signed the Protestation returns which makes it difficult......but it is only a matter of time before he is removed.' Gewen, though overtly displaying little emotion, was clearly relishing the thought of finally ejecting the wayward Rector. 'He has friends, but they cannot protect him for ever. But what of yourself, Robert? You will have read Christina's letter. Are you both in accord?'

Robert had been listening hard to Gewen's words but had difficulty concentrating. The politician spoke quickly, with little emphasis and without pause. 'We are both in accord, sir.'

'And are you aware of the priorities of the County Committee?' Gewen persisted.

'We are a little way off in Clymestone.' He had not meant to sound humble or apologetic, but could not avoid it.

'We were selected in July '44 to execute ordnances, deal with sequestrations, make weekly assessments...'

Robert could no longer keep pace, but found himself observing Gewen intently. He was clean-shaven, his light brown hair cut short in the 'roundhead.' fashion, his eyes small, a little too close together, his ruff brief and yellowish. This small, faceless, innocuous-looking man did not at all look the part he undoubtedly played.

'...and generally to preserve the County, as they say, 'from spoil and plunder'. Of course we issue warrants for sequestrations and so on. And we need reliable men...' Robert had begun to take notice again. '...agents, collectors and so on. Clarke will not be the only one to lose his living.' Gewen paused, perceiving something of Robert's difficulty. 'Are you with us or against us, Robert?'

'I am with you, sir.' Robert tried to express himself with conviction.

'Let us not then beat about the bush,' Gewen resumed, leaning back in his chair. 'There is money to be made. Why do you think the men in there are so patient?' He raised his eyebrows towards the closet where Robert had been waiting. 'Look, as you know there are remnants still of the King's supporters about the County. Naturally we seek them out. If you help us, you will benefit. I recommend it, sir.'

Robert nodded enthusiastically. So far he had not been required to act strenuously or against his own inclination. What was there to lose? This was exactly what Christina wanted.

'This is a list,' Gewen continued, passing a paper across the table, 'of men from Clymestone or its neighbouring parishes who are sought by Parliament. When discovered they will, in due course, be tried for treason.'

Robert picked up the paper which contained, in alphabetical order, about a dozen names, most of which were familiar to him. Most of them had long been presumed dead. But two names, occurring next to one another, Andrew Hampton and George Hawking, caused him to hesitate before replying.

'I know most of the names. I believe these men are dead or at least have not returned to Clymestone.'

'Any names you are unfamiliar with?'

'Andrew Hampton. I think he is not from Clymestone.'

'No, he is not from Clymestone. He is a Royalist officer of Colonel Edgcumbe's Regiment of Foot, wounded a month ago while escaping across the Tamar from Cotehele. He refused to surrender and so briefly had the distinction of being sought by both armies. We believe, by the way, that 'Hampton' is an alias. You do not know this man?'

'No.'

'Are there no names with which you have a particular familiarity?'

'No.'

Gewen looked disappointed as he retrieved the list, pursing his lips and slowly shaking his head. 'Come, Robert. Let me show you my birds!' He stood up and was still hardly head and shoulders taller than his visitor. 'Follow me.'

One of two doors, both panelled and neither of which Robert had previously noticed, led back into the forecourt. From there he was led through the hall, clearly the oldest part of the house with its huge fireplace and high, hammer-beamed ceiling, and then through another door to the yard.

'They are my sole delight, but I have so little time for them now.' Gewen had to raise his voice above the various noises of a busy farmyard. 'Are you a hawking man, Robert? No? I recommend it, sir. They are expensive and must be looked after...but I suppose you are content with your dogs.' Now they were walking side by side past the stables, barn and cowshed and a whole array of sheds the purpose of which, to Robert at least, was quite obscure.

In the far corner they came to a quieter place with a dovecote, but as they approached he became aware it was no ordinary dovecote. There was neither sight nor sound of a single pigeon and all that part of the cote facing into the yard, save for the topmost peak, was exposed and barred so as to give the appearance of a large cage.

'Before the war,' Gewen explained, 'we had the pigeons as you would expect and put the first squabs on the table every Easter, before they could fly. But now I hunt for them and enjoy them all the more!'

Robert had stopped listening again, overcome with admiration for the two magnificent peregrine falcons sitting proudly on their perches, motionless but for the innate nervous twitch of curiosity they could not contain. The larger of the two he knew to be the female, the blue and grey of her faintly barred back and breast, differing little from that of her diminutive partner.

'They are a pair but never squabble as do their human counterparts. As you see they have space.'

'They are fine birds! Robert exclaimed, relaxing at last.

Gewen signalled for a servant who had been tactfully hovering about the yard and who, a moment later, brought two leather gloves and a hood. Gewen slipped on one of the gloves and handed the other to his guest.

'Here, I will show you. The tiercel is less skittish,' he said, dismissing the servant with nod.

Gewen opened the cage and slipped the hood over the bird's head, then proferring his gloved hand, lifted the smaller bird out of the cage, at the same time skilfully untethering him from the perch. Gewen's small eyes positively glistened with excitement.

'I take them on the moors with the spaniels. They get impatient. Perhaps now the war is over........' He leant down to pick a torn piece of quail from the bottom of the cage. 'They will catch anything that flies,' He slipped off the leather hood, careful to hold the bird low and steady. Robert was bewitched by the falcon's noble bearing, its arrogance, its very proximity. 'Here.' Gewen passed him the quail. 'He will come to you.'

Robert held out his gloved hand close to that of Gewen and the peregrine transferred himself and took the quail between his talons, though not immediately bending his head to tear the flesh.

'You are a disappointment to me, Robert.'

Gewen's voice sounded suddenly harsh and uncompromising. He could only stand shocked and helpless with the bird tearing at the meat on his gloved hand. 'You have not been honest with me, sir.' The words were spoken in an undertone, so low he could hardly distinguish them. The politician's lips scarcely opened.

'Sir, I…'

'You take me for a fool. I am not a fool, sir. Your sister is married to a certain George Hawking, the name on the list with which you have no particular connection!' The bird was tearing furiously at the quail, as if only too aware of the implication. Inadvertently, he raised his arm away from his face. 'Have a care, sir! If he flies away now, you will owe me a replacement! Do you think I brought you here to view my precious peregrines?

He grew suddenly weak, a prickle of perspiration down his back, nausea mounting to his throat. Yet he could neither move for fear of losing the falcon nor speak for fear of offending the squat, insignificant-looking man who stood calmly before him.

'Walls have ears, Robert. If it were not for my niece, you would be under arrest. Now, what can you tell me about your brother-in-law, George Hawking?'

'He....he has not been seen for three years. He is thought to have been killed at Bristol,' Gewen said nothing, but after the manner of his birds, put his head to one side enquiringly. 'Everyone in the Parish believes him dead...except Mary, my sister.'

'Your sister takes him to be alive and well?'

'Yes, but....'

'Perhaps she has reason.......' Gewen appeared to be weighing his options. The remains of the meat from the quail had fallen to the ground. 'Whatever your belief, Robert, and that of your fellow parishioners, I can assure you George Hawking is indeed alive and well.' The look of of genuine surprise on Robert's confused and frightened face must, if nothing else, have convinced the politician of his innocence.

'George Hawking never went anywhere near Bristol. He was attached to Henrietta Maria's retinue, some time after the fall of that city. When the Queen fled from Exeter in '44 she, together with her most trusted Catholic coterie, she passed through Lanson, a fact with which you are doubtless cognisant, on her way to Pendennis. Hawking is known to have been one of that coterie, and so passed very close to his estate in Hampt and, for that matter, very close to Mary, his wife. He is now known to reside with the Queen's household at the Palace of St Germain in Paris, where he remains a trusted adviser. He is also known to have visited England, on the Queen's behalf, in recent months.'

Gewen, aware of the shock he had chosen to inflict, now became genuinely concerned for his falcon, which was growing increasingly restless. He slipped on the hood, took him quickly onto his glove and returned him to his perch.

'So, Robert, you understand my concern?' Robert nodded. 'The information I have given you regarding George Hawking was only recently received from Paris. It is not to be shared.' Robert nodded. 'I have chosen to trust you in spite of your...lack of truthfulness. It would not do for you or Christina to be associated with popishness, however indirectly.'

'I am no papist,' Robert murmured under his breath, unconsciously adopting Gewen's quiet, secretive manner.

'A warrant will be issued for the sequestration of Hawking's property in Hampt. Your visit here has been fortunate in that some matters have been clarified. I expect the warrant to be executed before the end of the week. If your sister is found on the property she will of course be arrested.' Robert saw that they were walking towards the stables. Gewen had indicated to a stable boy for his horse to be brought out. 'I recommend, sir, as one family member to another, that your sister not be discovered on the property. I leave that in your hands. As for Hawking, if you are found to be protecting him, you know what to expect.'

'Everything you have said is new to me.'

They had come to a halt a few yards from the stable, from which his horse was now being led.

'For the time being, Robert, I believe you. 'Gewen almost smiled. 'But you cannot expect to remain free from suspicion. There are others with greater influence than I. Think about it. You bring information to me about Clarke, but lie about Hawking. It remains for you to prove yourself. I tell you, there is money to be made, much work to be done. I recommend it, Robert. But first you must prove yourself trustworthy. If you have further information for me, take it to Captain Shaw.' Robert looked puzzled. 'The man who signed your pass. In my absence, he controls Lanson.

'Thank you sir, for..'

But Gewen had already turned his back and was walking purposefully back in the direction of the hall. He took the reins which were proffered. There was a narrow gateway to the rear of the yard. It was the only way out.

*

On his return to the house, Gewen motioned for Lilley, the general factotum with the superior air, to join him in his sanctum.

'Get rid of them, and then come back here.'

And so the three petitioners who had waited so patiently and who would now be unlikely to bring themselves to Gewen's attention in the foreseeable future, were summarily dismissed. Having done his duty, and not without a certain satisfaction, Lilley returned to his master's side.

'Now get me the report on the Hawking estate.'

And throughout the remainder of the afternoon, Gewen read and re-read the report. Having only recently been submitted, he had not hitherto given it the attention it deserved, especially in the light of the information received from Paris. Now he noted with interest, that the farmhouse had been broken into on 18th March. He noted further that nothing of much account had actually been stolen, a little food and some clothing, nothing more. Not, it seemed to Gewen, the act of a rational housebreaker. Nor had any door or window apparently been forced, entry having been by the buttery door the lock of which, according to a certain John Wright, had long been defective.

'Who is John Wright?'

Lilley was reliable and anxious to please. 'John Wright was questioned a week later sir. He appears to conduct the business of the farm in the absence of Mr Hawking. Mrs Hawking is said to have removed herself to a cottage belonging to the farm.'

The bars of sunlight, criss-crossing the politician's table, had faded away. Gewen hesitated, shuffling the two pages of the report between his hands.

'Tomorrow, have John Wright brought here. Nothing more. Understood?

Chapter 11

'I cannot help but love you.' Mary's tone was half playful, half apologetic, but there was no doubting its sincerity.

Andrew Hampton did not reply but he would answer her in due course. That was his way. She had not been able to detain him a moment longer in the cramped cottage which had become his prison. Soon after daybreak, they had set off for the 'Old Park' which she had judged as empty a place as they were likely to reach and return from in a day. In keeping with the season, there was a spring in her step as she led him along the fringe of trees which formed the western border of the meadow. In the middle distance, to their left, the Tamar wound its lazy way south to the sea.

'You stray too far!' His voice, in contrast to her own, was serious, almost a reprimand.

It was true, unthinking she had begun to lead him down the slope into the meadow. In silent recognition of her fault, she made her way back, at a tangent, to the ancient sheep track they had more or less been following. Momentarily, they came together at a cluster of beeches which marked the treeline, until Hampton motioned for her once more to take the lead.

He had insisted she wore her old blue shawl and cap, the way she always had, traipsing along the riverbank. She was to be as unobtrusive as possible though Hampton himself had no choice but to wear George's expensive, grey jerkin she had retrieved, almost as an afterthought, from the farmhouse. She pictured him now as he walked behind with his sword and satchel, now conveniently containing a flagon of ale and enough bread and cheese to last them the day.

'How far before we come to this park?'

'The 'Old Park'? Not far. We come to a stream and follow it up the combe to Hook Wood. It's a quiet place. Nobody lives there now. Is it of concern to you, my love?'

She imagined him behind her, watching her skirts trailing in the dew, her shawl and cap between them scarcely sufficient to contain her tumbling curls.

'You are a married woman.'

She turned her head a little so that he might properly hear. 'For three years they have told me I am a foolish widow. Now you say I am a married woman!'

Hampton was breathing more heavily, but she had not noticed, having quite forgotten the wound she had tended and from which he had not yet entirely recovered. 'Mary, a moment!' he gasped, stifling a cry.

She turned to face him, suddenly aware of her neglect. He gestured for her to go on, but the track having widened, she linked her arm in his and they continued slowly together until they came to the banks of the nameless stream which, out of sight and a little way to their left, flowed inconspicuously into the Tamar. It seemed natural then to sit together by the gently murmuring brook.

'You are foolish to care for me. You know I cannot stay. You may never see me again.'

'Does love then take account of convenience? Whether I be widowed or married, whether you stay or leave…It is all the same.' She shrugged. 'I love you.'

'And I you,' he confessed at last, albeit reluctantly.

'Then we are both equally foolish!' Mary laughed, her cheeks unusually flushed, and leant her head to his.

'I am two fooles I know,' he smiled. 'For loving and for saying so.'

'Sometimes,' She sat up straight to study his countenance which lately had seemed to disappear beneath the dark bushiness of his beard, 'you talk in riddles.'

'Then I shall not talk at all. Come.' He raised himself awkwardly, avoiding the pressure on his leg.

They followed the path by the water's edge, entering by degrees a thickly wooded and steep-sided combe.

'This is Hook Wood. A little further and the stream divides. We go to the left, deeper into the wood. The stream flows right down from Kit Hill.

By and by, they came to a clearing and on the far side of the stream, but still some way off, a large L-shaped building came unexpectedly into view.

'You said this place was unpopulated!'

'The Lodge,' Mary replied with an air of exaggerated patience. 'It's broken down. Nobody lives there now.'

'Then this was a deer park. So it is you call it the 'old park'..Kerrybullock, I remember.'

'A hundred years ago! You have a good memory. Nobody comes here now......only if someone is desperate, they might seek shelter....as you did once.'

Nevertheless, they left the path and entered the woods, Andrew anxious lest some poor soul, hiding in the Lodge, should spy them. But there was no sign of life, no smoke from the chimney. They passed on, out of sight, and re-joined the path where the stream divided. There was a rickety wooden bridge which they had to cross in order to follow the narrower channel deeper into the woods. Here and there the floor of the forest was sprinkled with spring flowers, yellow celandine, delicate blackthorn and, as the ground began to rise towards Kit Hill, a vast carpet of bluebells which, to Mary's fancy, seemed positively to delight in this, their secret expedition.

By unspoken consent, they followed the stream almost to its source, to where the shallow water narrowed to a mere rivulet tumbling impatiently around lichen covered stones, on its tortuous way to the river. So tempting was it that Mary knelt, cupping her hands to drink.

'No!' She looked up in surprise. 'Look, it is an old tinning stream. There is no telling what it might contain.'

'How do you know?'

'Look higher up where the banks have been hacked down. The stream was diverted.' He pointed across the channel to where the ground was strangely uneven. 'Old men's workings,' he announced, apparently relishing the discovery.'

'It is hard to believe.' She regarded him with a kind of wonder. 'You know such strange things.'

Hampton had not been listening but had taken to exploring the glade in which they found themselves, the little brook bubbling along for all the world as if it had not been disturbed in a thousand years.

'The water found its right way again, once they were gone, when they had no more use for it.' He was poking about in the undergrowth with his rapier. 'Dig a little and doubtless you would discover the remains of their picks and shovels and buckets....'

'I do not like this place,' she interrupted. 'Andrew!'

At last he listened and took her hand. 'You are right. The woods are gloomy. Let us go up the hill, into the light.'

They came to a spot, clear of the trees on the eastern slope of the hill from where they could see the Tamar itself, wending its way in great loops towards Calstock and Cotehele. They sat together and drank from the flagon of ale and the sky grew lighter from the east, but without the sun. She thought of the tinners long gone, and the mysterious passing of time. Was he thinking of that too?

She was afraid to ask. Like the river and the stream her thoughts meandered, but at last took their inevitable course. Did he truly care for her? And if so, why could he not express it in a less obscure way? Did he regard her as a married woman or a widow? He had certainly known the name, George Hawking. What else did he know? And at the back of her mind, continually present, his imminent leaving for Pendennis. He would not tell her when or why.

She took off her shawl and cap, rolling them up into a pillow, and lay down at his side, looking up into the grey sky.

'My father is dead. My mother is sick. My husband is missing and my lover is leaving. how about you?'

There was a long pause. She had wanted to shock him into revealing himself. Perhaps she had failed. Perhaps he would say nothing.

'My father lives. My mother is unknown to me. I am a bastard and I am about to leave,' He paused to regard her quizzically, 'my lover.'

They both laughed out loud at the incongruity of it but also with the sense of relief which accompanies disclosure. When they had calmed themselves, he took her in his arms and lay with her.

'Honour thy father and thy mother,' he mused, 'whether it be a Commandment or no, it is sound advice.'

'The sixth Commandment may have slipped your mind,' Mary retorted, not naturally amenable to what Hampton termed 'advice', 'Thou shalt not kill.'

'And, by the same token, I need not remind you of the seventh!' Hampton laughed, suddenly releasing her.

'George is dead!'

He could not help but kiss her, pushing back her curls, clutching her to him. And then, for a long time, they lay quietly. The sun had risen in earnest over the moor, dispersing the clouds which cast fleeting shadows over the hillside. Lazily she reached for his satchel and took out the bread and cheese.

'It rattles.' She shook the satchel to prove her point.

'Let me show you.' He took it from her and delved into the bag with both his hands. She heard the lining tear and he brought out one clenched fist. 'What do you think it is?'

'Money,' she replied without hesitation. 'I remember you said there was money.'

Hampton unclenched his fist to reveal a shining gold crown. 'They are not all crowns. There are sixpences and shillings too. You see. I will pay my way to Pendennis.'

She was not as impressed as he had expected. Where did a man in wartime, and amid such poverty and destruction, acquire such wealth? She did not want to think of it. So she tore up the bread and broke the cheese and handed him his share.

'What shall I do when you are gone?'

He cast the satchel to one side, mildly disappointed. 'You have a brother and a priest and, above all, you have a mother. Go back to her. Seek her love and it will be returned.'

'She cast me out.'

'It is easy to misunderstand a mother's love.'

'I wanted to see my father die, but she would not have it,'

'So? She had some other reason.'

The sound of chewing, licking of lips and occasional swigs from the flagon which accompanied the exchange, would have seemed to an outsider to belittle the words. But it was simply a way of sparring to which she had grown accustomed and which did not admit any kind of self-indulgence.

'She has buried herself, ' Mary tipped up the flagon until she had swallowed the last drop of ale, 'in the past.'

'It is a family trait.' His tone was more offhand than he had intended but it was too late. He had misjudged her. She would not look at him now. 'Mary....' He was not used to having to search for the right words. 'We cannot help the past, nor alter it. It is dead........ Nothing is forever.'

'Mary looked unconvinced. 'One short sleepe past, wee wake eternally,' You see Andrew, I remember everything you tell me. Your quotations are apt to contradict themselves.'

'Mary, he capitulated, 'you are too clever for me.' And so, cleverly rebuffed, he lay on his back and closed his eyes.

'Do you think the tinners will come back?

'No.'

'And you, will you come back, Andrew? Or is this the last time?' There was no reply. 'Sometimes I wonder if you protect me, or yourself. Perhaps I should come with you?'

But she could not goad him into a response and so they lay together and slept until the afternoon sunshine disappeared and an early evening chill settled on the hillside.

She awoke to find a goldfinch poking about the satchel. Gently, she lifted it away from him and shook out the crumbs of bread and cheese. Hampton had also stirred. She put a finger to her lips and they waited expectantly for the finch to return. In a moment he emerged in buoyant, dipping, airy flight from the undergrowth, and then another in the same manner, equally bold and unafraid.

'They have so much colour for so small a bird,' she whispered. 'Look, black, white, crimson, brown and they have a yellow streak on their wings!'

There was a chattering in the bushes and one tiny bird after another came dipping and swooping from every plant and branch.

'They come every year to the same spot to raise their young,' he whispered, 'even to the same nest. Today they are fortunate. A feast they could hardly have expected!'

'And next year too,' Mary thought, 'but we will not be here then to feed them........any more than the tinners.'

They waited until the last crumb had been consumed and then, arm in arm, made their way down the valley to the stream not, for once, dwelling on any other time or place.

***

Robert had left Gewen's yard in a state of shock, his head spinning, as no doubt Gewen had intended. it was not simply the information which the politician had chosen to reveal to him, but the manner with which he had been manipulated. He could not bring himself to face the streets of Lanson, the soldiers, the checks, the cautious bustle of the town, and so he took to the lanes, west and then south, guessing his way to Clymestone.

In contrast to the town, there was only the occasional packman and around the clusters of cottages which came his way, barely any sign of life. He sat slumped in the saddle, deep in thought and only vaguely aware of where his horse was taking him. He knew the longer his journey, the more time there would be to come to terms with what Gewen had told him, more time to consider his position.

He had been stunned by the knowledge that not only was George Hawking alive but that he was also being sought as a leading papist and close adviser to the Queen. Hawking had been presumed dead for years by everyone, except Mary who had stubbornly waited for him and been thoroughly mocked for her pains, not to say ostracised. Did Mary know her husband was alive? Was she a papist too? He could hardly credit it, but then he had ignored his sister for so long, had not even laid eyes on her since their father's funeral.

He had always thought of himself as being much older. Perhaps that was on account of her...her flightiness. And yet there were not five years between them. She had, after all, been a married woman since before the war. It was the war that had undone her. That she was a papist began to make sense. She never attended church, as you might have expected, to pray for her husband. but had deliberately isolated herself. George, he knew, had fought in the Low Countries. That experience must have raised him through the ranks in the Royalist army, but it had never occurred to him or, he imagined, to anyone else, that George must have fought for the papists, for the Spanish!

Gewen's words kept coming back to him, the words but not the man whose face, even now, he could hardly bring to mind. Gewen had seemed to know everything, even to the most trivial detail. 'I suppose you are content with your dogs.' Surely Christina could not have written to Gewen about his dogs! How he had gained his confidence and then threatened him with arrest! 'You are a disappointment to me Robert.' Had he not been trying to protect his sister? Was that not natural enough in a man? And Gewen had appeared to let him off the hook. 'I recommend it, as one family member to another, that your sister not be discovered on the property.'

The farm at Hampt was about to be sequestrated. He tried to slow his thoughts, to think more clearly. It was up to him to ensure that Mary was not found on the property. He must therefore warn her and help her to escape...but escape where? He had no idea. But perhaps that was not his concern. Only to escape. And what about Hawking? Gewen had seemed to believe that Hawking was in Cornwall..

They had found their way somehow to the Plymouth road. Before long he would be home and Christina, Christina would want to know. What could he say? Her letter. Gewen had been grateful for the letter. It would assist them in ejecting Clarke, the imposter, from his living. And what of himself? Well, there was money to be made. If more information could be provided, there was work, profitable work. Gewen had said something about agents and collectors. 'Are you for us or against us?' How otherwise could he have replied?

It had begun to drizzle, but he reined his horse to a standstill, anxious not to round the final bend into Whiteford. He must decide about Mary. He could go to her directly or perhaps speak to Francis. No, he must not involve anyone else, not Christina, not Francis. He would ride over to Hampt. But then he would have to explain himself. She had to leave because he had discovered that the farm would be confiscated. And the reason? The County Committee had learnt that her husband had been a papist. It would be safest to make no further reference to George. If she knew her husband to be alive, that was her business. If she thought him dead, he could not disabuse her. In that case, George had chosen to ignore her most cruelly, even passing through Lanson. He could not make Mary's life even more unbearable than it already was.

By the time Robert reached Whiteford, he was thoroughly bedraggled. Their only stable boy, not always on hand, was luckily there to look after his horse. His own yard, growing muddy in the rain, he could not help comparing with Gewen's. But the welcome was warm enough, there being a distinct air of anticipation which he was loathe to dissipate.

Thomas and Liddy were as much affected as Christina though Christina would have denied being anything other than her normal self. He changed from his wet clothes and then descended to the parlour. Thomas had found a pheasant in one of his traps and had to be congratulated, as had Liddy for cooking it. When they were done Christina despatched Thomas to help Liddy in the kitchen and then, without further ado, made it perfectly plain she awaited his report.

He told her how much Gewen had appreciated her letter which was certain to hasten the ejection of Clarke. And there was money to be made from the provision of more information. Agents and collectors were to be employed as Royalist land was sequestrated. Christina watched him closely across the parlour table, hardly blinking as he gave his account.

'Your uncle was kind enough to show me his birds.'

'They have long had a dovecote at Bradridge. It was there when you came to court me. Remember?

'No, he has converted it,' Robert was happy and relieved to be able to demonstrate this new found intimacy. 'He has peregrines now. Fine birds.'

'So what is amiss?' He could not help reflecting how Christina had a way, when she chose, of looking right through you so that, whatever you tried to conceal, you felt sure she already knew.'

'Amiss?'

'There is something amiss.'

Under Christina's unwavering interrogation, Robert visibly squirmed. 'I suppose I do not like to provide information about people. To be something akin to a spy.' And then one desperate throw of the dice. 'It does not seem Christian to me. That is the truth of it.'

'The guilty should not go unpunished.'

'But punishment could mean the scaffold. 'Thou shalt not kill'. Am I to be a party to that?'

Christina stood up impatiently and began to pace the room. 'The sixth Commandment forbiddeth the taking of our own life, or the life of our neighbour unjustly or whatsoever tendeth thereto. Unjustly, Robert. Therein lies the crux!'

He was beaten, as he expected to be, but in his defeat he had been considering how best he might approach Mary, without arousing Christina's suspicion.

'Your uncle showed me a list. Men who are wanted. I knew most of the names, but I think they are all dead now, men who fought for the King and never came back.'

As he had anticipated, Christina was quick to show interest. 'But some may have returned and are now quietly tending their fields, undiscovered!'

'It's possible.'

'You could find out!' Christina was pacing the room. 'Robert, find out, tomorrow. Make yourself useful to my uncle. Why not?

These men will be brought to account sooner or later..in this world....or the next.'

Robert made a feeble attempt to appear reluctant, but as Christina was not attending, the effort was wasted.

'Will you do that Robert? And then you might visit our neighbour, Minister Marten. Tell him you are an agent of the County Committee. Will you do that for me, Robert?' Now she regarded him in excited supplication.

'Sweetheart,' he replied, somewhat incongruously. 'Your wish is my command.'

If he had capitulated too easily, Christina did not appear to notice. Riding about the Parish, ostensibly in pursuit of Royalist miscreants, would give him the opportunity to visit Mary, and Marten too if that was what Christina wanted. Besides, apart from George Hawking and the single stranger on Gewen's list, Andrew Hampton, he was certain all the other men had already met their maker.

That night Christina was in forgiving, not to say rapacious mood, content that Robert had made such an agreeable impression on her uncle, and had agreed so easily with her proposal. He had explained to her satisfaction the reason for his misgivings. That was understandable. He was a sensitive man, irreligious and stubborn but sensitive nevertheless. Christina slept soundly.

But as if to confirm his sensitivity, Robert lay awake till dawn, wondering what on earth he would say to Mary and unable to escape the sensation of being sucked into a whirlpool of deception, over which he had no control.

Chapter 12

On April 2nd Hugh Peters, a Cornishman and only recently Thomas Fairfax's envoy to the Eastern Gentry, preached to both Houses of Parliament. Conveniently setting aside the uncomfortable fact that St. Michael's Mount and Pendennis Castle still held out for the King, Peters declared that, 'All Cornwall is yours without blood. The hills,' he persisted in typically exaggerated fashion, were 'rejoicing' and the 'valleys laughing.'

But even Peters had to admit, somewhat in contradiction of himself, that all was not entirely well. There were still those, the man of God reminded Parliament, who must not be forgotten; 'the disabled soldier, the widow and the orphan, beggars, prisoners and debtors. No doubt, Peters said, they would all come to be rewarded in due course.

Janella Golding, who was not present at the time, was neither disabled soldier, nor widow, orphan, beggar or debtor though she might well have considered herself a prisoner. At the beginning of the war, before Samuel's dreadful illness, she had been part of a more or less happy and prosperous household. It was only later that she had realised how much of that had come from Samuel himself, hard-working, good-humoured, affable Samuel, prone to outbursts of violent temper it was true but you learned to keep out of his way and anyway they soon subsided.

Now the war was over and Janella was left with the widow Alice who, though emerging at last from a year of confusion and torpor, still remained remote and uncommunicative. And Francis was little better, once 'Jack the Lad' and well known for it, he had flirted with her as well as everyone else. But by the time she had decided not to rebuff him so severely, he had lost interest and moved on. And then had come the lash of his father's tongue, overwhelming guilt and the Lostwithiel campaign.

Francis had come back obsessed with the horrors he had witnessed, only to find himself ignored by his mother and rejected by his dying father. Now he still kept to his room and still, when she came to clean the tiny attic which had once been hers, she would find scraps of screwed up, inky paper strewn across the floor.

Janella knew it was she who had kept together what remained of this unhappy household for so long. But she was thirty-one, not that any of her birthdays had been celebrated or even recognised. She had no family of her own. Was she to grow into a lonely old maid or should she escape now before it was too late? She found her thoughts tending ever more in the same direction. Perhaps it was the Spring and the end of the war, or more likely the renewed, more serious but less persistent attentions of Arthur. He was a few years older, hard-working, rough and ready and cynical yet he had held a candle for her, without encouragement, all through these troubled years. She knew in time he would give her up. He had told her so and she had shooed him away, but then called him back.

'Arthur, I know I am a harridan. I do not deserve you. Midsummer Day. On Midsummer Day, I'll give you my answer, once and for all.'

Arthur had simply looked sceptical and gone off to work. And she had thought of his acre of land and cottage at Tutwell where he lived with an elderly mother. If they married, that is where she would live. Perhaps they would have children. Life would be just as hard. She remembered her mother telling her what she was to expect;

'There's cookin' 'n washin' 'n milkin' 'n feedin'

"An whatever come into their 'ead.'

It was a long rhyme which her mother had no doubt composed herself.

'...when you'm maz'd an' long for your bed

'There's picklin' 'n scrapin' 'n curin' 'n cleanin'

"An' whatever come into their 'ead.'

'Whatever come into their 'ead.' She had never forgotten it nor questioned its accuracy. She allowed herself a smile. But if it was her own home, all the work would be for herself and her own family, not someone else's. It made sense to accept Arthur. What other offer could she hope for now? But before Midsummer, when the opportunity arose, she would at least tell Francis so that he would not be surprised when the time came. It would also of course, be the last chance Francis would ever have of making his own feelings known, if he had any,

***

The knock at the cottage door was hesitant, barely audible. Mary and Andrew looked at one another in alarm. John Wright they would have heard coming down the hill. In any case he was not expected, any more than Francis, their only other likely visitor. She gestured for Andrew to go into her room, then when he had made himself scarce, opened the door.

'Robert!'

'Mary.'

'You had better come in.' She saw he had tethered his horse to a tree some yards further up the slope. 'I did not expect you.'

'I'm sorry. I know we have long grown apart.'

Beside his sister, Robert looked tall and awkward. He had inherited his father's look, large, gangling almost and, had it not been for Christina, perhaps he too would have been jovial, good-humoured. They sat down opposite one another, the only option unless they were to remain standing. Mary took note of her brother's discomfort, but for one who had ignored her for years and was wed to an outrageous Puritan, she was not prepared to put him at ease.

'You look well,' Robert tried to break the ice, but it was true. While Mary was confident and bright he, the elder brother, was uncomfortable, uncertain how to proceed.

'I have come to warn you.'

'Mary furrowed her brows and put her head to one side in mock consternation. 'The Reverend Clarke has warned me, Francis has warned me. And now you have warned me. Robert, you may count me as thoroughly warned.'

'This is different.' Robert pressed on manfully. 'Listen to me and then I will be gone. Perhaps you do not regard me as a friend.' Mary made no dispute. 'Then all the more reason for you to consider what I have to say. You must admit I have nothing to gain.' Mary lowered her eyes, inviting him to continue. 'You are aware that Christina's uncle is Thomas Gewen, perhaps now the most influential man in Lanson?' Mary nodded slightly and Robert took some time to collect his thoughts. 'I have met Gewen……. He informed me that before the end of this week, your property will be confiscated and if you are found on it, you will be arrested.'

'Why? Why should they care about me?' She tried to be contemptuous but there was fear in her voice.

'George. They believe George,' He had reached the point of greatest difficulty, 'was or is a leading Catholic and particular supporter of the Queen. Cornwall is now under the control of Parliament. It is not unnatural that properties such as yours should now be sequestrated.'

Mary's countenance, if it were possible, had grown paler even than usual. Her voice trembled. 'George. Is George alive?'

'I do not believe so,' he lied. 'The point is his being a papist…Mary, I hope you know I care not one way or another, but if George was a papist, a leading papist, and you are his widow…that is the point. There is no doubt your land will be taken and sold off, for as much as they can get. If they find you here, they will arrest you.' Robert's voice had grown louder, shaking with emotion, frustrated lest Mary might not believe him. But he need not have been concerned. His sister had grown very quiet. So he relented a little. 'It is not to say you would be hanged like some papist priest, but you would be imprisoned until they decided what to do with you. George, you must understand, was not merely a papist, but a leading one, a favourite of the Queen's.'

'Thank you, Robert,' she said quietly. 'But what am I to do? Where am I to go?'

'I can't help you. I take a risk even in telling you this,' he lied again. Gewen had more or less instructed him to do exactly as he was doing now.

He stood up to go and Mary followed him to the door where she took his hand in both of hers.

'Perhaps when all this is over, we can be friends.' And as she spoke she could not help but notice, hanging by a nail to the back of the door, George's grey jerkin and red doublet and beneath them Andrew's leather satchel.

Robert followed her gaze as he turned away from her to lift the latch. He had seen them too. She was sure Robert had seen them too. But he said nothing and she watched him stride away to where his horse was tethered, mount and disappear in the direction of the farmhouse. Andrew emerged cautiously from her chamber.

'I heard everything.'

'He saw the clothes on the door, and your satchel.'

'We have no choice then. We must both leave at once.'

They were speaking in an undertone, as if someone was listening. And then there was silence as each of them, in their own way, considered the implications. Mary was the first to speak.

'Perhaps George is alive. Perhaps they know George is alive. Perhaps he is coming back for me! Strange… after so long, but now I couldn't bear it!'

They stood together by the door. 'Would Robert have recognised the jerkin as belonging to George?'

'I think so, but then he would have no other conclusion to draw. He would know nothing of you.'

'He has taken a risk, but even now might be on his way to Gewen. Think! It would be a feather in his cap. The arrest of George Hawking, or Andrew Hampton for that matter.'

'Then we have no time to lose!'

'Do you have horses?' It was odd that never before had they discussed the details of his own escape, imminent though it had been. 'There is a stable at the farmhouse?'

'There is the bay I used to ride...if he is still there. John Wright should have…and the working horse you have already seen, which he uses about the farm.'

'Saddles? Bridles?'

'In the stable. Andrew, I will come with you! I will come with you to Pendennis!'

'No! No!' He took hold of her. 'That would be more dangerous than remaining here. It is what they will expect, a man and a woman together. If I take both horses, it will further mislead them. You cannot come with me, Mary. All this has done is to hasten our parting.'

It sounded brutal. She wrenched herself free and stepped away from him. She was facing arrest. Or worse, George was about to come and spirit her away! And Andrew! Andrew thought only of his own escape to Pendennis and certain death! Tears both of despair and contempt rose up within her. She would not, would never plead with him. Let him go!

'Go then,' she almost stifled the words.

Hampton who was staring fixedly out of the little window facing the hill, did not hear. 'We must quit your cottage now, leaving whatever false trail we can.'

'Go then!' she screamed, at last rousing him from his calculations.

'Mary.' He took hold of her again. 'I will not desert you, I promise, until I know you are safe. But where are we to go now, until the time of our parting? That I cannot fathom.'

'The Lodge,' she said after a moment or two. 'You remember the Lodge?'

'The Lodge, yes, it is nearby and did not appear to be occupied. We will go there. But you will need help, Mary, when I am gone.'

'There is only Francis.'

'Will he come?'

She was thinking of how, by the old oak, she had confused and deceived him, had done everything possible to keep him away.

'Will he come?'

'If I get a message to him. There is a lad, Ned, who roams about the village, more often than not by the river. He used to carry messages for the Reverend Clarke. Perhaps I could find him…'

Hampton took from his satchel a handful of sixpences. 'These will help.'

'I am afraid if you leave me now, I will not see you again.'

'Mary, I will go to the Lodge and wait for you.' In his anxiety to leave, Hampton seemed to be growing increasingly impatient. He took the satchel and grey jerkin from the peg on the door. 'Let us leave the doublet. It will confuse them. And we must do something about your chamber.'

Mary's makeshift altar was still there in the corner. Silently she regarded it, a guilty expression on her face.

'Mary, I will bury the crucifix and candlesticks.' She nodded her consent as he laid them flat and folded over them her white linen cloth. Then without explanation, he deliberately ruffled up her bedding. 'I will put food in here,' he said, taking up one of the covers. 'We are sure to need it.'

She could hardly grasp what was happening to her. This was her home, her life. What was to become of her? She sank bewildered into her chair, by the empty grate.

'It is too quick, Andrew. I cannot bear it.'

He came and knelt at her side. 'You are right,' he said softly, after a while. 'It is better I wait here while you look for Ned, and then we will go to the Lodge together.' But he could not help but calculate. 'When you come back, change into your better clothes. There is a way to make you safe. I promise.'

'How is that possible?'

'First we must get away from this place. When Francis comes, I will explain.'

Curious but partially placated, Mary began to regain her spirits and before long left him to search for Ned by the riverbank.

After an hour of wandering up and down, as far as Tutwell and back, she had come to despair of ever finding him. There was nothing for it but to take a risk and walk into the village. It was then, on her final passing of the bridge, that she caught a glimpse of a giant shadow beneath the nearest arch. She slithered down the bank.

'Ned, is that you?'

He was paddling in the shadows, the water being exceptionally low, and was apparently engaged in a minute study of the bridge's construction. Reluctantly, he stepped into the light.

'You could blow'n up from 'ere, Miss Mary. Powder from a musket. Take a lot o' powder but I already got some.'

'Powder is dangerous, Ned.'

'Yes.' Into that single word, Ned managed to pack an inestimable sense of anticipation.

'Do you want a sixpence?'

'I'd rather a shillin."

'Sixpence now, and sixpence when I know it's done.'

Ned appeared to acquiesce but was now more interested in drying his feet on the grassy bank.

'You know my brother Francis, at Venterdon?' No response, but it was not a sensible question. Ned knew everyone. 'I want you to take him a message.' Ned put out his hand for the sixpence, which he duly received without acknowledgement. 'Just tell him 'The Lodge'.

'The Lodge.'

'Yes, he asked me and now I'm telling him, 'The Lodge'. but it's a secret. Not for anyone else's ears and I want him to know now, this afternoon.'

'And the other sixpence?'

She knew Ned might never see her again so handed him the other sixpence. 'I'll trust you.

Ned promptly wandered off in the direction of Venterdon and Mary hurried across the meadow to the cottage. Hampton was ready with the food wrapped in a blanket. While she had been away he had buried the crucifix and candlesticks. They were ready to leave.

***

Janella was carrying a heavy pail of milk to the kitchen when Ned wandered into the yard.

'Ned.' Janella put down the pail. 'You're on business, I expect.'

'Message for Mr Francis.'

'He's in the North Field.' Ned turned to go. 'Or,' she called after him, 'you can tell me if you want.' Ned didn't want.

Janella thought, as she took the milk through the kitchen to the buttery, it could only have been Mary. Alice was sitting by the fire she had lit earlier, but had nothing to say. Perhaps she had not heard Ned in the yard. She put the pail down, the milk slopping casually over the rim, and slipped through the brewhouse back into the yard. If Mary was in trouble, the first thing Francis would do would be to come back and make some excuse. He would need to avoid his mother. She did not have long to wait. First, his boots trudging up the lane. She recognised his step. And then there he was at the gate, motioning for her to come over, taking for granted she would be there.

'I got a message, he said in an undertone, 'from Mary. She must be in trouble.'

'What did Ned say?'

'He was very particular, wouldn't let Arthur hear. He just said 'The Lodge', and then asked for sixpence!'

'The Lodge in the Park?'

'There's no other I know of. Something's going on. When I saw her last, she did everything to keep me away.' He recalled Mary's strange confession by the old oak, the way she looked.... 'I think she must have fled to The Lodge. The Reverend Clarke was forever warning her. Something must have happened.'

Janella said nothing. Mary meant trouble. She would do better to come home to her mother who was sitting there in the kitchen, pining for her.

'I'll have to go, Janella. She may be in danger. But I'll wait till we finish so that Arthur…and if mother notices, tell her I'm in my room. I will not take the mare. If I'm not back…'

Janella could no longer restrain herself. 'I will not always be here to do these things, 'she said sharply. 'It would look better if you and your sister and your brothers paid more attention to your poor mother!'

She left him standing there, speechless by the gate. She might herself flee, whenever she felt inclined, and she wanted Francis to know it! What would happen if she were in trouble? But later that afternoon she was, nevertheless, careful to mention to Alice that Francis was a little unwell and might need a day or two's rest, not that Alice believed a word of it. For as dusk fell, she was waiting at her window and watching Francis as he scraped off his boots before continuing along the lane to the village.

*

At about the same time as Francis was leaving Venterdon for The Lodge, a portly figure leading a pony more lightly burdened than usual, might have been observed on his way down the hill from the farmhouse at Hampt. It is not the usual time of day for John Wright to make his deliveries but it may be that he has some additional purpose.

In the failing light, he knocks on the cottage door and then calls out in his usual manner.

'Mrs Hawking…Mrs Hawking!' No sound comes from within. No sign of life. 'Mrs Hawking!' This time he shouts so that there can be no mistake.

The cottage remains silent and so, perhaps to make sure all is well, Wright opens the door. No-one is about. The chairs are empty. The shelves are bare. Even the grate is bare. But oddly enough, there is a red doublet plainly not belonging to Mrs Hawking, hanging from a nail behind the door.

With growing confidence, he advances to the second room which is much darker as a piece of rough sacking hangs lop-sidedly at the window. It takes a moment for his eyes to become accustomed. The bed, in some disarray, has feather pillows and an expensive-looking cover. To his right a small, bare table is set against the wall. He makes a careful mental note of everything he has seen before leaving.

The pony waits. It has not been necessary to tether him. Wright takes up the rope around the pony's neck. There is a scampering of feet. A fresh loaf of bread is missing from the half-empty pack slung carelessly in place of the saddle.

'Is that you, Ned? he shouts up the hill. It is only a guess but even so an accurate one. 'Bring it back an' I'll give you a penny.' He hears Ned slowly descending the hill and waits patiently for him to emerge from the gloom. ''ere.' He holds out a penny which Ned takes and then quickly withdraws, retaining the loaf.

'Answer me truly an' you can 'ave the bread. You seen Mrs Hawking today?'

'No,' answers Ned stoutly. 'I 'a'n't seen 'er for a week!' And scampers away.

Chapter 13

Francis and Arthur had been preparing the North Field for sowing, backbreaking work which would take several more days. He could not have left Arthur in the lurch. He had done that often enough. As usual, they did not communicate more than was necessary, so for the remainder of the afternoon he had been free to wonder what had happened to his sister. Janella could be forgiven. She had never known how cast out Mary felt. After all, Mary was a widow too and a papist one at that. Janella should have been a little more understanding.

The shortest way to The Lodge was through the village, past the church and down the lane to Oldmill, where the nameless stream began its journey to the Tamar. In the gathering darkness, he followed the path down the combe and beside the babbling waters, the forest on either side now cautiously awakening to the night. He crossed the rickety bridge close to where the stream was met by another and approached The Lodge, faintly visible through the trees. It was one of those private, hidden, tumbledown places he and Mary had often frequented as children. He came round to where the two wings of the house partly enclosed an overgrown, cobbled area with a broken-down well at its centre. There was a barn set some way from the house, but long since derelict.

Mary stood like a ghost by the main entrance, motionless, bareheaded, slightly dishevelled, her fine, green cloak unfastened at the neck. Somehow she had an air of having always been there waiting for him, though it had been hardly a minute since, from a broken window of The Lodge, she had watched his familiar shadow crossing the rickety bridge. There was a single candle, like a sentinel, burning in the ground-floor window behind her. He hesitated. Why was she here? What had happened? She looked nervous now, avoiding his curious gaze, ensuring unnecessarily that the battered door behind her was properly closed. Then at some hidden cue, like actors on a stage, brother and sister approached one another. She took his arm. Her voice trembled.

'Francis, come with me a moment. I must explain.'

She led him across the greasy cobbles, past the stinking well and into the black, gaping entrance of the barn. Inside, the skeletal roof cast unexpected shadows on the dirt floor. There was a dank mustiness in the air and in dark corners the outline of shapeless, wooden instruments. They stood close together, each instinctively protective of the other.

Francis, exhausted after a long day in the fields, waited for Mary to speak, braced himself. When it came, Mary's tangled tale was almost beyond belief. Again and again, to make any sense of it, he had to interrupt.

'Robert came to see you?'

'Yes, I...'

'This morning?'

'Yes.'

'And he told you the farm was to be confiscated..because George was a papist?'

'Yes.'

'Is George alive?'

'No.' She faltered. 'I have never seen him. You know that.'

'And so you fled here?' Mary nodded impatiently. 'Then who is this other man, the man with you in The Lodge?'

Mary explained again. A royalist officer, Andrew Hampton, wounded by the royalists themselves and now wanted, wanted by both sides. He had been dying. She had saved him. What else was she supposed to have done?

'You have been living with him?' She could sense her brother's growing indignation.

'Yes, but..'

'Not as man and wife?' It was not really a question, more of a convenient assumption. He did not wait for an answer. 'But nonetheless you have been living together, a married woman!'

'George is dead!' Mary spat out the words. 'For God's sake, Francis!'

He had turned away from her in disgust, easily forgetting his own youthful debauchery. 'Mary, tell him to go. I will not speak with him.'

Mary did not reply. For a moment or two there were only the mysterious sounds of the night, the smell of old stones and rotting wood, shadows merging.

'He leaves tomorrow for Pendennis,' she whispered. 'There is no call for him to leave now.' A rush of air shook the ancient timbers, her voice dying in the wind. 'He,' she would not say his name lest it enrage him further, 'he has vowed to bring me to safety. Go now yourself, if you want no part of it...'

After what seemed an age, during which all thought and emotion seemed to dissipate helplessly into the darkness, through weariness rather than reason, Francis brought himself to concede.

'This is the last time, Mary.' He turned at last to face her. 'You must not toy with me again. I will see you made safe and that will be an end to it.'

He followed her back to the Lodge, barely discernible now, save for the solitary candle glimmering at the window. The battered door, like some strange forest miscreant, shrieked and squealed on its hinges. Rubble in the hallway had long since blocked the way to more than half the building but to their right was a plain door set low in the wall which Mary, ever fearful that Andrew might even now have deserted her, opened nervously.

Of course Andrew who had given his word was there, standing easily by the large stone fireplace in the flickering candlelight. Francis was not slow to recognise, behind the unkempt beard and soiled jerkin, the unmistakeable confidence and bearing of an officer. And when Hampton spoke first, as he was bound to do, Francis could not help but recall the officers of the King's army whom he had first encountered at Trecarrel, and then rushing in upon him, fleeting but all too vivid, the horrors he had witnessed at Lostwithiel.

'Francis.' With that single word, intended in friendship but delivered in the manner of a natural superior, he sensed his disadvantage. They shook hand but the words of the officer passed over his head. 'I hope Mary has told you truly. It is not given to everyone to save a life and at no small risk to their own.'

Mary was staring blindly through the cracked window towards the bridge, to all intents and purposes as if her brother had not yet arrived. Francis was not listening. His eyes wandered around the bare room, floorboards scattered with droppings and thick with dust, pieces of plaster broken away from mildewed walls, Hampton's satchel and rapier casually placed in a corner, a grey blanket, the candle quivering in the window overlooking the yard. Hampton was still trying patiently to engage his attention.

'I believe I can bring your sister to a place of safety. I will not leave until…' Hampton's voice was, considering their situation, unnaturally calm, unnaturally measured. 'Francis.' It sounded like an instruction this time. 'Will you hear me out?' He nodded and Mary, sensing his accord, visibly relaxed but still chose to remain in the shadows by the cracked window.

'I was at Cotehele,' Hampton continued, 'when the news of the surrender came. Edgcumbe was at the Mount.' The names meant little. Edgcumbe was one of those who had surrendered on their behalf. Cotehele was a great house on the Tamar. But Hampton persisted. 'Lady Margaret is Edgcumbe's aunt. She is very old, but still revered by the family. She was at Cotehele when I left. Like myself she was enraged by her nephew's cowardly submission.'

Mary turned away from the window, intrigued. 'You know her? You have spoken with her?'

Hampton shrugged. 'I know her well enough. We have an understanding.'

Francis too began to wonder. How could Hampton have been so intimate with one such as this 'Lady Margaret'? 'My sister tells me you leave for Pendennis. I do not understand. Fairfax cannot be beaten now.'

'Francis, we must do what they least expect. They will be looking for a man and a woman together, so I will take both horses from Hampt but ride to Pendennis alone. Mary will go to Cotehele. Lady Margaret will employ her.' He paused. 'Perhaps you know of a better way to ensure your sister's safety?'

Francis was aware Hampton had deliberately turned the conversation away from his own inexplicable intentions, compelling him to think first and foremost of his sister.

'You must not be in any doubt,' Hampton resumed. 'Mary's farm will be sequestrated. Arrest warrants for George and Mary Hawking may already have been served.'

'Why,' Mary interrupted, 'should Lady Margaret Edgcumbe take any account of me?'

By way of explanation, Hampton picked up his leather satchel from the corner and took out what appeared to be two identical silver discs.

'If one of these can be passed to Lady Margaret, I promise she will take you in. Her word will not be challenged even by Sir Piers. Give her one of these and you will be safe.'

Mary and Andrew stood together by the hearth. She took one of the discs in her hand and bent to the candlelight to examine it.

'A silver button,' she said, taking it by the shank between her thumb and forefinger, 'and there is some kind of pattern. What is it Andrew?'

'Lady Margaret will recognise it.'

'Why so mysterious?' She linked her arm in his, coquettishly and to her brother's mounting discomfort. 'They look like birds, swallows. Why should Lady Margaret recognise them?'

'I tell you Mary, she will. I have no cause to lie. Here, take them both. With one you may have to trust a servant.'

'If Mary goes to Cotehele…' Andrew and Mary looked up, surprised, as if they had forgotten he was there. Francis repeated, 'If Mary goes to Cotehele, it would be better if she arrived not on foot or even on horseback. She would be turned away. Mary, John is in Callington. He will know the way and might provide us with better means.' He turned to Hampton. 'My brother is a carpenter. Repairing carts and wagons is his business. I will take her.' It was Hampton's turn to acquiesce.

Of course Francis was right but to Mary the details now taking shape of how she would go to Cotehele left her no longer in doubt. Her fate was sealed. She would go to Cotehele and Andrew to Pendennis. The end had already come. It only remained for each of them to act out their allotted parts. Abruptly, she left Hampton's side and took up her former position on the window seat. She glanced at the two men. The ice had broken. They stood facing one another across the empty hearth, leaning on the mantle like figures in a painting. The candle had burned low. She had stopped listening to the words. It was all the same now. Andrew would never take her out of Cornwall to a new life, though there was nothing to prevent him, only that unnatural obsession of his, that need to continue his own private war.

***

Christina lay alongside her husband, puzzled. Robert did not usually disappoint her in this way. Now he was feigning sleep. It was certainly a pretence. When she had lured him earlier than usual to their chamber, he had not seemed in the least fatigued. His day she mused, fruitlessly examining his countenance for signs of strain, could hardly have been gruelling. Yet after supper he had appeared somewhat morose, praying with even less fervour than usual.

'Robert, what is amiss?'

'Nothing.'

'What did Minister Marten have to say?'

'He...asked after your health. Nothing. Nothing yet from the 'House of Lords'. He was learning to lie with increasing facility. After leaving Hampt, he had been unable even to countenance the Minister.

'The men on the list, they are all dead?'

'So it seems.'

'Then what is amiss?'

Robert had not opened his eyes. Perhaps she would desist. Perhaps she would just let him sleep or at least pretend to. Perhaps she would relent. Was he not humiliated enough?

'You are not yourself.' Christina's voice was low, guttural, impatient. He was conscious of her sitting up now, on top of the sheets, restless in her shift. Her cap would be somewhere on the floor. She would not be ignored. 'What happened today?'

He sat up next to her and opened his eyes. He had pondered all day whether he should tell her. Now she was pushing him against his will, against his better judgement.

'There is something…something your uncle told me. I have been waiting for the right time,' he lied again, this time with the fear she might explode. 'I was to keep it to myself. One of the names on the list is that of George Hawking.' Christina was just listening. 'Hawking, it appears, is a papist, a favourite of the Queen's…a leading man.'

'I thought Hawking was dead.'

'He is not dead. Gewen, your uncle, told me Hawking's property at Hampt is about to be sequestered, and that I should warn my sister so that she might make good her…escape'

'And today you did just that?'

'Yes.'

'I trust Mary was duly grateful.'

'Yes but, as I was leaving I saw, behind the door, a doublet and jerkin belonging to George. I recognised them.'

Without comment, Christina pulled back the canopy curtains and began to pace the room, as she always did wrestling with her conscience. She was, to Robert's infinite relief, surprisingly calm. He watched her like a prisoner in a courtroom waiting for the verdict, pacing to and fro, in and out of sight. When her energy finally began to wane she returned to his side.

'You have warned Mary. Understandably, that was my uncle's wish. There would be a scandal if she were arrested. My uncle would not have been able to conceal it. You have done your duty, but you must not be seen to be protecting the likes of George Hawking. If he is found to have been at Hampt, your own life will be in danger. We must inform my uncle at once.'

'But Mary may not have…found somewhere.'

'You have done what was required! What more can you do? I will write now to Captain Shaw. Tomorrow you must ride to Lanson and deliver it, before it is too late!'

***

At daybreak, Francis found himself in Callington. It had been a long night. When the candle had sputtered and died, Mary had spread the blanket in which Hampton had brought to the Lodge their few items of food. Now it seemed, they were all three to lie together. he had made some excuse. He would find some other place and then, in the morning, would leave early for Callington. But there had been nowhere else to sleep. First he had broken a window in the other wing of the Lodge but had been faced with a wall of debris, the smell of rotting flesh, the pit-pat of tiny feet on the boards. He had considered and rejected first the dirt floor of the barn and then the damp and cold of the woods. So cursing himself for a surfeit of delicacy and his sister for bringing him here, he had set off for Kit Hill to keep some warmth in his body and perhaps, he told himself, find somewhere to sleep on the way. But of course, the hill had offered no shelter and a biting wind had begun to blow from the east. Forlorn and shivering, he had finally struggled down to Kelly Bray and the Callington road.

Now standing before his brother's workshop as the sun rose invisibly behind a sullen sky, he could think only of food, warmth and above all sleep. The yard was cluttered, a pair of broken carts, a sawpit covered over with a tumble of logs, in a corner ash and elm seasoning beneath a makeshift roof.

There was no sign of life. An open doorway led into the workshop itself, where the morning light had hardly yet penetrated. Workbenches lined the walls, above them rack upon rack of carpenter's tools and in the rafters great lengths of timber waiting to be cut. Over all the inevitable odour of his brother's labour, of wood and iron and sweat. On end in a corner, three newly constructed coffins of varying length, and now from behind them, emerging silently into the half-light John, his brother.

Since their father's funeral they had not met but John's embrace was welcoming and warm.

'Something has happened,' he said in a matter-of-fact way. 'Come in.' Hidden behind the coffins was a door leading to a large, well-lit kitchen and pantry. 'Sit.' John produced two mugs and a jug of ale. 'Susan will be down in no time and make us breakfast. But something has happened. Is it our mother?'

There was a strong physical resemblance between the two men. It was like facing, across the kitchen table, an older, more settled version of himself, the thinning, brownish hair and neat beard, the cheeks a little fuller, the mouth unusually narrow like his own. Only their demeanours markedly differed. John had a kind of calm, purposeful intensity. But then John, he could not help thinking, had not fought in a war.

'No, our mother improves. Janella looks after her well. I think she is beginning to accept it all now...No.' He must grasp the nettle. 'It is Mary. Mary is in trouble.'

He had forgotten what he must say and what he must conceal, except that he could not reveal the existence of Andrew Hampton. He knew he must not do that. As for the rest, he had no idea what he and Hampton had agreed, or rather what Hampton had insisted upon. It did not seem so important now. He was comfortable with his brother.

'It is certain now that George was a papist and a well-known one at that. Mary's property will be sequestrated and Mary herself might even be arrested.' John did not look particularly shocked. 'Robert gave her a warning.' John nodded. Of course he would know the connection with Gewen. 'And so she came to me.'

'Where will she go?'

'We have found her a position,' he blundered on, 'at Cotehele. I would like to take her there tomorrow...but not on foot.'

'And so you came here, to borrow a cart or some such.' John had never been slow on the uptake. 'I can pay.' He rummaged awkwardly in his pockets, finally producing the two gold crowns Hampton had insisted on giving him. There was pause during which John drained his mug and Francis imagined him calculating some obscure pecuniary advantage.

'There is a wain in the yard, a broken felloe, belonging to a Callington man. He will not expect it yet. If I mend it today you can have it tomorrow. There is always a nag in the stables.'

Francis supped his ale to hide his relief. Perhaps John did not care for his sister but he knew a gold crown when he saw one. But even in that he was deceived. John picked up one of the crowns and pushed the other back across the table.

'You might need it, Francis.'

'You have no need...' he began, shamefaced for his assumption, but John waved away his protestation, mild though it had been.

Perhaps, the thought occurred to him vaguely, perhaps John was not at all obsessed with money. Perhaps he was merely hardworking, determined to succeed, cautious. Whatever the truth of it, everything now was set in motion. Hampton's plan would go ahead. There had never really been any alternative.

Susan, a small, bright, bustling woman he hardly knew came down the stairs and promptly set about making them a hearty breakfast. He had forgotten about Alice and John, their two small children, peeping now from behind their mother's skirts and generally making a nuisance of themselves.

There was no need for him to return at once to the Lodge so John took him upstairs to an attic room, of a kind all too familiar to him, to sleep, and then went out to the yard where his two apprentices were already at work.

He woke in the afternoon to the patter of rain on the tiled roof and to John tip-toeing softly past the end of his bed. Something else he had forgotten, that way his brother had of padding around soundlessly, like a cat ready to pounce.

'It's raining,' John had stopped at the window overlooking the yard where work had temporarily been suspended, 'but I'll have your cart ready in the morning.'

He felt under no obligation to return in the wet to the Lodge. His brother's welcome had shown no sign of running its course. Mary, no doubt, would prefer to be alone with Hampton. He could hardly blame them. Soon Hampton would be gone. Soon he would be back at Venterdon.

Waiting with John and Susan in the kitchen for the rain to cease, they spoke of their mother and of the end of the war. Perhaps there would be a good harvest. Perhaps taxation would turn out to be less burdensome than they expected. Perhaps Mary would begin a new and happy life at Cotehele. Francis found their natural optimism infectious. John was making his way in the world. The stables were beginning to pay off. 'Pellow's Stables'. John showed him the sign, just visible from the entrance to the workshop. A Callington gentleman in urgent need of a horse would not have to look far. Francis thought belatedly of Hampton, but then Hampton himself had insisted on secrecy. Above all it was necessary to mislead. To seek John's further help now would be to risk everything.

When the rain stopped he took his leave. In the morning he would pick up the wain and drive to Sevenstones on the Tavistock road where Mary would be waiting for him. From there to Cotehele was not far but through a maze of lanes which, with the best will in the world, John had failed to explain.

Patches of blue appeared in the sky as he took the track skirting the woods around the northern slopes of Kit Hill. But it was muddy underfoot, pools of water in the rutted lane. In the woods, it was drier and, after the rain, redolent of Spring. He approached the Lodge with caution. All was quiet. The room where Mary had spent the night with Hampton was empty. In a way he was relieved not to find them there, but they would not have strayed far. Hampton's plan would be carried out. Of that he had no doubt.

As the light went out of the sky he watched them surreptitiously as, hand in hand, they emerged from the trees. There was little to be said. Certain now that Francis would take Mary to Cotehele in the morning, when darkness fell, Hampton would leave. He would take both horses from Mary's stable and head for Pendennis.

'What if Wright has stolen the bay, or if the horse is unfit to ride?'

Hampton declined to answer and Mary, her face blotched and stained with tears, simply turned away. So it was already understood between them. Hampton would not be coming back. Francis found his patience to be running out. No doubt Hampton would walk to Pendennis if necessary. The sooner he was back at Venterdon the better.

Mary had once more perched herself on the window seat and was gazing out towards the bridge and the stream, taking pains to ignore them both. From time to time, the two men muttered to one another; the stable, the horses, the road to Cotehele, until darkness crept up on them. At last Hampton took up his sword and satchel packed with the remainder of the food.

'God be with you,' Francis mumbled without enthusiasm.

But it was more than Mary had to offer. She would not accompany him to the yard, nor even look up from her place at the window, though the bridge and the stream had surely faded now from view. Hampton did not stay to plead but abruptly turned his back and was gone.

*

Hampton took the path from which he and Mary had first seen the Lodge, back down the combe and alongside the stream until the trees petered out by the meadow. Then along the old sheep track to Hampt, past the cottage ghostly and abandoned now. Up the slope to the farmhouse, looming unexpectedly in the darkness, the first time he had laid eyes on it. The farmyard was unnaturally quiet, as if the animals had all been stolen or so neglected had left of their own accord, for a better life.

He came to the stable door which was heavily bolted. Not a sound from within. He drew back the bolts one by one and entered, leaving the door wide open to admit what little light there was from the moon and the stars. There were two stalls to the right. In the first, the small, labouring pony which Wright had used to bring food and logs to the cottage. She was still, docile, allowing herself to be led by the rope which permanently encircled her neck. From the other stall he could hear the bay beginning to stir. He could barely make out her shape, huddled in the darkness. Softly, patiently he coaxed her out, first from her stall and then into the yard to stand beside her companion. Her coat was a rough patchwork of light and reddish brown. It was not necessary to touch her. Even in the dark he could make out the bony ridge of her back and the distorted outline of her ribs and withers.

Of the two animals the pony, used regularly about the farm for transporting corn or pots of sand, was by far the healthier. But neither could be ridden. In the stable he found a tub almost empty of water and no more than a random sprinkling of hay, for the most part in the pony's stall. There was a saddle and a rudimentary bridle for the bay, but no bit or stirrups. He saddled her gently, hardly tightening the girth.

Francis had advised him to take the lane towards Horsebridge and then west to Linkinhorne and on to Bodmin. That way, Francis said, though it was longer he would avoid the village and it would not be necessary to muffle their hooves. But now speed was everything. He would have to risk the shortest way. To simply leave them would defeat the purpose. Hopefully no-one would be disturbed and those in pursuit of George and Mary Hawking would not consider the condition of their horses but simply register they were missing. All he could do now was to leave them in a place of safety beyond the village and then continue his way alone and on foot.

Chapter 14

Lady Margaret Denny, nee Edgcumbe, was unwell or at least had been unwell and was now prolonging her symptoms in order to keep Mrs Howard, her companion, on her toes. Philippa Howard whom she liked to think of as her 'esquire of the bedchamber' had become much too snooty of late. It would do her good to earn her keep for a change, empty a chamber pot or two.

Or perhaps it was simply that her stay at Cotehele had itself, after eighteen months, become intolerably tedious. When she had left Stortford, after Lostwithiel, it had seemed the obvious thing. The Rectory Manor, garrisoned permanently by Cromwell's troops, no longer seemed to be her own and though, on account of her advanced years and undisputed status, her wishes had generally been respected, she had sometimes felt like the only royalist in the whole of Hertfordshire. Whereas in the west, the county of her birth, the King's forces had been triumphant again and again. Cornwall had positively risen up for the King. It was only natural she had begun to hanker after the land of her birth.

Above all, she remembered Cotehele and the idyllic days of her youth beside the Tamar. She had badgered all of her sons, one after the other, to take her back. They had all been equally reluctant but it was Thomas, being unmarried, who was finally prevailed upon. It had seemed the best decision of her life. The coach journey across England had stimulated her beyond measure and she had been much admired at the time for her tenacity. It was not expected that an eighty-four year old woman would travel as she had done and especially not when the country was at war.

Her nephew Piers and his family had all been there at the South Front to welcome her. It was the first time she had set eyes on Cotehele in forty years. Nothing much appeared to have changed; the same hall, the courts, the chapel, the quays by the river. Only the tower, with which she had been especially impressed on learning that the King himself had stayed there en route for Tavistock, was new. Naturally she had insisted on occupying the same chamber on the third floor, in spite of the narrow, twisting staircase.

There had been something deeply satisfying about returning to Cotehele. It had been a kind of pilgrimage but not at all, as her family assumed, the inevitable desire of an old woman to return to her roots before she died. The idea of death hardly came into it. Although almost everyone from her own era and experience had passed away, although she had herself been a widow for forty-eight years, although two of her ten grandchildren had died in infancy, Lady Margaret never considered her own mortality. Perhaps it was precisely because she had survived so much and for so long that it had never really occurred to her that one day she too would meet her maker.

Lady Margaret's acuteness had not dimmed with age or, more recently, lack of occupation. She read newsbooks whenever she could get hold of them and was thoroughly aware of the changing military and political situation. Propaganda did not influence her as she was a passionate royalist. It was not something she had to weigh in the balance, not something that preyed on her conscience. The existence of an absolute monarch was simply part of the natural order though, having known three personally, she was not inclined to accept their divinity. Charles had not impressed her in the least and his French, papist wife had appalled her. It was not the thought of occupying the King's bedchamber that had appealed to her, rather the assumption that for her, only the best was appropriate.

But now she had grown bored. The family bored her. The children bored her. She was forever muddling the names; Mary, Catherine, Winifred. At first it had amused them. And never having taken an interest in domestic matters, Mary, Colonel

Piers' wife, was never a natural companion. Thomas had returned to Stortford and Philippa thought she was God Almighty. When Piers, Coryton and the rest had meekly trooped off to Bodmin to surrender, she had remonstrated with all and sundry, except that Mary, the children and Colonel Piers himself had long since fled to the Mount, whether in the face of Fairfax's army or Lady Margaret's ire was not clear. 'Colonel Piers Edgcumbe,' she had read somewhere, 'master of languages and sciences, a lover of the King and Church.' Poppycock! She knew perfectly well why they had done it. When the war was lost, Lady Margaret was a realist if nothing else, Fairfax, an honourable man, would be a valuable ally. There would be increased taxation and the potentially disastrous effects of compounding. Her nephew was not one to risk ruination. The eastern gentry were cutting their losses.

It was about that time she had become aware of Lieutenant Andrew Hampton, responsible amongst other things for a Company camped in the environs of Cotehele and protecting the Tamar. Apparently his men, informed of Fairfax's imminent arrival in Lanson, had been slipping away in the night. Hampton had come to the House in search of Colonel Piers and had been disappointed to discover his commanding officer had not only departed to the Mount but was already on his way to Plymouth to negotiate with an emissary from Fairfax. Hampton's angry voice disputing in the Hall Court had attracted her attention and she had immediately despatched her own emissary to discover what was amiss. Mrs Howard, on learning the reason for Hampton's outburst, had requested him to wait and subsequently brought him to her mistress in the tower.

And so had begun the short but mutually satisfying relationship between Lady Margaret Denny and Andrew Hampton. She had established without difficulty, Hampton being not at all reticent, the reason for his distress. Not only were his men disappearing but the Colonel himself was endeavouring to come to terms with General Fairfax, in defiance of Lord Hopton's specific orders to withdraw to the west.

Hampton had appeared not at all concerned that he was addressing Colonel Edgcumbe's aunt, an observation that had endeared him to her at once. Lady Margaret had found in Andrew Hampton a kindred spirit. She had enquired after his family and found her prejudices confirmed. He reminded her of her husband, of his loyalty to the Queen, of the price he had paid. After that they had met privately, two or three times, in her chamber. But then soldiers from the Mount had been sent to arrest him, and he had fled down to the quays and across the river.

Since then, Lady Margaret had largely kept to her chamber, studiously ignored by the family who remained at the Mount. She still picked up information regarding the course of the war, whatever Mrs Howard could extract from the servants. But she had privately resolved only to remain in Cornwall as long as Pendennis Castle still held out for the King.

***

There was no sign of Mary at Sevenstones. During the night they had lain together on the blanket, sleeping only fitfully, half expecting Hampton to return but knowing all the time that he wouldn't. At dawn he had left for Callington, telling her to leave as soon as she was ready. That way they would meet at Sevenstones.

He had picked up the wain as arranged at John's yard. More than a simple wain, in better times it had been fitted with a bow and seat and so could be driven as well as led along the wider lanes around Callington. And what John had dismissively referred to as the 'nag' was a sprightly grey mare, clearly used to the task and already being led to the shafts. Once more he had found himself beholden to his brother.

'Only to Cotehele and back,' he had assured him. 'I should not be long.'

But now Mary was not there, beside the road, as he had expected. He looked at the sky and predicted rain. Mary he could not predict. There were no half measures with her. First George, then Hampton. What did she expect? He was about to get down but then there she was, suddenly, in her green cloak and bonnet, pale and calm beside the wain. He helped her up and gave a flick to the reins.

'Cotehele is not far. If Hampton is right, you will sleep safe and sound tonight.'

She ignored him, and the mare was less lively now with the additional weight and the way was still muddy from the rain. Mary was in a world of her own. He chose not to disturb her. It was time to think of himself for a change. John had displayed a degree of friendship which had surprised him, but more than that, John had shown how you could pull yourself up by your bootstraps, make a life for yourself even in the midst of war. But was it necessary, he wondered, to turn your back on everything you had ever known? Even before their father's death, John had set up home in Callington, and had hardly ever returned to Clymestone. He had never understood that.

The mare took the turn to Norris Green of her own accord, and he gave her the benefit of the doubt. But John had warned him, it was easy to get lost in the lanes leading down to the river. A woman clearing her garden beside the road finally pointed the way to Trehill Farm. Trehill Farm, his brother had said, and you are almost there.

Mary seemed oblivious, hardly aware even of their destination, not caring if they were lost or not. But soon they would have to talk, prepare their story in advance.

But Mary was not at all, as she appeared to Francis, in some kind of stupor. It was bitter resentment rather than stupefaction that sustained her. When Francis had left them the previous day to seek John's help, she had begged and pleaded for Andrew to take her away, knowing in her heart of hearts that it was too late, that the dye was already cast.

When the rain had ceased they had walked out of the Lodge together for the last time, into the woods. There was a sunken lane leading to the southern edge of what had been the old deer park and here they had lingered. There had been no further protestations of love. Andrew had seemed only consumed by an anxiety to be gone as soon as possible. It had felt at times more like the final arrangements of a truce. They had barely touched.

'You will be safe at Cotehele.' It was a strategy, successfully conceived and now only to be implemented. 'Lady Margaret is a good woman and perfectly alert, considering her age...but like everyone else, she has her prejudices. I fear she has no more sympathy for papists than for Parliamentarians. It is the way she was brought up.' She could see he was about to be delicate. 'Mary, I'm sorry but you must take off your ring, put it to the left hand, otherwise she will notice.'

By then she had already distanced herself from him; now she turned on him with utter contempt. She pulled off George's ring and flung it onto the grassy bank. It was of no consequence. George was of no consequence. So what if he was dead! Only Lady Margaret mattered now! Andrew had scrabbled about in the grass, amidst the bluebells and white wild garlic and when he had retrieved it she had laughed in his face.

'Keep it....to remember me by. It is of no further use to me!'

The blood had drained from his face. She had touched a nerve, made him feel something at last. It had given her such sweet satisfaction.

'If you have no wedding ring,' his voice shook, then you must explain at Cotehele, that you have never wed.'

Andrew never left his reason far behind. She had turned on her heel, tears streaming in the dying light. And he had followed her back to the Lodge...

Francis had stopped the cart. They had passed the farm at Trehill and the tall chimneys of Cotehele were already in view.

'Mary...'

'I know what to do,' she interrupted. 'Lady Margaret has a companion, Mrs Howard. We must speak to her. I will explain. I will give her this. 'She unclasped her hand to reveal one of the two silver buttons Hampton had given her.

He made no dispute, concluding only that Mary did not intend to stray from the part she had been given to play, and urged the mare on across the meadow fringing the whole of the north and west side of the manor. To their left a farmer and his dog were encouraging a group of cows into the yard of a dairy. To their right an expanse of green culminated in a low wall encircling an elaborate garden. The house itself, snuggled as it was into the hillside, was less imposing than he had expected. Only the tower, draped in ivy and at least a storey higher than the rest of the building, asserted itself in the grand manner, its castellated roof reminding him, like the castle in Lanson, of another time only vaguely present in his imagination.

As they came to a halt before the entrance to the Court, a man in a long, black coat and stylish wide-brimmed hat stepped out to meet them. Francis realised that the gentleman now regarding them with an air of importance and the rough-looking farmer they had passed only minutes before were, astonishingly, one and the same. Though how the man could have arrived in advance of them and so completely transformed himself was a mystery.

'My sister is here by arrangement, to see Lady Margaret,' he said, alighting from the wain and determined to assert himself.

'Lady Margaret......' The gentleman knitted his brows, as if trying to recall the name.

Francis restated his case. 'Lady Margaret. Yes.'

'Lady Margaret is unwell.'

'Perhaps we could speak to Mrs Howard. She will understand. It is in order to take up a position.'

The gentleman, who was surprisingly elderly and clearly being required to fulfill more than one role, decided not to contest the matter and disappeared into the Court. It was some time before Mrs Howard came into view, but when she did her impact was rather greater than that of her predecessor. For the first time Mary was roused from sullen acceptance of whatever lay before her to something barely short of panic for Mrs Howard's appearance was not one to encourage familiarity. The expression on her face alone made it perfectly clear she was not accustomed to dealing with common people in a haywain. Above her scowl she wore a perfectly folded linen cap and below a lilac bodice with matching petticoats, the whole overlaid with a scrupulously casual layer of white silk. Her forearms were bare. Mary simply wanted to flee, whatever the consequences.

'Lady Margaret,' Mrs Howard spoke as one in severe shock, 'is indisposed.' And obviously deeming that piece of information sufficient, turned her back on them.

'My sister,' He had to raise his voice as Mrs Howard had already lifted her skirts to cross the lawn inside the Court, 'My sister requests that you give this small token to Lady Margaret...I am sorry she is unwell, but she will recognise this...' He had taken care to secure the silver button from Mary's clasped hand, 'and will I am sure, when she is recovered, be happy to receive her.' Mrs Howard hesitated, then turned to face him, an appraising look in her eye.

'Name?'

Francis decided, under the circumstances, to take a risk. 'Lady Margaret will know the name...Andrew Hampton.'

Mrs Howard gave not the slightest indication of being herself familiar with such a name, but nonetheless held out her hand.

'Wait.'

They waited. From inside the Court, the bell in the little bellcote over the chapel chimed the hour and time itself seemed to loiter with them. Mary descended from the wain and began to walk up and down. They caught sight of the farmer, as if by magic driving his little herd to another part of the meadow. Still Mrs Howard did not reappear. Perhaps she had forgotten. Perhaps, he thought with sudden horrror, Mrs Howard was some kind of informer. When the bell chimed again, Mary climbed back into the wain and insisted they return to Callington and then to the Lodge. It had all been a terrible mistake. Andrew Hampton had miscalculated. Lady Margaret was no longer even here, He was about to agree when he spied a diminutive but certainly more friendly-looking figure, a maid of some kind, crossing the Court to greet them.

'What a lovely mare you have, Mrs Hampton,' she said cheerfully, greeting the horse first rather than its apparent owners.

Mary began to correct her but Francis shook his head. The maid was stroking the mare's neck, examining her with an expert eye.

'She's thirsty. Before she leaves, Mrs Hampton, I'll fetch a pail for her.' The thought seemed to remind her of what she was supposed to be doing. 'Mrs Howard's busy so she told me..I'm Kate by the way.......to come and get you. Lady Margaret is unwell, but she'll see you tomorrow.'

Kate was all smiles, so pleased to meet them, her natural, unheeding way lifting Mary's despondency in spite of herself. He kissed Mary on the cheek.

'All will be well. If you have to, tell them 'Pellow's Stables', ' he whispered, before Kate whisked her away across the Court lawn.

He watched them as they disappeared beneath a further archway, Kate chattering nineteen to the dozen, as if they were already the best of friends. Before he left, a young lad brought a pail of water for the horse and a flagon of ale for himself. On the Callington road the sun came out, further raising his spirits. Before he knew it he was back at the wheelwright's yard. The grey was taken to the stables and the wain he saw being looked over for damage. John took him aside, anxious to know how he had fared, but also offering some comfort of his own.

'Sometimes, a Cotehele man will come to the yard. If I learn anything I will let you know.'

Walking home in the late afternoon sunshine, he began to experience an unexpected nostalgia for Callington and Cotehele and even the Lodge, a regret that his two day adventure was over. It was not something he could easily explain. The return to Venterdon to which he had looked forward only hours before, now seemed fraught with difficulty. He slowed his pace. Janella would want to know. His mother would want to know. Arthur would be furious, openly contemptuous, two days slaving in the North Field while he, Francis, had supposedly been ill.

He scraped off his boots outside the door, convinced he had seen his mother's shadow in the window above. Janella was in his father's chair by the fire. She too must have heard him coming. There was ale and bread and cheese on the table and Janella clearly had no intention of providing anything else. He felt beholden to speak first, Janella not being inclined in that direction either.

'Mary is safe...' No reply. He would have to explain. 'George Hawking was a papist. Mary believed her farm was about to be ..sequestrated. We decided Mary would be arrested.'

'We?'

'John and me. We had to get her to a safer place.'

Janella put another log on the fire. 'You did well. There have been soldiers at Hampt all day.'

He could scarcely credit what Janella had said. It had all seemed like Mary making a nuisance of herself, like something he had just had to do. He had never thought Mary was really in danger of arrest.

'So Robert was right. It was Robert that warned her.'

'There were soldiers everywhere, looking for papists they said, George and Mary Hawking,' Janella continued casually.

'Did they come here?'

'I sent them packing, said you were at work in the fields, that the family had nothing more to do with the Hawkings.'

'What would we do without you?' he thought, but said nothing. 'Did they speak to Arthur?'

'I can't answer for Arthur. I can't say what I would have done.' She regarded him pointedly,' clearing the North Field...Anyway, where is she?'

'I can't say. She is safe, safe as can be...not that you would care,' he added peevishly.

'I don't, any more than you care for your mother. You can explain it all to her, if not to me. She knows they have been looking for Mary. She knows you have been away. Imagine how a mother feels, if you can. I have had enough!'

She got up and crossed the room, not deigning to look at him. He heard her mount the stairs, her chamber door open, a stifled cry, and then the door slammed shut. Coming home. It was even worse than he had anticipated. Arthur might already have informed on him. He might himself be arrested. How was he to explain his absence of two days? Janella was right as usual. She was his conscience. He should have told her more. Now he was bound to tell his mother Mary was safe. He owed that to her at least. Somehow, in coming to terms with Samuel's death, she had seemingly transferred all her affection to Mary, all her hopes on Mary coming home at last. He could not bring Mary home, only assure his mother she was safe.

She was sitting in her usual chair at the window in a state, he would have said, of exaggerated tranquillity. He had knocked but still she feigned surprise as if, apart from Janella, it might just as well have been someone else.

'I have been to Callington to see John,' he began, judiciously. 'Between us we have made certain that Mary is safe.'

She looked him straight in the eyes, dignified, apparently composed, lucid. 'Where is she?'

'Cotehele,' he said. 'Mary is at Cotehele.'

Chapter 15

Alice sat by the window and watched the shadows lengthen in the yard. As she watched, the sun slipped below the horizon leaving behind a buttermilk sky and straggles of grey cloud tinged with crimson. Alice, naturally enough, was contemplating her son's words, weighing their significance in the uncertain balance of her mind. 'Mary is safe,' he had said. 'Mary is at Cotehele.'

As the light died in the sky, she stood up to undress, first adjusting the window so that it should be ajar by just the amount Samuel preferred. She would not be disturbed now until morning. She had heard Janella's door slam, not at all like Janella,, and then Francis when he had left her, as he ascended the creaking stairway to his attic room. She snuggled down under the covers, on her right hand side as usual, so that she could see the window and watch the sky. The sight of a bare wall was not to be tolerated.

Mary had always been her favourite. Mary had always been different. While John and Robert had each had, though in diverse ways, the look of their father and even sometimes of herself, Mary had borne not the slightest resemblance to either of them. Dark hair, dark eyes, darker skin, like a little gypsy and with such an excess of life! She was the 'cuckoo in the nest' they said, good-humouredly. But ribald remarks had never offended them. No-one could ever have doubted that Mary was born of her loins, nor that Samuel had planted the seed. Alice and Samuel Pellow were in the summer of their lives. And sometimes it seemed Mary had only ever lived her life in the spring and the summer.

Mary in the flickering firelight, too close to the Midsummer fire on Kit Hill. Mary black-berrying, a pot of blackberries between her small hands, her face and apron stained with their juice. Mary participating in everything with shrieks of delight and endless curiosity. Feeding the chickens, imitating the pigs. Mary on May Day with a garland of daisies ringing her long black hair. Mary bringing home the harvest, single-handed! Or having to keep away from the shearing. Mary delighting in everything, never crying. Mary standing here beside the bed, unable to sleep, her mind so full of all the excitement of the day.

Mary was not just Alice's favourite. Everybody loved Mary. They said she was like her mother when they stood together in identical caps and petticoats, all made from the same length of cheap material she had picked up at Callington market. But they were not at all the same. Mary was much more than a replica of her mother. Even as a child, though happy enough in her parent's home, Alice had never had Mary's lust for life. And even as a young woman, her eyes had not flashed with the same excitement, nor had she ever persisted with the same determination Mary had, with whatever happened to take her fancy.

Alice remembered one particular day, a Sunday in high summer. The Reverend Parker had been taken ill suddenly, and at the very last moment one of the churchwardens had announced to the restless congregation that Morning Service would have to be cancelled. The church had been full to overflowing, the Reverend Parker being every bit as popular as his successor, the Reverend Clarke, There had been much muttering, much genuine disappointment, but then as they had drifted away from the church something more akin to debate had taken hold. The more puritanical were determined to observe the Sabbath as the Lord intended and, as far as possible in the circumstances, resume their prayers, at home. Others, Alice and Samuel included, looked up at the blue sky. It was like an unexpected gift from Heaven. Labour on the Sabbath was forbidden. But soon it would be harvest time. soon they would be hard at work from dawn till dusk.

Together with others of a like mind, they had taken victuals and beer down to the river, and when they had been consumed had wandered lazily along the riverbank, John and Robert and Mary rushing up and down in noisy excitement. That day, to Alice, had seemed to be the best of their lives. They had walked on and on, heedless of the time or the place, past Hampt and Luckett.

But at last the shadows of the old oaks along the river had begun to lengthen and she was tired and thirsty. If anything Samuel had quickened his pace, striding on regardless, like a man possessed. And Mary rode high on Samuel's broad shoulders. And John and Robert were all for pressing on to Latchley and beyond. She had decided to return to Venterdon and wait for them, prepare a meal and rest.

A shadow passed over Alice's pale face and staring eyes, a precursor of the night. The rays from the setting sun no longer lightened the sky. It was time for sleep.

*

Samuel and the children had pushed on as far as Latchley where, Mary said, she had had enough of riding so high and lonely. So he had set her down and pausing, had settled himself in the shade of an oak close to the river. For a while he watched the three of them playing happily in the meadow. There was no-one else about. He stretched himself out, hardly a cloud in the sky. He could hear the delight in the voices of his children, and the steady, interminable flow of the river. He must have closed his eyes because, a moment later, John was shouting in his ear.

'Father, father, where is Mary? Where is Mary?'

He sat up, all his senses alert. 'I told you! I told you! You must keep an eye on her!'

It was more than a hundred yards to the woods. Surely she could not have strayed so far.

'John, look that way, he said, getting up, 'the way we have come. Down by the river. In the reeds. Where the bank is high. She must have fallen...Robert, come with me.'

They searched a hundred yards and more, along the river in both directions. And then into the woods. There was no sign of her. It had begun to grow dark. He had not dared ask John or Robert how long he had been sleeping or how long it had been since they had last seen her. Their guilt was shared and no more was said of it. He told them to hurry home. He would come when he had found Mary. He would not be long. She must have wandered further than they had thought. But they knew, all three of them, even then, that the river had taken her.

Hours later he had found himself in a tavern in Gunnislake, afraid to go home. Nobody could tell him of a four year old girl missing near the river. And then he was standing on Gunnislake bridge at the start of a new day. A man from Morwellham came over to him. A ferryman on his way to Cotehele Quay on the dawn tide, the man said, had found a girl in the river. It had taken him four hours to walk home. Alice had not slept. She stood at the door, bedraggled and tear-stained. 'Mary is at Cotehele,' he had said, his voice breaking. 'She is drowned.'

Everything else, Samuel thought, stemmed from that moment. He had confessed his guilt time and again to Alice, but he had known it would not suffice. When, a year later, Alice gave birth to another little girl, he had told her it was Mary come back to them. And they had baptised her Mary, in memory of her sister, drowned in the Tamar and taken by a ferryman to Cotehele. But Alice had not been convinced. This Mary was not dark and spirited and loved by all who knew her. She was not her sister's incarnation and, her sister being dead, Alice could not love her.

To those outside the family, after a decent interval, Samuel had become his old self again, good-hearted, reliable, inclined on occasion to lose his temper, but otherwise a shrewd farmer and a pillar of the community. It was all a pretence. There was an emptiness in Alice's heart and, working alone in the fields, it tore him apart.

John and Robert sensed it and Mary grew up estranged from her parents, never understanding her inadequacy. John had become apprenticed to a carpenter in Luckett and then set himself up in Callington. Robert had found himself a Puritan widow and Mary had married a hard-bitten soldier she did not love. His great hope had lain with their last born, Francis. They had, in hope of his advancement, sent him to the Grammar School in Lanson, but then Francis had brought shame upon them.

When Mary had taken to walking the riverbank, just as they had done on that fateful day, all those years ago, it had driven them almost beyond endurance. It was as if Mary had taken to searching for her own previous self, for the little girl they had lost and yet who still remained at the heart of their lives.

***

When Janella came in with her hot milk, Alice was already up, dressed and sitting by the window. It had begun to rain again, a damp, chilly drizzle, but Alice did not appear to mind.

The contrast between the two women was unusual. For once, it was Alice who seemed to be in control. Janella was, for her, dishevelled, the skin beneath her eyes dark, her cheeks pale. Alice was not in a mood to notice.

'Everybody has been looking for Mary,' Alice stated, with some satisfaction, watching Arthur with interest as he entered the barn. Janella did not answer, but turned to go. 'But I know where she is,' Alice continued, confident of securing Janella's attention. 'Francis told me. Did he tell you too, Janella?'

'No.'

'Mary is at Cotehele. A ferryman took her there. Samuel told me.'

'Samuel?'

'Francis, Francis told me last night. Francis has been away. It doesn't matter what you tell me, Janella. I know.'

'A ferryman took her, not Francis?'

'That's right, from Morwellham, I think. Ask Francis.' For the first time since Janella had come in, Alice looked up at her. 'You are ill.' It sounded like a reprimand. 'You have not slept. We have all been sick with worry. Francis did not tell you. Well, now I have told you. Mary is safe. Mary is at Cotehele.'

Janella picked up the pot which needed emptying, took her leave and stumbled down the stairs. Francis was standing at the door to the yard, still wide open from Arthur's leaving, as if wondering whether or not to follow. As she came into the kitchen he pushed the door shut and slumped onto the bench facing the door, his back to the table.

'Arthur turned his back on me,' he mumbled, so that she could hardly make out the words. 'I tried to explain...He knows I have been away.'

Janella went through to the back to empty the pot. When she returned, Francis had not moved and did not seem inclined to.

'Arthur is not stupid. He would not have told the soldiers. He has too much to lose,' she offered, by way of encouragement.

She thought that perhaps this was the time. She would tell him now. They both began to speak together and then both stopped, each more concerned perhaps for what the other had to say. Janella changed her mind.

'Last night, you spoke with your mother.'

'Yes.'

'She told me that Mary is safe. She is much relieved.........She told me Mary is at Cotehele.'

'I should have...'

'Master Francis,' Janella's sarcastic tone was not to be mistaken. 'It is not for me to say what you should have done…but if Mary is at Cotehele and if she is truly in danger, you must take heed. Your mother might just as well tell anyone as me. I did not even have to ask.'

Janella had sat herself astride the bench on the opposite side of the table, close to the fire and behind his back. She had her bowl of tallow and had begun to dip her rushes, with care and concentration. She seemed to be waiting for Francis to take himself away.

'How is mother?' Francis asked, avoiding his dilemma.

'You saw her last night,' Janella answered abruptly, but then could not help relenting. 'She was already up and dressed, pleased with herself. What you told her about Mary, it has settled her mind.' She heard his boots on the flags, not leaving but coming closer. She felt his hand on her shoulder and allowed the taper to slip into the bowl.

'Janella, I sometimes forget, you are my best friend, perhaps my only friend. It is time I made amends. I want to tell you everything.' She looked up and he saw how pale and tired she was. He would not normally have noticed. 'Now, no more concealment!' She glanced towards the stairs. Alice would come down when she had finished her milk.

He took the hint and motioned for her to follow him, through the buttery and into the larder which had its own back door, and into the yard. There was a makeshift lean-to which had been used for pails of water and empty churns and which in wintertime was stacked high with logs. The drizzle had turned to rain and looked set for the day, but the lean-to offered them shelter and a small but private space. He hardly knew where to begin. What had he already said? They could hear the rain splattering on the cobbles and drumming on the roof over their heads. Gently he touched her arm so that she should come to the driest space, against the wall.

'I believe last night I told you,' he began in a whisper so faint she could hardly hear above the sound of the rain. 'Mary, it is true, is a papist like her husband. I went to meet her at the Lodge in the old deer park. I think she must have left just in time. She was not alone, but it was not George she was with...'

And he went on to tell her about Andrew Hampton, also a wanted man, and how Mary had doubtless saved his life, about Hampton's escape and how he had set out to mislead his pursuers, how John had lent them the wain and about Lady Margaret at Cotehele.

'So now Janella, you know everything. I will not deceive you again.' He seemed to breathe more easily now, but was still anxious for her approval.

'You have done well by your sister. You have taken a risk for Mary...and this Hampton. Is she safe now?'

'I think so. There was something strange about Hampton. This Lady Margaret he spoke of as a friend. And why would he want to go to Pendennis, when the war is already lost? He took her hand. 'Mother may already be down.'

'Francis, there is something I do not understand. Alice said a ferryman took Mary from Morwellam to Cotehele. She was in no doubt about that.'

'She is getting confused again. I took Mary in the wain,' he reiterated patiently. 'We met at Sevenstones and I took her to Cotehele. We waited. Someone came for her. She was to see Lady Margaret today. Look Janella, He released her hand. 'the rain is easing off. I'll go now. I must make things right with Arthur.'

He went round the back of the house and then crossed unhurriedly to the barn conscious that, despite the rain, his mother might still be watching. Janella slipped back into the larder. She had again thought, too late, perhaps deliberately too late, that one piece of honesty deserving another, Francis should be told of her promise to Arthur. But now she and Francis had come closer again, it had seemed somehow self-defeating. She had hesitated again, lest she should drive a further wedge between them.

Chapter 16

At Cotehele, Mary woke to the chimes of the chapel clock, though she did not think to count them. She could not have known the morning was already well advanced. The window to her tiny chamber being little more than a slit, day and night were more or less indistinguishable. All she had understood from Kate was that Lady Margaret was to see her at nine o'clock.

She stood at the slit. What little she could see of the sky hung dark and low over Cotehele. To her left, a grey stone buttress, serving no obvious purpose, obscured much of her view. But leaning forward with her nose almost to the pane, she could look down through the tops of the trees and sense, if not quite make out, the ribbon of river beyond the quays. A flourish of pink and white cherry blossom, an improbable gash of colour, was just visible on the south-eastern slope above the treeline.

She could hardly collect her thoughts. She was, at one and the same time, saved and discarded. George was dead and perhaps by now, Andrew too. Wherever they were, they had both cared more for the war than for herself. Would they really take Hampt from her as well? Could it possibly be God's will that she should be so continuously deprived? And yet Francis, and Robert and John had all come to her aid. And Francis, whom she had led a merry dance, most of all.

The events of the previous day crowded into her mind. She had been quite prepared to return to Hampt whatever the consequences, until Kate with her heedless manner and infectious smile, had changed her mind. Talking nineteen to the dozen, she had led her across the small courtyard, past the chapel and then down some steps into what Kate said was the Hall Court. Then through the enormous Hall itself, so high it had reminded her of Clymestone church, through a huge pantry and finally into a kitchen the size of her cottage at Hampt.

There Kate had set her down and requested of Mrs Rundle, its only other occupant, to provide 'Mrs Hampton' who had travelled far, with some suitable refreshment. Mrs Rundle, though clearly unhappy with this intrusion into her less than strenuous routine, had nevertheless assented. She had tried not to stare in awe at the cavernous hearth, furnished with a dazzling variety of dogs, spits, trivets and pothooks, the like of which she had never even imagined. But she need not have bothered. Kate made no demands and being perfectly at ease with herself, expected no less of her new companion.

In due course, Mrs Rundle had grudgingly supplied them both with a bowl of game soup, a plate of cold meats and bread still warm from the oven. The house Kate explained, was not busy, the Colonel and his family being at the Mount. Apart from Lady Margaret and, Kate made a face, Mrs Howard in the New Tower, they had only themselves to see to. Since her illness, Kate enthusiastically explained, Lady Margaret had been confined to her chamber, leaving Mrs Howard to take her meals alone in the Parlour.

'I have never met Lady Margaret,' Mary began, clumsily implying that she moved in the same circles. Of course it was wasted on Kate, who went straight to the point.

'You need have no fear of Lady Margaret so long as you are straight with her,' she opined, judiciously selecting a particularly succulent piece of ham. 'She can be a faithful friend or a mortal enemy.' Mrs Rundle was conspicuously not listening, but Kate continued unabashed. 'Puritans and papists she condemns alike.' At this juncture Kate leant forward to whisper confidentially in Mary's ear. 'It is said that in Ireland, she had the whole crew of a Spanish ship hung on a gibbet!'

'Ireland?'

'Lady Margaret has had a long and interesting life, Mrs Hampton,' Kate said, reverting to her normal voice for Mrs Rundle's benefit. 'But you are already in her good books, I expect,' she said, grinning. 'Lady Margaret, if you don't mind me saying so, Mrs Hampton, took quite a shine to your husband.'

At this point, Mrs Rundle, giving up all pretence at disinterest, came over to them. 'Don't you mind Kate, Mrs Hampton. She's a little tartar and don't care what she says. She thinks she knows everything that one! And she's no more'n a child herself!'

Kate had adopted such a shocked expression at being so remonstrated with that all three had burst out laughing. Mary smiled to herself now, standing at the window in the half-light. How strange it had been to laugh out loud, how close to tears laughter was.

Later Kate had taken her through a maze of larders, sculleries and still rooms to a stone staircase which led up to a narrow, featureless corridor, running the entire length of the east wing. Finally she had unlocked one of the many plain, whitewashed, wooden doors and suddenly there she was, safe in her own room. It was small, dim, cell-like, a narrow window set deep into the wall, a small bedstead with a feather mattress and pillow, a pot underneath, a frail wooden stand for a basin and a ewer of cold water. Kate was apologetic, even a little embarrassed.

'If you are staying long, Mrs Hampton...'

'Mary.'

'Mary, if you are staying long, they'll find you something more comfortable.'

And then she had been left to while away the afternoon. She was to have gone to the kitchen for a meal but had preferred to spend the hours on her bed, staring at the ceiling and listening for the chimes of the chapel clock. Even in such straightened circumstances, she had no longing for home, only that familiar sense of dislocation that had come with the knowledge that George was nothing to her now. She thought of Andrew and wondered where he was, if he was still alive. She recalled his warning above all to conceal her Faith, a warning now confirmed in no uncertain terms, by Kate. She had stood for a while at the window and when even the tops of the trees had become invisible, had knelt to pray for Andrew, for Francis, for her father and, perhaps only in defiance of her new Protestant benefactor, for the Queen.

There was a tap at the door. Kate's voice.

'Mrs Hampton...Mary...it is nine o'clock. Are you awake?'

She stood in her shift, bareheaded and unwashed. It would not be seemly to admit her. She would not have Kate think ill of her. She took a step or two towards the door and spoke to it in a low voice.

'Kate, I am hardly awake. I wonder, can you find me a comb and a towel? You know I came with nothing...and I have only my bonnet.'

There was no reply. Kate was offended. Mary shrugged to herself and hurried to dress and wash as best she could. Again there came a tap at the door. She could hear Kate breathing heavily. Still in some disarray, she opened the door.

'Your Majesty!' Kate curtseyed extravagantly, and burst into shrieks of laughter. She had brought her own brush and comb, a fancy cap and a towel of a kind Mary had seen in the kitchen. 'I will get a maid,' Kate said, glancing under the bed, 'to empty your pot. A queen does not empty her own pot!'

A thought that would have set Kate giggling again had she not had a serious message to impart.

'Here, let me help.' Kate took the comb and brush and began the fruitless task of trying to straighten Mary's curls. 'I must take you to the Hall. Mrs Howard will meet you there.'

When she was ready and the fancy cap, which was rather to small, had been more or less secured, Kate stood back to inspect her work.

'You will improve in the full light of day,' she offered unflatteringly. 'Lady Margaret notices these things.'

Kate left her in the Hall and scurried off on some other errand or perhaps simply to avoid Mrs Howard. It was even grander, lighter than she had remembered from the previous day. Portraits, she supposed of family members, lined the walls. High arched windows, overlooking the Court, were emblazoned with unknown coats of arms. Looking up, she became mesmerised by the network of interlacing beams high above her head.

'Mrs Hampton.'

She must have entered through the archway from the Hall Court, but it took Mary a moment to recognise her, Mrs Howard, a vision in green silks, a short string of pearls about her still elegant neck, being so much transformed. But her expression at least was less antagonistic, and her voice softer, more conciliatory. Mary felt intolerably shabby.

'Mrs Hampton,' It was almost but not quite, a smile. 'Lady Margaret will see you now. Follow me.'

Without further ado, Mrs Howard picked up her skirts and led the way to a doorway in the far corner of the Hall. Mrs Howard moving at a statelier pace than Kate and not finding it necessary to engage in conversation, Mary had more time to observe her surroundings. They came to a large stairwell with more portraits on the walls but Mrs Howard ignored the wide oak staircase and led her instead into a large dining area, hung from floor to ceiling with magnificent tapestries. Mrs Howard looked so perfectly at home as she traversed the room, it was as if she had only now stepped from the walls to become flesh and blood.

Beside the fireplace was a steep flight of stone steps to a landing, and then a further flight and a further landing. It was clear they were ascending what Kate had called the 'New Tower'. Finally there was a winding staircase leading to an elaborately carved oak door conspicuously, it seemed to Mary, closed.

Mrs Howard knocked loudly and, without waiting for an answer, opened the door and led the way in. The room was large, light and airy with double casement windows all around. To her right, set between smaller windows and with linen hangings extravagantly embroidered in green and pink, protruded a large four poster bed. And sitting upright in the bed, supported by a plethora of pillows, was the object of her visit, the new arbiter of her fate, Lady Margaret Denny.

She heard the door click to behind her. Mrs Howard, presumably by prior arrangement, had departed, without speaking,

Lady Margaret motioned her to come forward and then gestured for her to bring one of the small chairs by the window, to her bedside. Mary sat where she was bid, determined not to be intimidated, trusting in Andrew Hampton's judgement.

Sitting close beside her, Lady Margaret looked, though Mary could never before have laid eyes on her, disconcertingly familiar. She wore a peaked, close-fitting cap, spreading behind like a cowl round a pale, flabby face. but, somewhat in contradiction of her age, she had an unusual wide-awake look, her eyebrows arched as if in a permanent state of surprise, her eyes intent, appraising.

Mary could not hold her gaze but looked away to the dark, velvet bedjacket, Lady Margaret's small, mottled hands on the white linen sheets, and to the folding table within easy reach of the bed on which stood an engraved wine glass, full to the brim.

'Purely medicinal, Mrs Hampton.' Mary flushed. 'But let us be open with one another.' Lady Margaret spoke from the back of her throat, with a sort of unintended chortle. 'It's not Mrs Hampton at all, is it?'

'No.' Lady Margaret waited patiently for Mary to order her thoughts. 'My name is Mary Hawking. Yesterday, my brother gave the name Hampton. It was meant only.......'

'What then is your connection with my good friend, Lieutenant Andrew Hampton?'

'He was wounded. I found him and helped him recover.' She looked Lady Margaret boldly in the eye. 'Andrew is now on his way to Pendennis.'

Lady Margaret did not seem particularly impressed. 'But he told you to come here?'

'My...Lady Margaret, my property is to be sequestrated. I faced arrest.'

'You look harmless enough to me.' Lady Margaret raised her eyebrows even further. 'Why on earth should you be arrested?'

'My husband, George Hawking was...I believe him killed at Bristol..an officer with Sir Bevil. I have heard from a reliable...they will take my property.'

'You have no wedding ring.'

'I..I..'

Lady Margaret did not insist but stroked her chin thoughtfully, tugging at the bristles, then switched the conversation.

'Did you lie with him?'

'My husb...'

'Andrew Hampton. I may be old but I am not foolish, Mary. Did you lie with him? I am a widow too, of forty-eight years! Can you imagine that? I can hardly imagine it myself.'

'He would not have me.'

Lady Margaret snorted. 'Ha! I can believe it! Just like Andrew Hampton. He must have cared for you then. Pendennis, you say. I can believe that too!' And then a pause. 'Did you know Hampton by any other name, Mary?'

'No.'

Lady Margaret fell silent for a while, then reached for her glass. When Mary took it away empty and returned it to its place on the table, she was conscious that something else had passed between them, something akin to friendship.

'I came here in forty-four, when Essex had his comeuppance, when the war was almost won. Now it seems I will return when the war is lost. This is not my home you see, Mrs Hawking…though perhaps for the time being 'Mrs Hampton' will suit you better. You are free to remain here at Cotehele for as long as Pendennis holds out. When Pendennis falls, as it surely will, I will return to Hertfordshire. After that I cannot guarantee your protection.'

'I ask for nothing.I do not deserve it.'

'I beg to differ, Mrs...Hampton. You saved a life, and one worth saving.' Mrs Howard had entered in a rustle of skirts. 'Philippa, find Mrs Hampton something to wear. Mrs Hampton, I have a mind to rise tomorrow. We will dine together in the Parlour.'

Mary returned the chair to its place by the window and took her leave. And without a word, Mrs Howard lifted her skirts and led the way down the spiral staircase to the landing below. There, a door she had not previously noticed opened into a chamber apparently occupied by Mrs Howard herself. She was requested to wait by the door while Mrs Howard stooped to rummage in a huge chest which stood beside her bed. After some minutes, she emerged a little flustered and presented her, unwillingly Mary thought, with a plain apron, buff-coloured bodice, petticoat and linen shift.

'These should fit you well enough Mrs Hampton. If you need more, you must ask Kate.' Mary muttered her appreciation and hesitantly took what was so reluctantly proffered. 'I will leave you to find your own way about. Lady Margaret always dines at midday. Listen for the chimes. The Parlour is on the floor below.' Mary must have looked confused. 'The chamber we passed through,' Mrs Howard added, her patience clearly wearing thin.

Her hand was already on the doorknob, so taking the hint, Mary thanked her again and clutching her new clothes, managed to retrace her steps through the Parlour and back into the Hall, where the family portraits on the white, plastered walls stared down at her once more in no less contempt of her insignificance. One in particular caught her eye and in an instant she knew who it was and why Lady Margaret had seemed so strangely familiar. The painting was of a young woman, with a high collar, ruff and revealing décolletage, her dark hair brushed tightly back, her face angular, eyebrows raised, brown eyes intent, inquisitive. Lady Margaret, perhaps sixty years ago, superior, contemplative, a beautiful young woman staring back at her from a time before even her parents had been born.

She looked away, confused, recalling Lady Margaret's words, 'I too am a widow, of forty-eight years. Can you imagine that?' Sunlight was streaming in through the open door to the Hall Court, beckoning. But she must take her new clothes to her room and she had not breakfasted.

In the kitchen, Kate was gossiping with Mrs Rundle, but offered to take Mary's clothes upstairs on condition of receiving a detailed account of her interview. Within limits and between the soup, sliced cold meat, game pie, fresh fruit and cheese, Mary did her best to comply.

'Is that Lady Margaret, near the fireplace in the Hall?' Mary asked when the opportunity eventually arose.

'Yes,' Mrs Rundle was getting up to scrape the leftovers into the fire. 'It's hard to imagine. I remember her from when I was little, maybe forty years ago. It was the last time she came here, newly widowed and much in demand, if you know what I mean.'

'Did you see her parchment on the wall?' Kate interrupted. "Charter of Protection', it says, and signed by the King!'

'Much good will it do her now,' Mrs Rundle rejoined philosophically. 'Now more likely it'll get her arrested.'

They asked her how long she would stay but that, she could only say, depended on her husband, Lieutenant Hampton. She was a lucky woman, they said. The Lieutenant was a fine man.

'The sun is out,' she said, to change the subject. 'Can I go down to the river? I miss the river.'

'I'll come with you!' Kate was enthusiastic. 'Pa will have to wait.'

And so Kate and Mary left promptly for the quays, down a dark passageway to a little used servants' entrance to the east wing, and then an equally dark track leading steeply down through the trees.

'Your pa?'

'You know him already. He farms the land for Edgcumbe. It was he that received you, remember?'

'When I came with my brother? Your pa has more than one job then, and so do you, I think?'

'I help on the farm and whatever comes up. When the Colonel and Lady Edgcumbe are here, I watch the children, anything they want.'

The track curled down, in wayward fashion, sometimes almost turning back on itself. When they eventually emerged into the light, it was to find the quays deserted. Kate was apologetic.

'Before the fighting there was boats here regular from Morwellam, Calstock and even Plymouth.'

'I used to walk by the river at Hampt. It is not so far away.'

'Where is your husband now, Mrs Hampton…Mary?'

'He is fighting for the King, Kate, though I fear it is a lost cause.'

'Lady Margaret would not agree.'

'You seem to know her well.'

'She says I am a free spirit and that's what the war is about.' And by way of confirmation, Kate twirled herself round by the edge of the water. 'Just look at her Charter on the wall, Mary. It is signed by the King. Once she asked me to read it to her. Nobody, it says shall do 'or suffer to be done any act of force or violence or offer any interruption or disturbance whatever to Lady Denny.' You see, I am more learned than you supposed!'

They walked a little by the river and then Kate said she must go to her pa, to take in the herd.

'As you are my friend,' said Mary suddenly, grasping Kate's hand as she was about to go, 'do not desert me.'

They embraced briefly and then Mary was left to wander the woods. The smell of bluebells and ramsons reminded her of Andrew and the last time they had been alone together in the sunken lane, of her last desperate attempt to prevent him leaving. He still had her ring. Lady Margaret had noticed its absence as he had said she would. It was only in recognition of Andrew Hampton's judgement that Lady Margaret had accepted her, at least for the time being. But she knew she had not been entirely believed. Lady Margaret might be a faithful friend or a deadly enemy.

But where was Andrew now? He could not already have reached Pendennis. Perhaps he had been arrested. She had no way of knowing what was happening beyond Cotehele. Could they already have taken away her land at Hampt?

*

Whether or not Lady Margaret suspected Mary Hawking of papistry was not clear. Whatever the case, she chose not to make enquiries. Had she done so she would have discovered that not only were George and Mary Hawking wanted for papistry but that a powerful sub-committee of the County Committee, most prominent member Thomas Gewen, had indeed issued warrants for the sequestration of the property at Hampt. Before the sale could take place and in order to deter miscreants, one John Wright had been allowed to occupy the farmhouse and cultivate the land.

It was only later in the month that confirmation of George Hawking's continued residence in Paris, as part of Henrietta Maria's retinue, was received. Hawking had not recently visited Cornwall. With the passage of time, the whereabouts of Mary Hawking and her partner, now presumed to be Andrew Hampton, was no longer considered to be of paramount importance.

By 11th April, Pendennis Castle was entirely cut off from the mainland. There were serious shortages of food and no money to pay any of the defenders. Desertions had become frequent. St Mawes Castle, on the opposite side of Falmouth harbour, had long since capitulated and St Michael's Mount soon followed suit. On 17th April, Sir John Arundell was called upon once more to surrender, 'the last garrison......betwixt Oxford and the Land's End for the King.'

'I place not honour in other men's opinions but the rules of Justice and Piety,' he replied, 'and rather to expire before than survive the ruine of King and Kingdom.'

Pendennis being also blockaded by sea, Vice-Admiral Batten's summons to surrender was likewise to be rejected by the seventy year old Governor, and in the same uncompromising terms. Pendennis still held out for the King.

As for Andrew Hampton, he had disappeared into thin air. True a Linkinhorne farmer had, one morning, found himself unexpectedly richer by a pair of miserable-looking horses and a handful of gold crowns. But otherwise, nothing.

Chapter 17

As the month progressed and threatened to draw to a close, Christina grew ever more despondent. There had been no reply to her letter, delivered faithfully by her husband to Captain Shaw. Had the letter ever been passed to her uncle? Had it simply arrived too late?

Though the Hawkings' farm had been sequestered, Mary and George had both eluded capture. Robert had been obsessed with the need for his sister, his papist sister, to escape justice. Perhaps he had lied to her. Perhaps her uncle had not been at all concerned for the safety of Mary Hawking who was, after all, no more than an obscure and distant relative.

Whatever the truth, in Thomas Gewen's eyes they must both have failed. Robert had discovered none of the wanted men on Gewen's list. Had he ever even troubled to search them out? That morning he had certainly not visited Minister Marten as he had claimed, not that she had sought to verify it personally. But she had drawn her own conclusions. She could not bear to face the Minister herself. Was it her place to offer comfort to a Minister of the Church, in all his trials and tribulations? Was it not rather the Minister's task to comfort her?

And besides, she could no longer tolerate the narrow lanes and high hedgerows of this God-forsaken place. Her home at Whiteford had become a prison. She hardly went beyond the yard now. She had not entered the church since Lady Day. The very thought of The Reverend Clarke peering over his pulpit, smoothly manipulating the simple aspirations of his credulous congregation, was enough to drive her to a blind fury. The imposter Clarke, long since ejected for ungodliness and superstition, still clinging like a leech to his living, still collecting his tithes! Though for some reason she could not properly explain, she still insisted on Robert taking Thomas and Liddy to Sunday morning service.

In the parlour when Robert was out with his dogs and Liddy and Thomas were confined to the kitchen, she would turn again and again to the Gospels. But the Gospels, in their turn, had failed her. She had begun to doubt even the Word of God and though she repented she had, at the same time, failed to repent. It was not enough, as Robert had claimed, simply to desire to be righteous. Robert did not understand. The world was changing about them. The old order was being swept away. It was necessary to comply with the Will of God.

At last she had turned to the sermons of the Minister, her late husband, the sermons she had once copied so reverently in her own hand, at his bidding. Yet it was those words, those that sprang from the page, which most haunted her, that we are 'sunk in the abyss.' It had been the Minister's constant refrain, 'the abyss of our fallen state'. Only by 'an act of free Grace from God' could we be saved. How was it that these words had once so inspired her? How was she now, so far from God, to attain His Grace?

'If we lose our estates,' her husband had solemnly intoned, 'we may recover them again; if we lose our friends, God may raise us up some other; if we lose our lives, we may exchange them for a better; but if we lose the faith once given to the saints, being once lost, it is lost forever.'

She had read them all now from beginning to end. A log tumbled against the grate. She looked up and became aware of her surroundings. The parlour from which she hardly strayed, and opposite, her husband's ungainly form. She had the impression he had been waiting patiently for her to finish.

'I have not been out with the dogs.' She shrugged inwardly but gave no outward sign. 'I went to Hampt and then to Burraton.' He was attempting to solicit her interest. Very well, she was listening. 'They have put John Wright in possession of the house, until it can be sold along with the land. I asked him about the rumours.'

'Rumours?'

'Rumours about Mary and George, that they could not have fled on horseback. I got the truth from Wright, though in the end I had to pay for it.' At least he had roused her interest. She had laid the sermon aside. 'Wright cared not a jot for Mary's horses. They were so ill-fed they could not possibly have been ridden.'

'Then how did they escape? She felt herself, albeit reluctantly, returning to what Robert would have called the real world.

'Wright couldn't explain it. The cottage was empty that night, not long after I went to warn her…And Wright said something else. It was not George. Now, they are not looking for George.'

They could hear the wind rushing down the lane, buffeting the doors in the yard, straining the rafters. The pair of candles on the the table flickered and threatened to expire. The fire spat and crackled in the grate. Robert leaned towards it and selected another log from the hearth. She could see he was not yet finished.

'So Wright is an informer for the Committee,' she muttered, resisting the temptation to rise and pace the room, in order to think. 'And Mary has a fancy man. Why did you go?'

'Not for Mary. She has brought it on herself. For you, Christina.' He was poking the fire, avoiding her eyes, 'All your plans. You have not stepped outside the house for a month. I want to get you back.' He looked past her to the papers strewn across the parlour table. 'I want to get you away from all those sermons.'

'And you went to Burraton too?'

'Marten was concerned for your health, but more optimistic now about his petition to the house of Lords. He has been told they are giving it some attention. Clarke, he says, cannot survive much longer.'

Now the temptation was too much for her, and though she would not pace the room as once had been her habit, she stood up to straighten her papers and when she had straightened them, straightened them again, before putting them away. Christina was thinking.

'Do you not see the hand of God in this?' She had come to stand at his side, her hand on his shoulder, her eyes shining. 'That you should take it upon yourself. It is God given.'

'I have done...'

'Robert, do you not see? Now is the moment!' Christina's voice trembled as she insisted on his attention. 'The Word of God is to be preached in Clymestone. The Royalists and preachers of superstition are to be driven out! Now is the time to play our part. We too can raise ourselves out of the abyss and be saved.'

'Christina....' Alarmed at her sudden zeal, he stood to hold her. 'Christina, we are already saved. The Will of God will take its course, cannot be suborned.'

'It is a sign, I tell you.' She released herself abruptly from his grasp. 'We must seek to further God's Will. We cannot ignore the knowledge we have. God invites us to carry out His Will!..Where is your sister?' He could no longer follow her train of thought. 'Are you not afraid for her?' Christina had begun to pace the room. 'Does she not live in sin?'

'George is dead,' he mumbled. 'Mary is a widow. I suppose her to be safe, and that is your uncle's wish.'

'The man she is with is a traitor, who will be hanged. Does that not concern you?' Christina was white with rage, her cap and kerchief flung to the floor.

'We do not know the man she is with.'

'The man on the list! You told me, the one you did not know.'

'Andrew Hampton.'

'Yes, she is with him, somewhere. We find her,' Christina smiled sarcastically, 'Your brotherly love would not deny you that, and so we find him. My uncle is appeased and so will come to rely on you, rather than the likes of John Wright, for his information. Is that not to be desired?'

'You ask me to betray my own sister!'

'No, I ask you to find your sister, and betray Hampton.'

'They could be many miles away, out of Cornwall.'

'Without horses, soldiers everywhere? Your brother, John. He has stables.'

'John has made too much money to risk losing it.'

'Then Francis. Brother and sister. They are the same age. He must have taken them somewhere.' She stamped her foot, her voice breaking with emotion. 'For my sake, Robert. You must do this! You must embrace the Will of God!'

***

At Venterdon, Alice continued to bask in the knowledge that Mary was safe at Cotehele. That she should on occasion reflect warmly on the prompt action of the ferryman, was a puzzle to Janella, but hardly disturbing. Occasionally too Alice would fuss about Samuel's will and Francis would have to remind her that the Reverend Clarke had everything in hand. The will had to be proved in the Bishop of Exeter's Court. The Reverend had explained. Such matters could not easily be dealt with, and especially not in times of war.

Francis and Arthur worked together on the North Field and then the lambing, not a prolonged affair as few healthy ewes remained. But Francis had never properly explained his absence in the days following Easter. Arthur knew he had not been sick and, as the news spread of the sequestration of Mary's property at Hampt, had doubtless put two and two together.

It would have been pointless to lie but equally, he could not take Arthur into his confidence. That would have been far too great a risk. The result was a grudging, surly, uncomfortable partnership, Arthur still awaiting Janella's word and having nowhere else to go, Francis dependant on him for the running of the farm. With Midsummer Day less than two months away, Janella knew she would soon have to tell Francis of her promise to Arthur. The passage of a few weeks had not caused her to deviate. If Francis would not have her, then Arthur surely would. She would not become an old maid, serving others until the day came she was of no more use, until she was cast off and alone. She would not be relied on for ever.

The moment came, inevitably perhaps, towards the end of the day when black clouds and torrential rain drove Arthur home to Tutwell, Alice to her room and Francis to dry off by the kitchen fire. Janella pretended to be busy in the scullery, remembering how Francis had once held her hand, before hurrying across the yard in the rain. Courage mustered, she sauntered into the kitchen. He was stretched out in Samuel's chair, barefoot, his stockings steaming on the hearth.

'Have you heard from Mary?' she asked, not expecting he would tell her, but just that he should speak.

'No.' He sounded weary. 'But John would tell me if anything was amiss.'

'And Arthur. Have you told Arthur?'

'No!' This time she had touched a nerve. 'I do not trust him...not as I do you. Arthur must not know.' His voice was raised. It was not Janella's business. 'Let that be an end to it.'

'Francis, he is not stupid.' Janella had an unsettling way, when she had a mind, of getting straight to the point. 'You were away when she disappeared. The whole village knows Mary's farm has been taken. Just be thankful Arthur has not betrayed you already!'

'Janella, what is it?' He had sensed there was something more on her mind. Janella was not easily aroused.

Now there was no going back. She had brought it to a head, but not in the way she had expected. 'I have promised him...'

'Promised?'

'I have promised him, come Midsummer Day, I will give him my answer.'

'Arthur?' She nodded.

He was stunned. He had not been in the least aware of Arthur's ambition, never given a thought to the idea that Janella might want a life of her own, that she would not always be devoted to her service at Venterdon. But he also knew Janella would not speak lightly. Janella always meant what she said.

'Janella, it is not possible. He does not deserve you. Nobody deserves you!' he spluttered, rising from his comfortable seat, cold feet on the flags.

'You expect me to wait on you till I am old?' she retorted, stepping away from him. 'Am I not to have my own home, children? Is that written down somewhere? I would make a good wife!' She flushed. 'Do you not think?'

It was done. She would not debate the matter further and so, on the flimsiest pretext, she made off to the scullery, leaving Francis in his bare feet and damp clothes, listening to the rain in the yard.

***

The last day of the month, mid-afternoon. The rain had ceased but the lanes were still muddy and there was drizzle in the air. Robert was slowly riding home, up the hill from Callington on the Lanson road, over his head tall beeches reaching towards each other, obscuring the dull sky. He had explained to Christina there was nothing more to be done. If Francis knew where Mary was he would keep it to himself, likewise John. And those who depended on Francis, Arthur and Janella, would, if they knew anything at all, support his motives and remain loyal. It might even be that Mary and Hampton, trusting no-one, had simply fled together in secret.

Christina had been contemptuous and then, abruptly, had lost interest and gone to bed. In the morning at first she had refused to rise, then once persuaded had, without a word, taken up her sermons again. For the first time he had feared for her sanity.

The stable boy was not to be found so he had saddled his horse alone in the yard, knowing he had to do something. In the end he had ridden to Hampt. John Wright would tell him anything for a shilling or two. He was a cunning, self-seeking man but, in his increasing desperation, Robert was compelled to recognise a kindred spirit. They were both practical men, both sought to insinuate themselves with the County Committee and both were equally curious to know the whereabouts of Mary Hawking. It would be difficult to enquire directly. Had Wright seen John or Francis or any other man at Mary's cottage? When had Mary left?

But Wright's palm, once greased, the two men had reached an understanding. As far as he could tell, Wright then told him all he knew.

'That night, I went to the cottage. To tell the truth, Mr Pellow, as there was no answer to my knocking, I went in. It was empty and bare. Even the food I 'ad brought the day before was all gone. I'm sure there was two of them.' Wright paused to weigh the odds. 'The bedchamber see, the bed was all mussed up like....an' there was men's clothes 'ung at the door.'

Later Wright had allowed himself to speculate further.

'You recall the robbery, sir? No, well there was someone broke in 'ere, at the 'ouse. There was food took and clothes, though I don't know what exactly. They 'ad it down for some poor so.....but then she started asking for more bread an' cheese, a flitch or two, like she was gettin' 'ungrier.'

'So there were two of them. but where could they have gone? You understand, I am only concerned for my sister. I do not want her arrested. I want her safe.'

'I understand, sir,' said Wright, smiling broadly. 'You can rely on me, sir.'

Wright had had nothing more to add, but promised to inform Robert in the unlikely event of Mary returning. Of course it would not be his place to reveal such an occurrence to the authorities in Lanson. Robert knew he was lying, that Wright was firmly under Gewen's control, but that was all part of the game, the game they were both playing.

After that, without admitting to himself the intention, he had ridden to Callington. He did not go there often. Sometimes he would meet his brother, sometimes not. He had entered the village from the Tavistock road and then, at the church, turned back towards Lanson. He saw the sign first, 'Pellows Stables', and then his brother, holding the reins to a fine sorrel stallion and in animated conversation with a prosperous looking farmer. As he approached, the farmer mounted and spurred the horse off in the direction of Lanson.

'Brother! How is business?'

'Robert! Good to see you!' John was always warmly welcoming, genuinely pleased to see him. 'Come in. I am not too busy.'

But the yard was bustling. John was always busy. And besides, he was in no state of mind to greet the family.

'I'll not trouble you John.' He tried to be equally hearty, equally friendly. 'Christina will be waiting.' And then he tried to be casual. 'I have not heard from Mary, since they took the farm. Do you know? She has not been arrested, I hope.'

John's face fell, his brows knitting briefly. Robert guessed what he was thinking. Were it within her power, Christina would herself have Mary arrested.

'I hope she is safe, Robert. I have not laid eyes on her, to tell the truth, not since our father died. She became so solitary.' John shook his head sadly. 'I think she was cruelly used by that husband of hers. It was never worth the waiting, Robert. I hope she is safe now, wherever she is.'

He had been convinced. John had never really lied. He had turned down a second invitation, honestly offered, feeling guilty for lying himself, for asking about Mary, when it was only Christina he cared about.

Now he was nearly home. Christina would not be waiting for him, did not even know where he had gone, or that he had gone at all. She had given up on him, not just him, given up on this life in her obsessive pursuit of the next. All he could say to her now, he practised the words;

'It's not John. I have spoken to him. And John Wright knows nothing.'

And Christina would look away, return to her sermons, a woman obsessed, or turn her back on him and retire early to her chamber.

Chapter 18

It is little more than an alehouse, one of a number not long established. But business is brisk. Since the arrival of Fairfax's regiments, Pennycomequick has acquired a new prominence. Drinkers come not only from the two regiments investing the Castle but also from their inevitable array of hangers-on, and not infrequently from those that have slipped out from the Castle walls, unable or unwilling to face the dangers and deprivations of a long siege.

And sometimes there are men you cannot quite put your finger on, messengers perhaps or spies for one side or another, gentlemen with some unspecified role difficult to classify but nonetheless involved with the siege and its ultimate outcome.

The tiny tavern, having been recently created through the amalgamation of a pair of fisherman's cottages, is modestly set back from the shore. At the back and barely visible through a cloud of tobacco smoke, a crude bar and behind it two hogsheads of beer, rows of tankards on a shelf and a motley collection of bottles and glasses. There is sawdust on the flagged floor and behind sturdy kitchen tables long benches line the newly whitewashed walls, already stained with grime and sweat and tobacco.

In the centre, somewhat incongruously, an elegant oak table with spiral legs and spindle chairs around, is more naturally occupied by the better class of customer.

In a corner by one of the windows overlooking the street and beyond that the shingle beach and expanse of bay, a soberly dressed, heavily-bearded man of uncertain origin. One of those you could not quite put your finger on. He is already known to the keeper behind the bar inasmuch as he pays for his beer, sits in the same place if it is not taken and causes no trouble.

While not especially averse to conversation, the man at the window is generally quiet and will, more often than not, leave after an hour or so. If asked his business he will more than likely reply that he is waiting only for the siege to be raised, as if that were explanation enough. For most it is, for all the talk in the tavern is of the siege. How many are in there? How long will they hold out? Some say a matter of days. Others insist, more likely it will be months. The Governor would die rather than surrender. And there is no shortage of powder and shot. We can all see how prodigal they are with their powder, whereas Fairfax, or rather Hammond now, only rarely bombards the Castle to remind the inmates, so to speak, that they have not gone away.

The runners, many of them Hopton's men sent to Pendennis after the surrender at Tresillian Bridge and who have neither shoes nor shirts to their name, are adamant. They insist, and shamefacedly some of them, those that remain will have to be starved into submission. Already the food is strictly rationed. The ale is foul and what remains of the beef is tainted. It will be horsemeat soon. For most, it is already bread and water and sixpence a day, if you're lucky. The heavily-bearded man merely nods and listens, making little comment, hedging his bets.

Against the same wall, closer to the bar, an older man in a blue, knitted cap, bulky, a man of experience even of authority you might say, has his own place and also listens without comment. Invariably, he smokes a pipe, drinks more than most and sometimes to excess. He is well-known to many of his fellow drinkers. Commonly addressed as 'Captain', he is commiserated with by some, congratulated by others. Impassive, he might give a nod of recognition here and there before picking up his beer and drinking long and deep.

'Captain,' a loud sneer of contempt. 'I had not thought to see you again!' It is a brutal looking, bare-headed fellow, shirt-sleeves, a dagger at the front of his belt, a tankard half-full held carelessly at his side like a weapon. 'They say a coward hides himself away, but 'ere you are bold as brass!' Momentarily between the bar and the window, conversation dies away. The newcomer raises his tankard. To drink or to dash it in the Captain's face? He glances round. There are soldiers coming in from the street. 'Aagh! You are not worth my trouble. Go back in your 'ole Captain.' The mood around them begins to relax as their fellow drinkers lose interest and turn away. But the cause of the commotion is reluctant to move away.

'You mark my words, Captain.' He leans over the table snarling into the Captain's face. 'Pendennis is not done yet, no matter how many runners!' And then as he turns to squeeze his way back through the crowd, 'I'll see your 'ead on a pike yet, Stephens!'

From the window he can be seen striding away alone in the direction of Penryn. And an hour later the Captain himself leaves, more worse for wear than usual, but for once not entirely alone. Staggering in the gloom up the narrow, cobbled lane away from the shore, he loses his footing. There is a helping hand.

'May I assist you, sir?'

'Are you come to murder me?' The Captain's speech is a little slurred and he is panting with the effort of the climb but, being accustomed to his condition, he is not at all unaware of his surroundings.

'Not at all Captain. I am here to assist you, perhaps in more ways than you can imagine.' They have come to a halt before a battered door, the last in a row of delapidated cottages. The door is unlocked. 'I will not enter against your will, sir.'

In a befuddled way, the Captain is considering whether or not to admit the stranger, a gentleman apparently and one he recognises from the alehouse, the man at the window. After some hesitation he decides to leave the door ajar. Fate will always have its way. Besides, there is nothing to steal, little of consequence to lose.

His companion closes the door behind them, espies the solitary candle on the mantelpiece and lights it with a flint. The room is in a piteous state. Plaster fallen from the bare walls lies undisturbed amidst the droppings of whatever creature it is that shares the Captain's lodgings. The Captain himself is already sprawled in an ancient armchair by the empty grate. There is one other farmhouse chair propped against the wall. The stranger opts to remain standing.

'Who was the man that threatened you?'

'Goes by the name of Honks.'

'Did he know you from Pendennis?'

'Yes.'

'You escaped?'

'Yes.' The Captain looks up suspiciously, less inebriated than one might have supposed. 'What business is that of yours?'

'And Honks?'

'Why do you want to know? Who are you anyway? Explain yourself, sir!' The Captain makes a half-hearted attempt to rise.

'My name is Hampton, Lieutenant Hampton. I am, through no fault of my own, sought after by both armies. My business is to break into the Castle, not out......'

'The Captain is too drunk or uncaring to express surprise. 'I would do the same if I could.' He bows his head. 'It is to my eternal shame that I ran away...Honks and those like him are right. At least they have their pride...'

'What happened? Who are you?'

'My name is Stephens. I was a Captain under Mohun. A month or so ago I was at Upton's Mount, a redoubt, the most forward position from the fort…In the daytime we gave them plenty of shot, but all the time they were extending their works, from Arwenack right across to the sea...' The Captain's speech is slow, deliberate but entirely coherent. 'The men began to talk of getting out, before it was too late. At nightfall we would be replaced. The men said it was our only chance…' Stephens reaches for an imaginary drink, but finding none shrugs and continues his tale. 'I told them,' Stephens shakes his head in abject despair. 'I told them, if we fled we would be traitors to the King. But they said it was all over. The war was all over.' He coughs and spits into the grate. 'In the end I led them out..They would have gone without me....'

Stephens begins to sob out loud. Hampton can only look away in distaste. The candle is almost burned to the mantle. This is a miserable, stinking hovel.

'Would you go back if you could?'

Stephens makes an effort to pull himself together. 'I am, as you can see Lieutenant, out of my mind. It is easy to say I would.'

'And this Honks?'

'Before Fairfax came, they tried to burn Arwenack down, but they were too late. Only the old hall was destroyed. When the Roundheads arrived, they had to withdraw to the Castle. Honks was one of the arsonists. He was trapped the wrong side of the Manor, but managed to escape.'

'So in his heart, he is not unlike you Captain, guilty for having got away.'

'There is no way in! The Castle is entirely cut off, by land and by sea. Look.' Stephens takes a poker from the fireside and begins, by the flickering light, to draw in the thick layer of dust which covers the hearth. 'The Carrick Roads, St Mawes here, Pendennis here, Batten's ships blocking the bay, the peninsula sealed by from Arwenack to the sea.'

'But Hampton has seen this explanation before. It is nothing new. 'Captain, I said I would help you. If you want to return to Pendennis. If you want to salvage your pride, I will help you. It is my intention to break the siege. I have travelled many miles with this in mind. Do you understand?'

Stephens nods, remarkably sober now. 'And you watched me. You picked me out. What drives you Lieutenant, your love for the King?'

Hampton ignores the question, but answers his own instead. 'You know the Castle. Now we must find someone who knows the sea…but first, where can I find Honks?'

'Honks?'

'Why not? From what I saw of him, Honks is exactly the man who would go back. And if there is to be a fight, not one to be trifled with. Where can I find him?'

Stephens looks dubious. 'You saw how he treated me…Penryn…somewhere in Penryn.'

'Then like you...' Hampton begins, but the candle sputters and dies leaving them in total darkness.

'I have a family in Truro.' Stephens' voice, clear as a bell, is sure of itself now that its owner has been rendered invisible. 'They believe...'

'And you cannot bear to tell them the truth,' Hampton interrupts, impatient now. 'If you come with me that little problem will be solved.' He prepares himself to leave. 'You will not betray me?'

'No, I will not betray you.'

'Then I will see you again in the alehouse, when we are ready.'

***

That Honks should be in Penryn was convenient and time was of the essence. Hampton himself had found a room in one of the innumerable Penryn taverns. Honks, having such an unmistakeable presence, would not be difficult to find. But he would have to be careful. Sympathy for Parliament, he had already learned, was strong in Penryn. An odd place for a man like Honks to choose.

The morning brought bright sunshine together with the sound of a heavy and prolonged exchange of fire from the direction of the Castle. Hampton wandered about the village looking for Honks but without success. Against his better judgement he began to ask discreetly here and there. About midday he was approached by a decrepit-looking beggar, barefoot and in rags.

'Honks is up there,' he said, putting his head to one side and holding out his hand.

Hampton tossed him a coin and crossed the lane to a narrow alleyway seeming to end, after only a few yards, in a high, crumbling wall. it was dank and dripping and stank of excrement, no hint of sunlight on the cobbles. There was a doorway to his left and then a strong arm under his chin, wrenching him back, thudding him to the ground. A knee on his chest driving the air from his lungs. A knife at his throat. Honks.

'Still. Move and I'll slit your throat. What do you want?'

He tried to speak but failed. The knee raised itself a fraction. 'I want help,' was all he could manage before beginning to breathe again more regularly. 'I want to get into the Castle.'

'There is no way in. What are you, some kind of agent? Do you take me for a fool! Honks now took hold of his coat and lifted him bodily to a sitting position in the doorway.

'I intend to get in...if you spare my life. I believe there is a way.'

'Who are you?' Honks relaxed his grip and returned the knife to his belt.

'My name is Hampton. I belonged to Edgcumbe's Foot...until they surrendered. I do not choose to surrender. I am a wanted man....as you are I think.' Honks glared and made to reach again for his knife. 'Is there somewhere we can talk?'

Honks paused to consider, then dragged Hampton to his feet and with one well-aimed boot kicked in the door and pushed him inside. A storeroom, abandoned, empty crates and barrels and from somewhere close the sound of running water. Hampton, once released, brushed himself down and began to explain. He had seen Honks before at Pennycomequick and had heard his story from Stephens. Honks frowned. He understood that while men were slipping out of Pendennis almost daily, there would not be many wanting to get in. But he believed Honks might be one of them and, whether he liked it or not, Stephens was another. With a half dozen men who knew the coastal waters and a small boat they could break the siege and take in much needed supplies.

'Batten has sealed the harbour.'

Hampton shrugged. 'We disregard the harbour.'

'Why should I believe you?'

'We are no threat to them. A few imbeciles like us. I know the siege will come to an end. We cannot make that much difference. It is more a matter of self-respect, don't you think? Or have I misjudged you?

"The King's Arms.' The keeper is a man called Stubbs. Before the war he worked for Killigrew. He knows these waters like the back of 'is 'and...He 'as two sons. 'Honks plucked thoughtfully at his meagre beard, ' and he may know of a boat. 'ave you got money?'

"Yes, I have. I have money to pay men and buy supplies.' Uncharacteristically, Hampton grinned. 'But not here with me you understand. I am not that much of an imbecile.'

***

At Cotehele, May Day came and went without celebration but not without recollections of happier times. 'We used to say nothing makes beautiful like kissing the dew on May morning,' Lady Margaret mused, 'but no-one believes that now. It is all 'heathenish vanity'. Fancy has been abolished.'

Mary was left much to her own devices, free to wander the courts and passages until she knew, or thought she knew, every nook and cranny. But she was neither mistress nor servant. Mrs Rundle would not allow her to help in the kitchen and whatever needed cooking, cleaning or mending was done by those whose job it was and Mary was not expected to interfere.

'We'll find you somethin' soon enough, when the Colonel gets back, Mrs Rundle warned darkly. 'Then everythin's topsy-turvy from dawn till dusk.'

Only on occasions would she be asked to dine with Lady Margaret and Mrs Howard and then would have to listen carefully for the midday chimes of the chapel clock. It was not something she enjoyed. Surrounded by the parlour tapestries, she found it difficult to concentrate. 'Classical scenes,' she was told but whatever they were they did little to aid her digestion. Lady Margaret at the head of the long, polished table talked and probed and ordered the servants about, and asked for more wine while Mrs Howard, serene and distant, spoke only when spoken to and at the first opportunity retired to her chamber.

Mary was altogether more comfortable with Kate and Mrs Rundle or one of the maids in the kitchen.

'Better food 'ere anyways,' said Mrs Rundle slyly.

If the sun shone she and Kate would go down to the quays or wander about the woods until, after a while, Kate would say, 'Pa will be expecting me' and disappear to the farm. But Mary soon concluded that her new friend, though a farmer's daughter, was not one habituated to work on a farm. Somehow Kate was not habituated to anything. An hour or so of her time here and there was all she had to give. It was just the way she was, 'a free spirit' as Lady Margaret said.

So Mary spent hours alone in the woods close to the house, or when it rained, in her room staring at the ceiling or peeping through her window at the distant stream, thoughts of Pendennis, of Andrew and of their last days together endlessly turning in her mind.

One morning in early May, sitting unladylike on the quay, her feet dangling over the river, there was a sudden scuffle on the gravel behind her and then Kate breezily calling out;

'News for Mrs Hampton...Mary, news!'

She scrambled to her feet. 'What? What news?'

Kate still several yards away, could hardly contain herself. 'Well, pa was in Callington, at the market..' She was still breathless from running down the hill. 'He was talking to a man at the stables who seemed to know you was here.' Kate took a deep breath. 'Mrs Hampton, he says, ah...I have a message from her brothers, all is well, he says.'

'Is that all?' Mary said, hardly concealing her disappointment.

'Your brothers. I think he said 'brothers', more than one...Your brothers are well and if you have a message, my pa can take it at the next market. The man at the stables...' Kate came to embrace her but Mary could not help but shrug her off.

'My pa can ask...'

'No! No! I have to be patient. I have to wait...I am well. That is my message. I am well.'

When she turned round a moment or two later Kate had gone, leaving her more bereft than ever. And then came the distant chimes of the chapel clock. Midday. She had forgotten. Lady Margaret would be waiting in the parlour. Hurriedly she picked up her skirts, in the manner of Mrs Howard which she had unconsciously adopted, and set off up the path to the house.

By the time she entered the parlour, red-faced and flustered, the chimes had long since ceased. Mrs Howard was in her usual place but Lady Margaret was nowhere to be seen.

'Lady Margaret is indisposed,' Mrs Howard stated bluntly, without looking up from her soup.

She was as distantly superior as ever and clearly had not the slightest inclination to engage in conversation. Mary seated herself and put her soup to one side, though in the kitchen she would have relished it, and began to pick at her meat.

'Is Lady Margaret sick?'

'Indisposed.'

Mary could no longer restrain herself. 'Mrs Howard, I recognise you are a woman of some...substance, but is it necessary to disregard me so...thoroughly? I am an officer's wife,' she lied, 'and accustomed to a certain degree of respect!'

Mary thought she had phrased that rather well but Mrs Howard only looked at her as if she could hardly believe she were an officer's wife or that she had managed to string so many words together at once.

'Perhaps you would feel more at home in the kitchen. We are not bound to eat together.'

Mary stood up, sending her chair to the floor. Mrs Howard cut herself another slice of ham.

'Too true, Mrs Howard. Do not doubt it! This is the last time!

Had she stayed a moment longer, she would have resorted to some kind of violence. Instead she turned her back on the parlour and, in her own mind, on everything it represented. In her miserable, cell-like room she cast off each one of her voluminous skirts so grudgingly donated by Mrs Howard, and flung herself on the bed. Wrapping herself tight beneath the thin counterpane and despite the cold anonymity of her chamber, she willed herself to a fitful sleep.

There was a knock on the door. Her chamber was in darkness. A maid she had not seen before.

'Lady Margaret is waiting for you.'

She assented, closed the door, dressed and straightened herself, pinned back her hair as best she could, settled her cap, a splash of ice-cold water to wake her up. No doubt she had incurred Lady Margaret's displeasure. Well, that could not be helped. When she pulled open the door, the maid was still there.

'I know the way,' she said and watched the girl hesitate before melting away into the shadows.

There was no other sign of life as she made her way through the sculleries, across the empty hall and through the parlour to the spiral staircase, the landing, the door to Mrs Howard's room and then the narrow twisting stairs to Lady Margaret's chamber. She knocked and detecting a murmur from within, pushed open the door.

Surprisingly, Lady Margaret was not in her bed but fully dressed and standing by one long row of curtainless windows. There was a candle on the small, round table in the corner and another by the bed. For the first time she noticed the King's 'Charter of Protection' on the wall and beside it a steel, ebony-framed mirror which reminded her of the one in her old bedchamber at Hampt. She closed the door. She would not be intimidated. Mrs Howard had wronged her. It was not her place to apologise.

'Your brothers are well, I hear.' Lady Margaret settled herself in the more comfortable of the two chairs beside the table. Her speech had seemed unnaturally subdued.

'Yes.' Her only thought was that Kate, whom she had come to rely on as her only true friend, had an even greater friend in Lady Margaret.

'Sit.' Lady Margaret gestured vaguely to the empty chair. 'I have something to say to you.' There was a glass of red wine full to the brim on the table. Lady Margaret changed tack. 'But I see you object to Kate being so much in my confidence?' Mary said nothing. 'That is true, but she is also in yours, I think?' Well, Kate has nothing to hide. No secrets. It is part of her charm. She has told you, I suppose, that I had the crew of a Spanish man o' war hung on a gibbet?'

'She has told me that.'

'Did she tell you they were all papist scum?' Lady Margaret took a delicate sip from her glass by way of emphasising her point.

'No.'

'You see Mary, nothing is ever what it seems. No-one is ever what they seem. It is something you have yet to learn. Mrs Howard is not what she seems. Snooty? I will grant you. Contemptuous? Perhaps. Overdressed? Without a doubt.' Mary felt herself flushing. 'But it will not have occurred to you, that is only the masque she presents to the world. She does not speak to you, and so you are offended?' Mary nodded. 'And so you think her superior. But have you ever listened to her, when she speaks? Have you ever listened to the manner of her speech?'

'She ignores me, avoids me, Lady Margaret. I am nothing to her........nor she to me.'

'But the manner of her speech, Mary. You do not listen. There is a lilt to her voice which she cannot hide.' Lady Margaret picked up her glass and almost drained it dry. 'Once we had a castle in Tralee, besieged like Pendennis is now, but in the Irish Rebellion, not so long ago Mary, not so very long ago...I am not accustomed to reminisce but you see, Mary...sometimes...My grandson died in that rebellion. Only by a miracle his family survived....' Lady Margaret drained the last of her wine. She appeared to Mary to have lost her thread.

'You must.....'

'The papists burned the castle at Tralee to the ground. Mrs Howard, whom you so detest, was assaulted in the presence of her husband and then required to witness his execution........hung from a gibbet. It is a cruel world is it not, Mary? There was a sudden lash of rain against the row of night black windows. 'But Mrs Howard, despite her ordeal, assisted my grandson's family to escape to England.' Lady Margaret seemed about to rise from her seat. Her voice trembled. 'She is the most courageous woman I know!'

The rain came and went against the window panes. Black night shut them in. Mary was only conscious of an old woman's black widow's weeds which were not widow's weeds at all, and in a flickering light Lady Margaret's white, flaccid features still impassive, hovering over the flame.

'I will leave.'

Lady Margaret leant back and motioned towards the folding table at her bedside. She did not appear to have heard. Mary went over to fetch the bottle and emptied it into the glass.

'The Catholics laid siege for six months. It was my home once, a long time ago. A siege is ten a penny these days. Pendennis will not hold out long.' Lady Margaret brought her small, dull eyes temporarily into focus. 'I am a woman who keeps her word, Mary. When Pendennis falls and your fancy man,' she sniggered, 'comes back, I will return to Herdof...Herd..Hertford..shire. Ha! Till then, you have nowhere to go..so you...stay here.'

The last image Mary had as she closed the door at the top of the spiral staircase was of Lady Margaret picking up her glass with great care and a steady hand to ensure that not a single drop should be lost. At the door to Mrs Howard's chamber she paused, wondering if she should alert her to Lady Margaret's condition. But then decided it was not her business, nor Mrs Howard's. For all she knew, Lady Margaret drank every night at this time. Perhaps it helped her to sleep.

Back in her own chamber, she sat lifeless on the bed. Lady Margaret would not hesitate to have her hung if she came to know of her Faith. Mrs Howard, for all her travails, continued to regard her with contempt. Kate, who said whatever came into her head, could not be trusted. Her life at Cotehele had suddenly become much more precarious. She felt an overwhelming urge to flee, not to Hampt, not to Venterdon, not even to Pendennis, but simply to float down the river to the open sea, to disappear.

Chapter 19

'Every night, Batten has ten large boats and barges, well-manned, before the mouth of the harbour. But he draws them off in the morning, just as day breaks. That is the moment.'

It is mid-afternoon, Monday 21st May at the 'King's Arms', their one and only time together. The room is small, windowless, unrolled on the table a detailed, coloured map of the coastline and clustered around, six chairs, all occupied. It is the sort of nondescript room Stubbs has undoubtedly used before, perhaps for purposes of a more nefarious nature.

'Why not earlier? If we come from the west and ignore the 'Roads', we would hardly be noticed.' Stephens tries but fails to exert the authority to which he had once been accustomed.

'We would put ourselves against the tide.' Stubbs explains patiently. 'We must go out on the ebb. Besides, when we pass the Dennis it will still be dark.'

'But when, Stubbs? I do not wish to delay.' This time it is Hampton's voice, calm, insistent.

'Simon and Luke will look over her and load up tomorrow and Wednesday. As I told you, they will have to make two journeys. The wagon will not take the lanes around Constantine and Port Navas. Out of Penryn, they will have to turn the mare into a pack animal. It all takes time. The earliest would be Thursday, on the dawn tide. And people get curious so we go separately. James, you go with Honks and Luke with Stephen. I'll keep an eye on Mr Hampton here..'

'Stubbs,' It was Hampton again. 'Show me again on the map and then you, Stephens, again. We must not be in any doubt.'

Stubbs was only too pleased. "The 'Mary Jane' lies here, a little in from the creek, but not too close to the village. We cast off as the tide turns and row as far as the Passage. James and Luke will have muffled the oars. By the 'Head' we'll have the sails raised. Then straight across to Pendennis, with a following wind if we're lucky. Couldn't be easier.'

'Stephens.'

'The siege-works are here, all the way across from Arwenack House to the sea.' Stephens' delivery is slower, almost ponderous but no less to the point. 'We sail onto the shore here, on the seaward side of the ditch and earthwork. Until we are behind the earthwork, we are exposed to fire from the near end of the Parliamentary line. There is nothing we can do about that. Further out to sea and we risk being spotted by Batten. We have to get the provisions up and along this side of the earthwork. But they are sure to see us from the Horse Pool Bastion here and so will send out for us. The drawbridge will be lowered. At the highest point of the earthwork, we make a run for it, across the bridge and through the ramparts.' By now Stephens is perspiring visibly. Apart from his own, there are four solemn faces around the table. All except for Stubbs who appears only to relish the prospect of danger.

'Let us hope,' he says, a smile on his face and to break the silence, 'we are spotted early from the Castle and not fired on too hastily from the siege-works.'

'The only pity is the 'Mary Jane' will be lost for good...'

'When we cast off at Port Navas,' Hampton breaks in, 'I pay each man five gold crowns, and when we reach Pendennis through that gate, five more.' There is no response. Hampton is apologetic. 'It is all I have left.'

But it is not the money. He knows it is not the money. Honks and more especially Stephens are here to salvage some self-respect. Only Stubbs is different. For Stubbs it is the prospect of a return to the old ways before the war when smuggling was rife and piracy not entirely unknown. Once a trusted lieutenant of that most notorious of Cornish families, the Killigrews, Stubbs is nothing if not familiar with the coastline around the Fal and the Helford Passage. Superficially, keeper of the 'King's Arms', secretly he suffers that peculiar frustration of all born seamen who find themselves bound to the land.

His two sons, Luke and James, taller, younger versions of their father and darker still in complexion, give credence to the rumour, never denied, that Stubbs had once been wed to a Saracen.

When Honks had arranged for Hampton and Stubbs to meet, Stubbs, anxious for privacy, had led him into the stable-yard and down a steep flight of stone steps to the cellar. It was a cool, orderly place, with long, narrow windows peeping surreptitiously over the cobbles and into the yard. Already briefed by Honks, Stubbs had been typically enthusiastic, stimulated by the challenge, but also understandably suspicious and not to be fobbed off by Hampton's vague explanations of himself.

Stubbs already knew Honks and even, by repute, Stephens, but nothing he insisted, nothing at all of Hampton. He would not become involved in any scheme without some assurance of what he called Hampton's 'interest'.

Stubbs' suspicion was entirely justified. Hampton had become a man almost divested of identity. He would have been suspicious himself. There was little now to connect him with the officer who had been shot escaping from Cotehele. His satchel and even George Hawking's clothes stolen from the farmhouse at Hampt had long since been discarded. All that remained was the rapier. Hampton had decided to take a risk.

'Do not be alarmed,' he said unnecessarily, slowly drawing the thin blade into the light.

Stubbs, distinctly unalarmed, had taken the hilt in his hand and, holding it up to the window, studied the brightly decorated cup with interest.

'Hirondelles,' he murmured appreciatively. 'And the money?'

Hampton took a handful of coins from his jerkin and laid them on top of a barrel.

'To pay for food, drink, tobacco, whatever you can lay your hands on.'

Stubbs took up the money without bothering to count. 'There is a shallop, 'The Mary Jane', moored near to Port Navas. She has not been sailed since before the war, but I think she is seaworthy.' Stubbs cast a casual glance around the cellar. 'Two or three barrels of beer, some firkins of Portuguese wine, a barrel or two of beef, salted hogs, tobacco......More and she would be too low in the water.'

'Your sons...'

'They will come. Six men. It is a balance. Fewer than six we could not handle her....'

'And the more of us there are the more we risk discovery. I would like to see her, 'The Mary Jane', as soon as possible.'

Stubbs put out his hand. 'Come here tomorrow, same time.'

They had borrowed a pair of unremarkable nags from the stables. Stubbs, he observed with good humour, could lay his hands on anything he wanted, and without much difficulty. Once out of Penryn, they had entered a maze of lanes and tracks he would never be able to remember but Stubbs, he suspected, had already thought of that. Certainly, they could not have been taking the most direct route for they passed not a single dwelling nor came across the smallest sign of human life.

After a while, he had sensed they were close to water and sure enough Stubbs indicated for him to dismount and follow him down an invisible path through a tangle of heavily-scented yellow gorse. In a well-secluded, grassy area they had left the horses and pressed on through a cluster of old hawthorns.

And then all at once, the undergrowth fell away in front of them, to reveal the 'Mary Jane', apparently moored in the middle of a forest. Hampton had to look beyond her to convince himself she was actually afloat in a narrow stretch of water, lapping gently against her hull. A willow leant lazily over her bow and another conveniently at her stern, obscuring her almost entirely from any other vessel small enough to navigate the narrow channel in which she lay.

A hundred yards to their right, Stubbs explained, was Port Navas and to their left the creek which opened out into the Helford Passage. Hampton could sense Stubbs' excitement as, lasciviously almost, his gaze raked 'The Mary Jane' from stem to stern.

'She is almost dry, Stubbs said, slipping nimbly over her side, the better to examine her.

Unused to nautical considerations, Hampton remained where he was. 'She is smaller than I had expected. Has she no mast?'

'Stowed here see, along with the sprit. They are easy enough to raise. The sails are safe with me. James and Luke'll bring them. She's small, I grant ye..' Stubbs looked slightly offended. 'Two..two and a half tons, twenty -two foot, short for one of these, but bigger and we couldn't handle her, not in bad weather. See there's the oars and there's six rowlocks, not that we need 'em all. My boys'll get her shipshape, Lieutenant. Don't you be alarmed. She can be rowed and she can be sailed and a shallow draught see, she can go anywhere...barrels' go under the bow and under the transom...but we have to catch the ebb, Lieutenant, or we're done for.' Stubbs could hardly contain his enthusiasm as he checked the tiller and taffrail, smacking his lips with eager anticipation. What do you think, Lieutenant?

'I think,' Hampton replied, smiling his appreciation, 'there is nothing on God's earth...or sea that can stop us.'

And now as the meeting disperses, and he recalls Stubbs' unbounded enthusiasm Hampton's doubts, in spite of the dangers spelled out by Stephens, are once more dispelled.. He is convinced, as he surely has been all along, that they will succeed. It is true, nothing on God's earth will stop them now.

***

Mary wandered further and further from the quays, downriver to another nameless stream, like the one at Kerrybullock, and another bridge but more substantial than the rickety one at Deer Park Lodge. She crossed into the woods and all at once was reminded of Hook Combe and what Andrew had called 'the old workings', the tinners who would never come back and the goldfinch who always would. But this time there were no delicate clusters of white wild garlic hidden amongst the bluebells. the forest was already bereft of those subtle, delicious aromas of Spring. And Andrew Hampton was no more than a distant memory. Not even that. She could no longer picture him, picture his face. It was almost as if he had never been, a figment merely of her old imagination.

Here, beyond the chimes of the chapel clock, she felt even more alone than when she had tramped her way along the riverbank, waiting for George and knowing all the time he would never come. But her path across the meadow to Horsebridge had at least been her own. She had made it her own. It had become what was expected of her. Now in these strange woods, unknown and misunderstood, she was beginning to lose all sense of her own existence. Perhaps she was losing her mind.

She thought of kneeling down alone in the forest to pray but instead merely cast her mind back to her life before the war, before her father's death, before George. She could hardly grasp that there had been such a time. Her mind would only allow her the barest impressions: her father's powerful voice ringing out across the yard, John and Robert growing up beyond her reach, Francis, once the darling of them all scampering off down the lane, and then her mother watching silently, sadly but without reproof, knowing she had cast her out.

She became aware of the river rushing noisily by. Somehow, she had come out of the woods to a curve of shingle along the shore. She took off her cap to shake out her curls, then on impulse flung it into the water, too fancy anyway. She turned back towards the bridge, then over the nameless stream to the quays and almost at once heard the sound of the chapel clock echoing down the hill.

'Lady Margaret wants to see you.' It was Kate rushing down to the quays with a message, just as she had once before. 'She is in the Great Chamber, a funny place to see you but…Mary, she is impatient.'

The Great Chamber occupied the first floor of the Tower. It was certainly odd that Lady Margaret should want to see her there, odd that she should want to see her at all. Since the night she had been called to Lady Margaret's bedchamber, she had not laid eyes on her, or on Mrs Howard. But without a word she picked up her skirts and solemnly followed Kate up to the House.

Lady Margaret, an effigy in black, stood motionless beside an ancient tapestry which had been pulled to one side. There was an opening set deep in the wall, in the form of a cross.

'I saw you come in. At least you did not dawdle.'

Lady Margaret stepped back to allow her to peer through the opening, which provided a perfect view from above of the Great Hall. How many times had Lady Margaret observed her from this very spot?

'There is another into the chapel.' Lady Margaret allowed the arras to fall back into place.

The chapel, Mary knew, was locked, the chaplain having accompanied the family to the Mount, but Kate had shown her the winding stair leading from the parlour to the very foot of the altar. Now on the opposite side of the Great Chamber, Lady Margaret revealed a small recess and a further opening in the form of a cross, but this time with a perfect view of the interior of the tiny chapel.

Mrs Howard, in unexpectedly sober dress, was kneeling on the black and white tiled floor, just where the rood screen opened to the altar and half-hidden by the lectern.

'She comes here daily,' Lady Margaret whispered. 'She does not know I observe her. You take my meaning now, Mary. Mrs Howard is not at all what she seems.'

They could hear her praying. Mary felt like an intruder but curiosity had the better of her.

'...dimitte nobis debita nostra. Libera nos ab igne inferni.'

'Forgive us our sins,' Lady Margaret translated softly. 'Save us from the fires of hell.'

'....requiem aeternam dona ei...'

'Eternal rest grant unto him.' She prays for her husband, hanged in her presence, as I told you Mary.'

Mary could no longer bear it and insisted on coming away. 'Lady Margaret, Why do you show me this?'

'I want you to see Mrs Hawking, she is a papist and yet I defend her. Her husband is already in Heaven or in Hell and yet she persists in praying for his soul. It is mere superstition and yet it is a fine thing, is it not? I want you to know Mary that I am a

tolerant woman. I do not hang papist scum merely for sport.'
Mary said nothing but bowed her head, and prepared to take her leave. 'Do you pray for the dead, Mary?

'I remember them.'

'But do you pray?'

'I pray in my chamber, Lady Margaret.' She smiled in spite of herself. 'If I pray in the chapel, you may observe me.'

***

They set off separately from the 'King's Arms', in pairs as Stubbs has instructed. Hampton and Stubbs are the last to leave. How will the inn continue to function, Hampton wonders, without its keeper? Stubbs only answers in a roundabout way. Something about a woman. Everything is taken care of, Stubbs says, grinning broadly. He will take up where he has left off. Hampton has the impression this is not the first time.

When they arrive the others are already aboard. All that they can carry is neatly stowed at the bows and the stern. The rowlocks are muffled, the mast fixed in position and the main and staysails ready to be raised. James, the elder of Stubbs' two sons, wades knee-deep in the shallows to push them free of the mooring, before heaving himself over the gunwales and taking up his oar.

The little boat noses its way into the narrow channel. A moonless and starless night as Stubbs has predicted and there is a mist on the water. At first there is an irregular splashing as the rowers; Hampton and James to starboard, Honks and Luke to port, struggle to co-ordinate the dip and pull of their oars. Stephens in the bow, in his blue cap is to keep a look-out. Stubbs' sense of humour for, in the mist, there is nothing to see.

As the rowers settle, Stubbs steers them unerringly into the wider waters of the creek. They are surprisingly low in the water. Stephens, inevitably unemployed at the bow, anxiously allows his hand to drift in the stream. At the tiller, Stubbs is a man in his element, supremely unconcerned, only on occasion issuing some incoherent instruction or comment to one or other of his sons. As they turn into the Passage, they sense the ebb tide swell beneath them.

'Rest on your oars,' says Stubbs, perhaps aware that Honks and Hampton are already feeling the strain.

A lone gull startles those unused to the sea as it screeches past their stern, unseen above the mist. Looking round, they become aware of the near shore rising up darkly from the waves.

'Another mile or so lads,' The salt tang in the air has given Stubbs an extra jauntiness, 'should take us past the Dennis. Then we raise the sails...Alright lads, we have the ebb with us. Set to your oars!'

The dawn tide is with them but now there is a stiff, cold breeze blowing in from the sea, part of Stubbs' calculations he has omitted so far to mention. The waves begin to slap more insistently against the bows and the oars, at least fully visible now, no longer strike the surface smoothly and in unison. The mist has all but cleared, enabling Stubbs and Stephens simultaneously to pick out on the far headland, the distinctive silhouette of the Dennis Fort. Stubbs nods to his sons, who know what to do.

'Ship your oars lads. Honks, Lieutenant, make yourselves scarce to the bow and lie low. You too Captain.'

Stubbs heads them directly into the wind as James and Luke raise first the stays'l and then the main. Honks and Hampton lie opposite one another with a pair of salted hogs for company, while Stephens can only sway this way and that to avoid the flapping jib.

'We have to beat into the wind,' Stubbs shouts above the rush of the sea and as the sails fill. 'Round the Head, away from the Fort and then out to sea, as far as we dare. Then I will run her in.....Stephens...' They are picking up speed now, heeling over to port, the sea slamming into her bow, salt spray lashing their faces...'Stephens keep your eyes peeled for a man o' war.'

The dirty, dun-coloured sails, though visible from the Dennis, have not been spotted. Before long they are round Rosemullion Head and, as the sky brightens, Stephens picks out the embattled turret of Pendennis on the horizon. But as they change tack and move further away from the shore, they begin to take in more water. Stubbs has a wooden pail by his feet but does not yet see fit to use it. Stephens remonstrates that they are sailing away from Pendennis.

'Here.' With his foot Stubbs moves the pail towards James. 'Hampton, Honks. One of you bail out, but mind the sprit!'

Hampton takes the pail but it leaks and does not seem to have much effect. Much to Stephens' relief, they change tack again and Pendennis comes once more into his line of sight. Hampton offers the pail to Honks but Honks is too busy clinging on to the gunwales for dear life, not half the man he was on land.

'One of Batten's ships!' Stephens points excitedly, his eyes fixed on the horizon.

'He has not seen us,' Stubbs murmurs, barely audible above the wind and the waves.

Hampton looks at Stubbs. Batten's man o' war lies to their south and east. But Stubbs, more concerned with the Parliamentary batteries onshore, does not alter course. Now they are almost abreast of the tower with its turreted lookout, but still heading out to sea.

'I'm going to run her in now, ' Stubbs raises his voice just enough to be heard. 'Keep your heads down lads!'

They swing round to face the shore, now with the wind astern, they pick up speed. Luke lowers the stays'l.

'Stephens, where do we go in?'

'There! There! See the earthwork, from the ramparts down to the rocks. Just before...'

'James, mains'l. '

James struggles for a moment with the rigging before the mainsail and sprit are lowered neatly into the well. Stubbs is on his feet at the tiller.

'Now!' Stephens screams.

There are heads peering over the parapet, muskets. Stubbs pushes the tiller sharply to port. A loud scraping as her keel hits the rocks. Hampton looks up to the parapet. More heads. Someone shouts an order. Luke and James are already tumbling barrels onto the shore. Honks and Stephens are scrambling onto the slippery rocks. Stephens has lost his footing. A familiar whine above his head. Hampton looks towards the Parliamentary lines.

A puff of smoke. Then another. Stephens does not get up. A pool of bright red staining the sand and weed circling at his neck. Hampton kneels at his side, momentarily losing track of the time and the place. He watches as Mary, herself kneeling, tends to his bloodied thigh. An angel in a pigsty. Stubbs lays a hand on his shoulder.

'Leave him, Lieutenant. he is dead.'

A heavy grating noise from high above them as the drawbridge is lowered. From Upton's Mount a retaliatory outbreak of musket fire. And then a party of men are hurrying down towards them through the furze and alongside the earthwork. A young officer, distinguished more by his bearing than by what remains of his uniform, approaches Hampton and salutes.

'Lieutenant Shipman. You are a welcome sight, sir. The best we have had in months.'

Hampton gestures towards Stephens lying at his side, apparently unaware of the musket balls peppering the rocks about 'The Mary Jane'.

'I fear he is dead, sir.'

Hampton's only response is to set about heaving Stephens out of the water. The young Lieutenant, seeing no alternative, goes to his aid. The barrels of food and beer, the firkins of Portuguese wine and the two salted hogs are all being carried up the slope alongside the earthwork. Shipman and Hampton are the last to climb over the mud wall, manhandling Stephens as best they can and then supporting the corpse upright between them as they stagger across the drawbridge to safety.

Immediately they are surrounded by hundreds of cheering soldiers, a stinking, bedraggled, ragtag army, and by their womenfolk too, with children in their arms and about their feet. Smoke from celebratory cannon fire drifts across the chemise. In the confusion, Stephens is unceremoniously taken away for burial. Hampton looks around to make sure Stubbs and the others are safe, before turning to Shipman.

'Lieutenant Hampton,' he says, 'previously of Colonel Edgcumbe's Foot.'

Shipman leads them across the horn-works to the Round Tower, across another drawbridge, a glimpse of the Gunroom crowded with sick and wounded and then up a winding stairway.

'Wait, a moment please. I have a private obligation to fulfil.' Shipman bows and withdraws. Hampton reaches into his doublet and takes out all that remains of his wealth. 'I know this is not the reason, but it was our bargain nevertheless. In such a place as this, you must keep it well-hidden.' And Hampton places the last of his gold crowns in the hands of each of his companions.

Then Shipman leads them up a second set of spiral stairs to the officers' quarters, high above the chemise and facing north towards the siege-works. There are the inevitable, noisy congratulations and many a toast to the King before Arundell himself enters from his private chamber, to shake each man by the hand.

'You have shown by your courageous action that the King's cause in Cornwall is alive and well. I will personally ensure you are each commended by name to His Majesty'...and not forgetting your fallen comrade.'

Whereupon the Governor, not unnaturally, invites Hampton to his private quarters, where the two men remain closeted for some time.

Chapter 20

The Reverend Clarke had much on his mind but had never been anything if not decisive. It was not in his nature to brood and besides now that there was so little time, there were a number of matters which demanded his attention. The church had been empty as it always was at such an early hour. He had prayed briefly before the altar before entering the vestry, neat and equally empty apart from his white surplice on its usual hook, the folding table folded neatly to the wall. He had not left by the south porch as was his habit but by the tower door, the better to conceal his intention.

On his return, the Rectory too had been empty. For a few days, he had explained to the maid, her services would not be required. She should not be concerned. Soon everything would return to normal. He regarded himself critically in the mirror but left his silver hairbrushes untouched. Enough of vanity! He had places to go, people to see. First to the Pellows in Venterdon, one family amongst many with whom he could not help feeling a special bond.

Where was Mary Hawking now? Did she still hold to the Faith? He knew the farm had been sequestrated but only the Pellows perhaps knew where she was and, if they had any sense, they would keep that to themselves. And there was that other matter. Had Alice fully recovered her mind? He hoped she had. Samuel's passing had laid her so low. If only she had turned to the true Faith as Mary had, she might then have confessed and relieved the burden from her shoulders.

It was Janella as always who opened the door.

'I have come to see your mistress, Janella. Is she well?

The Reverend, Janella thought, did not seem quite his usual self. Perhaps it was the cold, early morning light, but his face was more deeply lined than Janella could remember and there was a sadness in his eyes, belying the practised, jovial tone of his voice. Alice sat by the fire, small and alert in Samuel's old chair. To her the Reverend was no different, brisk and dapper as ever. He handed her a rolled parchment with a bright red seal.

'At last it has been proved Alice, in the Bishop of Exeter's Court.' Alice looked confused, causing the Reverend to wonder if she really was recovered. 'Your husband Samuel's Last Will and Testament.'

In truth, Alice was trying desperately to remember whether that was the reason she had been waiting to see the Reverend Clarke. Perhaps it was. She could think of no other. Janella offered him something to drink but the Reverend declined. Time was of the essence, he said. There was a noise at the door. Janella saw through the window it was Arthur, come to pester her again. She excused herself and turned away to open the door.

'The Reverend is here,' she hissed, glad for once to have an excuse to shoo Arthur away.

She could hear the Reverend behind her, making some polite enquiry of Alice and then Alice's shrill voice;

'Mary is at Cotehele, Reverend, at Cotehele.'

She closed the door in Arthur's face and then, almost immediately, had to open it again as the Reverend took his leave. Alice had stuffed the will down the side of her chair. Both her head and her hands were shaking, as they sometimes did, but she would not be comforted. So Janella went about her business.

Francis had been to Lidwell to help the pigman and for his trouble brought home a piece of pork. She had thought to hang roast it. From the scullery, she could hear Alice, anxious apparently to conceal the will, creeping up the stairs to her bed. With mixed feelings she abandoned the pork, brought more logs in for the fire and looked for her bowl of tallow. With Alice out of the way and dipping her rushes, she began to think.

She could not get out of her mind the expression on Arthur's face. It had not simply been that she was shutting him out. Arthur was used to that. But there had been a sharp look in his eyes. She was certain he had heard. Alice's voice was not loud but shrill, high-pitched. You could not help but hear her. 'Mary is at Cotehele.' Something mist have clicked in Arthur's mind. He would have put two and two together. Francis away from the fields, the sequestration of the farm at Hampt, Mary's disappearance. Everybody knew Mary and George Hawking were wanted and now Arthur knew for certain that Francis was implicated, that Francis had taken Mary to Cotehele. Arthur in one chance moment had acquired over them all, a deadly power. And in three weeks, Midsummer Day, when she would have to give him her answer.

Betrothed to her, Arthur would have no cause to harm Francis. Rejected, there was no telling what he might do, out of sheer spite. Perhaps he already suspected she had a soft spot for Francis., more than that. Not that Francis cared. She remembered how they had sheltered in the lynhay, the rain drumming on the roof, splattering on the cobbles. 'I will not deceive you again,' he had said and they had seemed so close. And then she had finally brought herself to tell him of her promise to Arthur. Again it had been the rain, sending them home early from the fields. 'He does not deserve you!'

Well perhaps not, but that is sometimes the way.

Since then, the weeks had slipped by and they had hardly spoken. Mary was safe, he said. There had been a message from John, and that was all. And on the farm, Francis and Arthur had continued to work together in an atmosphere of mutual suspicion. She could see the distrust in the way they avoided one another, in the way they hardly spoke. Yet she would not deviate from her purpose. If Francis would not have her, then Arthur would. She had prepared herself for both eventualities, thought of little else if truth be told.

Alice had said she was ill, little suspecting that Janella might soon be lost to her for ever. Francis said nothing but she had sensed, even in his silence, he was thinking of her, imagining perhaps the rest of his life when she was gone.

Sometimes, when it seemed she was too busy to notice, he would look at her askance. And once, by chance, he had come upon her in the scullery, pinning back her hair in that graceful, womanly way she had, and the colour had risen to her cheeks and she had turned away. And once, though she was ashamed to think of it now, she had brushed against him on the stairs, and then it had been no accident. Her mother had warned her never to flaunt herself but then her mother had been unfortunate in her choice of men, and had never been an old maid. Before the war, Francis had lusted after her but she had not been so foolish as to submit. He had been different then, before Lostwithiel, before the death of his father.

Alice stayed in her bed but did not refuse the warm milk and bread she brought to her. As for the will, it was nowhere to be seen and Alice had nothing to say on the subject.

Janella prepared the pork and hung it to roast. She had looked forward to that, preparing for Francis a wholesome supper, but Arthur's coming had changed all that.

The sun had not yet sunk below the rim of the moor when she heard Francis scraping off his boots in the yard. He came in more pleased with himself than usual.

'Smells good!'

'You have the pigman to thank for that.'

She went to the scullery to cut some bread. Then while he sat waiting, cut down the roast and brought it to the table.

'Mother...'

'She went to lie down. The Reverend came this morning and brought your father's will. Your mother just took it to her room.'

Francis, half-rising from the bench and facing the fire, had begun to slice the meat.

'It reminds me of the shearing. We've finished now, every last one of them, not that there were many to start with...Why don't you have some Janella? You look tired.'

'I'm not hungry.' She sat down nevertheless. 'Arthur came too.'

'He said he was coming back, something about the shears. Really you he came to see, was it?' Francis was beginning to lose his good humour, but there was nothing she could do about that.

She sat in silence, at the corner of the table, allowing him to eat. It was the least she could do. Then she brought him his customary jug of ale and surreptitiously watched him as he ate and drank, taking pleasure in his pleasure. Without knowing it, she had taken to examining him; unkempt like his father after a day's work, light brown hair prematurely thinning, narrow beard, a man she would have said without pretension. But he was also a man who had fought for the King and was still at risk of his life for rescuing his sister. Francis, she thought in a roundabout way, was more than the sum of his parts. She knew what he was thinking...

'Pestering you, was he?'

'No….but he came to the door just as the Reverend was leaving. The Reverend was asking after Mary. Your mother said, 'Mary is at Cotehele' and Arthur was at the door. I think he heard.'

Francis was using what remained of his bread to mop up the juice from the meat. Sometimes, she thought, he is unwilling to face the truth.

'Are you sure?'

'Yes, he was next to me at the door. I told you before. He will put two and two together. You were away. Mary disappeared. The farm at Hampt was sequestrated. Francis, he knows! He could have you and Mary arrested, any time he wants!'

'Are you going to marry him?' Francis was apparently engaged in studying his now empty plate.

'If we are wed, he will have no cause to betray you or Mary. He will have what he wants.'

'And if you don't?'

'If I don't he will think, it might have something to do with you...you know, he is suspicious.

'If you are married, will you...'

She was beginning to find him tiresome. 'Francis, I think there is nothing will stop me now! If I make Arthur happy, you and Mary will be safe, and that is an end to it.'

He poured out the last of his ale and took a long draught. 'I do not wish you to marry him.'

'I have made up my mind. On Midsummer Day he will have my answer. I will not skivvy for you Francis, or your mother, for the rest of my life!'

'Is that so bad?'

Why was he being so pig-headed? 'What are you talking about? Either we will be wed or not. I think we must be Francis, if only to save your sister from Lanson prison. Have you thought of that? And I am supposed to be the one cannot abide her!'

'It is not black and white.'

'It is.'

'Would you...Janella, would you....' For the first time their eyes met. His voice was trembling, 'take Arthur rather than me?'

'There is no question...'

'If Mary was safe, if there were to be no arrests, no question of arrests?'

'I would take you.' She had risen and turned her back on him, so that the words were barely audible. She went to the window to look into the yard but there was nothing there. 'Then that is what we must do,' she heard him say. But that was not enough. It was mere convenience. He could not risk Mary's life. She waited, refusing to respond, and suddenly he was close to her.

'I think I need you, Janella..'

She could not remember the rest of it. In her chamber. In her bed. Alice who might hear them from across the landing. It was not at all what she had expected. Afterwards they lay awake far into the night, hardly able to believe that the curtain of doubt which had hung between them for so long had been torn to shreds. And long before the break of day, listening to the house martins in the eaves, boldly anticipating the dawn.

'Arthur,' she whispered. But he placed a finger to her lips.

'Mary will have to leave Cotehele,' he said without conviction and after a long silence. But the spell was already broken.

'Francis, there is nowhere else. Nowhere else would be safe. It would be better to pretend this never happened. I will not hold you to it...'

'I will not turn my back on you! I never thought.. How could I? You are...you are not to leave me now.' He held her fiercely. 'We will think of a way. Just tell him, when the time comes, tell him you cannot decide. We still have time to think.'

'Three weeks, and there is no telling what he might do, if I refuse him. Perhaps I should simply tell him the truth, persuade him he has nothing to gain. He is not an evil man. Perhaps I was mistaken. Perhaps he heard nothing...'

The sky had begun to lighten. Whatever the new day might bring it would, they both knew, contain more hope for the future than the last.

***

Coat and boots dusty from the dry lanes, the Reverend Clarke returned late to the Rectory. Clymestone was a great, sprawling parish and he had visited each and every one of those who shared the Faith and all of those whom he took to be his friends. He had taken care to warn them of the changes that were certain to come. They had not known it was his final leave-taking, but soon, for news or even rumour of a momentous kind always spreads quickly, the whole Parish would know.

There was a letter lying on the hall tiles which he guessed would be from Marten. In the dying light, he took it into the parlour and drew the curtains. The grate was bare and there was a chill in the air. Too tired to light a fire he lit a candle instead and brought it to the oak dining table. Marten's letter was brief and to the point. He too had received a letter from the County Sheriff confirming the success of his petition and of his appointment as Rector by ordinance of Parliament. He was to take up his duties from Sunday Morning Service the day after tomorrow. With reluctance he accepted the Reverend Clarke's request that he be allowed to retain possession of the Rectory until Monday morning. The letter was signed, 'Minister James Marten. Burraton.'

He was sorely tempted to burn the mealy-mouthed missive in the flame of his candle, but resisted the impulse. He might yet have recourse to it. Instead he picked up his own letter from the County Sheriff, timed no doubt to be received simultaneously with Marten's. The words were all too familiar to him. He was 'ejected' according to the 'ordinance of July 1644' addressed to all clergy found to be 'scandalous in their lives or ill-affected to the Parliament.' He was also warned in peremptory fashion that should he resist this ordinance, the County Committee had the authority to remove him forcibly from the Rectory and place him under arrest. He had one week's grace.

He set both letters aside. His own battered Bible, once much perused, lay on the table unopened but within his reach. It was not yet dark but increasingly chilly out of the sun. It did not occur to him to remove his coat and boots, still soiled from tramping the lanes. In front of him the polished oak surface of the table. A thin veil of dust but a fine piece of workmanship. He had not always appreciated such things. He opened the Bible at random. Once he had consulted it daily but in the face of his congregation he had chosen to communicate its message in his own way, through his own voice. He peered at the text as if for the first time, as if curious to know what it might now say.

But he was too tired. Besides, had he not once been able to recite the Gospels, almost word for word? Had he not, year after year, imparted their meaning in all good faith to the people of Clymestone? It had involved, he had to admit, a certain amount of concealment, a certain amount of hypocrisy. He had falsely sworn the Protestation Oath and promised to defend the 'true Reformed Protestant religion against all Popery.' That had been an outright lie. Yet had he not dissembled, he would have felt the hangman's noose a long time ago. If he had been honest he could not have given succour to all those who had remained true to the Catholic Faith. He could not have brought consolation to so many of his parishioners for so long. Was it cowardice? Was pretence, however well-intentioned, a sin?

In a different age, if the war had taken a different course, he would have been lauded. The King himself was tolerant of papists. Some say, like the Queen he is a papist himself. It could not conceivably be true that right and wrong were simply to be determined by those in power. There was a Higher Authority and it was only to that Authority he, Richard Clarke, had ever deferred.

But he had misjudged the course of events. Even with the coming of Fairfax, he had thought himself invulnerable. Even though he was perfectly aware that injustice had always flourished everywhere since the beginning of time, he had considered himself shielded, by the Will of God perhaps. But reason is nothing without Faith. The idea brought with it an overwhelming urge to confirm to himself the nature, the tools of that Faith. 'I am nothing,' he muttered aloud, 'if not what I have chosen to be.'

The parlour, a humble enough room, yet contained within it one other notable piece of furniture, an oak sideboard covering the whole of the inner wall. At head height were two doors opening to left and right and between them a narrow, blank panel of no obvious significance. The Reverend Clarke opened the door to the right and inside his fingers found the place. There was a click and the panel sprang open.

Here lay the sacraments, the secret articles of his Faith. He drew them out, one by one. A square of white linen which he opened out on the table, a silver crucifix, patens, a silver chalice, one of many agnus dei. 'Behold the Lamb of God,' he murmured, 'who takes away the sin of the world,' and homilies for distribution to the faithful. Finally a purple stole, richly decorated with images of the cross and which he solemnly draped around himself in the manner to which he had been accustomed.

He hesitated, caught up in admiration of the display, gleaming in the candlelight, and then nervously reached once more into the space between the doors to draw out a bottle of Communion wine, as yet unopened. He placed it on the white linen beside the chalice as if in confirmation of its authenticity and picked it up again and twisted out the cork. In a moment he had filled the chalice almost to the brim and the bottle was already half empty.

He sat down and picked up one of the patens. 'This is my body,' and then, taking care not to spill the wine, the chalice. 'This is the cup of my blood.' He took a long draught and began to examine at length the objects of his piety, sipping repeatedly from the silver chalice. 'Am I now become one with Jesus?' he muttered, a little incoherently, as he studied the crucifix which lay in his palm. 'One with Jesus? If I am a sinner...' He poured out what remained of the wine, 'then this is no more the blood of Christ than....' he sniggered involuntarily, 'than a pot of piss.'

But he continued to finger the objects of his faith as if he might somehow determine the truth from their very texture and the light from the candle gleamed knowingly on the smooth surface of the table around the square of white linen. He picked up the bottle but found it to be empty and the panel between the two doors, he noticed with some distress, was still open. He stood up to close it and the Holy Bible, opened at random, came unexpectedly into view. He placed his hands on either side to steady himself and brought his eyes closer to the words.

'Matthew: Chapter 28, Verse 20 - I am with you even unto the end of the world.'

He looked up to the ceiling to consider their significance and then made his way uncertainly across the room to close the panel. It could not be left ajar. He was the only one, after all, who knew of its existence.

The hallway was by far the largest single space in the Rectory, giving promise of a much grander building than the one which actually surrounded it. There was the heavy, studded door, the immaculate black and white diamond tiles and above all the fine oak staircase leading straight up alongside the panelled wall before turning abruptly right to the landing above.

'I have not always appreciated such things,' he mumbled privately to himself.

At the foot of the stairs he positioned himself for the ascent. There was some kind of carpet running up the middle which he had never before remarked upon. His foot slipped. It must be that he was not used to wearing his boots, not to ascend the stairs, and his coat and stole seemed forever to be getting in the way. He fell forward and decided to make use of his hands as well as his feet. That way he would be less likely to fall. At the last spindle before the stairs turned to the right, he paused to regain his breath. Looking down he could see the stool where he would sit to put on his boots, and the lower part of the door which opened into the lane.

The staircase, being steeper than usual, he felt a little nauseous and so took to examining the spindle at his side, a fine piece of craftsmanship, turned and twisted at its centre, elegant in its way yet, he noted with interest, firmly fixed at the base.

Chapter 21

As the Reverend Clarke had anticipated, rumours that he had finally been ejected by the County Committee, spread rapidly throughout the village. Late on Saturday morning he had woken from a deep slumber, still in his dusty coat, his boots soiling the counterpane. In recollection of his drunkenness and with a profound sense of revulsion, he had kicked off his boots, torn off his coat and flung them together into a corner.

His head ached. There had been a loud knocking on the door to the lane, which had probably woken him. He would not answer anyone today, but he must not forget to draw back the parlour curtains, otherwise they would think him unwell. Brushing back his hair with customary vigour, he remembered that in his inebriated state he had omitted to extinguish the candle. The hot wax would have dribbled onto the smooth, polished surface of the parlour table. Even now it offended his sense of propriety. He would have to clean the table, wash out the chalice, dispose of the empty bottle and return everything to its secret place in the sideboard.

Then he would spend the day alone, in contemplation. The Holy Bible still lay open on the table, inviting his attention. But instead, when the time came, he fell to thinking of how he had first come to Clymestone. The living, at that time in the gift of the Duke of Cornwall who was later to be King, had been much sought after. He still had the letter of his appointment and well remembered the words: 'The parsonage of Clymestone having lately fallen void and the Council of the Duchy having strongly commended you in respect of your learning and pains in our service...'

'My learning and pains,' he muttered, without drawing any conclusion. It was strange to think how his own fate had been so closely bound with that of the King.

And so it was that the day passed, not as he had intended in contemplation of the Gospels, but of all the years he had spent as Rector in Clymestone, by far the greatest portion of his life. Beset by reminiscence, he took a morsel of food or a cup of water only as it occurred to him, and resolutely ignored the occasional, intrusive knock at his door. When darkness came he went heavy-hearted to his bed, but was unable to rest. Only with the dawning of a new day did he close his eyes at last and lapse into a dreamless sleep.

*

At Burraton, Minister Marten had risen at first light and, despite the early morning mist, had hardly delayed before setting out on foot for the village. There had been little enough time to prepare since receiving the Sheriff's instruction but the plan for this, his first Sunday morning service in Clymestone, had long been forming in his mind. Painstakingly, Minister Marten had now transcribed every word of every prayer, every word of the sermon he was about to preach. It's theme, long nurtured and, in the Minister's view, the only possible one now that the war was over, the overwhelming need for reconciliation.

Having preached often enough in London, the experience would not be entirely unfamiliar to him. But he knew he would have to adjust. The congregation in Clymestone would be much less knowing than any in the capital. He would have, to a certain extent, to restrain his natural inclinations, not rail against the Church of Rome nor against the bishops, that they should lay aside their spirit of pride and envy. No, he would not harangue them, not confuse them with obscure matters of doctrine. From the Reverend Clarke, they had been used to nothing more than homely platitudes and superstitious nonsense. He must take care to wean them gently from their misconceptions, not crudely bludgeon them into the path of righteousness.

At first he would not be widely recognised. There would be some resentment. That was only natural. The Reverend Clarke had assiduously cultivated his more influential parishioners. There would be a period of transition. But in time they would come to appreciate his calm and principled demeanour and recognise his humility, his essential Godliness. He already had friends in the Parish. Christina Pellow, for one, had shown an immovable faith in him, even when all had seemed lost. And the successes of General Fairfax had done much to turn the common people, weary of war, in favour of the Parliament.

He halted in his tracks as the church came into view. The early mist had dispersed. The sun was rising in a clear blue sky. This was the moment he had been waiting for. He must grasp the opportunity with both hands. His message of reconciliation and forgiveness would fall on fertile ground. Even those who had suffered most would learn to forgive, all passions would be buried, all suspicions of injuries. 'We are all brethren,' he declaimed aloud as he passed through the south porch to open the great door to his new realm.

It was quiet as only an empty church can be, the early morning sunlight dappling the empty pews. Now that all civil strife had ceased, his message would be impossible to resist. Disdainfully, he turned away from the chancel, the graven images which so polluted this place of worship. In the fullness of time, he promised himself, they would be replaced. But he would be patient.

In the vestry, he refrained from tearing down from its hook, the Reverend Clarke's white surplice. Beneath it the huge parish chest containing countless records of births, deaths and marriages, minutes of vestry meetings, records of visitations. Would they all be in order, according to the Bishop's instructions? He doubted it. The Reverend Clarke was not that kind of man. He must remember to acquire the keys before Clarke was gone from the Rectory for good.

He became aware of the bellringers deep in conversation at the far end of the church. Soon the church would be full. He would rise to the occasion. Of that he had no doubt. Belying his natural humility, he felt his heart swell with pride. The bells began to ring.

It was those same bells for Sunday morning service which woke the Reverend Clarke from his short sleep. From where he lay he could see the topmost part of the church tower, detect almost the very movement of the bells in their chamber. He had never before lain in his bed and listened to the bells. Soon there began a bustling in the lane below his window. Incongruously, the sun was shining as they came in their twos and threes or in whole families to the south porch of the church, as they had always done.

Today there was an added sense of anticipation in the air. For Christina Pellow it was more a sense of justification than anticipation, a sense that her view of the world, the new order had at last come to prevail in Clymestone. Not since Lady Day had she entered Clymestone Church. She had kept her word. It was her moment too.

When the bells ceased, the congregation turned their eyes to the pulpit or, if they were close enough, to the small, whitewashed door of the vestry. Three hundred pairs of eyes watching for the white surplice, for the figure they hardly knew to cross in front of them and ascend to his proper place.

There was a lanky, beetle-browed man standing in the transept before the central aisle, tightly clutching a battered Bible and some papers. Even Christina, from her privileged position close to the pulpit, had not noticed him emerge from the vestry. Only slowly did she come to realise that Minister Marten already stood before them, spurning the pulpit, spurning even the cassock and surplice. As any other man attending Sunday service, he wore dark stockings, breeches and a full, sober, unfitted doublet. He looked steadfast, she thought, and not at all nervous despite the extraordinary position in which he had so boldly placed himself.

In a kind of panic, Christina looked around her. Hardly anyone had noticed and yet, bit by bit, one by one, the congregation were becoming aware, were ceasing there whispered chatter, were beginning to wonder what on earth they were about to witness.

The Reverend Clarke in black cassock, shiny, buckled shoes and with an elaborate crucifix about his neck, was pottering about the Rectory kitchen. As he had expected, a rope of the kind he required had been lying about in the bell chamber. There were always bits and pieces up there. Now it lay on the drab, unvarnished surface of the kitchen table. Perhaps it was too thick or not long enough? And the knot would be a struggle though he had seen it done at least once before, in Lanson prison.

The rope lay in an 'S' shape, the longer end trailing on the floor. He pulled it together at the centre and wrapped the shorter end round and round so that there was a kind of double loop. So far so good...

When the congregation had settled, Minister Marten introduced himself. His voice was much lower than the Reverend Clarke's, much calmer, so that that the church itself became calmer and quieter too as each and every one of them strained to listen. Minister Marten held up his little, battered Bible. It was the Word of God, he said and his purpose was no more no less than to bring the Word of God, unsullied by superstition or cant, into the hearts and minds of the people.

He had come among them for he was one of them, and would not take a higher place. The pulpit no longer had a purpose. On this, his first day as their Minister, he would read to them from the Book of Genesis. He would begin at Chapter 13, Verse 7. Whereupon Minister Marten opened his Bible and, holding it in one large, bony hand, began to read:

'And there was a strife between the herdmen of Abram's cattle and the herdmen of Lot's cattle. And the Canaanite and the Perizzite dwelt then in the land.

And Abram said unto Lot, Let there be no strife, I pray thee between me and thee, and between my herdmen and thy herdmen, for we be brethren.'

Still dumbfounded at the unexpected appearance of their new Minister and then further confounded by the flat, expressionless style of his delivery, the congregation were finding it difficult to attend to the words, though Christina did try. Robert, sitting at

Christina's side, was only anxious that the service should be a success for her sake. Liddy was too bemused to notice that Thomas was using the smallest of her kitchen knives to carve his initials into the side of the pew.

'Just as Abraham and Lot made peace so should we.' Minister Marten was making a serious point, if only they had been paying proper attention. 'In the Bible there is strife amongst herdmen with overlapping claims, just as there are pastors today that compete for each other's flocks...'

One of those competing pastors, the Reverend Clarke, had meanwhile found a way of slipping the longest section of the rope through the knot. Held up over the kitchen table, the noose closed neatly on itself. Apparently satisfied, the Reverend carried the rope into the hall and up the stairs as far as the spindle which had previously caught his eye, at the point where the stairs turned right towards the landing.

'The whole kingdom has been infected with the spirit of division. Nowhere hath it not breathed some malignant distemper.'

Without turning her head too obviously, Christina was attempting to gauge the reaction but saw only row upon row of expressionless faces. She had herself now begun to lose the Minister's drift. Minister Marten, she had to admit, was unconscionably slow in getting to the point.

'Abraham for peace because of the Canaanites and Perrizites that dwell in the land, and because they were brethren. Today there are Canaanites who scoff at all religion and Perrizites who make it their design to divide.....' To his profound satisfaction, Thomas had now completed a 'T'. 'T' for Thomas. 'Some on both sides are brethren truly Godly,' Minister Marten conceded, but without any noticeable change in intonation. 'Why then so bitter, one against the other?'

The more alert members of the congregation were beginning to appreciate Minister Marten's message but could not understand why they were being accused of bitterness towards one another. There had been war, true enough, but within the village had there not been unanimity rather than conflict? Had they not all loyally supported the King? There were some who had even sacrificed their lives. The Reverend Clarke had understood all that. The Reverend Clarke had been, at heart, one of them. But Minister Marten doggedly persisted in his theme:

'What means the gall and wormwood?' he asked, barely raising his voice.

The Reverend Clarke tied the rope tightly round the base of the spindle. Though a tough and wiry man, sitting on the stair and leaning awkwardly against the banister, he had become a little breathless. 'Not the same as walking,' he muttered. As everybody knew he could walk for miles. It was just this swivelling in his cassock and with his crucifix clattering against the spindles. He would have to rest, then take a pull on the rope from the hallway below, to make sure it was well secured.

'My brethren, my brethren, did our Lord Christ wash his Apostles' feet and amongst them a Judas' feet, and shall we throw dirt in one another's faces? Is this Christ like? Doth this become Christians?'

The stool was not as high as he would have liked. Everything had to be so precise. He could not risk failure. But there was no other piece of furniture more suitable, one which, alone, he could have manoeuvred into position. Recovered, he descended the stairs and picked up the stool. How often, he wondered vaguely, had he sat there in the hallway, pulling on his boots?

He placed the stool where the rope was dangling into empty space. Grasping one of the lower spindles for support, it was easy enough to climb up and determine the height of the noose. Too low, as he had half-expected. He would have to make adjustments.

'Did he pour out his precious blood to purchase our peace and shall we draw out one another's blood in breaking our peace?'

Minister Marten was warming to his theme, though for most the theme itself remained obscure. Christina had seemed to settle. Liddy had given up. Robert was slyly observing Thomas's less than successful attempt at a 'P'.

The Reverend Clarke had successfully adjusted the rope. He had had to untie it and then, having marked an imaginary spot, re-attach it to the base of the spindle. He could feel the sweat trickling down his back, moistening the sleeves of his cassock. He paused to draw breath and then once more descended to the hall. Mounted on the stool and holding on to the staircase with his left hand, he was able to pull down hard on the rope. As far as he could judge, this time everything was in order.

'Where there is brotherly strife all possible and speedy means must be used for reconciliation.'

As far as Robert could judge the sermon was nearing its conclusion and not before time. The congregation were becoming restive. Was Marten aware there was a point beyond which he could not go? He glanced at Christina. As the sermon had progressed and as the members of the congregation had increasingly begun to seek out other subjects of interest, a friendly neighbour, a pretty face, Christina had only become more and more wrapt in her attention, more and more oblivious of her surroundings.

For the Reverend Clarke, one last glance at the Bible, still lying seductively on the parlour table. With a certain inevitability, his eyes were drawn to the words he had read in his drunkenness. 'I am with you even unto the end of the world.' The Reverend Clarke shrugged and returned to the vast, cold expanse of the hallway. He looked round as if expecting someone else to be there and then climbed onto the stool. The knot he remembered should be behind the left ear, and so he shuffled round until he was facing a blank wall, his back to the Rectory door.

'Father, into your hands I commend my spirit,' he said, and kicked away the stool.'

'Are we brethren? Are we Godly?'

And thus it was that the Minister came to the end of his sermon, just as the Reverend Clarke came to the end of his life, only leaving in the minds of his audience a question, when they had been accustomed to a solution. The congregation, stunned as it were into submission, remained in their seats. The Minister's rambling discourse, delivered in a low monotone, had provided them with little warning as to its conclusion, let alone to the conclusion of the service itself. Perhaps they had thought the end would never come. At any rate, now they were caught unawares, and for a minute or two nobody moved.

The Minister had already disappeared into the vestry. He would not, they concluded, be waiting for them in the porch, to wish them well or enquire after their health. It was over. It was all over.

And so they began to sigh and cough and stretch and then made their way, shuffling past the tower screen, into the porch and out into the open air. And not a few of them were puzzled that now they knew so little of the Scripture, when once they had known so much. The Reverend Clarke had made it all so clear. Perhaps for all these years, he had been deceiving them.

Christina was of a mind to waylay the Minister in order to congratulate him after such an inspiring sermon but, for once, Robert would not have it. They were standing in the main aisle as the last of the congregation were leaving. Thomas and Liddy had already made good their escape. After such a sermon, Robert whispered loudly, the Minister was sure to be exhausted. She should wait, visit the Minister once he had moved into the Rectory. There she would be welcomed with open arms. Christina reluctantly concurred but, as they walked down the aisle, could not help looking back wistfully to the vestry door, hoping against hope that the Minister might yet appear.

In fact the Minister was elated rather than exhausted and might even have welcomed Christina's congratulation. But after such a triumph his thoughts were already turning towards his imminent occupation of the Rectory. He had already written to London and made arrangements for Lucy and his daughters to join him as soon as practicable. The overdue revival in Clymestone of the true Protestant Faith had begun, exactly as he had intended.

Beyond the confines of the vestry, the members of his congregation meanwhile were making their way home in a state of bewilderment, to their various parts of the Parish. One or two stopped at the Rectory, wondering perhaps if the Reverend was still there. A neighbour remarked that he had not set eyes on him for several days and was, on those meagre enough grounds, persuaded to knock. There was no answer. The curtains to the parlour window were drawn back. No need for concern. It was just curiosity. The Reverend not being in his usual place on a Sunday morning, where then was he?

It was not until Monday morning when Minister Marten, cognisant of the fact that he had not yet received from the Reverend, the keys to his new home, and determined there should be no further delay, decided in a state of some impatience, to make a call on the Constable.

The letter from the County Sheriff, together with Clarke's note, clearly indicated that he was now indisputably within his rights to take possession of the Rectory. The elderly Constable had therefore no alternative but to accompany Minister Marten to the Rectory where the heavy brass knocker was again brought down, but this time with somewhat greater purpose than previously.

Forcefully and repeatedly the Constable knocked, until the sound resounded down the lane, bringing curious faces to the cottage windows and disturbing curious children in their play. Again the Constable knocked. There was no answer. They peered through the parlour window. All they could see was a Bible lying open on the table. A reliable-looking boy was eventually deputed to climb over the gate at the back and try the door to the kitchen. No answer.

No doubt the Reverend, humiliated and depressed by his ejection, had simply disappeared, leaving Minister Marten to pick up the pieces. Neither door was of a kind to be easily broken down. The Constable, acutely aware of the Minister at his elbow, was compelled to make a decision. The window to the parlour would have to be broken and as, even then, it would be too small to admit a fully grown man, the same reliable-looking boy would have to be put through to unlock the door to the lane, and let them in.

There being no obvious alternative, the plan was put into operation amidst a gaggle of increasingly inquisitive onlookers. The Constable, all too anxious for the matter to be resolved, broke the window with his distaff and pushed the small boy through into the parlour.

Moments later they heard the grating of the bolts as they were withdrawn and the sharp click as the huge key turned in the lock. The door opened and Minister Marten strode purposefully into the hallway. It took him a moment to get used to the light. There had been no cause to expect anything untoward. The small boy, keen for a sixpence, had gone straight to the door to let them in, mercifully unaware of the Reverend Clarke's presence.

Now the gust of air from the opening wide of the great studded door had caused the Reverend's body to revolve slowly towards the staircase. His face was hardly visible and his feet had somehow disappeared beneath the cassock, so that the corpse appeared to float of its own accord above the tiles. Next to the overturned stool lay one well-polished, buckled shoe.

Minister Marten turned to face the Constable immediately on his heels, and showed by no more than the panic-stricken expression on his face that the door must be closed and the onlookers dispersed. Then in the stillness of the hallway, they stood together by the closed door, as far away from the gently swaying corpse as possible. Minister Marten, white-faced, his breath coming only in sudden starts, could barely bring himself to speak.

'Constable...the body...must be taken down. The window...sealed. Then I must have the key.'

'The body, Minister. what must I do with the body?'

'The body? A carpenter. A coffin, here..and then I must decide..the burial. Only, when the man is in his coffin, bring me the key.'

And with that the Minister fled to Burraton. Self-murder. The Sixth Commandment. 'Thou shalt not kill.' It was beyond belief that the Reverend Clarke should have committed such an act. Yet he alone would have to deal with the consequences, according to his own conscience and with the utmost haste. In a matter of days he would be joined by his dear wife and beloved daughters. By then the Reverend Clarke, even down to his memory, would have to be expunged, and the Rectory thoroughly cleansed from his awful presence.

Chapter 22

The Reverend Clarke's death brought about a great deal of speculation, in particular regarding the extent to which Minister Marten might have been involved. The people of Clymestone could not help but reflect that the Reverend had died almost exactly at the moment of his replacement by Minister Marten. Moreover, they had lost a much loved Rector and only gained one who spoke to them in a strange language of things they knew nothing about, one who harangued them to make peace, when peace was all they knew.

It was hard to believe that the Reverend Clarke had, as the Constable assured anyone who cared to ask, committed self-murder by hanging himself in his own Rectory, even as they prayed not a hundred yards away. Only two days before he had been amongst them, had been quite his usual self.

Perhaps the Constable was mistaken. Minister Marten had, after all, fled to Burraton and not taken up his place at the Rectory. Perhaps, in due course, the Minister would be chased out of Burraton altogether. Perhaps the Reverend Clarke was alive and well and at the next Sunday morning service would return to his proper place, in the pulpit.

Minister Marten was all too aware of his predicament. Despite his self-imposed isolation, he knew there would be rumours which would need to be scotched. Clarke would have to be buried. His peers would say, not in consecrated ground. He had broken the Sixth Commandment. But they did not have to deal with the consequences. If it became known that he had supervised the Reverend Clarke's interment in some shabby piece of land, set apart from the church, there might even be those in the village who would rise against him.

Once again he found himself admitting that the Reverend Clarke had been, though corrupt, a popular man. In the end he had lost his mind. It had been God's Will. Was it prudent that he should jeopardise his whole future, the whole community, for what was no more than superstition? What was 'consecrated ground'? A bishop had said a prayer, that was all.

On the other hand, Clarke must not be buried in too prominent a position. That could equally have the effect of undermining his ministry, the ministry he had coveted for so long. There would have to be some kind of compromise.

The constable brought the key to the Rectory as instructed, together with a bill from a local carpenter. The Reverend Clarke had been transferred to his coffin which now, according to the Constable, lay on the parlour table awaiting removal. Unbidden, a woman from the village had washed the body and clothed it in a white shroud. A simple cross, together with the Reverend's Bible, had been placed with him in the coffin.

Minister Marten, having determined a course of action, asked the constable to return at his convenience, bringing with him the only churchwarden with whom he had had some, though fleeting, contact. The Reverend Clarke, he explained, would have to be removed from the Rectory and interred with all possible expedition.

*

At Venterdon, Janella and Francis, basking in their new found intimacy, were both shocked and saddened by the Reverend Clarke's self-murder. Neither of them doubted the circumstances. The Reverend had been living a lie for too long. The strain had been apparent to Francis when he had spoken to him in the vestry. And Janella recalled how, only two days earlier when he had brought Samuel's will, there had been a sense of his carrying out some final duty. Time was of the essence, he had said. The knowledge that he had been ejected and replaced by Minister Marten would have been the final straw. His calling had been his life.

'Janella, I think my mother must not be told, not yet. It would only confuse her, and so soon after his visit. It makes me wonder how the will could have been proved in Exeter, just at this time, and how......you know...how my father...'

'I think the Reverend knew just what he was doing, Francis. The will was on her bed this morning, just where I would have noticed it, still unopened. Perhaps she wants you to read it to her.'

'She was always asking for the will, but why? My father, somehow or other, will have left everything to her. The Reverend would hardly have falsified my father's wishes...I think they were friends, of a kind. She can read well enough, but I will ask her.'

He came home early, leaving Arthur alone in the North Field. He needed to make repairs to the barn, he said, knowing Arthur would not believe him. Alice was sitting at her window. The will lay unopened on the bed.

'Do you want me to read it to you, mother?' Alice nodded, but continued to look out into the yard. 'John and Robert?'

'Janella,' Alice said. 'Janella is my friend.'

Janella, not feeling it to be her place, came reluctantly and sat on the bed near the door. Francis sat with his mother at her little table and then broke the seal and unrolled the parchment.

'Every word,' Alice insisted tremulously and still looking away. 'Do not spare me.'

Francis glanced over the parchment. It had every appearance of being genuine. He need not have been concerned. At the bottom, Samuel's scrawled signature witnessed by four well-known and reliable men from Clymestone. It would have been easy enough for the Reverend to persuade them.

'In the name of God, Amen,' he began, slowly and gently for his mother's sake. 'The thirteenth day of July in the Reign of our Sovereign Lord, Charles, by the Grace of God of England, Scotland, France and Ireland, King and Defender of the Faith.' Alice seemed not to be listening. 'And in the year of our Lord God one thousand six hundred and forty-five, I Samuel Pellow...' Alice began to shiver, prompting Janella to rise from the bed and take her hand. '...of the Parish of Clymestone, having my right mind and perfect understanding through the goodness of God, commend my soul and commit my body to the Christian burial.'

Francis paused but Alice he could see, was impatient '...I give two shillings to the reparation of the Parish Church of Clymestone and one shilling to the poor people of the said Parish. I give and bequeath unto my son Robert's child twelve pence and unto my son John's children twelve pence apiece.

My will is also that my executrix shall deliver unto Mary Hawking, from time to time, such portion of goods as she shall think fit for her maintenance hereafter.'

For the first time Alice was looking at her son as he read the will, her brow knitted in concentration.

'Mary, your daughter Mary,' Janella whispered, to engage her attention.

'It is almost finished mother......'All the residue of my goods and chattels I give and bequeath to Alice, my dear wife whom I appoint whole and sole executrix of this my last will and testament.'

'Mary,' Alice said, her hands fluttering over the will which now lay between them on the table. 'Mary,' she repeated, and picked up the will, begging him to read again.

Francis read again the part concerning his sister, Mary Hawking. 'Father wanted you to look after Mary,' he explained, apparently convinced his mother had lost the capacity to understand plain English.

'Mary is at Cotehele. The ferryman took her there...'

'No, mother. I took her with John, to make sure she was safe.'

'John, John and Robert, but not you Francis.' Alice smiled thinly. 'You were not even born.'

Janella began to understand. Francis, she could tell, had no idea. 'Alice, how old was Mary, when the ferryman took her? How old was she? Can you remember?'

'Four. Mary was only four. Samuel said the ferryman found her. She was...Samuel said, she was drowned.'

'And then,' Janella held both her hands, insisting on all of her attention. 'And then later, another Mary, another Mary was born.'

'Not the same....'

'What was the first Mary like, Alice?' Instinctively Janella seemed to know that what had been suppressed for so long must be allowed to come to the surface. Francis was only staring at them like an outsider, listening to a conversation he knew nothing about, between strangers he had never met.

"Mary was different,' Alice replied brightly. 'The cuckoo in the nest, they said. Dark, dark skin, dark hair, dark eyes. Everybody loved her. Everybody in Clymestone loved her. The Reverend Parker said she was blessed and...always in the summer. It was always summer then...Samuel's favourite too.' She turned to her son, with a superior look. 'Before you were even born, Francis. You should have seen her, Janella, always in the summer...'

'And then another Mary.'

'Samuel said it was Mary reborn,' Alice pouted, 'just to please me, I suppose.....but she was not the same.'

'But now, Alice,' Janella persisted. 'Now Samuel, in his will, has asked you to care for her. She is alive and well.'

'And will soon be home,' Francis interrupted.' I will bring her home.'

'She took to walking along the river. People said. I thought she was looking for....'

'No,' said Janella firmly, dragging Alice back to reality. 'She was waiting for George to come home after the war. George Hawking. But George never came back. So Mary has nowhere to go now, except here to Venterdon. Francis will bring her home soon, when the war is well and truly over and everything is safe.'

Alice was struggling hard to remember this second daughter who, just like the first, had failed to come home and was now safe at Cotehele. 'What did Samuel say about Mary? Tell me again, Francis.' Alice seemed to be growing more lucid.

'You are to deliver to her...'such portion of goods as you shall think fit for her maintenance hereafter.' He says you are.' Francis ostentatiously searched for the words, 'Alice, my dear wife' and 'sole executrix.'

Alice clenched her little fist on the table. 'I heard the soldiers, tramp, tramp, the jingle of the horses...gone. I waited all day, all day long. Francis went to the church to look. I waited. 'Woman', he said. He pushed me away. I think I wanted him dead then, and that is the truth...They found him under a hedge and brought him back in a cart.'

The late afternoon sun had broken up the yard into incoherent patterns of light and shade. In Alice's chamber, their own shadows lay still on the wall.

'If I had gone to look for him, he might have been saved. he might have spoken to me. But I waited and waited. I did not care enough.' Alice's thin, shrill voice faltered and caught in her throat. 'Perhaps I blamed him still.'

'You looked after him.'

'I bathed his face and lay with him till morning. Remember, Janella? Remember what we did?'

'You stayed with him.'

'The Reverend Clarke said, 'He has made his wishes known.'

'And here they are, mother.' Francis was at a loss.

'I will carry out his wishes,' Alice said, dry-eyed, knowing, unable to weep.

'Come down. We will eat together,' Janella proposed boldly. 'You and Francis must decide how best to fulfil his wishes. There is nothing more to be done now.'

'I will go to bed now, Janella. Bring me some warm milk and then I will sleep.'

'I will stay,' Francis began, but his mother looked as if she did not care whether he stayed or not and Janella shook her head, faintly so that Alice would not see.

When the sun faded they left her alone to sleep. By the fireside, as if they were already man and wife, they sat opposite one another, overcome with exhaustion.

'Francis did not know what to think of his mother. 'Mary always said she was cast out. Now we know why. Unloved from the moment she was born, and mother could only think of that other Mary, who was drowned...and Robert, John, they all knew! And nobody said a word. All of this so long ago, before I was born, before Mary was born, before even the Reverend Clarke...'

'She told me once about the ferryman. It didn't make sense.'
'But why the secrecy? And for so long?'
'Some things are just too painful, Francis.' Janella tried not to show how much more she understood. 'Everybody just protects everybody else.'

'But in the end, it drove Mary out of the house, to marry a papist twice her age and now this other man...Janella, I tried to bring her home, but she would never come.'

'At least she is safe at Cotehele.'

But Francis was following his own train of thought. 'And to think of my father, in his dying breath...he was thinking of Mary...or do you think that was Clarke's doing? Papists together.

'I think the reason is of no account,' Janella said gently. 'It is done.'

'When all this is over, I will bring her home.'

'But not yet. It is too soon. And Arthur might do anything.'

They listened to the crackling of the fire and Francis saw how much he depended on her.

'I will write to my brothers. They will have to know about the will,'

'And then, ' Janella hesitated, 'will you come to me?'

'Without you, Janella,' He took her up from her chair and into his arms. 'I would be a poor excuse for a man.'

***

Minister Marten had been busy. Both the Constable and the churchwarden, a young man unusually sympathetic to the new order, had shown an unexpected understanding of his predicament. He had explained his wishes succinctly. The coffin containing the Reverend Clarke was to be removed to the church after dark, when it was less likely to be noticed. The grave was to be dug without attracting undue attention. Here the Minister sought the advice of the young churchwarden.

The Reverend Clarke, Minister Marten began uncomfortably, had committed a mortal sin, but were he to be buried in unconsecrated ground...The churchwarden understood perfectly. He would himself instruct the gravediggers. There were two in particular who could be relied upon, and there was a plot on the north eastern periphery of the churchyard which would be, sufficiently ambiguous.

Much relieved, the Minister went on to explain that the interment would be most conveniently conducted at break of day, before the village came thoroughly to life. The young churchwarden sagely concurred. The matter would thereby be concluded before the facts of the case could be disputed. All concerned, the Minister assured them, would be well rewarded for their pains.

The churchwarden departed, eager to carry out the Minister's instructions. His efficiency, his alacrity would be appreciated. It would, he thought, stand him in good stead.

For his part, the Minister felt that he had taken all necessary steps, given the circumstances. Once the interment was concluded, he would be able to turn his attention to the Rectory. But haunted still by the image of his predecessor, the minister slept only fitfully. Long before sunrise he began to prepare for his walk into Clymestone.

It was misty in the lanes, just as it had been when he had set out to preach his message of reconciliation. Where the lanes dipped between the high hedgerows, it was still dark, the only sound that of his boots stumbling in the ruts. Like Christina Pellow, in the lanes he felt himself lost in an alien land. When he entered the church, the sun had still not risen over the rim of the moor.

The pale wooden coffin lay across a pair of trestles at the very spot from which he had preached so successfully. In the half-light he stood for a moment by the coffin, mesmerised by the swirling pattern of the elm. The Reverend Clarke lay directly between himself and the altar, still obstinately usurping his place. He tried without success to make sense of the symbolism.

Outside, the helpful churchwarden, together with the Constable, was already waiting beside a heap of newly dug earth and an open grave. They stood at the furthest extent of the churchyard, where a ragged hedge of hawthorn marked, in a haphazard way, its northern boundary. From a side-door to the nave, two men brought out the coffin and laid it without ceremony in the long, wet grass at their feet. The light, new wood was already soiled. As they attached the ropes the sun rose over the moor, chief witness of the dubious act they were about to perform.

Minister Marten nodded to the churchwarden and then watched as the four men manoeuvred, then lifted the coffin, tipping awkwardly over the empty grave. There were strained gasps and inarticulate instructions from one to another. The Minister had a sudden vision of the Reverend Clarke, spilled on the grass in his white, woollen shroud, refusing to be buried, before the frail, wooden box was finally lowered into the pit. The gravediggers pulled up the ropes and Minister Marten stepped forward, clutching his Bible, a symbol of his office if nothing else.

They listened, heads bowed, as he intoned the familiar words of the Lord's Prayer '.....for thine is the kingdom, the power and the glory, for ever and ever. Amen.'

The gravediggers were paid. (The Constable and the churchwarden had already been handsomely rewarded). The Minister repeated his wish that it be generally known, throughout the Parish, that the Reverend Clarke, despite having committed a mortal sin, had been buried with proper Christian ceremony. The grave was to be filled and in the fullness of time he would arrange for a suitable headstone to be erected. The gravediggers were left to complete their work, the churchwarden was especially thanked for his invaluable assistance. And then the Constable was taken to one side.

'The Rectory. Do you have the key, Constable?' The Constable nodded. 'You understand, I must take up residence as soon as possible.'

The parlour window had been repaired. The glazier, he was reminded apologetically, would need to be reimbursed for his trouble. Inside, the hallway gave no indication of its earlier, gruesome occupant, except perhaps in the imaginations of both men as they looked along the row of climbing spindles, half-expecting the Reverend Clarke's corpse to swing into view.

In the parlour, the Reverend's two silver-backed hairbrushes lay together on a shelf. The table and sideboard had been cleaned and polished. Minister Marten opened the doors to the sideboard. Apart from some ancient crockery, it was empty.

'I will retain the furniture, of course,' the Minister muttered. 'Nothing else.'

The Constable eyed the two brushes with renewed interest. 'The Overseer will see to the remainder, Minister.'

In the kitchen, there were utensils of various kinds, for which neither the Minister nor Lucy, his wife would have any need.

'The Overseer.....'

'Yes, the poor, the needy,' Marten agreed, with some impatience, 'everything apart from the furniture. Everything must be taken away.'

Upstairs they found clothing and bedding in an old chest. The Minister could not bring himself to investigate.

'Is there a will, Minister?'

'A will...No. But tell me if you find one...And a carter.' The Constable did not always find it easy to follow the Minister's train of thought. 'Tomorrow my wife will be in Lanson. By tomorrow everything must be moved. A carter, at Burraton. Can you see to it?' The Minister was acutely aware he knew no-one. There was nowhere for him to turn except to these officials, these local worthies, churchwardens, overseers, carpenters...'

'Minister, you will need a mason.'

'A mason?'

'For the stone. For the grave.'

'It will have to wait, Constable. Of course I will attend to it myself, when the time comes.'

Again the Minister was forced to leave the key with the Constable, and then return to Burraton to consider which of his meagre possessions would have to be transported to the Rectory. And then to the most difficult task of all, the preparation of a sermon, not one word of which had begun to form in his mind.

Chapter 23

Minister Marten's second Sunday morning service in Clymestone passed without incident. The congregation were subdued but curious to know how the Minister would explain the death of his predecessor, and in his roundabout way he gave them satisfaction. He was respectful. The Reverend Clarke, he said, had served them well, but he would not hide the fact that the Reverend had committed a grievous sin. In taking his own life he had clearly broken the Sixth Commandment, 'Thou shalt not kill.' The Reverend Clarke, though he had striven to conceal the truth from his loyal parishioners, had for long been sick in his mind. Nevertheless, his body had been interred with due Christian ceremony. As for the fate of his soul, that lay not within his power, but rather in the hands of the Lord.

Christina was relieved. Robert could sense the tension falling away from her and therefore was also relieved. The new Minister's survival, like Fairfax's military triumphs or his own uncertain advancement meant so much to her. More and more now she seemed to care, when she cared at all, for things which meant nothing to him.

By way of contrast, Liddy and even Thomas were a little disappointed and would have preferred some kind of reaction, but it was not to be. And Thomas did not even have the compensation afforded by Liddy's kitchen knife, having been thoroughly searched before leaving home.

Neither was there criticism of the way in which the Reverend Clarke's interment had been quietly taken in hand by the Minister. If anything the Minister had, in this respect, been rather admired for his diligence. Those old enough to have known the Reverend Clarke through all the trials and tribulations of their lives, truly lamented his passing. But it was only those few who had clung stubbornly to the old Faith who now, without the Reverend Clarke, faced the future with fear and trepidation. Who would protect them now? With whom would they celebrate Holy Communion? To whom would they confess their sins? How would they ever become one with Jesus?

In his sermon, Minister Marten made no reference to Midsummer Day, now almost upon them. Under Parliamentary rule, such ancient, pagan festivals were no longer recognised, no bonfires on the hills, no propitiation of the sun, now in imminent decline, no marking of the longest day and the shortest shadows at noon. That was all gone. Before the war there had been flowers in the church. The 'Feast of St John the Baptist', the Reverend Clarke had told them and they had believed him.

Now, in this particular year, it was simply the day on which the Royalist capital of Oxford finally surrendered to General Fairfax, and closer to home, in Clymestone, the day Janella Golding would give her answer, once and for all, to Arthur Doidge.

*

Lying beneath the eaves with Janella in his arms, Francis could easily have willed the problem of Arthur out of existence. But Janella would not allow that and so they would whisper together and consider what they should do from every viewpoint, as if in so doing they were bound to reach a rational conclusion.

Perhaps Arthur had not overheard at all. Perhaps Janella should just say nothing. Perhaps she should simply refuse him. But then should she say why? Would Arthur be shameless enough to have Mary, even Francis, arrested? Perhaps Janella should accept him after all. Or should Mary be warned? But where then would they take her? It was all too much for Francis. By the morning of the longest day, they had still come to no conclusion.

When he awoke in Janella's bed, it was already light and Janella had gone down to the kitchen. It had been raining during the night. He heard Arthur's boots, heavy and wet, in the yard and leapt to his feet. At least Janella would say nothing in his presence. He dressed quickly, closed the door softly behind him and tiptoed down the stairs.

Arthur had already made himself comfortable at the table, eating and drinking in his usual slovenly fashion. The fire was lit and Janella was busying herself in the scullery. Arthur gave him a cursory nod as was his habit. Janella could have said nothing.

'Corn is in ear,' Arthur said, wiping his lips with the back of his hand. 'There's the traps to be laid.' Francis nodded. Arthur was not usually so forthcoming. 'You'll be seein' to the sand we brought up to Old Clims, I suppose?'

They had brought up pots of sea-sand from Calstock to dress the fields before the next ploughing. Arthur was planning, thinking ahead, getting things in order. Attend to the present crop and think about the next. Without Arthur, Francis was once more reminded, they would hardly get from one year to the next. If he went to spread the sand, that would put them at opposite ends of the farm, also no doubt part of Arthur's intention. Perhaps Janella had already told him to expect her.

'I'll do the spreading,' he said. 'You're better with the traps.'

Arthur nodded and then left, without another word. Francis, he knew, was hardly likely to disagree. Janella had a pail in her hand at the door to the buttery, transparently avoiding him.

'What did you say?'

'Just that I'd see him later.' Janella made a move towards the yard, but Francis stopped her. 'I'm going to tell him the truth, Francis, rely on his better nature. He'll find out soon enough...unless you want me to marry him?'

'If he...if he threatens...' Francis began weakly. 'Mary...'

'Francis, if Arthur knows anything, he wouldn't even know who to tell. General Fairfax? Minister Marten? The County Committee? And why, why should he betray you? He has nothing to gain, everything to lose.'

'Just for his own satisfaction, I suppose,' he said, pecking her on the cheek to mollify her.

Janella had nothing more to say and so left him, pulling at his beard by the buttery door. There was nothing for it but to pick up his shovel from the lynhay and head for the most distant part of the farm, to Old Clims where they had dumped the sand.

Janella watched him go from the barn and heaved a sigh of relief. Francis would not have understood, but she had to think of Arthur now and what she was going to tell him. Arthur had pursued her for so long. He did not deserve it to end like this. She remembered how she had wanted the roof mending, to stop the rain dribbling down her bedroom wall. How Arthur, with a twinkle in his eye, had said she would have to take him up, show him where everything was. She could not help smiling to herself. Arthur had wanted more than she was prepared to give, at least without a ring on her finger.

And then she remembered how the winter had seemed endless, all the winters. The hunger, the vagrants at the door, Alice out of her mind and Francis ignoring her, neglecting the farm, writing about the war as if that made any difference. And all that time, Arthur had held a candle for her. He was not a bad man, had never abused her. He was the kind of man who said little and understood a lot. He might even have married her. But now all that was changed.

Now she would milk the one remaining cow, should the animal prove willing, which was by no means certain, scrub the floors and wash the spare bedding. It would dry quickly on the hedge at the back of the yard. And then Arthur would be expecting her. It was something she could not avoid.

At midday the sun shone high and bright and Janella took a napkin of fresh bread and cheese and a flagon of ale out to the North Field, where she knew she would find Arthur, laying his traps. She saw him as she opened the gate in the low wall, his wide-brimmed hat steadily descending the slope.

'Wouldn't want to get caught in one of those,' she said, a little breathless as she came up to him. Not that Arthur was one to banter. 'Brought you some ale and a bit more cheese.'

If Arthur could guess from her manner what she was going to say, he gave no indication. But he dropped the trap he was carrying and settled himself on a broken part of the wall, to receive the flagon of ale. The field of corn was on a rise, looking down over the hedgerows, and offered no shade from the midday sun.. The cheese would do later.

'It's Midsummer. I promised I'd give you my answer.' Arthur sat with his head tipped back, swigging from the flagon, the ale trickling down his beard. His wide-brimmed hat crumpled against the wall.

'Corn is in ear,' he said, putting down the flagon and staring out across the field, 'Earlier than usual.'

'I can't marry you, Arthur.' Arthur took another swig from the flagon. 'It's Francis.' Arthur's face did not betray the slightest emotion. He knows, she thought. He has known all along. 'I'm sorry.' Arthur put the empty flagon aside and picked up the trap. 'What will you do?'

'I still have my mother to feed.' Arthur thought for a moment.' I will stay out of your way.'

He was already walking away but she stumbled after him, on the margin of the corn. 'Alice.' Janella was flustered, breathless. 'Alice asked me. Perhaps you know where her daughter is, where Mary is? They took her farm...'

Arthur did not look back. 'How should I know? None of my business.'

Janella wandered back, none the wiser. She felt sorry for him. She might have given him the rest of her life, children. It seemed as if he had known all along. And if he had known, she reasoned to herself, and had not betrayed Mary, then why should he now? And by the time she reached the farm and the yard, the future had altogether taken on a much brighter aspect. Perhaps, was it too much to hope, all would be well.

As the sun sank over the moor and the sky began to darken, when all the sand had been spread at Old Clims and all the traps had been laid in the North Field, Francis and Janella sat outside in the yard, to catch the last warmth of the sun.

Arthur, for his part, had had enough of the sun for one day and was making his way to the 'Packhorse Inn' at Horsebridge. It was closer than the 'Half Moon' in Clymestone and a welcome sanctuary after a long day in the fields. Arthur, though not a sociable man, knew the place well.

He sat alone by the door, a pipe in his mouth, a large mug of beer before him on the table. The sun still lay shimmering on the stone flags, behind him smoke rising from innumerable pipes, a sense of contentment, men who knew one another. Men who knew what they were about. From time to time he went out to look across the river, towards the setting sun. Now and again a man would cross the bridge, this way or that, according to the rhythm of his life, the need to be home or out at the 'Packhorse', as the case might be. Now a large, paunchy man in a green doublet and greasy, shapeless hat.

'John.'

'Arthur.'

'Drink?'

'Don' min' if I do, Arthur.'

John Wright preferred to sit inside by one of the high arched windows, last vestige of the nunnery, now devoted to more earthly pleasures.

'A'ead of ourselves with the corn,' Arthur remarked, after allowing his companion to take a long draught.

'That's good, Arthur. That's good,' Wright replied ambiguously.

'Hawking's place'll be sold. What'll you do then, John?'

'Perhaps I'll buy it.' Wright laughed, in a serious sort of way. 'You never know, Arthur. You never know.'

'An' what's become of that Mary? Off 'er 'ead, I 'eard.'

'Disappeared, Arthur, into thin air.' Wright looked quizzical. 'But you're not askin' for the good of your 'ealth. What's brought all this on?'

Arthur looked round, as if to ensure they were not being overheard, then leaned forward. 'Word 'as it, John, that you're in with that Committee, what's in charge o' things, nowadays.'

'Don' deny it Arthur. I'm a man they can trust, see, man of my word.'

'Those Hawkings,' Arthur could not refrain from appearing surreptitious. 'Committee still after 'em?'

'Arthur, you are leadin' somewhere as I'm not sure I've a min' to follow.... but on the other hand, it is no secret. George Hawking, they say, is in France, with that papist Queen. Papist 'imself, by all accounts. Strange thing is there was two 'orses taken, not that either of 'em was much good, and Hawking's clothes was in that cottage. So you see, she was with a man, but it wasn't George Hawking.'

'Question is, John...question I'm askin'...are they sought, Mary Hawking and this man?'

'Yes, Arthur. I can safely say, they are sought. But wherever they are and whoever the man is, I have no idea.'

Arthur rose from the table to secure another drink. John Wright, being curious to know what Arthur Doidge had on his mind, expressed himself not averse to one more.

'She's a Pellow,' Arthur said bluntly, returning the mugs to the table.

'An' you work for 'em.'

'Funny lot.' Arthur took a long draught. 'That Francis don' know 'is arse from 'is elbow, an' Alice, mad as a 'atter.' Wright said nothing. Arthur would come to his point, all in good time. 'Funny family,' Arthur continued, looking into his beer. 'Don' even know where one another is.'

'But perhaps they know where Mary is. Is that what you're 'ere to tell me, Arthur? You know where Mary Hawking might be?'

'I might.'

'That is privileged information, Arthur. That Robert was askin' me only the other day.'

'She's a tartar.'

'Christina? Oh yes, a tartar alright. 'as 'im where she wants 'im, if you ask me. Under 'er thumb. Uncle on the Committee min'. Would pay I think, for the knowledge you 'ave, Arthur.'

'Pay me or you, John?'

Wright looked at the window. Night had well and truly fallen. There was nothing to see. 'Bit o' both, I reckon. If I let it be known, that there is one,' Wright's speech had slowed, 'as can furnish certain information, but that should 'e come forward, that would be more'n 'is life were worth...'

'She's at Cotehele.'

'An' the man she's with?'

'More'n likely. Can't be sure. I 'eard the old woman tellin' Reverend Clarke. There can be no mistake, an' Francis more'n likely was the one that took 'er.'

Wright received the information casually, as if these were matters he was quite used to dealing with. 'Robert Pellow will want to know, if not the Committee itself. Look,' He could see Arthur was already losing his resolve. 'I will make it clear,' He placed one large hand on Arthur's shoulder. 'I will make it clear there is a certain person that will not be named...but that he expects to be rewarded. I will say nothing, Arthur, before I 'ave some money for it. You can be assured o' that.'

'Janella...'

'Ah, that you was sweet on? Don' do to be sweet on 'em, Arthur. This is what they do to you. They Pellows 'as 'ad it comin' for a long time. Don' you fret. I'll get Ned to take a message. That Robert'd spill 'is own sister, for next to nothin'.'

'Nothin' to do with me, John.' Arthur got up to leave, already regretting what moments before had seemed nothing more than natural justice.

'Except for what I can get you, eh Arthur?' Wright called out cheerily, as his companion made hurriedly for the door.

***

At Pendennis, the nightly bonfire was not in celebration of Midsummer, but rather to guide the relief ships, which never came. Already, in early June, they had watched helplessly as a ship carrying ammunition, provisions and letters, had been intercepted and captured by Batten's Parliamentary fleet.

Later in the month, a message intended for the Prince of Wales was successfully smuggled out. If the Castle were not relieved, it stated, surrender was inevitable within three weeks. The garrison was 'reduced to the last extremity.' They were never to know that when the letter reached Jersey on 13th July, the Prince had already left to join his mother in Paris. By then soldiers were said to be 'running out' daily. The Governor, Sir John Arundell, gave instructions that did not bode well:

'General Buckly and Major Brittayne are hereby desired and appointed to view all the horses within this Garrison, and that they take particular notice of all such horses as are fit to be killed for beefe, for provisions for this Garrison, and that they give an account of their doings herein..etc.'

But horseflesh alone, as the Governor well understood, could bring no permanent solution. Another shallop did miraculously manage to break the siege but the paltry provisions it brought did little to alleviate the hunger. In desperation, a last throw of the dice, the governor ordered a sally, out of Pendennis by boat, in search of provisions onshore. The attempt, which resulted in a number of deaths, was always doomed to fail.

Throughout July surrender was anticipated daily. All of the West Country had long since submitted. The King himself was in the hands of a Presbyterian Scottish army. And the stench of fear and disease from the Tower Gunroom, where women and children, wounded and dying, were crammed together for safety, had already become intolerable.

It was then, at the end of the month, that the first signs began to appear. Plague....

Chapter 24

Christina was still in bed. The note which Liddy had found under the door now lay on the parlour table. It was ill-written and the paper looked as if it had been torn from the back of a newsbook. But its message was clear. John Wright had some information and this morning could be found at Mary's old cottage at Hampt. Robert debated with himself whether or not to wake Christina. On balance, he decided it would be better for her to be told once he had secured the information from Wright, if it existed. Otherwise she might simply become impatient or worse, disinterested.

He told Liddy he was going out. By the time he returned, Christina would be up and about and ready to face the day. Or perhaps not. Apart from attending Minister Marten's services, she had hardly left the house, on some days not even their chamber. And now that Minister Marten was safely ensconced in the Rectory, with all his family around him, she no longer felt the need to seek his advice. In Christina's mind, he would only irritate her. Though satisfied that the Minister should have achieved his rightful place, Christina knew he could bring her no personal solace. And what else was there to take her out of Whiteford? The ways of Clymestone people were not her ways, and inevitably the longer she shunned the narrow lanes and high hedgerows, the more she held them in abhorrence. And at home she no longer read the Gospels nor derived comfort from her first husband's sermons.

Whenever pressed by Robert, at a loss to understand her, she would only say, 'You do not know it Robert, but we are sunk in the abyss. Only an act of free Grace from God..,' and then she would knit her brows and shake her head, puzzled beyond endurance at God's silent intransigence. and where once they had spoken freely now, he could tell, she distrusted him and no longer gave herself to him, willingly, in that delicious way she once had.

Even Thomas no longer sought his mother's attention, but turned to Liddy for all his needs, all his small, childish pleasures. His father was just as distant, would not take him out with the dogs as he had promised, so consumed was he with Christina's mounting despair.

Mary's farmhouse was locked up and the farm, nominally managed by John Wright, had an air of abandonment. He rode slowly down the hill until the cottage came into view and then tethered his horse, as he had before. The door was ajar and Wright was sitting in Mary's upholstered chair, boots splayed on the rush matting where once Hampton had lain to cut out the dark, poisoned flesh, and where Mary had tended him.

The room, the hearth, the shelves, everything was bare. He glanced over his shoulder. No grey jerkin either, or red doublet hanging prophetically at the door. Wright had a faintly amused, insolent look. Robert chose to remain standing.

'Well?'

'Your sister, Mary. It 'as come to my attention....'

'You know where she is?'

'It is a delicate matter.' Robert placed two shillings on the mantelpiece. He had come prepared.

'The person who 'as informed me, takes a risk.'

Robert placed two more shillings on the mantelpiece. 'That is all I have,' he said, between gritted teeth. 'If you refuse to tell me, I will break...'

Wright went to the mantelpiece to ensure the money was within his grasp. 'She is at Cotehele.'

'Cotehele? How do you know?'

'My informant.'

'And the man, Hampton, or whoever it is?'

'More'n likely.'

'If you are mistaken,' He took him by the grubby kerchief at his neck. 'be sure, I will come back for my money.'

He rode back to Whiteford, furious at having paid four shillings they could ill-afford to such a miserable specimen of humanity as John Wright, but equally, elated at the thought of bringing Christina the news of Mary's whereabouts. He had almost forgotten that Mary was his sister or that, not very long ago, he had saved her from certain arrest.

He found Liddy scrubbing the flags in the kitchen, with Thomas assigned to a mop and bucket and trailing in her wake. Liddy sat back on her heels and indicated, with a raising of eyebrows and a slight movement of her head, that Christina had not yet risen.

He left them and hurried up the stairs to their chamber. The curtains were still drawn round the bed and at the window. He could tell she was awake even before he pulled back the curtains, but not that she would be sitting up, impatient for his return. Her shift was unbuttoned, her cap discarded, and judging from her exasperated expression, she was in no mood to be placated.

'I heard you go,' she said, accusingly. 'And come back.'

'I went to Hampt.' He sat down at the end of the bed.' There was a message from Wright.' Christina expressed no opinion. 'He told me where Mary...and most likely her lover, are in hiding. You wanted me to find out, remember?'

'Well?'

'She is at Cotehele.'

'And the man, Hampton?'

'It is likely.'

Christina seemed to consider. 'I want to leave here, remember? You said we could leave. Is that another promise you intend to fulfil?' Her voice had become unnaturally deep, guttural, dragged out of her as if she could hardly bear to articulate what she felt.

'It was not a promise. I never promised, Christina. Do you want me to inform your uncle or not? It is not an easy thing, to betray my own sister.'

'She is harmless enough!' Christina retorted dismissively. 'It is Hampton they want...it was a promise, Robert. The day you came home with a rabbit. Do you not recall? Or do you only remember what is convenient?'

'It was a hare, not a rabbit.' He slid closer so that he could feel the warmth of her body beneath the sheets. 'But you relented then, as perhaps you will now.'

But Christina shrank from him. 'I was foolish enough to believe you then. You do not understand. My place is in Lanson. I have had enough! This God-forsaken place..'

He stood up frustrated and went to the window. 'I watched Liddy skinning the hare in the yard.'

Christina too was remembering the hare, but on the parlour table, not in the yard. It was what it represented that so offended her, the way Robert drew such pleasure from the mundane things of life, the way he struggled to understand. He had impressed her momentarily. 'He who desires to be righteous is righteous.' Minister Marten had almost laughed in her face. Robert would just say anything to try and please her, but what did he ever do, but go out with his dogs?

'I will go to Bradridge, whether you like it or not. You are right. It is not Mary they want.' He had returned to the bed, sitting close to her. 'I did what your uncle asked, helped Mary escape, looked for the names on the list. George is in France. I could not help that. It is only Hampton they want.'

'My uncle may be in London.'

'Bradridge is not far.'

'Then do as you wish.'

'It is what you wanted!'

'Do as you wish, Robert. Keep the promises that are most convenient.' Christina slipped down beneath the covers and turned her back on him.

'I will go tomorrow.'

'Tomorrow?' All he could see was her yellow hair, dishevelled on the pillow. Her voice was muffled but her meaning clear enough. He could not resist placing his hand on her shoulder and then over the sheets, along the whole length of her body. 'Today,' he said with a sigh. 'I'll go today.'

He could not settle and so it was with a sense of fatefulness that, after only the smallest delay, he returned to the stable to resaddle his horse. Christina's manifest contempt was no deterrent. He would do her bidding because there was no alternative. He was not thinking of Mary or even of himself. It was only that he should bring some satisfaction to Christina. He knew he had no other purpose but to please her. Perhaps he had never had any other purpose. And yet somehow she had come to regard him only with distrust and disdain. Would she ever regard him thus?

It was accompanied by thoughts and musings such as these and hardly aware of his surroundings, that he rode dejectedly in the bright sunshine towards Lanson.

The town was quite back to its normal self and so did little to disturb his train of thought. No soldiers at the South Gate, no clatter of muskets in the square or stamp of heavy feet, no red uniforms in the summer sun.

Little noticing the way from Lanson to Bradridge, he came upon Gewen's manor almost unawares. Then all at once a jumble of uncomfortable recollections of his previous visit; the same bright afternoon, feeling nervously for Christina's letter in his doublet, the falcons, and then his ignominious retreat. This time though there was no sign of the soldiers lounging about the court. Perhaps Gewen was in London, as Christina had said.

But the gate to the courtyard was open and as he dismounted Gewen's pompous factotum appeared as before to ask him his business.

'Robert Pellow to see Thomas Gewen,' he said, trying to make something of himself.

'He is occupied,' Lilley responded neutrally, giving himself time to recall the circumstance of their previous encounter. 'He may see you if you wait, but I warn you, he is likely to be some time.'

Robert indicated his willingness to wait, whereupon a stable boy was summoned to take his horse. Lilley ushered him portentously into the same panelled room with the blue, upholstered bench. This time it was empty but the wait was interminable. He sat facing the single window set high in the panelling. As the sun sank further to the west the room, despite the season, grew chill and grey. At least, he told himself, Gewen is here and not in London, but then wondered if that was what he really wanted.

With difficulty he clung to the reason for what now seemed an importunate intrusion into Gewen's affairs. He had valuable information for the County Committee. He was here to prove himself a useful agent, to establish himself and Christina as upholders of the new order. And most of all so that Christina...

The door to Gewen's inner sanctum had opened quietly. Gewen himself, squat, inconspicuous, bareheaded and cleanshaven, was observing him mildly with those small eyes, just a little too close together. He stood up, towering awkwardly over the smaller, more powerful man.

'Come in, Robert. An unanticipated pleasure.' Gewen's deep, manly, authoritative voice surprised him again. He had forgotten the sheer presence of the man. 'I have been out with my peregrines....ah, I recall, you have already been introduced.' Gewen smiled. 'Fine birds...a pair of woodpigeons and then some rabbits, already being plucked and skinned for supper!' Robert saw that he was still flushed and dusty from the chase. 'Sit down....sit down. If I seem a little tired, you must have patience. I have been all day in the saddle.' All the uncomfortable details of their previous interview came flooding into his mind. He was taking some time to organise his thoughts. Gewen did not seem to notice. 'Tomorrow would have been too late. I have to leave for the capital, unfortunately. The House will soon be in session. Well, Robert, what brings you here?'

'Christina wishes you well, sir.' Gewen nodded. 'But I believe I may have information of interest to the Committee...The list, the last time I came, you showed me a list. One of the names was Andrew Hampton.' Gewen nodded. 'I believe him to be at Cotehele, sir...with my sister, Mary Hawking.'

Gewen frowned. 'Are you comfortable, Robert, in revealing to me the whereabouts of your sister? I seem to remember requesting you specifically to ensure her safety. And yet now, on a whim, you betray her.'

'No, but I am persuaded, sir,' Gewen had picked up a quill, 'that..,'

'Do you want her arrested?' Gewen dipped the quill carefully in a pot of ink. 'I can request solicitor Stephen Revell to issue an arrest warrant immediately, or shall I defer the matter?'

'Sir, I do not wish my sister arrested,' Robert blustered. 'Only Andrew Hampton. He is a wanted man. You asked me to find any of the men that were being sought.'

'Mary is a papist.' Gewen leaned back, his hands comfortably interlaced on his belly. 'Her husband is a leading Catholic in the pay of Henrietta Maria. There is a war. What do you expect me to do?'

'Can you not reprieve my sister, sir?. Surely she represents no danger now.' He wished he had never come. It had not been his intention to betray Mary. Had he not been instrumental in her escape? 'What about this man, Hampton?'

With a certain degree of pleasure, Gewen watched him squirm in his confusion, before replying. 'Hampton is not at Cotehele.'

'How do you know? How can you be sure? Have you searched?'

'There is evidence Mary Hawking and Andrew Hampton parted when they left Clymestone. It appears Hampton fled to the west.'

'And Mary?'

'Mary Hawking is at Cotehele, as you say but,' Gewen appeared to stare right through him, 'I would have preferred you not to betray her.'

There was a long silence during which Gewen seemed to be considering what to do with the man facing him. Robert was having difficulty coming to terms with the fact that Gewen already knew where Mary was, even where Hampton was likely to be.

'Would you believe it!' Gewen had become suddenly quite animated. 'The Central Committee of Compounding is in dispute with the Committee of Sequestration. That estates should be redeemable at two years of pre-war value and naturally in proportion to the delinquency, seems reasonable enough to me. What do you think, Robert?'

'I can...hardly say, sir.'

'Sometimes I think it would have been easier to leave the King where he was.' Gewen sighed and scratched his head. 'We would not have these difficulties. Robert, stay a while longer. I need to think this over.'

So saying, Gewen rose abruptly and left by one of the doors leading into the courtyard, abandoning Robert, whether by accident or design, to ponder his shame. Now that Gewen had so succinctly pointed it out, he could not conceive how he could possibly have betrayed his sister in such a way. How could he have risked consigning Mary to Lanson prison, when before he had prompted her flight? It was fortunate that Gewen had already divined Mary's whereabouts. Or was it? Did the shame not lie rather in the act than its result? Gewen was right about one thing. How much simpler if the war had been lost.

By chance, he had been one of the first to learn of Fairfax's crossing into Cornwall. He had been riding to Lanson to make some purchases, without a care in the world, when he had come across a column of footsoldiers and a troop of horse led by Sir Thomas Bassett. It was the last orderly withdrawal from Lanson, before Fairfax had occupied the town. He had received the news from Sir Thomas with equanimity, quickly turning to pleasure at the thought of how Christina would welcome it.

Of course, she had been delighted and almost at once had set off for Burraton to tell the Minister. He had gone out with the dogs. Only six months ago. And then there had been Clarke's Lady Day sermon. Without that, Christina might never have written to her uncle. By then all of Cornwall, save for Pendennis, had capitulated. His humiliation, twice now at the hands of Gewen, might never have occurred. And then Mary's flight, so much scheming. It had never been part of his nature to scheme.

And now, Christina repeatedly reminded him, her husband the Minister's money was fast running out. Would they have to give up the house at Whiteford? Had it really been necessary to cultivate Gewen and Marten? Had there been no alternative? It was not as if they were of any use to either of them now.

He glanced out of the window. The summer nights were drawing in. He would not wait indefinitely, a glutton for humiliation. Then, without a sound, Lilley entered with a branched candlestick which he placed on the corner of Gewen's huge desk, lit the candles and then departed, without a word.

When, a moment or two later, Gewen himself returned, he looked somehow neater, his sober attire no longer dusty from the chase. Perhaps he had changed, though his ruff still had the same yellowish tinge. Perhaps, Robert thought, with no small amount of resentment, he has had his supper. It was only then, as Gewen entered, that it occurred to him. Wright had first been rewarded by Gewen and then had extracted a further four shillings from him at Mary's cottage. That was how Gewen was so well informed.

'I will not detain you longer than necessary, Robert.' Gewen made no apology for his absence. 'You will be anxious to return to Whiteford, before nightfall. But it is time, is it not, that we came to an understanding?' There was a pause for Gewen to assure himself that Robert was paying attention. 'Your sister is unlikely to be arrested. It is of course, not entirely my responsibility. I do not issue warrants, but it has to be said, Mary Hawking is not now perceived as a threat. Her husband is in France. Her property is sequestrated and her priest...is dead.' Gewen gave Robert sufficient time to absorb what he had said. 'All of that being the case the emphasis shifts, as you correctly observe, onto her companion, Andrew Hampton. And here lies the rub, Robert. If, as seems likely, your sister returns to Clymestone unmolested, I request simply that you take account of her actions so that we may continue to be assured of her, let us say...innocence. In particular, I request that you inform me, or some other representative of the Committee, should she be found once more in the company of Lieutenant Hampton. Do you take my meaning, Robert?....You hesitate.'

'I take your meaning, sir. If my sister is to remain secure, I have no compunction in drawing this man, Hampton, to your attention. He has brought enough trouble.'

'Good, then in that case, I have a further proposition, Robert, which I do not expect you to decline. Within a week or two the Hawking property will be sold. With your agreement and for an appropriate fee, I am prepared to recommend you to the Committee for the supervision of the sale. I recommend it, sir! What do you say?'

Robert had few misgivings. That he should become responsible for the sale of his sister's property, summarily appropriated by the state, did not seem too much of a burden to bear. And keeping an eye on Mary, once she had returned to Clymestone, could hardly be troublesome. George Hawking, after all, was in Paris and likely to remain there. Hampton, he thought, was probably dead.

Gewen had arranged for his horse to be well-fed and watered. The picture which remained in his mind was of the politician turned slightly towards him, his face glowing in the candlelight, one elbow on the table, chin between thumb and forefinger, in the other hand a quill poised. There was a contemplative, almost serene expression on his face, only marred by the eyes, small and slightly too close together.

In fact Gewen was already going through the motions of debating with himself whether or not he had made the right decision with regard to Mary Hawking. This re-assessment of his own rationale always brought him satisfaction, the satisfaction of knowing he was right. Colonel Edgcumbe, Gewen reasoned, together with his fellow gentry of aristocratic pretension, had reached in Bodmin a gentleman's agreement with General Fairfax. And Fairfax, a trusted friend of Cromwell and an honourable man, would adhere to it. Once they had capitulated, Edgcumbe, Coryton and the rest would not expect to be hounded by the bureaucracy. There was little danger of Cotehele being sequestrated and then compounded for at punitive rates. With or without the King, the establishment would re-assert itself. It would serve no purpose now to rock the boat.

Hawking himself was not at all an honourable man, rather the antithesis of Fairfax. He would be staying in Paris with the Queen to whom, by all accounts, he was committed to an unseemly degree. He would have no inclination, nor be foolish enough, to take up with his wife again, in Clymestone. As for Hampton, he was lost in the mist and fog of war and, given his connections, might already have perished needlessly at Pendennis.

Satisfied, he returned the quill to its holder, as if that somehow concluded the matter. He had not been intending to write. It was merely a habit. At an appropriate juncture in Gewen's silent recapitulation, Lilley had entered, sensing, as always, the time when he would be needed.

'Mary Hawking is to be left alone,' Gewen murmured, as if the thought had just occurred to him. 'There is no reason to offend Edgcumbe. Her brother will keep an eye on her. I have asked Pellow to supervise the sale at Hampt. He has no understanding of compounding, sequestration or even the general assessment, but it would be a pity not to make use of him. Besides it will put Wright out of joint. He is getting too big for his boots. Let him make a greater effort to secure our favour. And you never know, Pellow may turn out to be worth more than impressions would indicate. If nothing else, my niece will keep him in order, keep his nose to the grindstone'.

Chapter 25

It was harvest time but at Pendennis the eternal rhythms of the countryside were not much in evidence. On 10th August, starvation and plague finally compelled the Governor to accept the inevitable and negotiations for the surrender began, only to be delayed when some amongst Arundell's officers suggested that all their ordnance should be blown up so that, as they put it, 'victors and vanquished might perish together.' Only once they had been overruled were negotiations able to resume in earnest.

On the 15th of the month, Arundell agreed to treat simultaneously with Vice-Admiral Batten and Colonel Fortescue, who had by now replaced Colonel Hammond. The terms of the surrender were generous. Passes were to be provided for those returning to their homes in Devon and Cornwall and also for those returning to Wales or into exile. Local men were to be 'shipt and landed at Looe'. None were to be 'plunder'd, searched or injured' and five hundred pounds was made available for the care of the sick and wounded. Officers 'in commission' were allowed to retain their weapons and all prisoners of war on both sides were to be released. The seventy year old Governor signed the treaty on 16th August. 'Condescended unto', he wrote at the bottom of the page, 'by me, John Arundell'.

And so it was, at 2pm on 17th August and according to the terms of the treaty, the garrison marched out, every soldier with twelve charges of powder, drums beating, colours flying and trumpets sounding. Seven hundred and thirty-two soldiers led by one hundred and fifty-four officers crossed the drawbridge and marched proudly towards the Parliamentary lines at Arwenack.

Inside the Castle walls were many more, too ill to march and including two hundred women and children. The garrison had not been short of ammunition, but the horses had all been butchered or were themselves starving to death. The Castle had been entirely without sustenance.

***

The harvest was poor throughout the length and breadth of the County, presaging another hard winter. But Clymestone in the east was fortunate. The spell of warm weather continued until the wheat was ready. From time immemorial, three small farms around Lidwell and Venterdon had worked together to bring the harvest in. Francis, Arthur and Janella had already spent a week on the other two farms, before it was the Pellows' turn. Alice had been left alone for much of the time but the risk, Francis and Janella persuaded themselves, was only slight. Perhaps it was good for her anyway, to potter about, make her own drinks and do some of the less taxing jobs about the house and the yard.

Arthur worked on in his usual way, but since Midsummer had refrained from breakfasting at the farm, staying firmly out of Janella's way, as he had said he would.

After a week or two, Francis had sent a message to John. Was Mary still safe at Cotehele? The answer soon came back. All was well. There was no cause for concern. But Janella could not help wondering if Arthur might still betray them. Arthur, in typical fashion, gave nothing away, and would not even look her in the eye.

He had taken up his traps the night before. Now the three of them stood silently waiting at the gate to the North Field. The sun was already up and warming the corn. It was a welcome relief when they heard the trudge of heavy boots in the lane and a chattering along the hedgerows. A greater relief still when the men and women from Lidwell appeared at the bend, bearing their scythes and rakes and sickles.

After the usual perfunctory greetings they set to work, the men with their scythes, spacing themselves evenly across the field. Francis, who was clumsy, came in for the usual banter.

"e'll 'ave 'is feet off 'afore 'e's finished.'

Francis took it all in his stride and, the new affection between Francis and Janella being impossible to conceal, they all knew why. Francis was easy enough to bait. Janella would have given them the lash of her tongue.

Once they had started, the women followed on behind to rake and bind and shock. The two fields of corn on the Pellow farm would not take long, if the weather held, and once the sheaves had been piled high into the mows, it would be back to Lidwell to bring in their harvest first.

Alice waited patiently for them to return to Lidwell for the bringing in. Then there would be no risk of Janella coming back on some pretext or other, but really to make sure she was alright. There was a shower of rain, but it passed and the sky cleared quickly. She supposed the corn would not have been damaged. Her bonnet and cloak were folded neatly away. She had not touched them for years, not since she and Samuel had last been to the Reverend Clarke's Sunday morning service.

When she left, the yard was already drying in the sun, but the lane into Clymestone was wet and shady and the hedges rustled and swayed and in their darkest places still dripped noisily after the rain. She had forgotten what it was like to walk the lanes, splashing and stumbling occasionally in the ruts.

When Minister Marten came upon her, she was close to the lych-gate, kneeling awkwardly, almost prostrating herself before one of the more recent graves. Hardly more than a heap of clothing. It might have been a child. At first he did not speak but stood behind her, tall and gangling and now, reluctantly, wearing his cassock. The congregation, his churchwardens had told him, would never credit him as a Minister if he did not look like one. He had been humble enough to take their advice.

He leaned over her, his shadow briefly touching the stone where it entered the earth.

Here lies the body
of
Samuel Pellow
who departed this life
21st July 1645

He thought of Christina, her husband, Robert. More than likely it was his mother.

'Mrs Pellow,' he said, as softly as he was able. 'Do not grieve so.' She had not heard. He bent closer, touched her shoulder. Something like a whimper emanated from the bundle of clothing, scarcely a sound at all. When she turned to him, her bonnet was tipped ridiculously to one side, her face ashen and streaked with tears. 'Come,' he said, and with some difficulty, helped her to her feet.

'My husband,' she said, straightening herself and a defiant look in her eyes.

'He is in Heaven now, Mrs Pellow.'

Alice looked puzzled. 'Where is the Reverend? I came to see the Reverend.'

'Also in Heaven,' Minister Marten explained, with some discomfort. 'He has passed away. Mrs Pellow, come with me and rest yourself.'

She allowed the Minister to take her into the porch, as he had intended, but then something persuaded him to open the door to the church and lead her in. Alice looked about her with a kind of wonder, as if it were a revelation, as if she had never before entered such a place, though it was here that she had married and here that all five of her children had been baptised.

But something was different and it was not until they approached the chancel that she realised the rood screen had been taken away. And the altar in front of her was bare, not even a cross. But she had never been so close!

Boldly, the Minister took her to the very steps and knelt with her. and together they said the Lord's Prayer. And then they sat together in one of the pews. It was like a miracle. She observed the Minister out of the corner of her eye. Where was the Reverend Clarke? Why had they not told her? It was all very strange.

The Minister too thought it strange. He was wondering what the Reverend Clarke would have done, unconsciously measuring himself against the man who had chosen to risk everything rather than relinquish his parish.

'But I waited,' Alice whispered.

'Waited?'

'Samuel went out to fight and then did not come back. I waited. I did not look for him. Why did I not look for him?' Alice answered her own question. 'I did not care enough,' she said.' And then they found him in a hedge, struck down.'

'Did they bring him home?'

'Yes. I cared for him. But it was too late. I might have saved him, but I did not care enough.'

'If you truly repent,' the Minister said solemnly, taking her hand, 'you will be saved and will join your husband, Samuel, in Heaven.'

'What must I do now?'

'Go home to your family. Live for the living and count your blessings.'

'Live for the living?'

'This world, Mrs Pellow, is often one of tribulation. We must bear it and look forward to the next. More than that, we must nurture those who need our nurturing.'

'Mary, I know. I nurtured her but she was not…reborn.'

'If she died, then she is in Heaven.' It was not exactly what Minister Marten believed, but in speaking to this woman he had, in his wish to comfort her, for once cast belief aside. Was that what the Reverend Clarke would have done? 'And she was not reborn?'

'No, we baptised her Mary, but it was not Mary. We expected too much of her.'

'Where is Mary now?'

'She is at Cotehele. They say she is at Cotehele.'

'But Mary died. The first one.'

It had not occurred to her, not in so many words. Mary was dead. Like Samuel, there would be a grave. She had not thought to look. 'She was drowned. A ferryman found her and took her to Cotehele.'

'Then she is buried here, at Clymestone?'

She had never dared visit her daughter's grave. It had been the same with Samuel. She had stayed at home, unable to face the funeral, the interment. She had not been able to face the reality of their deaths. Only now, Minister Marten seemed to understand.

'Come, your daughter's stone will not be far from your husband's.' Minister Marten was slowly coming to understand Alice's painful conundrum. He stood up to take her hand. 'Let us find it together.'

Alice kept her hand to herself but followed him back, down the aisle to the tower screen and the porch. By the lych-gate, the Minister wandered this way and that until he found what he was looking for.

Here lies the body
of
Mary Pellow
aged four years
who departed this life
June 14th 1619

It was a small stone set back, almost against the wall. Where they stood was high up overlooking the place where the lanes met, at the heart of the village.

'I will take you home now.' Minister Marten had not only put aside his beliefs, but had discovered something else, inside himself. Now, this woman's pain was all that concerned him. 'I will take you home.'

But Alice was not yet ready. 'They are bringing the harvest in at Lidwell. Do you think Mary will come home?'

'Your daughter Mary is in Heaven, together with your husband.'

'And my new daughter, will she come home?'

'Your new daughter will come home,' Minister Marten confirmed.

'Then I am ready,' Alice said decisively.

They made an odd couple, emerging from the churchyard; Alice small and pale, unused to the outside world, Minister Marten tall, beetle-browed and serious, awkward in his long cassock. The sun shone and the Minister insisted he would accompany her all the way to Venterdon. It was no more than a few hundred yards he said, from the church.

'They are at the harvest,' Alice told him again, gaining in confidence. He held her arm so she would not stumble.

'On Sunday, you will come to morning service. I will expect you.' the Minister said.

At the gate to the yard, they parted. For each of them it had been an unexpected but welcome encounter. The Minister returned to the vestry with a sense of having accomplished something, but not without the nagging thought that this was what the Reverend Clarke had always done.

Alice felt a powerful release, not questioning for a moment the Minister's words. Nobody had seen her come or go. Nobody would know. She scraped her shoes at the door and took them off. She would take care to wipe them before they came back from Lidwell. And then she took off her bonnet and cloak and returned them, neatly folded, to their place.

There was no need to reveal what had happened. It would mean nothing to them. But they would be tired. There was time now to prepare a meal for them and see to the washing, sweep the floor, bring more logs to the hearth. There was a definite nip in the air and besides, Janella could not be expected to do everything.

Sometimes, she knew, Janella attended Sunday morning service. Would she think it odd, Alice wondered, if she were to join her?

***

At Cotehele, it was generally known, though evidence was only circumstantial, that Lady Margaret was anxious to leave. She had been keeping very much to her room and it was constantly rumoured that Sir Piers and all his family were on the way from the 'Mount'. Lady Margaret and Sir Piers had not parted on the best of terms.

Mary had neither seen nor spoken to Lady Margaret since the day they had peeped together at Mrs Howard, praying in the chapel. Since then she had taken every opportunity to be out of the house in the sunshine but, crossing the Great Hall, would anxiously look up to that other cross-shaped peephole and wonder if Lady Margaret was observing her too. But it was unlikely. Lady Margaret had indeed lost all interest in Cotehele, not even condescending to eat in the Edgcumbes' magnificent Parlour, a relief to Mary who was so much more comfortable with Kate and Mrs Rundle in the kitchen.

There had been no news from Clymestone so she had no idea what had happened to the farm at Hampt, no idea that the Reverend Clarke had hung himself in the Rectory, no idea that her whereabouts were known to those that had sought her arrest. No news either from Hampton or the progress of the siege at Pendennis. But then she had become used to being cut off from the rest of the world. She told herself she preferred it that way, knowing it to be a lie.

The spectacle of Mrs Howard desperately praying for the soul of her dead husband had somehow renewed her own faith. Was that what Lady Margaret had intended? Did Lady Margaret know she was a papist? Whatever the truth, praying secretly in her tiny chamber gave her a strength she would not otherwise have had. She prayed for Andrew Hampton, that he might still be alive, and for the soul of her father, but no longer for George Hawking or his Catholic Queen.

One afternoon she had been caught in a shower and was drying herself by the kitchen hearth. Kate had been helping her father with the harvest and was nowhere to be seen. It was Mrs Rundle who brought her the message;

'My Lady upstairs wants to see you. Better go on up. Looks like somethin's 'appened.'

Mary waited until she was dry. She was not there to be ignored for weeks on end, and then to be at anybody's beck and call. She sauntered wilfully through the Great Hall and the Parlour, no longer intimidated by their magnificence. At the top of the spiral staircase, she knocked on Lady Margaret's door and then, in the manner of Mrs Howard, opened it without waiting.

Lady Margaret was on her bed, sitting upright on her covers, propped up by an elaborate arrangement of pillows. Mary had almost forgotten her striking, wide-awake look, her black, peaked cap, spreading like a cowl, her large floury face. Lady Margaret had not altered one jot, but in Mary's mind, as the weeks went by, she had passed somehow from reality to imagination. It had been as if the elderly woman in the tower, no longer existed in the flesh.

She wore the same black, velvet bedjacket as she had at their first meeting and one of her small, mottled hands clutched the familiar glass, full to the brim. She could not resist glancing at the bottle, which stood within easy reach on the folding table.

'Yesterday's bottle,' Lady Margaret protested indignantly. 'It's empty.'

'You...' Lady Margaret nodded for her to bring up a chair, so that Mary quite forgot what she was going to say.

'Thomas will be here in a few days.'

'But you said....'

'I know. Pendennis. The news came only today.' Lady Margaret was nervously fiddling with her jacket so that her wine was in danger of spilling. Mary took away the glass and waited patiently for her to settle. Though at the word 'Pendennis' her heart had leapt in awful anticipation. 'They couldn't hold out, Mary. I told you, it would only be a matter of time. Over a thousand men, they say, marched out...but it's all over. Arundell couldn't hold out, you see. They say the terms are fair.'

Lady Margaret would not look her in the eye, sounded offhand, even brutal, but Mary could see it was only her way. 'Lieutenant....'

'Andrew Hampton? I can't say. More than likely he was never there. It was a desperate enough plan.' Then Lady Margaret appeared to relax and relent a little. 'I don't know, Mary. There aren't any names. You must...'

'Wait.' The little colour she had, had gone from her cheeks. She felt sick. 'I know, wait, wait, wait...'

'It was a siege, Mary, not a battle.' Lady Margaret reached again for her glass.' They do not fight. It is always the same, just a matter of time.' For once she seemed genuinely concerned for Mary and for her friend, Andrew Hampton. But at the back of her mind she was only thinking of Hertfordshire, of going home to her family, her granddaughter and all her great-grandchildren from whom she had fled but now with whom she longed to be re-united. She tugged at her bristles and adjusted her pillows unnecessarily. She could not easily connect with this secondary matter of Mary Hawking and Andrew Hampton. She had not looked forward to this. Now Mary was ready to put away her chair and leave. 'Andrew.' She took hold of Mary's arm. 'If Andrew is...well, he will come here. There is nowhere else for him to go.'

'He is not Andrew Hampton though, is he? Mary held back her tears.

'No, he is not. He is a bastard and proud of it. Did he not tell you?'

Mary thought back to the day they had spent at the old deer park. How they had laughed. 'He told me once he knew his father, but not his mother.'

Lady Margaret lay back on her pillows. 'His father is a man of power and influence, Mary. But Andrew would not take his name.'

She had wiped away her tears. He was not dead. There was no cause to think him dead. 'Then he might have taken his father's name, if he had wished?'

'He held in low esteem the advantages that come with a name. He wanted to make his own name.' Now Lady Margaret was thinking of her husband who had been the same kind of man. 'He wanted to be beholden to no-one.' Lady Margaret shook her head and chortled. 'That's what he told me. I told him he was a fool. You see Mary, he was never what he seemed, like Mrs Howard who is also, as you know, not what she seems.'

'I am not surprised. I knew there was something different about him. I understand him better now.'

'Even you,' Lady Margaret would not be deflected, 'are not what you seem. To everyone here you are Mrs Hampton, but we know different, don't we?'

'And you, Lady Margaret.' Mary flashed. 'Are you what you seem?'

Lady Margaret laughed out loud, but her laughter had a hollow ring. 'No Mary, you are right. I am not what I seem either. I am the woman you pass every day in the Great Hall, not this decrepit baggage you see before you now!'

'I did not mean to offend.'

'Anybody my age would tell you the same, portrait or no portrait. Though it jogs the memory when I would rather forget. Underneath, I am the same as you Mary, in the prime of life.'

'And Kate, Lady Margaret. Is she at least what she seems?'

'Yes, life has not affected her yet. It will soon enough and perhaps when she least expects it. She reminds me of myself, a young slip of a thing, at court.'

'I will go now.'

'No, Mary.' Lady Margaret put out her hand. 'It had slipped my mind. Kate, I have asked Kate to enquire. You know her father goes to Callington. I am not the callous old woman you imagine. You cannot return to Clymestone unless it is safe. Kate's father will enquire. The stables in Callington, she said.'

'You need not concern yourself, Lady Margaret. Besides, I have no real home now.'

'But I do Mary, I do.' Lady Margaret was wondering, as she had been for some time, whether or not Cromwell's soldiers were still garrisoned at her manor in Stortford. 'If it is not safe, you will have to accompany me to Stortford. My 'Charter of Protection,' Lady Margaret pointed to the framed proclamation on the wall, signed by the King, 'still counts for something. They would not dare touch you.'

'You are generous, Lady Margaret,' Mary stammered, 'but..'

'Andrew Hampton, I understand, but you must also prepare yourself for the worst. If you are not safe in Clymestone and if Andrew is not here by the time Thomas arrives with the coach, you will have no alternative.'

'Do you think he will come back?'

'If he is alive, my dear, I am sure of it.' But there was no softness in Lady Margaret's eyes. Andrew Hampton, she thought, was not the sort of man who came back.

Mary touched her hand where it lay on the pillow, a way of thanking her as much for the lie as for the protection she had been afforded for so long. Lady Margaret pretended not to notice. As Mary put away her chair, she was certain they would not see each other again.

'Tell Mrs Howard,' Lady Margaret called out as Mary turned to the door. 'Another bottle, the woman forgets herself.'

Chapter 26

It was Lady Margaret who was the first to observe him, striding purposefully across the meadow towards Cotehele. She could tell, even at a distance, that he was no gentleman nor even a pauper come to beg. He was rather a man with a mission, a mission which he would do all within his power to fulfil. Lady Margaret watched him closely until he disappeared from view below the Tower. By then she was in no doubt as to the man's purpose.

Kate's pa appeared as usual at the entrance to the Retainers' Court, to ask the man his business. The chapel clock chimed indifferently. The man who was lean, unusually dark-skinned and with dark, intelligent eyes had, he said, a package for Mrs Hawking. Kate's father was dismissive. There was no-one of that name. He was mistaken. He should be on his way. But the man, who was calm and determined, would not budge. There was no doubt, he said, that Mrs Hawking was resident here, at Cotehele. He had it on the best authority.

There was a rustle of petticoats and the sound of quick feet coming towards them across the Court. Mrs Howard gave the immediate impression, to both of them, that the matter would soon be resolved. Apparently she had already grasped the gist of the dispute.

'Perhaps it is Mrs Hampton you are come about?'

'Mrs Hampton, yes,' he answered slowly. 'Perhaps it is. Is it Mary...Mary Hampton?' For all James Stubbs knew, this exquisitely dressed woman, with her low-cut bodice and bare arms, was herself the woman in question. To his mind, she would not have been at all out of place on the arm of Andrew Hampton.

'Mary Hampton is not here, not in the house.' Mrs Howard waved Kate's father away. 'If you have a message, I will take it to her. What is your name?'

'My name is James Stubbs.' He was not at all intimidated. 'But I have clear instructions. I must speak with Mrs Hampton. I am prepared to wait.'

James was polite but undeterred. Like his father and brother, he spoke with a mild West Country accent. As Lady Margaret had already deduced, he was no gentleman, but neither was he a man in awe of his superiors. He was just the kind of man, Mrs Howard perceived, who would have been admired by Andrew Hampton. Just the kind of man Hampton would have entrusted with the news of his death.

'You may wait then, Mr Stubbs,' she said condescendingly, 'in here.'

There was a small room, formerly known as the Lodge, to the right of the entrance, and which was still occupied regularly for that purpose whenever Colonel Piers and his family were in residence. Now it was a clutter of chairs and tables which Kate's pa had never quite got round to repairing, and in the corners evidence of its connection to the farm, a broken harness, a rake, a battered hat and coat on a hook.

Mrs Howard knew Mary would be down at the quays or roaming the woods along the river. Now the only question was who was going to tell her.

'Is Andrew Hampton dead?'

'You are....?'

'Mrs Howard. I am a friend of the Edgcumbes. I live here. ' Mrs Howard replied, rather stretching the truth.

Suddenly overcome with weariness, James sat down heavily on one of the less rickety-looking chairs. He had come a long way, with little food or sleep. 'Yes, Andrew Hampton is dead,' he said, looking up boldly and in such a way that Mrs Howard could see he would not elaborate further.

'Then I will find Mrs Hampton. Wait here. I will order you something from the kitchen.'

Mrs Howard was careful to close the door. He could hear her issuing instructions to the elderly man he had first encountered. He was tired and grateful for a moment to himself. It would not be easy, this interview with Mary Hawking. He was certain that was her name. Why she should have taken Hampton's name, he could not imagine.

At least he had been relieved of the burden of telling her Hampton was dead, but then she would want to know everything. She would not be satisfied with the bald statement. That much he had learned about women. Not that there was much more he could say. It was his father who had been there in the gunroom, his father who had taken the package and promised to deliver it. It was his father who had insisted. 'James, you are the fittest. I must get back to the 'Arms', before we are dispossessed.' So he had, as the treaty specified, been 'shipt to Looe' where, being like his father more comfortable on water than on land, he had found another ship leaving for Plymouth and calling at Saltash.

He had been able to pay his way with Hampton's gold crowns. At Saltash he had taken a wherry, transporting sea-sand up the Tamar to Calstock. Cotehele was on the Tamar and Hampton's woman was at Cotehele. That was all his father had been able to tell him. The worst part of the journey had been from Calstock, walking the tangle of lanes, constantly asking the way. Only when he had started showing his pass had the people in the villages been truly helpful, regarding him with awe and perhaps a little shame at their own abject surrender, now that the new regime was taking hold.

A short time after Mrs Howard's departure, Mrs Rundle herself brought him a tray of bread and cheese and cold meats, and a jug of beer. Everyone, apart from Mary, already knew who he was and why he was there.

Mrs Howard was in no hurry. Lady Margaret had told her, perhaps because her own small deception had become apparent, that she wanted no part of it. She had always known it was not 'Hampton'. Lieutenant Hampton had not even been married. So it was 'Hawking'. Lady Margaret had kept that to herself. It was of no concern to her. Lady Margaret had taken her in. Lady Margaret had a habit of taking people under her wing. She herself had been only one of many. Mary Hawking must have been in more trouble than she had realised. And now she was to be told her lover was dead. Mrs Howard was glad, in spite of their falling out, that she was to be the one. Women, she persuaded herself, understood grief.

There was, she fancied, a hint of Autumn in the air. It would be chilly by the river. The sombre-shaded cloak she selected and pulled around her shoulders, was lined with fur and would serve well enough to keep out the cold. She passed through the Parlour, the Great Hall, the gardens, and then carefully picking up her skirts, descended to the quays.

At first, there was no sign of Mary who had crossed the stream into the woods and was now meandering along the fringe of trees close to the river. Shamelessly bare-headed, her unruly curls straggled waywardly over her shoulders and down her back. Unlike Mrs Howard, she had not noticed the chill and wore only the bodice and petticoats Mrs Howard had herself provided.

It was Mary who first caught sight of Mrs Howard, her elegant figure on the quays. She had never seen Lady Margaret's companion anywhere near the river. There could only be one reason. Mrs Howard must have news of Andrew. She slipped into the wood, out of sight. Soon she would know. There was no avoiding it. She would know from the expression on Mrs Howard's face, even before she spoke. She walked back across the bridge, as prepared as ever she would be. As she approached, she saw Mrs Howard turn towards her and even in that movement, knew he was dead.

The two women stood facing one another. There was no animosity now, but equally, no natural sympathy between them.

'He's dead.'

'Mrs Hampton,' Mrs Howard chose to keep up the pretence. 'I am also a widow. I understand your grief.'

'How do you know?'

'There is a man at the Lodge, from Pendennis. He has just brought the news. He has a message, a package, he said. He would not say more. I will take you to him.'

At the Lodge, James was draining the last of his beer. The dish in front of him was wiped clean of Mrs Rundle's generous fayre. He looked refreshed, at least as much as any man might after so many months of dreadful privation. Mary closed the door firmly behind her.

'James Stubbs,' he said courteously, rising to offer his hand.

'Mary Hawking,' she replied automatically. His grip was warm, genuine, somehow expected. Andrew would not have allowed an insensitive man on such a cruel mission. They sat facing one another, amidst the lumber, both equally uncertain where to begin. To conceal his discomfort, he pushed the dish to one side, drew a small package from his doublet and placed it between them on the table.

'I have been asked to bring you this.'

She read the words above the seal, 'Mrs Mary Hawking'. She did not recognise the hand, but then she had never seen him write. She left the package untouched and tried not to meet the man's eyes.

'She told you?' he asked gently. Mary gave the slightest of nods. 'It was about two weeks ago, shortly before the surrender. The Lieutenant was at a place called Upton's Mount, our most forward position. There was little exchange of fire, but he caught a stray musket ball...' Mary sat motionless, expressionless, avoiding his eyes. 'They took him back to the gunroom. He gave this....' James put his hand on the package, as if to remind her. 'He gave this to my father....' He could not help but feel an excess of tenderness towards this pretty, young woman who could not bear to raise her eyes. 'He was thinking of you, my father said, right to the last.' James lied, 'He did not suffer much.'

'Did you know him?' Mary whispered

'Yes. Everybody did. He was a fine man.'

And then he told her how they had first met. How, together with Stevens and Honks, he and his father and brother had plotted with Hampton how to break the siege, how, against all the odds, they had succeeded, and how, without the inspiration of Andrew Hampton, they would never even have tried. He spoke softly, gently, proudly and at last succeeded in drawing her eyes to his own.

'He said he was going to Pendennis. He said nothing would stop him.' Her eyes blazed with pride.

'Nothing did, Mrs Hawking. Lieutenant Hampton was not one to be put off by such as a Parliamentary siege-works or Batten's little armada. That was why my father took to him.'

'Your father was with him, Mr...'

'Stubbs...yes, but he had to get back to the 'Arms' and he said I was the fittest, so here I am. I will be pleased to tell him that I found you.'

'The 'Arms'?'

''The King's Arms', in Penryn. My father is the keeper. The terms of the treaty were fair, but they are taking property all over now. We must try and avoid it, so father must take care of the 'Arms', or he would have come himself. They were close, my father and Lieutenant Hampton. That's the way it is, when you are bombarded every day.'

'How will you get back?

'Same way I came. The river and then the sea, Plymouth to Pennycomequick. I reckon they'll be sailing that way, for the new garrison if nothing else.'

James seemed to be preparing himself to leave. She could see he had the longing for home in his eyes, or perhaps it was the call of the sea. James and Luke had both inherited their father's discomfort with the land. What else could she say? There might never be another opportunity.

'Mr Stubbs,' she began hesitantly, as he stood to leave. 'Did Lieutenant Hampton ever give another name? Was he known by any other name, or rank?'

'No, he was very particular about that. He did not even like to be called 'Lieutenant'. He would not have any favours and would always take orders from those of the same rank, those who had been at Pendennis before him.' Mary's eyes had fallen again to the package on the table. Would the package perhaps contain the truth that Lady Margaret had alluded to? But James had not quite finished. 'I think my father knew who he was, and that was why he agreed to go along. Hampton always carried a rapier and in the cup there was a pattern, a pattern of swallows. My father set great store by that.'

'Swallows...' She remembered the silver button she had presented here, at Cotehele, and something made her look again at the package lying provocatively on the table. She picked it up. Imprinted on the seal, the same pattern, a pattern of swallows.

'And the Governor, he would come to the gunroom often, the women and children, the sick and wounded. That's why…I expect you know…that's why we had to surrender. The Governor, my father said, was very upset. When he came the last time, Hampton had already passed.'

'Where is he buried? Did they bury him? Where?'

'There is nothing more I can tell you, Mrs Hawking.' James put out his hand. 'One day,' he said, in a rush of feeling, 'you may come to the 'Arms', meet my father. Stay as long as you like. There will always be ships from Plymouth or Looe, but now I must get to Calstock before nightfall. Perhaps there will be a wherry going downriver tonight.'

They shook hands and without further ado James left, striding away across the meadow. She watched him go, before walking around the side of the house to the gardens, and then back down to the quays, the package, still unopened, grasped tightly in her hand.

She walked in a daze, her heart bursting, her mind a flurry of disconnected thoughts, each one rapidly succeeding the last. She had never really expected him to come back. Something had driven him away from her. Something more powerful than mere loyalty to the King.

And from the beginning, there had been a pattern of swallows. Without it she would not have been here. And this man Stubbs had recognised it too. Andrew had no more surrendered at Pendennis than at Cotehele. Perhaps he had wanted to die. A powerful and influential man, Lady Margaret had said, and then declined to say more. A powerful and influential Royalist. It could hardly have been a Parliamentarian. And one like Andrew, with the determination to hold out for the King, whatever the cost. And why had he been so anxious to break the siege? The Governor had been very upset, Stubbs had said. 'I am a bastard…I know my father.' She slowed her pace. The bastard son of Sir John Arundell, Governor of Pendennis?

She could not be certain. It all seemed to make sense, but did it matter now, who Andrew Hampton really was? He was dead and that was all there was to it. As she stood on the quay, she remembered that in her hand she was still clutching the package, clutching so tightly the tips of her fingers had pierced the outer skin. The red seal, the same pattern of swallows.

She looked around as if, even here, she might be secretly observed and then, not quite trusting the evidence of her eyes, took the path away from the quays and down the riverbank towards the stream.

She came to the fringe of trees and, almost with reluctance, broke the red seal. Something fell to her feet. It took her a moment to recover it from the long grass. It was a ring, George's ring. 'Keep it to remember me by!' Her own words came screaming back to her, as she flung it away in the sunken lane, his expression of shock and then watching him scrabble amongst the white, wild garlic and the bluebells.

There was something else, in her other hand. Only the paper which had been folded around the ring to form the package. Some writing, faint and spidery, though she could read it well enough. After the first words, she had no need.

'For I had rather owner bee
Of thee one houre, than all else ever.'

She had never forgotten, but why did he have to address her in verse? What was wrong with ordinary human discourse? And then she remembered he was no longer there to defend himself and they were, if Stubbs was to be believed, the very last words which had come to his mind. Overwhelmed, she sank to her knees on the turf.

After a while, with great deliberation, and for the second time, she flung the ring away to where it could never again be found, to the bottom of a nameless stream. What useful purpose could it serve now? She had told him to keep it, to remember her by, and that's what he had done. George had given it as a token of his undying love and then left her for good. Andrew had sent it back for no reason she could understand. It was better to be rid of it.

The words of the poem gave her greater pause for thought. Was poetry of such a kind no more than a gentleman's pastime or did it mean something? She could not decide. In the end, as evening drew on, she did not know what to think, or to feel.

Except that there was a chill in the air and Mrs Howard's petticoats were green with dew.

She wanted, above all to be alone. She would walk up through the trees, the way Kate had showed her all that time ago, and enter by the servants' door in the east wing, through the sculleries and up the stone steps to her chamber. She would not have to stay much longer, had no idea what would become of her and was not at all sure that she cared.

In her tiny chamber, she took her cloak from its hook on the wall and pulled it around her. It was colder here than on the riverbank. From her narrow window-slit she could still see the river through the trees and somehow its permanence gave her a measure of comfort. There was a tap on the door. Someone must have seen her, followed her, but not just someone, she had recognised the tap. Reluctantly she opened the door.

'Come in, Kate.'

Kate was a little breathless and uncertain, tremulous. It was written on her face. Dissimulation was so alien to her.

'Mary...Mrs Hampton..'

'Mary.'

'Mary, you had a visitor. My father said. I fear it is not good news.'

'Lieutenant Hampton died at Pendennis,' she managed, smiling wanly.

'Oh!' Kate took a step towards her and they embraced, but only briefly.

She thought of explaining her deception, explaining that she was not Mrs Hampton, but then it all seemed far too complicated and perhaps Kate, who revelled so much in gossip, already knew anyway. Perhaps by now everybody knew. James Stubbs had asked for Mrs Hawking, not Mrs Hampton.

She disentangled herself impatiently from Kate's arms. Kate was taken aback. Mary was dry-eyed, severe.

'You are not sad?'

'Kate, I don't know what I am, just tired, I think.'

Kate was gently re-arranging the cloak which had slipped from her shoulders. They stood together, almost in darkness. She had not troubled to light a candle. The light from her slit of a window was all she had needed. Soon she would be gone from this place.

'We are still friends?'

'Yes, of course. We are friends always, but you know Lady Margaret is soon to leave and...'

'You will not be here much longer, I know.' There were tears in Kate's eyes. 'I came to give you a message. My father has been to the stables in Callington.' Mary turned away to the window. The river was no longer visible through the trees. 'There is a message from your brother.' Kate stood away from her, hardly able to articulate the words. 'It is safe for you to go back, but not to Hampt, only to Venterdon. Your brother will come tomorrow at ten o'clock...and so you will leave...just as you came.' Kate's words trailed to a whisper. 'Mary, do you remember when you came and Lady Margaret said...'

'You were more interested in the mare.' Mary turned to face her friend. 'I cannot imagine my life here, without you Kate. I would have run away. Truly, I do not wish to leave now, but I have no choice. I cannot stay, only to be ejected by the Colonel who would not welcome me as you have done.'

'You may come back secretly. We will hide you!' Kate was almost hysterical. 'But tomorrow, Mary. I will see you tomorrow, when you leave.'

Mary embraced her warmly, moved by her simple open-heartedness. Kate was, as Lady Margaret said, what she seemed to be and was worth loving for that alone. They parted friends and she was finally left alone, as she had wanted to be. But now more alone than ever, more alone than walking the riverbank, more alone than when Andrew had left her at Deer Park Lodge, more alone than when her mother had cast her out.

It was true, she would have preferred to remain here at Cotehele. How did they know she would be safe at Venterdon? Did she even want to be safe? Andrew Hampton had displayed no preference for safety. He had risked all, for something or other. To prove himself to his father? To prove that even a bastard is worth something?

And here she was, a legitimate daughter, dreading to return to her childhood home. It was a contradiction she could not fathom and so, in the dying light, by the side of her narrow bed, obstinately, she knelt down to pray.

Chapter 27

When the chapel clock chimed the hour, she was standing at the entrance to the Retainers' Court, looking northwards across the meadow towards Trehill. It had been four long months since Francis had brought her in the wain, four long months since Andrew had turned his back on her at Deer Park Lodge. But then, she bit her lip to hold back the memory, he had not been the only one. There was no sign of Francis and the wain. And perhaps Kate had misunderstood, for there was no Kate either, though she had promised faithfully. Kate, Lady Margaret, Mrs Howard. It seemed they had all said their goodbyes, but not really said them at all, not in so many words.

The sky was grey. There was no sign of life, not even in the sky. The chimes had briefly kept her company. She had counted them and had made no mistake as to the hour. When they ceased, it was all too easy for her, once again, to feel herself cast to one side.

She had hardly slept, had deliberately risen late and dressed in her own clothes, leaving Mrs Howard's petticoats and bodice neatly folded on the bed. And then, as if to assure herself of its continuing existence, one last look at the river through her window-slit. Ready, in her green cloak and bonnet, she had entered the warmth of Mrs Rundle's kitchen. At least Mrs Rundle had been able to say goodbye and wish her well, in the normal way.

'I 'eard your news, Mrs 'ampton,' she said, embracing her awkwardly. 'Your 'usband was a brave man. You must be proud of 'im. Pity they aren't all like that. An' you be sure to come back, whenever you're settled. There'll always be a welcome in my kitchen.'

There was movement at the far end of the track, where the meadow disappeared into the trees. A wagon of some sort, a grey mare, the same four-wheeled wain that had brought her. She glanced up to the windows of Lady Margaret's chamber, and then behind to the arch of the Hall Court, from where Kate had first appeared. There was still no sign of life. The wain was approaching fast, but there was something different. It was not Francis, but John. What had happened? Why had Francis not come? She stood still, watching as John got down from the wain.

'You expected Francis.'

He dispelled her fears, as much by the natural warmth of his voice as the meaning of the words, and her troubled expression faded. They embraced and she remembered how reassuring, how reliable John had always been.

'Where is he?'

'We decided it was simpler for me. I can always make the time. And besides, they have had long days with the harvest.' John surveyed the scene. 'No baggage? No-one to wish you on your way?'

'No.'

John helped her up to the seat in the bow. 'You are looking well, Mary,' he said, incongruously. 'I am glad to see you well.' Once at her side, he gave an easy flick of the reins and the mare turned reluctantly. No pail of water this time.

'How is…?'

'Susan and the children? They are well, Mary, well. I am blessed.'

She was uncomfortable. Not since their father's funeral had they so much as laid eyes on one another. Yet John was calm and relaxed beside her, as they set off across the meadow. Exceptionally for a Pellow she thought, he has always known what to do with his life and simply gone ahead, even from the time of his apprenticeship in Luckett, all those years ago. Slyly, she observed him from the corner of her eye, his self-confidence, his ability to get things done.

'I don't want to go to Venterdon, John.'

John, deliberately or otherwise, misunderstood. 'They have sequestrated your farm at Hampt, Mary, but you will be safe at Venterdon.'

'Safe? How do you know? Robert told me George was, alive or dead, he would not say, a wanted man...and so I would be wanted to.'

'Robert knows Thomas Gewen. You know he is Christina's uncle. Gewen told him you would be safe.'

'Robert is well-informed.'

'Do you wait still, for George?'

'No...If he is dead, there is no point. If he is alive, then he set me aside long ago.' She surprised both herself and her brother, at the simple logic.

John was familiar with the lanes and it was not long before they came out on the Callington road. Once they were through Callington and on the way to Clymestone, there would be no going back. It was all happening much too fast.

'John, safe or not, I do not wish to go to Venterdon. I do not have to. My course is not set in stone. I have money...I am thankful, John, but you have to listen.'

For a while John did not reply, but she became aware he had allowed the mare to relax her pace. He was listening. He was not ignoring her.

'Yesterday, I went to Clymestone myself. Francis and me had a long talk...'

'But....'

'I will listen, Mary, but listen to me first. We had a long talk. There are some things you do not yet know.' John took a deep breath. 'Francis and Janella have posted their banns.'

'Banns? They are to be wed?' Mary was incredulous.

'I know. It has happened all at once.'

'Then she is with child.' Mary could not imagine any other explanation.

'I think not. They are happy together. It is plain to see.'

'And you expect to take me there! A mother that cast me out! And Janella, the woman of the house, presiding? John, she has always disliked me. No wonder they sent you, to smooth the way. God in Heaven! I refuse, John. I absolutely refuse!'

The mare by now was ambling so slowly along the Callington road, he thought she would jump down there and then. But it was true. He was there to smooth the way. And Mary's outburst was entirely justified. But he would have to finish what he had agreed and then try to persuade her. He put out one confident, capable hand to reassure her and then continued, unaware that his own calm temperament would do nothing now but arouse her further.

'While you were at Cotehele, the Reverend Clarke delivered our father's will.' He would make no mention of the Reverend's awful self-murder. 'Of course, everything goes to our mother, but our father willed that special provision be made to you, whenever you needed...'

'In case she forgot me,' Mary laughed bitterly. 'That was thoughtful...thoughtful of somebody, perhaps the Reverend Clarke cares more than either of them.'

'She wants you back, Mary.' He was trying hard not to betray his frustration. 'She has thought of nothing else. Do you not recall, how Francis came to you, and you would have nothing of it? Mary, our mother is much improved. She no longer takes to her bed. She has regained her memory. And as for the will, I think you are wrong. Father knew you were alone, waiting for George, who would never come back. He knew all that.'

'She threw us all out, John, remember? Her voice had shrunk to a whisper. 'She denied us our own father...and before that, I was already cast out. I just made the best of it, and married George…without even knowing my own mind.'

'She will be waiting for you now. She knows you are coming, today...and, and Mary, she did not throw us out. It was to protect our father. Janella told me. He was ashamed. Their chamber stank. He had no control..'

'And you are the loving son, now?' She interrupted, with vicious sarcasm.

He no longer knew what to expect from her. Now, instead of losing control, she was merely contemptuous. 'No, I have not been a loving son.'

'You chose to leave as soon as you could, to serve your apprenticeship. And since then John, you have feathered your own nest. So do not preach to me. Just set me down in Callington. I will go my own way.'

'There is one more thing I have to tell you, ' John persisted. 'Whatever you choose to do, it may help to explain...'

'You do not have much longer.'

'It was a Sunday in July, just before harvest time, before you or Francis were born. The Reverend Parker was ill and at the last minute the morning service was cancelled. The sun was shining. It was a beautiful summer's day. Many went down to the river.' The mare, since John no longer urged her on, had decided to stop in the shade of a hedgerow, perhaps to listen. 'One family walked along the river much further than the others. In the afternoon, the mother turned back but the father and the children carried on as far as Latchley.

At last they stopped and the father lay down to rest while the children played along the riverbank. There were two boys and a girl. After a while, one of the boys came to his father and asked where the girl had gone. She had disappeared and however much they searched along the river, they could not find her. The boys went back to their mother and the father continued to search throughout the night. She was found by a ferryman, drowned in the river, and he took her to Cotehele.'

'Cotehele?'

'I think you have already guessed. Her name was Mary. She was your sister and she was four years old.'

'Why are you telling me now? Why has nobody told me before?'

'Our father was ashamed, but it was mother who really suffered. She never properly recovered. I think at first, she tried to pretend that you were somehow your sister, tried to pretend that Mary was not drowned at all. It would have been better had they christened you differently, but then it is a common mistake. Of course, you could never replace your sister and so she resented you. You were always a disappointment and,' John took hold of her hand, 'you came to think of yourself as cast out.'

'What was she like?'

'Mary?' John flicked the reins, urging the mare on. 'She was different, different from any of us, like a gypsy, lively and loving. But no better nor worse than the rest of us, just so young, when she drowned. So you see, they never got over it. It was always there between them, and what could me and Robert do? What could we say? I suppose I was old enough to understand a little, feel guilty too, and you are right I suppose, that is why I left home as soon as I could.'

They had entered Callington and were approaching 'Pellows' Stables', already on the road to Clymestone.

'Stop, John. It is a pretty story. But it is no excuse. Nothing you have told me excuses her...and Janella! How could I bear it? I have money. I can look after myself. Set me down here.

***

At Venterdon, there was a sense of expectation, not to say nervousness, at the prospect of Mary's coming. Francis thought that once again she might disappoint, might somehow find a way of avoiding what to everyone else seemed inevitable. Yet he knew now how much courage it would take. Janella, long accustomed to difficulty, was prepared for the worst. She knew she would have to curb her natural antipathy. Perhaps her love for Francis had already curbed it. But how would Mary regard their betrothal? Would she feel ousted once again? Janella would have to tread carefully, take nothing for granted.

Alice, for her part, had no such doubts or concerns. Her only daughter was coming home at last. John was bringing her from Callington and John would not let her down. Besides, she had been feeling much better of late, had even attended Sunday morning service with Janella where she had, like the most zealous of Puritans, hung on Minister Marten's every word. Still no-one had seen fit to tell her of the Reverend Clarke's suicide, only that he had passed away and been replaced by Minister Marten. That was something to be regretted but then the Reverend had always had more time for Samuel than herself. Minister Marten, on the other hand, had singled her out, paid her special attention.

All the preparations had been made. Mary would take the chamber opposite her mother's, once belonging to Francis and then Janella. Francis and Janella would squeeze into the attic, but not find that in the least incommoding. At midday Francis had come in from the fields. Arthur had greatly surprised him when, on hearing of Mary's imminent arrival, he had seemed to relax, had seemed to welcome it as if a burden had been lifted from his shoulders.

But now Mary was still not come and Francis could take no further advantage of Arthur's new-found goodwill. He would have to return to the field at Old Clims, where Arthur would still be at work.

'Perhaps she will not come after all,' he whispered, out of his mother's earshot. 'But if she does, try to make her welcome Janella. I know she is difficult but it is with good reason and I think mother wishes so much to make amends.'

Alice, in her restlessness, went up to her chamber, so they kissed without restraint, before Francis put on his boots and left. When he had gone, Alice came tiptoeing down the stairs into the kitchen, a guilty look on her face and unexpectedly dressed in her best Sunday clothes.

'Janella, I have decided to meet them on the way. Just by the church, you know. They are bound to come that way.

'But Alice, you will tire yourself. And it looks like rain. Wait here by the fire. They will not be long.'

'I have decided, Janella. You will not stop me.'

Janella was familiar enough with that particular tone of voice Alice had, whenever she had made up her mind, but she could not allow her to go alone, though much improved, she was still frail. Frail but determined, Janella thought resignedly. She would have to go with her. She could not allow her to be alone and distraught in the lanes. There was still the possibility that Mary would not come.

*

'I can look after myself. Let me down here.' Her own words rang stridently in her ear from somewhere far away.

She was clutching something tightly between her two small hands; she looked down, a small pewter mug. And John was standing over her, encouraging her to drink. It was strong, a taste she did not recognise. Gradually she became aware of the warmth from the fire. Her cloak lay over a chair. John sat down next to her and made her drink some more, before taking the mug away.

'I can look after myself,' she repeated stubbornly, though the evidence clearly suggested otherwise.

'You nearly fell from the wain. I caught you just in time. It was lucky we were so close.' John's voice was soothing, gentle, penetrating the mist in her mind. 'Susan will make you something to eat and then we must decide what to do.'

So she was in John's parlour. She remembered seeing the sign, 'Pellows' Stables'. 'I am imposing on you.'

'You can stay here for a time, if you wish.' John did not sound enthusiastic.

'I have money. I will be alright.' she stammered, trying to recall the precise nature of her circumstances.

'How much?'

'I don't know.' She reached down to her skirts and drew out a handful of coins, three gold crowns, a shilling and a few sixpences, all that Andrew had given her. It did not seem much.

'It will not last long,' John said bluntly. 'There is only here or Venterdon, Mary. You have nowhere else to go.'

She felt herself regaining strength. 'You told me a story, John, about my mother,' she began slowly. But let me tell you another one, before I go. It is of a young woman that walked the riverbank, waiting for her husband to come back from the war.' Mary was staring into the flames of fire. 'Three years she walked the riverbank, but her husband never returned. Whenever it rained, she would seek shelter in a little ruined cottage. There was just one dry space in the corner, where the roof had not yet fallen in.' Mary looked round for her drink and John passed it to her.

'One day she came to the ruin and found a stranger sleeping in that one dry spot. It was a soldier who had been wounded, an officer who had not accepted the surrender to Fairfax, and was then being sought by both sides. If the woman had left him, he would surely have died, so instead she took him to her cottage and tended to his wound.

And when they came to confiscate her land, the woman fled to Cotehele and the officer, despite the danger, made his way to Pendennis. Together with five other men, they broke the siege and, at great risk to themselves, brought desperately needed supplies into the Castle.' At last she turned away from the fire which had so mesmerised her.

John's expression was one of curiosity mixed with concern. Susan, together with her children, had come silently into the parlour to listen. Francis never told them, she thought and was moved to tears. 'Yesterday, the young woman received news that the officer, Lieutenant Andrew Hampton, had been killed at Pendennis.'

John stood up. 'You loved this man?' It sounded like an accusation, but he had not meant it that way.

'Yes.'

'And he you?'

She hesitated. 'Yes.'

'What do you want to do, Mary?'

'I want to go to Pendennis.'

'You would be alone. Here you have your family...whatever you might think of them.'

Each of her brothers had helped her, in their own way and however reluctantly. She could not deny that. And her mother no doubt loved her, in her own way. 'The man who brought the news was called James Stubbs. His father was there...at the end. He is an innkeeper at Penryn. So you see, I do have somewhere else to go. Can you not take me, John, to Looe? There are ships. He told me.'

She did not hold out much hope, but she did not see and would not have understood, the look that John and Susan had exchanged.

'Mary'. He came to sit by her again and took her hand. 'I will take you to Looe, or by some other means bring you to Pendennis, before the month, before September is out and the winters sets in. I will take you if you will go to Venterdon now and be re-united with our mother. Is that not a fair bargain?'

*

At the crossroads in Clymestone, rain still threatened and there were gusts of strong wind from the west. Alice and Janella were huddled in the hedgerow at the corner of the lane to Venterdon. The church was not a hundred yards away and Alice kept looking in that direction, as if seeking some of the same assurance the Minister had once given her. Janella wanted her to come home. It did not seem likely now. Mary would disappoint her once again. But Alice would not be moved.

A few heavy spots of rain blowing in the wind and then, between the gusts, the heavy creaking of a wagon and the clip-clop of hooves. Up the lane from Callington a grey mare. Two figures in the wain, which was drawing to a halt even as it came into view. Alice started forward. The young woman in the wain got down. The words, 'John, you promised,' and the reply, 'I promise' were lost on the wind.

Her mother was walking towards her, arms outstretched. One last glance up to John in the bow of the wain, and then Mary took a step forward.

About the Author

Russ Hawton is a retired English lecturer with a passionate interest in Cornish history. He has long been interested in his own family's history in the county. His research has particularly focused on life in Cornwall during the English Civil War.

Printed in Great Britain
by Amazon